W 2/14

CODE

OF

DARKNESS

CODE

OF

DARKNESS

CHRIS LINDBERG

ISBN 978-1-257-80263-0

Acknowledgements

To my good friends Katie Telser and Ed Braun, both of whom did the heavy lifting in editing the book cover to cover. This is a better novel thanks to you. To OJ Adkins, who provided great insight on the mentality of a Chicago cop, and helped give the action scenes a sharper edge. To Jill Pollack at StoryStudio Chicago, who taught me to push detail, scene, and character beyond what I thought I was capable of. To Mom and Sandy, for reading the story only because of who'd written it. And to my wife and companion Jenny, without you this book would have never seen the light of day.

For Jenny, Luke and Emma

Prologue

Rage knew that this was the end.

He held the unconscious federal agent in front of him as a shield, his only protection from being shot again. His legs buckled; he felt more unsteady by the second. The remaining armored troopers had moved in, taking positions. He was surrounded.

He turned to see that the large agent had advanced on him as well. This man was the leader, beyond a doubt. Rage looked into his eyes: cold, murderous, clear and blue, like slicks of ice. A flash of familiarity gripped Rage, elusively – then let go before he could understand. They had known each other somewhere, or sometime, before.

The agent smiled malevolently, nodding at him. As if issuing a challenge. Rage somehow knew that taking him out would present his one chance to escape.

He had to do it now, before his consciousness slipped away completely.

Without hesitation, he dropped the agent and leapt forward. In a blinding motion, the enormous man reached out, caught him mid-leap by the neck, and swiftly threw him down to the pavement.

Dazed, head pounding, Rage looked up at the night sky, which faded in and out as a blur of darkness and the faint glow of street lamps. He saw the man appear in his view, staring down from above, then abruptly had the wind knocked out of him as a massive foot planted itself across his chest.

"I'll gather you're not used to this," the man said smugly, leveling the rifle.

The agent fired, and everything went black.

1

Inception

It happened on a Saturday morning, with no warning that it would change their lives forever.

Inside the Edgewater branch of Chicago Savings and Loan, the clock on the wall had just struck nine o'clock. The page-a-day calendar that hung next to it read March 12th. Early spring sunshine had set the bank lobby with a soft, warming glow.

Rage pushed through the front double-doors and entered the teller line. There was only one window open, and he was second in line behind an elderly couple. He'd glanced around to see a young woman had also just walked in, now behind him in line.

Somehow, the sight of this woman got him thinking about her again; how she had died quietly just days before, in her bed just before dawn, her hollow, sad, tired eyes closing for the final time, her soft, wrinkled hand going limp in his, the sun rising emptily on the windowsill.

A loud bang echoed through the room as the front doors burst open. Rage looked over to see the first man club the door security guard with the butt-end of a shotgun. The second man fired into the ceiling. Both were wearing black stockings over their heads. Everyone about him scattered to the floor. The first man shouted at the teller to keep her finger off the silent alarm. The second man fired the shotgun again, blowing to bits the teller window next to hers to make the first man's point.

"Everyone on the floor!" the first one shouted, waving his gun. The second man barred the front double doors with a crowbar. "Get *down* I said!" he screamed, shoving one of the bankers to the floor.

Rage crouched down, his eyes moving to the elderly couple, huddled against each other on the floor, both terrified. He swiveled his head back toward the woman, whose eyes met his. Though her dangling auburn hair obscured part of her face, he could see she shared the couple's frightened expression.

He closed his eyes and thought about his gift.

He had used it only once before, years ago. Since then he'd sworn to her he would never use it to harm another.

And this was a public place … with witnesses …

No. The thieves would take the money and leave.

It was that simple. It *would* be that simple.

The first robber, the smaller of the two, pushed a large burlap sack across to the teller. "Fill this," he barked, pointing the gun at the terrified woman.

The second robber kept the shotgun pointed at the group, telling everyone to stay calm, stay where they were, and it would all be over in a matter of minutes.

Mira Givens huddled on the lobby's tile floor, too frightened to move. She was starting a new job on Monday, and had only come in to put in a direct deposit slip for her first paycheck. Now she was face down on the floor, while above her men were pointing guns at her and the others around her.

From the floor she saw the black boot of the second robber pivot in her direction. She did not look up but imagined him looking down at her.

She then caught the eye of the man who'd been in front of her in line, and she was briefly struck from the moment. Aside from his rugged features and rumpled hair, his eyes were the blackest, coldest eyes she'd ever seen. Those black eyes locked with hers, then quickly looked away. But in that instant, in those eyes, she felt an odd calm, an inexplicable, momentary reprieve from the dire situation they were all in, as if somehow, everything would be all right.

Her thoughts were interrupted when the black boot tapped her ribcage. "You. Up," the gruff voice came from above.

The usual Saturday morning buzz of Nick's Diner on Chicago's far north side was interrupted by the dispatcher's voice crackling through the portable radio. Seated at the counter, Lawrence Parker took the call. A hostage situation at the Chicago Savings and Loan's Edgewater branch. Negotiators were being called, but since he and his partner Gino were closest to the scene, they set down their forks, flipped a pair of ten-dollar bills on the counter, and headed out the front door toward their squad car.

Hopping into the passenger seat, Larry called in the response to dispatch, his heart hammering behind the Kevlar vest as it began to sink in. His ten years on the force had exposed him to more shootouts, robberies, and drug busts than he'd cared to count. But this was different. Janna had been lost in a hostage standoff four years ago. Two bastards, two guns. Two seven-year-old sons left without a mother, a husband without a wife.

As the cruiser sped eastbound, he felt his head begin to pound.

Gino Urrutia had been Larry's partner since his rookie days. "Hey," he said, glancing over at Larry from behind the wheel. "Gonna be fine. Standard procedure. Hold 'em there 'til the negotiators arrive. They'll find out what these shitheads want, they free the hostages, we nail 'em. You know the drill. Just follow my lead, okay?"

Larry looked out the window at the streets moving by in a blur. "Everything's cool," he said under his breath.

As the frantic teller pulled the stacks of bills from the drawers and dropped them in the smaller man's burlap sack, the large man kept one eye on Rage and the others.

The teller's drawers empty, the small man took the sack from the counter and moved toward his accomplice. At this, the large man grabbed the young woman's arm and pulled her up to him. "Gimme your purse. Now," he said to her, then addressed everyone else. "That goes for all o'you. Take 'em out, put 'em on the floor. Do it now."

Face to face with the large robber, her right wrist being held tightly, Mira handed her handbag to the man, who tossed it into the burlap sack. The small one picked up the wallets, purses, and handbags the others had laid on the floor.

The large man eyed Mira, a smile coming to his face. "Lucky for you we ain't got room for ya in the bag," he sneered.

The small man folded up the sack and took it under his arm, still pointing the shotgun, and nodded to his partner. As the two men made their way toward the front doors, a screech of tires came from the front parking lot.

"Son of a bitch, the cops!" the small man roared.

Outside, Larry and Gino took up positions behind the squad car. Through tinted bank windows and glaring morning sun, he made out about nine or ten figures inside. Larry radioed in for backup, ordering units to every possible exit. The hostage negotiators would be arriving any second.

Inside the lobby, the small robber barked to his partner, "We gotta get outta here before they surround us. We need leverage. Take the broad and head for the back."

Cocking the shotgun, the large robber pulled Mira tight. "Looks like you'll be comin' with us, after all."

At this Rage stood up and grabbed the large man's forearm. "If you're gonna take someone, take me."

BANG. The shotgun went off. Startled by Rage's sudden move, the large man had fired it inadvertently, right into Rage's stomach. The lobby seemed to freeze in time. Rage fell backward. The teller screamed. The elderly woman fainted.

"Shit!" yelled the small man. "Head for the back, now!"

The large man pulled Mira, squeezing her under her right arm, overpowering her struggles. They made their way toward the rear exit as more sirens approached outside.

Outside, Larry heard the gunfire erupt inside the bank. Signaling to Gino, he rushed toward the back entrance, taking cover at the alley's edge.

The emergency exit door boomed open, and two men with black stockings over their heads emerged, the second much taller than the first. Both were armed. Larry pivoted into the alley entrance, his revolver pointed directly at them.

"Freeze!" he screamed at the two men.

Larry saw the young woman being held under the large man's arm.

"Drop your guns, and let the woman go," he ordered them.

Without warning the small man pointed the gun at Larry and fired. From out of nowhere a third man appeared between Larry and the robber, taking the shotgun blast in his right shoulder. In one blinding motion, the newcomer ripped the gun from the small man's hand then spun into a kick that connected with the large man's jaw. Larry could hear the sickening crunch as the jawbone shattered. Completing his full spin, he rounded up on the small man and punched him square in the chest, sending him flying into a brick wall. As the large man fell, he turned back to pull the woman free while kicking the shotgun from the robber's limp hand.

Larry stood there, thunderstruck. His gun was still pointed at the spot where the two bank robbers once stood, both now lying unconscious on the worn pavement. The intervener set the stunned woman down near the alley wall.

The man, maybe mid-twenties, was wearing a black t-shirt and torn jeans. Both his right shoulder and lower abdomen were bleeding, as if he'd been shot moments before also. He wore a shocked expression, but showed not even the slightest sign of pain. He was maybe five-foot-six, with matted black hair. He looked down at the two unconscious bank robbers, then over to Larry, as if analyzing whether Larry would become a threat himself. He took up the burlap sack and pulled out what looked to be a wallet, then tossed the sack in Larry's direction. Then, before Larry could utter a word, the man leapt all the way up onto the adjacent building's roof, and was gone.

2

Asset One

Along the unlit suburban streets of Washington, D.C., all was still. A soft night wind whispered through ancient trees.

The deep, precise hum of an engine gradually broke the silence, gaining volume as it drew nearer. Headlights came into view, their bright beams cutting forth through the darkness.

The red Lamborghini Murcielago rounded the corner onto 16th Street. It was headed toward Washington's affluent Fortuna Estates district. It moved along streets lined with ancient maples and oaks, and perennial flora adorning the high red brick curb lines. Street lights illuminated the silky curves of the exotic sports car as it downshifted into second gear, making its turn onto South Hillside Avenue. A tall, black wrought iron fence ran along the front of the estate. It took up the entire first block of South Hillside: a clear partition from the rest of the already exclusive neighborhood.

The car approached the front entrance. A tiny infrared security badge on the upper left edge of the windshield triggered the front gates to open, permitting the vehicle to pass through to the estate grounds.

The car downshifted into first gear, navigating the winding driveway, passing a vast expanse of lush landscaping. Groves of imported trees and shrubs, rare plants in full bloom mixed in with verdant floral gardens, stretched from either side of the paved path. A small driving range was flanked by tennis courts off to the far right. To the left, a massive, almost castle-like greystone estate house, complete with towering ornate windows, twenty-five foot high pillars along the facade, and gigantic limestone gargoyles at each corner of the roof, loomed forebodingly against the moonlit sky.

The Lamborghini slowed as it arrived at the far set of quadruple garage doors to the side of the house. The infrared trigger once again activated, opening the garage door programmed for that car.

Elias Todd pulled into the rear garages of his expansive home with a shrewd grin on his face. Tonight's job could not have been easier: posing as a waiter at a fundraiser, slipping an undetectable poison pill in an old geezer's drink. The autopsies would show the man had died of a heart attack; no signs of foul play. All so the man's twenty-something wife could collect more quickly on his billion-dollar estate.

Two hours of work, netting a half-million-dollar payout.

If they could all be that simple, he thought to himself.

It was just before midnight on Monday. He switched off the ignition and climbed out of the Lamborghini, adjusting the cuffs of his black tuxedo as he made his way to the connecting door to his house.

He switched on the light to the large, wrap-around kitchen. Black marble countertops reflected the soft glare from the rows of recessed lighting above. Stained oak cabinets lined each wall surrounding him, stretching up toward the eleven-foot ceiling. He opened his liquor cabinet and poured himself a glass of scotch, walking the glass to the kitchen's large center island and pulling off his bow tie. Taking a sip, he glanced down at the Monday edition of *The Washington Post*, scanning the review of his work from Sunday evening. A foreign dignitary from Ghana, shot in the head. Front page this time.

After scanning his iPhone for after-hours activity on his stocks, Todd downed the rest of the scotch and decided to head off to sleep. Grabbing his tie from the counter, he flipped off the kitchen lights and headed toward the living room stairway.

Rounding the corner into the massive living room, Todd switched on the overhead chandelier light, revealing the twenty men in full-body SWAT gear who'd been waiting for him.

An exceptionally large man, tall and broad-shouldered with thinning, steel-gray hair and a long, visible scar down his right temple, stepped forward and addressed him: "Mr. Todd, we'd like a word with you."

Without hesitation, Todd pulled the automatic pistol from inside his vest and began firing in their direction, then pushed off into a backflip toward the kitchen. He lowered himself into a somersault, using the kitchen counters as cover, and tore the knife rack down off the end counter wall. Popping up from behind the counter, he threw each of the twelve carving knives at his pursuers in rapid succession, then immediately ducked back down. He needed to force them to take cover; give himself time to get to the garage and make his escape. Judging from the screams, he knew he'd connected with at least eight to ten of them.

Staying low, he pushed the door open and rolled backward into the garage, firing a few more rounds into the kitchen before kicking the door shut. In the blackness of the garage he made his way to his industrial tool stand against the near wall. He grabbed it at the corners, heaving it high into the air, lodging it against the door. He switched on the light only to find another group of armored agents surrounding him, all with rifles pointed.

"Drop your weapon. Hands in the air, behind your head," an agent in front ordered him.

Raising his arms slowly, Todd surveyed the situation around him. There were about ten or twelve of them, all armored and heavily armed, complete with night-vision lenses. Even with his unique abilities, escape would be a near impossible task without the element of surprise.

He slowly lowered the automatic pistol, setting it on the garage floor before placing his hands behind his head.

A series of thuds came from behind him: the agents inside the house were trying to force their way through the door from the kitchen. A booming voice called through the door, ordering those in the garage to open it. Two of the men went to shift the tool stand away from the door but were unable to move its six hundred pound mass. Three more agents joined them, and began to slowly push the tool stand off to the side.

Seizing the opening, Todd roundhouse-kicked a rifle from one of the agents' hands, then, grabbing it in mid-air, opened fire on the unit. The agents scrambled for cover, erratically returning fire. The pounding of automatic-machine-gun fire filled the garage.

Suddenly the house door gave way, abruptly smashed open from the other side. The large man appeared in the doorway and immediately fired at Todd three times, connecting twice with Todd's neck, and once with his upper chest.

Todd jerked backward, clutching his neck. He began to feel his consciousness slip away. As his strength left him, the gun slid from his hands and made a flat clack as it hit the floor. He leaned against the car nearest him, trying to keep his balance. Eyes rolling back, he finally dropped to the floor.

Colonel Nolan Hayes did not lower his weapon as he entered the garage. Several of his men lay dead or stunned around the smooth concrete floor, while others cautiously emerged from behind cover of Todd's now bullet-riddled collection of expensive cars.

He looked down at Elias Todd's still body on the floor. "He's definitely one of them," he said quietly to himself, examining the wounds that the three oversized tranquilizer darts had left on Todd's neck and chest.

Hayes turned to his Second Lieutenant. "Contact the Ops group at the Pentagon; let them know Asset One has been secured."

"Right away, sir," the agent replied, then stepped away to make the call.

Hayes then called over to four of his other men. "Clark. Rogers. Assemble the Box and get him inside it immediately. Avin and Worley, watch the subject and keep your firearm pointed at him at all times. If he so much as twitches, put another dart in him."

"Yes, sir," they replied.

Seconds later, Argon Clive, Hayes' Lead Investigator, entered the garage. "Colonel Hayes," he said as he approached him. "I think you'll want to have a look at his private records. Much of the contents appear to be encoded, but from what I've seen thus far, his history is quite extensive. He also has a large file full of newspaper clippings of assassinations and high-profile hits. From what I'm able to gather, the subject appears to have been a hired killer of some sort."

Glancing around the garage, Hayes pondered this development. "Do a thorough search, then impound all evidence immediately. That information could be useful to us, but it's of secondary importance right now. Ops has already worked out Mr. Todd's "death" for the local authorities and press – but we don't want to leave anything that might lead to a larger investigation at that level. We need this, as well as our other acquisition, to be clean."

"Understood, I'll get my men on it."

As Clive walked away, Nolan Hayes stepped out of the garage and headed down the driveway. His heart rate had begun to pick up; the urge was returning. Glancing behind him cautiously, he strode toward a thicket of trees.

When no one was in view, he rolled up his sleeve. Again looking around him, he dug into a pouch in the side of his belt and drew out a small syringe.

Removing the cap, he took a breath, then plunged the tiny needle into his forearm.

3

Nightstalker

Rage had spent the past several moments staring down at his hands.

Outside, a cool breeze swept gently across the Edgewater neighborhood. A full moon presided quietly over the clear night sky.

Inside, the time had come for him to decide again.

As he had done many times since that fateful morning weeks ago, he found himself staring closely at his hands, turning them over every few seconds, examining them. As if the lines and patterns presented some sort of code from which he could draw answers to his questions.

The bank incident had caused a divergence in his mind. He'd sworn to her never to use his gift to harm another, and yet he had done just that.

It was to save a life, he told himself. There was no other way.

But he had felt something else in those lucid moments. Something unmistakable.

Bloodlust.

And this was what was feeding it. The engine that pushed him along.

And was the reason he'd gone out since that morning weeks ago. Several times.

Into the night, wearing a mask.

It was a transformation for him. From what he had always been and not been, into something more.

As if a veil had been lifted, revealing his true calling, right before his very eyes.

And it was only beginning; this he knew. Whether he wanted to accept it or not.

And it was for a greater good. He knew this. Lives had been saved. Wrongs righted. Justices served. Again and again.

It was better this way. For him and for the world around him.

And she would understand it too. Perhaps her passing was an unspoken permission for him to begin a new life. Forge his own path. Find his way.

And now once again, it was time to decide.

Night was coming. *His* time. It beckoned to him.

Would he stop this? *Could* he?

There was a part of him that *knew* he must stop; it had gone farther than he'd originally intended.

Now lives had been ended. At his hands.

They had been wrongdoers, yes, but lives nonetheless.

But the Lesson had been taught to those who remained.

But there had been joy in the punishment.

At this thought he felt the urge swell within him.

Perhaps he could stop this … perhaps he would, soon …

But not tonight.

No, there was too much to do.

He stood from the couch. It was time to go to work.

His new mission. His new life's work.

As he got up he pulled off his shirt and glanced down at his midsection. He remembered the shotgun blasts to his stomach and shoulder. And he'd been shot twice since then, once just last night. But as they'd done each time, his wounds had healed within hours, leaving behind only trace remnants of blood and nothing more.

As he went to his closet, his thoughts wandered to her.

Georgia Fay.

She had taken him in at thirteen, after a series of orphanages and foster homes.

A retired schoolteacher in Evanston, she would be the closest thing to a mother he would ever have. She kept him grounded. For every cruelty life had dealt him, she was the counterbalance of kindness. In their years together, she'd built within him a sense of right and wrong, and had helped him discover his humanity.

Only weeks before, she had died in her bed, with him at her side.

Now only blackness and despair remained.

He shook his head, putting away those thoughts. It was time to focus.

Moments later he had changed into his night clothes, the transformation complete. Jeans, t-shirt, athletic shoes, and ski mask. All in his favorite color: black.

He wrapped the heavy-duty belt around his waist, clipped the rope on its hook at his back; the brass knuckles into their hook at his side.

He went over to his sixth story window, pulled it wide open, and leaned out. Gazing out at the street and alley below, he took in the night, took a deep breath of it, and pulled himself out onto the fire escape. He leapt onto the building next to his and climbed its fire escape up to the roof. He crouched at the edge facing Granville Street, and sat quietly, watching over the city block ahead of him.

As he crouched, he thought about what had happened weeks before at the bank.

Thanks to his gift, no one had been hurt.

His gift.

He had never questioned his gift. Never wondered where it had come from. Or exactly what it was, even. He was fast and strong, but how fast or how strong, he did not know. It had always seemed to be the right amount, right when he needed it. He'd had it for as long as he could remember.

Why question it further, he thought.

Only Georgia Fay had known. She had always encouraged him to see a doctor. See if there could be any adverse effects. He refused. He'd never been ill his entire life, not even a common cold. He had no need for doctors.

He continued to scan the streets below, deep in thought.

The night was still around him. Too still. He would need to move.

Moving to the center of the roof, he got a running start and leapt onto the next building, and the next, and the next, scaled down a fire escape, scaled up another. He finally found himself at the corner of Lawrence and Broadway. From the rooftop edge, he scanned his surroundings. He would wait here.

A scream came from behind him. He turned, following the sound.

The scene came into view: two young men, sporting leather and waving handguns in the air, and a third person he couldn't make out, ran through the alley below him. It was clear this third person was the victim.

He crept along the edge of the roof, listening to the voices below:

"We gotchou now, bitch!" a male voice shouted. "No more pepper spray! Do you know what we're gonna do to you? Do you wanna know?"

The young woman backed into the wall. She had run out of room. "No, please!" she cried, trembling, tears streaming down her face. "I -- I haven't done anythi--"

Rage slammed down onto the first man at full force of gravity, then immediately landed the killing blow. The first attacker lying dead beneath him, Rage turned to the other attacker-now-turned-prey, black eyes glowing with fury. The man began to run, but Rage launched into a high jump over him, landing directly in his path. He made for his gun but Rage kicked it from his hand. It skidded harmlessly across the alley, disappearing into a heap of trash. Rage delivered a roundhouse kick to the man's face, cracking his jawbone, sending him cascading backward before crumpling to the ground.

He pulled his prey with him as he headed for the woman.

"Are you okay," he asked her.

The woman tried to stammer something, but couldn't form the words. Rage turned to the unconscious man and the dead one, then returned his gaze to her.

"Do you know these two?"

She made a n-n-n-ing sound. He understood well enough.

He would need to take her to a police station. He carried the unconscious man behind a dumpster where he wouldn't be seen. As he started back toward the woman, he saw she had gone. He turned toward the street to see her running away as fast as she could.

He sighed. "You're welcome."

He walked back over to the man behind the dumpster, who was still unconscious. When the man woke moments later, he cried in terror at Rage's dark visage in front of him. Rage slapped him. "Shut up. If I wanted you dead, you would be. I want answers. The girl – why were you after her?"

The young man looked at him vacantly. "W-why, man?" he asked.

Rage's eyes grew darker as his voice lowered. "Yes. Why."

"Shit, man, I don't know. Why *not* is more the question, right? I mean-"

Rage put a finger over the man's bloody mouth. He shook his head and took the young man's right hand in his. Beneath the mask his lips curled into a smile as he crushed the hand.

The man screamed. Rage hit him in the stomach to knock the wind out of him.

"Let's try this again," Rage demanded.

Several seconds later the young man, no longer gasping but still wheezing, raised his head and looked at Rage. "M-man, shit. W-we had to do what we d-did tonight."

"And I'm asking why," Rage said darkly.

The man stammered something inaudibly, then stopped.

Rage shook his head. "Not such a badass now, are you," Rage whispered viciously. "How does it feel to be at someone else's mercy, to be like that girl?"

His voice settled to a calm whisper: "Now. Continue."

"W-we had to do it, man," he stammered. "To be in the family … you got to earn your way in, you know … show you're a man … you know what I'm sayin'?"

"What family?"

"You know, man, the rulers of this neighborhood. The Clan Killers. To get in … you gotta do a female and then kill her, man. You know what I'm sayin'?"

Rage felt the urge race through him like electricity. His eyes grew darker. It was time. He picked the man up by his jacket collar and held him high in the air. He roared, causing some within earshot to come to their windows, then immediately draw their shades and bolt their doors. He threw the man down hard onto the pavement.

"Let this be known," Rage spat as he lurched down and snarled into the man's face. "That I am the new ruler of this city; the Protector of its People. You were doing evil tonight. On my watch there will be no evil, and that means no violence, no rapes, no drugs, no gangs. I will hunt down anyone I see, anyone I even *suspect* of doing evil and teach them The Lesson they will never forget. They know me and fear me, and when I am done there will be no more evil. Make no mistake: I will stop at nothing. So let it be known. You are poison if you are doing evil. You are bad for the world. You will be removed."

Rage slammed the man in the face with his left fist, rendering him unconscious once again. He pulled the man several feet, dropping him alongside the body of the other. Finding some heavy twine in the dumpster, he bound them together, hanging them from a nearby streetlight. He plucked a can of spray paint from the dead one and sprayed a message on the ground under them, for all to see. The Lesson was now complete.

He pulled a cell phone from the man's pocket and dialed 911. The attacker had sustained serious injuries while committing the crime, and thus needed immediate medical attention.

He leapt up onto the roof of the building facing him and looked down upon his prey, then turned and headed for home.

Less than a block away from his building, he stopped at the edge of a rooftop, taking one last breath of the crisp night air. Taking off his mask, he listened to the breeze gently rustling through the trees along the parkways. The city had gone quiet once again.

He was about to pull his mask back on when he heard a faint sound coming from the alley below him. He stopped and listened closely. A dog whimpering.

Grunting irritably, he pulled the mask on and raced toward the edge of the rooftop, making the final few leaps toward his building. From the fire escape he climbed into his open window, yanked off the mask and belt, and went to the fridge.

Examining its sparse white wire shelves, he found a few uncooked hot dogs and the remnants of a loaf of bread. Grabbing them, he went to the window and leapt across the alleyway, across a few rooftops, then dropped into the breezeway next to the building he'd stood atop just moments before.

As he strode through the breezeway, he could hear the dog's whimpering growing more fervent. Rounding the corner past a garage and into the alley itself, he looked to his right and saw them across the alley not ten feet away. The old man sat back against a garage door, skinny legs jutting out into the alleyway's pocked concrete surface, his Welsh Corgi laying on its side against his right leg. He was in the same denim overalls and flannel shirt Rage had always seen him in, the faded red baseball cap sitting cockeyed atop his long, grayed hair. Underneath them was a filthy plaid blanket, and a shopping cart full of junk a few feet to their left.

As Rage approached them, the haggard man's eyes, white as pearls against the layers of dust and grime which covered his face, darted hungrily to the food in Rage's right hand. The dog's old, sad eyes stayed fixed on

Rage's, its short, stubby tail wagging weakly as it panted. The tip of its tongue hung over the edge of its bottom jaw before licking its nose hopefully.

"Here," Rage said, tossing the food onto the man's lap. "Make sure he gets half."

"I will," the old man said, nodding his head. "I sure appreciate you doing this."

"You know I don't do it for you," Rage said flatly, turning away. "See you around," he added over his shoulder before disappearing into the breezeway.

After swinging back into his apartment through the open window, Rage had begun taking off his night clothes when he realized he'd become hungry himself. Tossing his shirt onto the couch behind him, he went to the kitchen counter and switched on the old AM radio. The radio was one of only two things he'd kept of Georgia Fay's, along with the lone painting on his wall. The radio had been stuck on the 1940s station since the tuning knob had stopped working years before. Rage didn't mind though; the music reminded him of her, and because of that, it soothed his fiery soul like so few other things could.

Duke Ellington squeaked out of the radio's single, ancient speaker as Rage opened the fridge. Glancing around inside, he realized he'd probably given the old bum the only edible things he had.

Grumbling, he turned to the cabinet above the counter and rummaged through it, finding an opened box of saltines and a can of Cheez Whiz. With a sigh he pulled the two items down and strode lazily over to the couch, its battered springs almost collapsing with a twang as he plunked down onto the center cushion. He opened the saltines, flipped the cap off the Cheez Whiz, and began to devour his makeshift meal.

Later that night while sleeping, Rage began to have a strange dream.

He was somewhere he couldn't recognize, a large, dark cavern of some sort. He looked about him. A rumbling began in the distance. It became gradually louder, creating tremors in the cavern floor below him.

Suddenly something had leapt upon him, smashing his face onto the hard rock floor. Twisting upward, he kicked his assailant off and turned to face him, when he found he couldn't – as much as he tried to force his gaze in the direction of whomever stood across from him, his eyes would defy him, remaining locked to the cavern floor. Before he could react further he was struck by another powerful blow, then picked up and thrown down once again onto the cavern's biting surface. There was no chance to recover: his attacker was once again on top of him and began landing crushing blows to his face, pounding him into submission…

Rage awoke abruptly, covered in a cold sweat. He realized he'd been screaming.

Heart racing, he sat up, glancing at the clock next to his bed. 3:33 a.m.

The nightmare again.

Shaking his head, he let out a deep sigh of relief. It was over.

He pulled the covers back over him and stared at the ceiling.

Slowly, cautiously, he drifted back to sleep.

4

Larry

The tiny bears swayed happily from side to side with every step, unaware they were being watched.

The building at 4333 North Damen Avenue was one of the only greystones in the entire neighborhood. Cracked concrete steps led up to a three-story structure with street-side bay windows on each level and a stone-spire roof façade. The open third-floor window reflected the sunset of the warm spring evening, and let in a slight breeze. Across Damen, a spike-haired young woman, dressed in a three-quarter length gray t-shirt and baggy cargo pants, walked northbound toward Montrose.

Crammed into the open window, Marcus and Daniel Parker sat with binoculars locked onto the woman, as if catching a glimpse of one for the very first time. Mouths open, their heads slowly turning in unison with her progress up the street, they remained oblivious of her mesmerizing effect on them.

"Dude, d'you think she smokes pot?" Marcus asked, following her closely as she continued along.

"What are you talking about?" Daniel replied, keeping his gaze on her as well.

"The bears, see 'em?"

"Bears?"

"The tattoo. The dancing bears tattoo," Marcus clarified. "On her lower back."

"What does that have to do with anything?"

"You know, the Grateful Dead. All their fans smoked pot."

"How do you . . . Give me those. Yours are better than mine."

Marcus handed Daniel his set of binoculars and stepped away from the window, heading to the kitchen to get a Coke. Both of them were still in their wool, green plaid school uniforms, even though it was an unseasonably warm April evening. "Want one?" he asked as he opened the fridge.

"Nah," Daniel replied absently, trying to focus on the woman's tattoo as she continued down the street. The screens hadn't been put in yet, so he leaned out the window a bit. She was too far away now.

Marcus sat back down next to his brother and scanned the street again. They heard the soft click of the front door lock behind them. "Dad's home," he said.

Lawrence Parker walked through the front door and regarded the two boys with a quizzical look. He was not a large man, but those meeting him for the first time usually found him a bit intimidating. His demeanor was not the reason; he was about as low-key as they came. Nor was it his abnormally wide chest. More likely it was the lungs behind the chest, surely the two largest ever given a man, expelling a booming voice that resonated with authority. Or maybe the dark green eyes which, despite a usual tenor of kindness, were known to pierce easily through any falsehood set in front of them. Or perhaps it was the way he carried himself, with a quiet air of self-assuredness, leaving a hint that there was much more to him than met the eye.

"What's going on here, guys?" he asked, raising an eyebrow as he hung his keys, took off his jacket, and walked over to the kitchen cabinet. He pulled his favorite short glass with the 1985 Bears Super Bowl logo from the top shelf, turned to the fridge, and poured his evening orange juice.

"Hey Dad, just having a look out the window," Daniel half-turned in reply to him. Marcus kept looking out the window.

"Really, now," Larry said, taking a drink from the glass and walking over to the window. "What's so interesting out there?"

"Nothing much," Daniel said, turning back to the window. "Just people walking by."

"Looks to me like you're being a couple of peeping Toms, maybe," Larry observed. "Probably not a good idea."

"Not peeping Toms," Daniel turned around, throwing an indignant look at his father. "That'd mean violating someone's privacy. We're just watching people walk by, on a public street. There's no crime there that I know of."

"It's a nice night out," Larry gestured to the window with the glass before taking another drink. "Why don't you guys go out and play or something?"

"Dad, we're eleven," Daniel replied, looking back out onto the street. "We don't 'play' anymore."

"Well, what do eleven year olds do, then?" Larry asked. "Whatever it is, you should be doing that."

"Can't do that either," Daniel shrugged. "We live with a cop who'll rat us out."

"Got that right," Larry said matter-of-factly, downing another gulp of orange juice. "Well then, what do *good* eleven year olds do."

"Not sure," Daniel shrugged again. "We don't know any."

"You trying to get rid of us?" Marcus finally piped in, but still peering out onto Damen Avenue. "Got a hot date or something?"

"Yeah," Larry chuckled to himself. "That's it."

"Come on, Marcus," Daniel said, seeming to catch on. "He probably just needs some chill time. How bout you give us twenty bucks, and we'll hit a movie?"

"It's a school night," he reminded them, digging his wallet from his back pocket. "Here's ten bucks, go get a couple of burgers at Wally's at the corner. He's probably got the Cubs game on. Sit at the booth by the bar, where he can see you. Be home by eight."

"Sure you don't wanna come with us?" Marcus asked.

"Thanks, but I'm beat. Go enjoy the game. And shouldn't you change clothes? You'll look like a couple of idiots walking around in your school uniforms at this hour."

"Oh, right," Daniel said, giving himself and his brother a once-over. "C'mon Marcus, let's throw some shorts on and head out."

Within a minute, the boys were changed and out the door.

Larry shook his head, smirking as he watched the boys yank the front door open and bound down the stairway like two newly released jailbirds. He closed the front door.

He walked to his bedroom to unload his gear. At the end of every work day, as he'd done since they day she had died, he picked up the picture of Janna on his nightstand and held it to his chest. He gently set it back down.

As he locked his gun in the wooden gun box on top of the dresser, he noticed the old lock on it was really starting to wear out. He made a mental note to get a new one, then wandered to the kitchen to make his dinner.

5

Mira

Looking up from her files, Mira happened to notice the clock. It was lunchtime already.

It was her third day of work at the newly-opened Chicago Loop branch of Beacon Therapeutic Social Services, and Mira had been asked to lunch by her co-workers Bernice, Edna, and Kim. Bernice was a black woman of about sixty who'd spent the past fourteen years at Beacon's Longwood location. She was at least six feet tall, with a lean frame and bushy gray hair that wrapped around a kind but steely face. Wire-rimmed glasses always rested about two-thirds down the bridge of her nose.

Edna and Kim had worked together at the Calumet Park campus. Both lived on the north side, so they had jumped at the chance to move to the Loop location. Edna was a witty lady whose neatly-styled white hair complemented her always-fashionable clothes, and who moved through life much faster than her short, 63-year old frame should have allowed. Kim, considerably younger than Bernice and Edna, carried a rougher edge through her day. Mira observed that Kim took on the most difficult cases, from child abuse to trauma. The circles under her eyes were but one sign that her cases had taken a long-term effect on her. She'd always schedule ten-minute intervals between clients to allow her to go outside and smoke at least two cigarettes. "One to detox from the last meeting, one to prepare for the next," she'd say.

The four of them found a booth right by the front window, and consuming helpings of pad Thai and pot stickers, chatted about their new clientele.

At a break in conversation, Edna piped in: "Mira dear, do you have a boyfriend?"

Mira froze in her chair, forcing a smile in response. She fought off the hot rush of embarrassment rising in her face. Why, she thought, did people feel the need to break the ice with her using the topic of men? She was single, but had learned that saying so usually led to back-handed compliments ("How on earth could *you* be single?"), followed by the prospective introduction to someone or another. It was flattering for a while, but even the most genuine of compliments aged quickly when repeated too often.

"Hmm, well, why do you ask?" she smiled back at Edna, trying to hide the slight bit of frustration her expression had surely given away.

"Oh, no reason," Edna replied, retreating a bit, still with a genuine smile. "I guess we were just wondering, that's all."

"*I* don't care," Bernice grinned at Mira, taking a sip of her iced tea.

"I think what our friend Edna's getting at," Kim started, "is something about her nephew. Isn't that right Edna? See, we know all about him. I even met him myself. Nice guy, a cop. Low-thirties, lost his wife years ago. Sad story. Still, he's handsome, nice tush. Built like an ox, but wouldn't hurt a fly. So, you wanna meet him?"

Edna flushed, taking a sip of her tea. "Okay, something like that," she admitted.

After hearing about her nephew's wife, Mira decided to humor Edna a little. "Has he dated often since?"

"Not a one," Kim cut in before Edna could respond. "Fussy one he is, if you ask me. Or can't move on, one or the other."

"Let's give Edna a chance here," Mira offered. "Continue, Edna."

"I think," Edna exhaled, putting her palms on the table, "that you've all made your point clear. How about we change the subject? Did you know, the city is going to offer special group therapy sessions at city hall starting week after next, paying moderators $1,000 for each course. It runs six weeks, just two nights a week. There are slots open if any of you girls is interested."

"Something to think about," Kim sat back in her chair, "if you can't get enough of this job during the day. Thanks, I'll keep my evenings to myself."

Bernice had started to flip through the day's edition of the newspaper. "Will you look at that," she said. "Another one of those murders. Just like the others – gang members. One dead, one left alive. Guy all in black, with a ski mask. This is like the fifth one, isn't it?"

"Fifth, sixth," Kim commented passively. "Who's counting?"

"It says here," Bernice continued to read, "that in the last two cases now, the words 'Protector of the People' were found spray painted on the ground underneath the victims. What do you think that means?"

"Well, whatever it means," Edna added, "I'm sure the police are doing their best to catch him."

"I suppose," replied Bernice, scanning down the story. "But apparently whoever it is, they're not leaving much of a trail to follow."

The subject then changed to the weather and other small talk. Soon afterwards, the four of them finished up lunch and headed back to the clinic for their afternoon appointments.

6

Chief Asset Recovery

The man walked in silence along the outer hallway of the Pentagon's southeast section.

The early morning sun cast a faint glare through the heavily tinted windows that lined the wide fourth-floor passageway. Halfway down the passageway, the man stopped in front of a large door. A placard next to it read:

DEPARTMENT OF DEFENSE

SPECIAL PROJECTS DIVISION

Just below the placard was a small touchpad and card-swipe reader. The man placed his left and right thumbs against the touchpad, then swiped his photo-ID card through the reader. A small green light blinked, and the door lock disengaged with a tight clack. He glanced behind him to see a second man, dressed in a blue suit just as he was, walking up. They nodded to one another. The second man reached the touchpad and repeated the process before both proceeded through the door.

"Any advance news you've heard beyond these briefings?" asked David Tolson, stepping up to speak quietly with his colleague.

"Nothing," replied Ferguson Millett, looking straight ahead as he spoke. "Pentagon brass wants to keep a tight lid on this. Nothing outside the inner circle."

"Still no word on CIA or FBI getting involved?" Tolson asked.

"Not that I'm aware of," Millett answered. "From what I've heard, both were specifically locked *out*. Just Defense and NSA. And as far as NSA goes, it's you and me. No one above or below us."

"Gotta love plausible deniability," Tolson remarked.

They turned right at a junction before stopping in front of another door, which was marked with another placard:

SPECIAL OPERATIONS BRIEFING ROOM

ABSOLUTELY NO ADMITTANCE WITHOUT PRIOR CLEARANCE

A guard seated at a desk greeted them. "Badges, please."

Millett and Tolson held up their badges, and the guard waved them through.

They proceeded inside, shutting the sound-proof door behind them.

The large, windowless briefing room was completely insulated: almost a cocoon. Fluorescent light glared over the entry area where the two men stood, but the rest of the room remained in shadow. At the center was a long table with at least ten chairs lining each side, above which was a projector mounted to the ceiling. A podium stood at the far wall, an American flag draped down a pole next to it. On the wall behind the long table was a small camera, mounted just below the ceiling.

Millett and Tolson aside, four other men were in the room: two were seated at the far end of the table, engaged in quiet discussion. The first was Secretary of Defense Aaron Collins; the second was Edward Armstrong, Senior Advisor to Collins.

The other two men in the meeting, Dr. Klaus Johannsen, Chief Scientist of the Advanced Sciences Group within the Special Projects Division, and Marine Colonel Nolan Hayes, who was heading up the asset recovery phase, were back toward the podium area, engulfed in shadow. Johannsen appeared to be poring over something spread across the podium, the small podium light illuminating a small section of whatever he was reading. Hayes stood behind him, dwarfing him by at least a foot.

Upon hearing the door closing, Armstrong turned toward Millett and Tolson, and stood up to greet them.

"Undersecretary Millett, Undersecretary Tolson, welcome back," he said.

"Thank you," Millett answered for both of them.

"Please, have a seat," Armstrong nodded back. "We'll be starting momentarily."

With that, Armstrong turned from them and once again took his seat next to the Defense Secretary, who never turned to acknowledge either of them.

Millett and Tolson exchanged brief looks before approaching the long table, taking a seat next to one another a few chairs down from Armstrong.

Moments later Johannsen switched on the projector, bathing the far wall in pale light. The lights went down, plunging the room into semi-darkness.

The Department of Defense logo appeared on the screen, underneath which read the words in massive black type:

PROJECT SAFEGUARD

Phase I – CHIEF ASSET RECOVERY

PROGRESS UPDATE BRIEFING

Johannsen stepped to the podium to address the group. He was an older man: at least sixty, with a slight build and of average height, bald and bespectacled, wearing a long white lab coat and dark-colored tie. Hayes remained several feet behind the podium, his hulking silhouette remaining still.

"Mr. Secretary, everyone, good morning," he began. His mild, flowing voice spoke with the precise enunciation more of a scientist than a military man. "Today we'll be providing a progress update on the joint initiative between the Department of Defense and NSA, code named Project Safeguard. Does anyone have any initial questions before we get started?"

The room was silent.

"Very well," Johannsen said. He clicked to the next slide. "Then let's begin."

7

The Underground Labs

Elias Todd awoke.

Consciousness returning to him, he opened his eyes slowly, then lifted his head to look around.

He was lying flat on his back, at about a forty-five degree angle, unable to move. His arms and legs were spread and locked into place on a massive table, shackled at the wrists and ankles. A large belt also surrounded his waist. All of it metal. He then noticed the IV drip going into his right forearm.

He began to thrash about, trying to wrench free of his bindings.

He couldn't even budge them.

He glanced once again at the IV and understood: it was weakening him.

Lifting his head once more, he looked beyond the table he was on, taking in the cavernous space around him.

The room was at least twenty-five feet high and stretched perhaps two hundred feet to the far wall. The walls were steel with some areas paneled in white, and a second-level observation room hovered over the lab to his left. A pair of mainframe computers buzzed down toward the end of the room, while two heavily armed soldiers stood by a double-glass door exit about halfway down the right-side wall.

To his right he noticed a second table, identical to the one he was laying on, complete with metal shackles as well.

He took another breath. The air was naturally cool, as if he were underground.

He remembered the SWAT troopers in his home. He'd assumed he'd finally been made, and the authorities had come for him.

But instead of a holding cell, he'd awoken in this high-tech lab.

His thoughts were interrupted by the slow hiss of an air-tight seal being disengaged. He looked up toward the right wall to see the two guards standing at attention, one at each side of the doors. Slowly the heavy doors pushed apart, and two more guards came through, each of them holding a door open. Two men in white lab coats made their way into the room, followed by someone Todd immediately recognized: the large man with the scar.

Todd's face tensed at the sight of him.

Dressed in full military garb, he walked with a powerful air toward the table, ignoring all others around him, his eyes fixated on Todd the entire way, as if sizing up a target. Again, Todd instinctively struggled against his bindings, again to no avail. The man reached the table, regarding Todd with a look of keen curiosity.

"Mr. Todd," he began. "You've been an extremely difficult man to track down, which is no small feat when it's the U. S. Government who's been looking for you."

Todd merely glared back at him, offering no response.

The large man paced for a moment, then stopped and stared silently back at Todd, peering into him intently, as if trying to pry his thoughts from his mind. "Now, I'm sure you have many questions," he continued matter-of-factly. "And while there are some I will not answer, you may ask anyway if you wish."

Todd kept his eyes on the man, saying nothing.

The large man resumed pacing. "Very well," he started again. "Then I'll answer your questions for you. First, who am I. My name is Colonel Nolan Hayes, Executive Special Agent to the NSA. I am the head of Operation C.A.R., short for Chief Asset Recovery; part of a larger undertaking by the Pentagon called Project Safeguard."

He watched Todd closely for reaction, then continued: "Which leads us to your next question: why are you here. You, Elias Masters Todd, aged twenty-eight, are Chief Asset Number One. You have been recovered as a matter of National Security, and are now the indefinite 'guest' of the NSA and Pentagon. Do you understand why?"

After another silence, Hayes moved to Todd's right side, leaning in close. "Mr. Todd," he said in a low voice, a knowing smile on his face. "Haven't you ever wondered just how it is you're able to *do* the things you do?"

A trickle of expression appeared on Todd's face.

"Yes, we know everything about it," Hayes pressed forward. "Your 'abilities' if you will. Speed, strength, stamina, cell regeneration. All of it. Perhaps even some things *you* don't yet know of."

As Hayes was about to continue, a tiny beep sounded. He drew a small transceiver from a clip on his belt and pushed a button to speak: "Hayes."

"Sir," the voice through the tiny speaker said. "We've got a lead on Chief Asset Number Two. You'd better come have a look."

"Copy," Hayes replied, then clipped the small device back into his belt. "Dr. Ingramov," he bellowed to his right. "You may commence with testing. Asset One will soon have some company down here."

Asset Two? Todd thought. For the first time, the possibility dawned on him: were there others out there like him?

The revelation was clearly transparent in Todd's expression, for when Hayes once again turned to look at him, he smiled mockingly once again and said, "Mr. Todd, surely you didn't think you were one of a kind?"

Hayes turned and strode out of the room, leaving Todd alone with his thoughts.

Just then, a second man appeared in front of the table. He had sharp facial features and short, receding reddish-grey hair, completed by a tightly maintained goatee. His white lab coat bore a small plastic tag that read "Ingramov." He was examining Todd very closely, making small markings on a clipboard. As he did this, a pair of lab technicians wheeled a large, gray machine with several wired attachments toward the table, stopping just to his right.

"Mr. Todd," he began in a cordial yet eager tone, with an accent Todd couldn't quite identify. "My name is Dr. Ingramov. I hope you are well rested and ready. We have quite a busy few days ahead of us."

8

Bumps in the Night

A knock came at Rage's door.

"Who the hell is it?" Rage bellowed at the door from the couch.

"Rage it's me, Morty," came the voice through the door. "Open up, I need to talk to you."

The Super. Great, Rage thought as he got up and headed for the door, turning down the mellow sounds of Count Basie from the radio as he did so. Opening the door, he was greeted by the sullen face of Morty Wilkerson. Morty constantly appeared as if he'd just been woken up and wasn't happy about it. His half-tucked shirts, the shuffling of his feet when he walked, and the oil-black comb-over were just a narrow sample of Morty's dead-of-winter demeanor. His trademark was handling tenant complaints with a long sigh and even longer response time. He'd been the Super for the entire three years Rage had lived in the building, and he had visited Rage's unit a total of three times, all in the past two weeks. This was his third and final warning.

"Rage, you know why I'm here. The neighbors are still complaining –"

"One," Rage interrupted. "One neighbor is complaining."

"That's not what's important. Problem is, you got noises coming from your apartment all hours of the night. Screaming and yelling. No one knows what it is or why it's happening. You say you don't even know. But it's loud, and frankly it's scaring the hell outta people."

"Nightmares," Rage said flatly. "That's all. Nobody's damn business."

"Well you've made it *my* damn business," Morty shot back. "I got tenants complaining –"

"ONE," Rage snarled, raising his index finger in front of Morty's face. "You got ONE freakin' tenant complaining. That's it. And you know George Leary is a lying S.O.B. How do you know he's not exaggerating, or even making it up. You don't."

"Rage," Morty said resignedly. "There's more than one now. There're others who've complained. And it's gotten louder. Christ, I heard it myself last night, and I'm two floors above you. I came down here, pounded on your door, even tried to get in, but you'd added all these extra deadbolts here – which by the way you've gotta remove, like *now*. I was about to call the police, but then the noise stopped. Wasn't for your damned loud snoring let me know you're still alive, I'd still have called them. Anyway, tonight is it, Rage. If it happens again tonight, I gotta evict you. I can't have everyone in the building on my ass about this."

Rage stared at him. "You're gonna throw me out, just for that."

"Rage, I got no choice. I'm sorry." And with that, Morty's drooped face turned and then disappeared as he closed Rage's door behind him.

Rage stood at the door for a moment, clenching and releasing his fists. He took a deep breath, turned, and wandered to the kitchen. He then realized he hadn't gotten the day's mail. Grabbing his keys, he walked out his front door and down the steps to the mail boxes in the building's front vestibule.

Coming down the stairs, Rage saw a tall, portly figure in the vestibule, getting the mail as well. It was George Leary.

Rage's scowl spread into a wide, malevolent grin.

9

Altercation

L arry groggily hit the button on the alarm clock, then pulled the window shade to let the early evening light into the bedroom.

Today was a split shift, so Larry had napped away the afternoon and was getting ready to go back on for the evening. He wandered back into the kitchen and opened the fridge. Sparsely positioned among the white wire shelves were a small tub of margarine, four cans of Coke, a carton of orange juice, and three slightly bruised red apples. He turned to the freezer and settled on a TV dinner. After setting it into the microwave and cranking the worn timer knob to four minutes, he flipped on the radio for the evening news. He had to get the TV fixed soon, or maybe get a new one when he could afford it. No wonder the boys had resorted to looking out the window. He made a mental list: grocery shopping. TV. Gun cabinet lock.

He slumped down in his recliner and looked around at the apartment, which for some reason seemed smaller lately. He surveyed with some dissatisfaction the busted TV on the makeshift file-cabinet stand in front of him, to the right of which yawned the bay window. To the right were the four doors leading to the outer hallway, his bedroom, the boys' bedroom, and the bathroom. Finally over his right shoulder, he noted the worn loveseat couch and the small, dingy kitchen, above which he noticed the glued-on plastic light fixture was slowly separating itself from the plaster ceiling.

He leaned his head back and thought of the boys. He'd done his best to raise them since their mother had died. But four years into it he still didn't know what the hell he was doing. He felt he'd been an adequate father, but knew he needed to be a better provider. Not just with normal household items like a TV; but even with the basics, like having more food in the fridge. He'd be able to better fulfill this duty if most of his meager city paycheck didn't already go to fund their private schooling.

Larry was finishing his last bite of dinner when a knock came at his door.

As he got up he smelled a familiar, inviting aroma. He opened the door to find his Aunt Edna, clutching one of her famous fresh-baked apple pies.

Married to Larry's father's only cousin, Aunt Edna was the sole remaining Parker of her generation, by marriage or blood. She'd lost her husband ten years prior, just six weeks after Larry's parents were killed in a car crash. Although they'd never known each other well prior to these events, the proximity of those losses had drawn them closer.

Always popping with energy, Edna had a way of spreading her liveliness evenly throughout a room. She lived toward the west end of their neighborhood, in a small house just off Western and Belle Plaine.

"Hello, dear," she said with a pat to his cheek as she entered the apartment, not waiting to be invited in. She scuttled past him to the far side of the kitchen counter, set the pie down, pulled a kitchen knife from the top drawer, and began to cut it before glancing around the apartment. "Oh, where are the boys? I was hoping to get to visit with all of you!"

"Hello, Aunt Edna," Larry finally managed, walking to the kitchen cabinet and retrieving two plates. "I told them to get out for a bit. You know, cause some trouble."

"Lawrence Parker!" she glared at him. "How many times must I say this, you should not kid around with an old lady. We're likely to believe anything you say."

"Yes'm," he grinned, setting a piece of pie on her plate and then another on his own. "Never again. Promise."

"Well," she added. "I still know well enough not to believe that … but seriously, where are they? It's a school night."

"I sent them down to the corner to get some burgers," Larry said.

"Larry, I thought we talked about this! Sending the boys out to fend for themselves, and on a school night!"

"Aunt Edna, they'll be fine," Larry said, waving a hand dismissively. "It's just at the corner, we've been there a million times. The owner knows 'em, and he'll take good care of them for the hour they're there. Plus the Cubs game is on."

"But what about nutrition? Burgers, again? They're growing boys, they need something healthier! Why don't you all come over three nights a week? I'll make sure you all leave full and happy."

"Aunt Edna, I—" he started.

"Oh, just think about it, will you?" she interrupted.

"Okay," Larry said. "Come sit down, make yourself comfortable. So, how's the new job going? The shorter trip's gotta be nice."

"Oh, that's going along well. You know," she paused and took a bite of pie before continuing, "there's a nice young lady at my clinic. She and I've been chatting, and it appears to me she's single."

Larry stifled a groan. So *this* was the reason for her visit. "Aunt Edna, please, you don't need to--"

"Larry, my goodness," she cut him off. "You're thirty-three years old. It's been four years since we lost Janna, and you've barely dated. You need to start to move on. You're such a handsome young man; it's a crime that you're not making yourself available to nice women. And if you're not going to do it yourself, I'm going to get the ball rolling for you."

He looked up at the clock. "Listen, I need to get going," he said, getting up from the chair abruptly. "You can stay here and wait for the boys if you'd like."

"That's fine, then, Larry," she said, sighing. "Well then, what's on TV tonight?"

"Very funny," he replied, and went into his bedroom to change.

Larry pulled his gray 1987 Buick Regal into the open parallel spot across from the station just in time for his shift. Just as he slammed the driver's side door shut, the side view mirror snapped off, falling to the street with a clang. Larry looked up to see a couple of teenage boys across the street, stopped in their tracks, laughing at him.

"Hey, don't get any ideas," he said, standing up straight and pointing at them. "You try and steal this, I'll find you."

This made the boys laugh even harder. "Man, we ain't big enough to push that thing home!" one of them said, continuing to laugh as they walked away.

Larry picked up the mirror and tossed it on the front seat. With a resigned sigh, he headed into the station to check in.

Inside, Larry's partner Gino was pouring himself a cup of coffee when he saw Larry walking up.

"Ready for another glamorous night," he said, yawning openly.

"Let's hit it," Larry replied.

Larry and Gino had just begun their nightly patrol when the first call of the night came in. "Units, three-eight, report of a disturbance, 1615 West Granville Avenue. Possible assault situation. Altercation is over, subjects have returned to their respective apartments inside the building. Requesting officer to subjects' apartments to question and file report. Units respond."

Larry picked up the handset. "Unit three-nine. Ten-four. En route."

"Ten-four."

10

Old Acquaintances

Larry and Gino parked the cruiser and entered the building at 1615 West Granville.

Looking around the lobby, they could see no signs of a struggle, as was reported.

"So, which one you wanna take," Gino commented tiredly.

"Let's flip," Larry responded.

Moments later, Larry was heading up the stairwell to the alleged assailant's unit, Gino to the victim's. As he ascended, he couldn't help but notice the overall dankness of the building's interior. The failing overhead lights, the dark puddles in the corners of most landings, and the broken railings all made him wonder how anyone could even be living in this place. He made a mental note to call the city and have them see if the building was even up to code.

As he emerged from the stairwell onto the sixth floor, the overhead hallway light went out. He unclipped his flashlight and turned it on. He slowly made his way down the corridor to apartment 611, the residence of the reported assailant. Finding the door, he stepped to one side, briskly knocked three times, and announced himself: "Police."

Nothing from inside. He knocked again.

A few noises came from behind the door, then: "Who is it?"

"Sir, this is the police," Larry replied. "I need to ask you a few questions. Please open the door."

Larry could hear annoyed rumblings inside, then footsteps coming toward the door. Within seconds, it creaked open to reveal a short, muscular figure with matted hair and a scowl on his unshaven face. He was barefoot and wearing a faded red t-shirt and torn jeans. As Larry got his first look into the cold, dark eyes before him, he immediately recognized the man, and fought back a shocked gasp.

The man from the bank robbery; who had intervened in the alley but had disappeared before Larry could question him.

"You," he let escape from his lips.

The man stared back, expressionless. He seemed to identify Larry as well, but he appeared unmoved.

"May I come in," Larry said, reminding himself he still had an immediate duty.

The short, rumpled man hesitated for a moment. "Yeah, sure," he finally replied, stepping aside so Larry could enter. "Have a seat wherever."

Larry stepped in and looked around. The apartment was small and mostly barren; the room's light came from a single bulb with a pull chain hanging from the center of the ceiling, leaving the place relatively dim. The hardwood floor was filthy, and creaked loudly in protest when walked upon. A wooden table and chair were pushed up against the wall just off the tiny kitchenette at the back of the room, next to which was a door that Larry assumed was a closet. A beaten couch and dark wooden coffee table rested in the middle. Peeling, dark green-patterned wallpaper adorned the four walls, giving the place an even darker feel. On the far wall, a faded painting hung crookedly just to the right of the apartment's lone window. A row of cows feeding at a trough.

"Thanks; I'll stand." Larry acknowledged.

"Suit yourself," the man replied, walking to the kitchenette and leaning back against the counter, arms crossed.

Larry thought for a moment, still feeling a strong urge to talk to the man about the bank incident, but knowing he needed to discuss tonight's matter first. He pulled out his notepad and began by stating the facts. "You probably know why I'm here. We received a call this evening about a disturbance in your building. One of your neighbors claims you were involved, so I need to ask you a few questions. First off, the name on your mailbox only says, 'Rage' – is that your last name?"

"It's my only name."

"You don't have a first name?"

"Like I said, one name."

"Do you know a George Leary?"

"Yes," Rage said flatly.

"Were you involved in an altercation with him this evening?"

"Yeah."

"Okay. Mr. Leary claims you attacked him, causing him injury. Is this true?"

"No."

"By your account then, what happened," Larry asked, jotting down notes.

Rage uncrossed his arms, putting his palms on the edge of the counter behind him. "He was getting his mail, I was getting mine. We had words. He made to hit me. I caught his hand and pushed him. He fell and hit his head on the wall."

Larry stared at Rage a long moment, not writing anything down. Being on the force as long as he had, he'd developed a knack for spotting lies. But he couldn't read this one. By all measures the man seemed to be telling the truth, but Larry had a feeling that if George Leary had cracked his head open on that brick wall, this guy would be all the happier for it.

Larry looked back down at the notepad, putting down a few more notes. "Are you aware that your neighbor wants to press charges?"

Rage exhaled through his nostrils. "First off, he's not a neighbor. Just because we live in the same building doesn't qualify him for that. Neighbors are friendly. This guy's a piece of crap."

"Aside from that," Larry continued, waving off the comment. "At this point we're not going to make any arrests, and we don't need to bring you in for questioning. But if he does follow through with charges, it'll likely be for aggravated assault, and it'll be his word against yours. So you'll need to secure an attorney. Do you understand?"

Rage said nothing for a moment, then: "The front hall has a security camera. They keep the memory disk for a week, before erasing it, in case there's a break-in. Why don't you just take it and see for yourself what happened," he said matter-of-factly.

Larry stopped writing. He hadn't recalled seeing a camera in the lobby, and he thought he would have noticed one if it was there.

"Where is this camera?"

"Hidden," Rage replied. "Under the bottom stair of the second landing. Red light is covered so people don't see it there. Building had a problem with earlier ones getting broken once they were noticed."

"You seem to know an awful lot about this building," Larry commented.

"Stands to reason one should know some things about where one is living, don't you think?" Rage said plainly.

"I suppose," Larry muttered, taking down more notes. "We'll certainly have a look at it."

Once he'd finished writing down everything he needed for the report, Larry put away his notepad and glanced over at the door before looking back at Rage.

"Got everything you need?" Rage asked, a clear attempt to bid Larry goodnight.

"Yes," Larry acknowledged. "But … I need to ask you a few more questions."

"About what?" Rage said knowingly, crossing his arms again.

"I think you know perfectly well what," Larry replied.

"Okay, suit yourself," Rage shrugged indifferently.

Larry glanced down to his notepad again, but he didn't pick it up this time. He looked back up at Rage and said plainly, "There are a lot of questions. First, I want to know why you did what you did, and then, how."

Rage went to the sink and poured himself a glass of water. Picking up a second glass, he gestured in offer to Larry as well.

"No, thanks," Larry replied.

Rage downed the glass of water, set it on the counter, wiped his mouth, and said matter-of-factly, "A woman was gonna die. Something had to be done."

"And what if the officer on the scene had the situation under control?" Larry commented.

"My right shoulder would argue that he didn't," Rage replied.

"I'll need to ask you about that in a moment. But first I need to know how."

"I know Martial Arts."

"Is that all? Because I know quite a few things myself, and what you did, I've never seen anything like that before."

"I make things up as I go."

"I see," Larry wondered, examining Rage's expression. "Then how, when you hit the first perpetrator in the chest, did you send him flying ten feet into a wall? As I recall from the hospital report, the man had several cracked and broken ribs. From one punch. You could've killed him."

Rage held back a cold smile. "So?"

"So, I've never seen anyone land a punch that sent someone flying like that."

"I work out. And he was off-balance."

"Right," Larry replied, increasingly skeptical. "Your shoulder," he continued, pointing to Rage's right shoulder. "We checked every ER in the area looking for you. Where did you go?"

"What does any of this have to do with your case?" Rage noted.

"YOU have everything to do with it," Larry shot back. "You were a key witness, and more importantly a participant. You fled a crime scene, which is in violation of the law. You were needed for questioning. For that alone I could bring you in right now."

"You threatening me for what I did?" Rage said quietly.

"I'm stating the facts," Larry replied. "There's due process, and you were a part of that process. You leaving the scene left open holes in the case. We needed answers -- from you -- to fill those holes."

"I think I've given you what you needed," Rage said thoughtfully.

"We can do this one of two ways," Larry said. "I can come back with a warrant if need be."

"Then do that."

Larry exhaled, keeping mind of the situation. He knew he had cause to arrest Rage, just based off George Leary's accusations. He could roll the incident from weeks ago into the one arrest and get a warrant from there.

But he felt an odd sense of obligation to this man, for his actions in the alley …

"Let me remind you that these are just questions," Larry said, making his decision. "You're making this harder than it needs to be."

"You asked questions. 1 gave answers. End of story. You wanna make it into something more, go back and get a warrant."

The two exchanged a long stare. Finally, Larry broke the silence. "Then I'll be back. You have a good evening."

And with that, he left the apartment.

Back in the lobby, Larry arrived to find Gino waiting for him. "Took you so long?" he asked, leaning up against the mailboxes with arms crossed.

"Guy'd been sleeping. Took him awhile to get to the door," Larry lied. "What'd your guy have to say?"

Gino grinned. "Guy's a real piece of work. Had a lot of conflicting details, was real dramatic, seems he really hates the other guy. You ask me, I think he's full of it."

Larry pondered that for a moment. "My guy claims he just reacted in self-defense ... gut tells me he's telling the truth, but ... I don't know," he trailed off.

They made to leave, then Larry stopped. "Wait," he said, walking over to where Rage had told him the security camera was. Sure enough there it hung, just under the stairs. "We need to talk to the Super, get the memory disk from this camera."

"Fine, but then we're outta here," Gino exhaled. "This place gives me the creeps."

Larry smirked; in all their years as partners, he'd never heard Gino say anything like that. He headed for the stairs. "Come on," he said, and the two made their way to the Super's apartment.

11

Learnings

The lights were low in the Underground Labs. The night guard kept watch by the door.

Elias Todd remained still on the examination table, the hair on the back of his neck bristling against the table's smooth, cold titanium surface.

He'd kept quiet and still since arriving two days before, listening to all that was being said around him. Learning.

What this facility was. What was in store for him. Who they were.

It turned out the facility was a testing ground for some top-secret military project. Apparently Elias was both prototype and sample base for the project.

Ingramov was the head scientist on the project. Another – named Barnes – was second in rank. Ingramov took the samples, Barnes tested and reported on them.

Then there was Ingramov's assistant, Polosky. A rotund, bald, bearded, flaccid-faced man, Polosky was both frightened of Todd and intimidated by Ingramov. His pathetic, almost nervous actions made it clear he was in over his head. Todd wondered how the imbecile had even been allowed in the building.

Todd wanted to hiss at him just to get a reaction from the man; or perhaps give him a heart attack.

Ingramov was a different story completely. He seemed to delight in Todd's pain and suffering. Todd couldn't wait to tear him limb from limb.

He'd often heard Ingramov refer to a "Project Safeguard," but he had no idea what it actually meant.

Lifting his head once more, he glanced around the low-lit room. The guard remained in his chair. He'd begun to nod off.

Todd thought about what had been done to him thus far.

Electric shocks. Continuous currents. Pressure points. Needles, large and small. Probes. Biopsies. All without anesthesia.

Through all of it Todd kept his pain inside of him, gritting his teeth through the agony, letting his anger build within him. He would get an opening, he knew he would; and when it came, he would kill them all.

First Polosky, then Ingramov, and finally Hayes.

But he wouldn't stop with them.

There were dozens, perhaps hundreds of people inside the complex. All of them.

His face twitched, then twisted into a disturbed grin.

If his life as he had known it was over ... if his vast riches, his estate, his life's work were already out of reach ... then he truly had nothing to lose.

He would kill them all. Wipe the facility off the map.

It would be the mark he would leave on the world.

12

Cautious Endeavor

Deep within the Pentagon, Edward Armstrong was making edits to a border defense plan when his secretary buzzed him.

"What is it, Marlene," he exhaled, setting down the red-ink pen.

"A General Dunlap here to see you, sir," the voice replied through the speakerphone.

"Hmm," Armstrong paused, stroking his chin. "All right then, send him in," he finally said, stacking the papers strewn across his desk and setting them in his inbox.

The heavy steel door opened, ushering in the tall, broad frame of General Jack Dunlap. He was dressed in full uniform as always, presenting the many service marks and medals packed tightly across his lapels. His clean-shaven, bald head and neatly trimmed mustache belied his gray, bushy eyebrows. A thirty-year Marine veteran and decorated war hero, Dunlap had been Armstrong's acquaintance since the Somalian missions they'd worked on together some fifteen years before, when Armstrong had been a military strategist, and Dunlap a Lieutenant. Now heading up the Pentagon's special task forces unit, Dunlap was viewed by many as next in line for promotion to Joint Chiefs.

Armstrong rose to greet him, then motioned for him to have a seat.

"Edward," Dunlap said, nodding as he sat down.

"Jack," Armstrong replied. "Haven't seen you since the North Korea debrief in December. How's the family?"

"Good, Edward, good," Dunlap said, a look on his face Armstrong couldn't identify. He appeared ready to speak when Armstrong cut in.

"So, what can I do for you?" he said curiously.

"Edward," Dunlap began. "One of the men under my command was recently tapped for a top-secret operation within our borders. Colonel Nolan Hayes. I was wondering if you knew anything about it."

Armstrong paused, leaning back in his chair.

"I might," he answered carefully, folding his hands together.

"Don't play games," Dunlap said sharply. "You either know or you don't."

"I do," Armstrong admitted.

"What are you doing running an operation within the homeland?" Dunlap questioned. "Is this in a *civilian* environment?"

"Jack, as you've already said," Armstrong replied. "It's top secret. I'm prohibited from speaking about it."

"But Hayes," Dunlap pressed. "He's one of my men. Why didn't you come to me first? At least for a POV? Do you understand the implications of deploying him inside our borders?"

"We've read the file on him, yes," Armstrong answered. "He's the perfect fit for this mission."

"He's also extremely *dangerous,"* Dunlap shot back, leaning forward. "Placing him in a civilian atmosphere puts us at incredible risk."

"We know what we're doing," Armstrong said flatly. "His skills make him the only one who can carry out the operation the way it needs to be done."

"Edward, listen to me," Dunlap said, his tone urgent. "If it's not too late already, you need to pull the plug, *now.* Hayes should only be deployed in hot zones, deep behind enemy borders, on the other side of the *world.* There are plenty of those missions to keep him busy. Under no circumstances should he be anywhere *near* U.S. civilians, innocents, or even *cameras*, for that matter."

"Jack, I don't understand," Armstrong said, flabbergasted. "He's the best soldier this country has; a decorated war hero, just like yourself."

"He's the best soldier we have," Dunlap said. "Because he is a killing *machine.* Yes, he's killed a lot of our most dangerous enemies. Hundreds, maybe a *thousand.* But there have also been scores of civilian casualties, even American soldiers."

"That's part of war," Armstrong said. "You know that."

"Not this way," Dunlap countered. "He has no regard for human life. *Any* human life. If you could only see what I've seen, you'd understand."

"Jack," Armstrong said, "I hate to put this argument to bed. But it's a moot point. The field leg of the mission began several days ago, without incident, I might add. The SRC created an antidote to his condition. To control these ... *urges* he has."

"Antidote?" Dunlap asked curiously.

"Yes," Armstrong answered. "There's a shot; he injects himself twice a day."

Dunlap paused, an almost hopeful expression on his face, as if he wanted nothing more than to be wrong about what he'd said. "Has the field leg concluded?" he asked.

"No," Armstrong answered. "But we're halfway there."

"Then I hope you're right; that he's taking the meds as you say he is," Dunlap said, standing up to leave. "And if for any reason he stops ... God help us all."

13

Lies and Videotape

Larry and Gino were headed northbound on Wabash Avenue when the call came in from the station.

Larry picked up the handset. "Three-nine responding."

"The lab's finished with the security footage you dropped off last night. Report will be ready when you return to the station," replied the voice.

"Can we see the footage?" Larry asked.

"Affirmative, just stop by the lab when you're in."

"Ten-four," Larry responded, then placed the handset back in its cradle.

Gino glanced over at him. "So, you wanna go back to the station."

"Yup. We've gotta head back up toward that way anyway."

They sat in silence for a moment as Gino turned onto Jackson toward Grant Park. Finally, he exclaimed, "I mean, what's so interesting about this case? You know *we* don't need to see the video; only the court does – *if* the guy decides to press charges."

"I need to see something," Larry said quietly.

"See what? A guy get shoved into a wall?"

"No. There's something about this guy," Larry thought aloud.

"The assailant?"

"Yeah," he replied, still immersed in his thoughts.

"Will you quit talking like that and just spit it out?"

"You remember the bank robbery. Weeks back."

"Course I do."

"In the alley. The guy who intervened and then disappeared."

"Yeah," Gino said expectantly.

"That was him."

"The assailant," Gino repeated. "From last night."

"Yes."

"Is the guy from the bank robbery," Gino said. "Are you sure."

"Without a doubt."

"Hrrmmm," Gino mumbled, unsure of what to make of it. "He recognize you?"

"Yep. I asked him about it."

"What'd he say?"

"Not much. Admitted being there, gave a lame explanation on how he took apart the bank robbers, then told me to go get a warrant if I wanted to know more."

"Clever son of a bitch, eh," Gino said. "So, that's where it left off?"

"Yes."

"And what are you gonna do?"

"I'm going to get a warrant."

"Fine," Gino said, bothered. "But let's think about this. The bad guys are locked up and awaiting trial. Prosecution has enough witnesses to win the case, hands down. What could this guy possibly have to add?"

"Just let me do this, okay?"

"Whatever," Gino relented. "But the Chief's gonna bust your balls about wanting to chase this guy while we're supposed to be tracking the vigilante serial killer, or whatever he's supposed to be. And I sure as hell wouldn't blame him."

They drove in silence the rest of the way to the station, where Gino parked the cruiser in its spot on Addison just west of Halsted. Larry kept his gaze straight ahead of him, but he could still feel Gino's glances as they got out of the car and climbed the front steps. He knew his partner had a lot more to say on the topic – Gino would sometimes force out a sigh through his nostrils when fighting the urge to speak his mind. The more sighs, the more he had to say. Since getting onto Lake Shore Drive, Larry had counted about twenty of them.

Once inside the station, Larry and Gino proceeded through the precinct's main room, heading in the direction of the lab.

The windowless lab at the precinct was housed in the basement, the coolest part of the building. It was a small room, not much more than a holding area for evidence waiting to be transferred to one of the city's bigger investigative facilities, but it had the essentials: two examination tables, two computer workstations, a basic chem set, two microscopes, and a very anal retentive lab technician: Robby Morton.

Larry and Gino entered to see Robby in the corner of the room, hovering over his computer screen, gazing at it fixedly, his tiny, recessed eyes squinting as they scanned down the screen. His thin frame was straddling a high stool, his shoulder-length curly brown hair pulled back neatly in a short ponytail and his long lab coat as white as ever.

"Robby," Larry said in greeting as he approached from the left, making Robby just about jump off his stool.

"Jesus, Parker," Robby protested. "Can't you guys knock or something when you come into my lab?"

"*Your* lab, eh?" Gino smirked. "Come on Robby, you're a cop. Can't be jumpy in this line of work."

"Hey, I'm a lab guy," Robby replied defensively. "You guys take care of the streets; I'll stick with the heady stuff in here."

Gino glanced over at the chem set, noticing that many of the bottles were on the far examination table and out of their specifically marked slots on the shelves. "Looks to me like you're keeping things a little less tidy these days," he said, pointing at the table. "Maybe a little time back on the streets'd keep you more on your toes here in the lab."

Robby glanced at Gino with annoyance, then back over to Larry. "You want to see the video stream, right?"

"That's why we're here," Larry acknowledged.

"Let me cue it up for you," Robby replied hastily, stepping over to the second workstation. "This is just a basic altercation, nothing special or interesting about it."

"Maybe not for everyone," Larry said patiently.

Robby sighed to the room as he clicked to open the video file. "I've edited this copy down to the ninety or so seconds you're interested in," he explained. Stepping back from the table, he motioned exaggeratedly to the screen. "There you go, see for yourself."

Larry stepped forward to the workstation, watching closely as the grainy, black and white video clip began to run. The first few seconds show the witness, a large, portly man named George Leary, walking up to the mailboxes mounted into the vestibule's far wall. He produces a key and opens the small metal door to collect his mail. The man stands with his back to the camera for a few more seconds, seemingly thumbing through the mail. He carelessly tosses a few pieces toward the small plastic wastebasket in the corner by the front vestibule door, missing the basket both times, and not attempting to pick up either piece. He then moves to his left and watches a second, much smaller figure approach the row of mailboxes, about four feet to his right. The assailant.

At first, the second figure does not seem to acknowledge Leary, but then he turns his head slightly in Leary's direction, as if saying something to him. Leary seems to say something in reply, his body language becoming more rigid, more exasperated. While this is happening the assailant appears calm, barely reacting to this sudden change in the larger man's demeanor.

As the second man turns to walk away toward the stairs, Leary appears to cock his right arm, then lunges, throwing a punch toward the back of the smaller man's head. Almost too quickly for the low-resolution camera to capture, the smaller man turns and catches Leary's fist in mid-swing. Inexplicably, Leary begins to stumble backward and slips on a piece of mail he'd previously tossed onto the floor. He falls into the row of mailboxes on the far wall, appearing to hit the back of his head on its steel surface.

The second man observes this for a split second before turning back toward the stairs and disappearing from view. Leary can be seen rubbing the back of his head profusely for the next several seconds. Finally he gathers himself up and walks slowly back toward the stairs.

"Satisfied?" both Gino and Robby said in unison from behind Larry, then exchanged inquiring glances at each other.

"No," Larry replied quietly, mostly to himself. "How do you rewind this?"

"Seriously?" Robby asked. "If you can't figure this out, how are you going to learn the Niss?"

"Niss …?" Gino asked.

"You know," Robby glanced sideways at him. "National Information Sharing System. You know, the new data interface with the FBI. Part of the Patriot Act. The program you guys are supposed to be learning."

"One partner per team is s'posed to be learning it, not both," Gino said. "And I don't do technology. So Larry, you mean."

"Come on, Robby," Larry said, getting impatient. "Show me how to rewind it."

"Technically it's digital, so there's no rewind," Robby said shrewdly. "But do you see the progress bar at the bottom of the screen? Just drag the cursor to where you want it, and then hit the 'play' button at left."

"Thanks," Larry responded, beginning to drag the cursor backward to the point he wanted to view again.

"You'll see the other buttons just below 'play' – 'stop', 'pause', 'rewind'; just think of it as a new age VCR," Robby continued.

"Enough, smart guy. He's got a DVD player," Gino cracked.

"Well, welcome to the '90s then," Robby said as he walked away, then began to replace the chem bottles in their marked slots on the shelves.

Larry restarted the video clip at the point where Leary was about to swing at the back of the smaller man's head. He paused it just as the right arm had begun to move forward, with the second man still walking away from him. "Now how do I get this to run very slowly," he asked.

Robby replaced the bottle he was holding into its slot, wiped off his hands with a small towel, and walked back over to Larry. "What do you need to see?"

"When the assailant turns around," Larry explained. "I want to see in detail what happens next."

"Frame by frame," Robby said, nodding. "Hang on, that's a different setting." Walking to Larry's right and palming the mouse, Robby opened a few menus and made some adjustments to the viewer's settings, then pointed the cursor back to the 'play' button. "Whenever you're ready," he said.

"What did you just do?" Larry asked curiously.

"I just reset the player to go frame by frame for you," Robby explained. "You'll need to click the play button each time you want to advance it one frame. See the backward arrow next to it? That'll take you back one frame."

"Thanks," Larry said. "Don't think I could've figured that out myself?"

"Unlikely," Robby said with a sigh, turning around and heading back to the chem set.

Larry clicked the play button once. Twice. A third time, advancing the clip one frame at a time. "Hey," he asked. "How many frames a second you think this is?"

"Oh, I don't know … most good quality digitals go at about 120 frames a second. That one is probably thirty," Robby said casually, continuing to clean the bottles and replace them on the shelf.

Larry continued to advance the clip shot by shot. On the eighth frame, the smaller man's position changed dramatically: he had gone from a normal walking stance, both arms at his sides, to a full defensive position, turned completely around, his right hand grabbing the larger man's extended fist in mid-swing. Larry clicked the back arrow one frame to be sure: the seventh frame, as he'd thought, showed the smaller man in mid-stride, walking away, no indication of the move he was about to make.

"Gino," Larry said slowly. "Take a look at this."

Gino, who'd walked over to the far table to glance at the newspaper's sports section, exhaled and sauntered back over toward the workstation, stopping just behind Larry. "Let's see," he said plainly.

Larry went back a few frames and forwarded them for Gino one at a time. "This is frame by frame—"

"Yeah, I heard that," Gino interrupted him.

"Hang on," Larry said. Getting to the seventh frame, he continued: "In this shot, the assailant is walking away. See? But if I advance it just once, look at this."

Gino watched the screen. "That's one frame?"

"Yes."

Robby, whose interest had been re-captured by this comment, walked over to the screen as well.

"Advance it one more," Gino said, moving up so he was directly to Larry's right.

Larry clicked forward to frame nine. Not much change from the previous shot, with one exception that Gino immediately noticed.

"Is he *smiling*?" he asked, astonished.

Larry went back to frame eight, then forward again to nine. Sure enough, the pose hadn't changed, but the smaller man, who'd seemed to show no expression in the previous frame, appeared to be smiling in this one. It was an oblique angle at best, but even through the grainy video, it was unmistakable.

"What the hell," Gino whispered aloud.

Larry stared into the screen, then clicked to the next shot. The smaller man's arm had moved slightly: an inch at most, as if he were flicking his wrist. Alongside this change, Leary's head had jerked forward two to three inches, as if he were being pushed.

Frame eleven followed through on the movement shown in frame ten: Leary's head jerked slightly further forward, his body beginning to move backward toward the far wall. Frames twelve through twenty-five showed the remainder of the incident, as Leary stumbled backward, slipped on the piece of mail on the floor and fell into the far wall, hitting his head hard on the row of mailboxes.

Larry turned back to Robby. "Thirty frames a second, you said?"

"Yes," Robby acknowledged, eyes glued to the screen as well. "I mean, that's got to be what it is. It can't be any slower."

Larry turned back to the screen and thought hard for a moment. If in fact thirty frames per second was the right pace of the video stream – and he trusted Robby's judgment – the smaller man appeared to be moving at almost inhuman speed.

Addressing the current situation, the video definitely confirmed that the smaller man's story was in fact true, and that Leary had been lying. But on a broader scale, and of more interest to Larry, was the fact that this evidence demonstrated how this man was able to incapacitate the two bank robbers in the alley several weeks ago.

But there was also something else; something Larry couldn't quite place …

Gino, sensing Larry's thought process, chimed in. "Okay. So now what?"

"I told you now what," Larry said, turning around to face Gino.

"Fine then," he said resignedly. "Need anything else in here?" he added, gesturing to the room.

"Nope."

"Then let's get on with it. Maybe once you get this done, you'll get your head back out of the clouds."

Robby Morton had wandered back over by the chem set, but he watched curiously as Gino and Larry walked out of the lab. With a dismissive sigh, he turned his attention back to the bottles.

14

Strangers on a Train

Twilight had spread across the sky by the time Rage began his walk to the northbound Red Line station.

Earlier in the day he'd heard the contractor tell a colleague they'd found a buyer willing to pay a premium if the building could be completed fifteen days ahead of schedule, so they'd asked the crew to double efforts and stay longer hours in return for the promise of double-time pay. Rage decided he could use the money, and he didn't really have anything better to do during the day, so he'd agreed to take on the extra hours.

As he walked, he pulled a small piece of paper from his inside jacket pocket. He unfolded it and held it open in his hand, reading the words silently to himself.

Mira looked over at the clock on her desk: coming up on eight-thirty. She was exhausted. She'd been in the office over twelve hours now, trying to catch up on paperwork. The place was dead quiet; she'd turned on a few lights in the lobby as well as the desk lamp in her office, but the office was largely unlit.

Her schedule was completely full for Monday, which was the reason she'd come into the office tonight, so as to not fall too far behind. She wiped her eyes, took a sip of stale coffee, and resumed entering case notes into her computer. Four down, one to go.

As he approached the Monroe Red Line stop, Rage tucked the piece of paper back into his jacket pocket. The night had become cooler, and it was starting to sprinkle rain. The street was dark and mostly empty, the stores along State Street having closed.

Pulling his jacket closer around him, he descended the stairs into the station.

Mira closed the door to her office and walked to the reception desk. Stopping just short of the door, she fished in the shoulder bag for cab money.

She pulled out a few singles and eventually discovered a five-dollar bill, but the grand sum of eight dollars she'd found would never get her all the way back to her neighborhood. Frowning, she tried to remember where the closest ATM was – usually the city had one every fifty feet, but for some reason the city block surrounding her office had none – save for the convenience store which had already closed at eight o'clock.

She looked outside. Raining. She remembered the rule of thumb about cabs in any city: whenever it rains, they're never to be found. Either way, it was wet outside, so she pulled her umbrella from the satchel, and in the process her CTA transit card flipped out of the bag high into the air, dropping to the floor. Believing it to be a sign, she picked up the card and pushed her way outside, locking the door behind her.

Rage slipped his card through the reader and pushed through the turnstile into the Monroe station. Far underground, the station was protected from the elements, but it was damp and grimy. And it smelled a mix of raw sewage combined with rotting food.

He looked around. The station was mostly empty; only a young couple and an older man stood waiting on the platform. The overhead lights flickered, causing the few other waiting passengers to look up toward the ceiling.

Suddenly feeling tired, Rage sat down on a wooden bench. He ran his palms through his matted hair several times. No Lessons tonight. He finally leaned forward, placed his face in his hands, and waited for the train.

Mira descended the steps into the Monroe Red Line stop, entering through the turnstile at the base of the stairs. Hearing the rumble of the northbound train as it rolled into the station below, she hurried down the second set of steps toward the platform.

As the train pulled into the station, Rage wearily got up and shuffled toward the opening doors. Less than a foot from the door he felt something grasp the sleeve of his jacket. He looked down to see a bony, gnarled hand; then turned back to meet the expectant eyes. It was an old woman. Nodding awkwardly, he held out his arm to assist the woman onto the train.

Getting to the bottom of the stairs, Mira walked quickly across the stone floor, stepping into the rear car just as the doors were about to close. She glanced around the train, noting it was about half full. Quiet for this time on a Friday night, she thought.

Taking a seat by the window just inside the vestibule, she removed from her bag the paperback she was reading and flipped to the bookmarked page. She settled into her seat, placing her bag on the empty seat next to her.

Rage sat down to the right of the doors. Inexplicably the trains were still heated even this far into spring, and the vent above was blowing hot air right on him. He grunted irritably and pulled off his jacket, scrunching it between him and the wall.

The train made several stops before Mira looked up to see how far they'd come. As the train slowed, the loudspeaker announced they were approaching the North and Clybourn stop. She looked out the window, relieved she hadn't missed her stop. Then, with a tiny sigh of relief, she turned back to the paperback.

As the doors opened, her attention was torn from the story as someone ran by her seat, grabbing her satchel and sprinting out the doors. Before she could react, a second person got up from his seat across the vestibule and bolted for the door as well. Her eyes followed as they ran for the stairs. With a speed her eyes could barely follow, the second man tackled the first, causing the contents of the satchel to spill all over the stone floor. She saw the second man get up and plant a hard kick to the first man's stomach, then quickly move to gather the loose items. Mira made for the door, and as she did, the man finished replacing the items into her bag and turned back toward the doors. When she was a mere foot from the doorway, the two doors closed, and she stood face to face with the second man, still on the other side of the door, looking in at her.

As the train began to move she caught sight of his eyes, those black eyes she'd seen weeks before. She stood riveted to the floor, watching him watching her, her bag still in his hand, as the train pulled from the station into the blackness of the tunnel.

15

Samples and Strands

The tap of heeled shoes on tile floor was the only sound that echoed throughout the otherwise dark and silent hallway.

The underground halls of the Department of Defense's Strategic Research Complex, also known as the SRC, had fallen quiet since the last shift departed hours before. The clack of each step reverberated off the floors and brick walls as the steps approached the north end labs, announcing the arrival of the newest member of the Project Safeguard research team.

Dr. Loretta Barnes was wrapping up her second week, and in all her years in biochemistry, she'd never seen anything like this place. The technology, the security, the wide array of equipment. All of it was far more advanced than anything she'd worked with in the private sector.

She'd worked late into the night each of the past four days. The massive amounts of data the samples team had compiled was keeping her more than occupied, and she was motivated to discover more. Even this late on a Friday evening, she was reluctant to go home.

She was close to a medical breakthrough: to replicate a unique strand of DNA that could potentially provide cures for a range of medical conditions, including many which had been called untreatable. After her first week of debriefing and signing her life away to secrecy, her second week had begun with a series of sample testing and advanced modeling on the project's chief subject.

Her only concern was on the moral grounds of the project. While the goal of the research was beneficial for all, the means by which they were doing it were questionable in her mind. The source of the DNA strand, a 28-year old male, was being held on a specially-constructed titanium observation table in the main lab, never once being allowed to move. This precaution was something she didn't fully understand, and whenever she inquired about it to the lead scientist or Executive Special Agent in charge of the project, they would merely say that it was for everyone's protection, and that she was advised to refrain from asking further questions.

With that in mind, Loretta had decided to look further into the case file herself. Though her job entailed nothing more than analyzing and modeling samples taken from the subject, if she were ever questioned, she'd claim she needed to better understand the subject to further her analysis.

She'd learned his name, Elias Todd, and much of his history: he had no surviving family, no close friends or associates, and he worked alone, which meant no one on the outside would immediately be looking for him.

But there was something else odd about the case file.

For one, she could tell that large chunks of information had been removed from the file, leading her to believe there was much more to his story than was in the official records. Exactly *what* was being kept secret she had no idea.

The veil of secrecy around him truly puzzled her.

Arriving at her lab desk, she pulled over a stool to sit down. Tying her shoulder-length, sandy-blond hair into a ponytail, she began to pore over the day's data: arrays of detailed graphs, digital micro-images, and multi-directional charts.

The subject was truly an amazing specimen. The sample tests showed many abnormalities from a normal human nervous system: a staggering resistance to disease, incredibly rapid cell regeneration, and several other anomalies.

Exactly what it all meant she didn't yet know. Thus far, she'd been focused only on the regenerative traits of Todd's DNA. That, and nothing else, was what she'd been assigned to pursue.

But to uncover how exactly all of these anomalies were possible ... She needed to run more analysis – with or without prior clearance.

She glanced around the lab, trying to decide whether she wanted to go down that path.

The data in front of her could only take her so far; she would need to obtain more information from the samples themselves.

On that note, she made her decision.

She pushed back the stool and walked over to the refrigeration chamber in the corner of the lab. Inside, hundreds of samples adorned the walls, taken from a number of subjects over the years. She pulled down the newest plastic container, marked "Todd, Elias M." and opened it, pulling out one of the five tiny vials half-filled with the subject's blood. She examined it closely, as if trying to spot anything unique about it just by plain sight, then walked over to the microscope stations at the other end of the lab. She extracted a miniscule amount with an eye dropper and carefully squeezed it onto a clear strip of plastic. She then pressed another strip on top and placed the sample in the microscope's examination tray.

Loretta hopped up onto the stool, pulled herself up close, and began to adjust the high-powered microscope into focus.

She was ready for a long night.

16

The Night Caller

The night sky loomed large over Mira as she scaled down the stairs of the Wilson Red Line stop.

It had stopped raining, but the wind continued to pick up. Mira ran along Wilson Avenue and then up Clark Street as fast as she could, gasping for air as she reached her apartment building. Praying the spare key to her unit was still where she'd hidden it, she buzzed the Super's apartment to let her in the front door, explaining she'd misplaced the key. After reminding her of the $50 replacement fee, he buzzed her in. She raced up the four flights of stairs to her landing, budged the old wooden door to the hallway open, and dropped to her knees as she reached her own door halfway down the hallway. Her long fingers scraped the bottom of the dark wood molding as she reached underneath it to retrieve the key. Grasping it, she pulled the key out of the small hidden cubbyhole and, still on her knees, pushed it into the door lock. She flung the door open, scooting into the apartment before immediately slamming the door shut behind her.

Once inside, she felt her heartbeat start to slow back to normal. She fell back onto the couch, closing her eyes to shut out the images, which only became more vivid. The room began to spin; too many thoughts rushed at her, taking turns at the forefront of her mind …

As the train pulled out of the station she stood there at the doors, watching the mysterious figure she'd seen at the bank weeks before, holding her satchel, staring back at her, clearly recognizing her as well.

Still in the vestibule as the train went into the tunnel, she stood, indecisive, when she noticed the man's black denim jacket was stuffed into the corner of the seat where he'd been sitting. Instinctively she went to the seat and picked up the jacket, holding it for a moment, still uncertain.

He had everything of hers, she knew: her keys, wallet, all her identification, everything. Although he'd tried to return the bag to her at the train stop, she had no idea when or even if he would try again.

Digging through his jacket, she looked for any way she might be able to contact him: driver's license, cell phone, credit card, anything.

The outside pockets contained nothing: a few coins and lint.

When she reached the first inside pocket, her hand found something soft. She pulled it out. It was a black ski mask.

Odd, she thought; why a ski mask in April?

Stuffing it back into the pocket, she went to the other inside pocket and found a small piece of paper. Unfolding it, she mouthed the words scrawled at the top: 'Protector of the People.'

Not making a connection but now curious, she began to read down the sheet of paper. It appeared to be some kind of manifesto or speech.

Her eyes widened as the revelation swept across her mind like a chilling wind.

Was this *him?*

The man who'd saved her life at the bank ... was *he* the serial killer?

Those horrible black eyes ... she recognized him, and she could now identify him.

He recognized her as well ... and it wouldn't take him long to figure out the situation. And now he knew where she lived.

He'd rescued her ... but now he's wanted for murder, and he would know she could identify him ... and now he knew how to find her.

She opened her eyes. The thoughts continued to spin in her head, whirling around without pause, without mercy. They branched and spread into more thoughts, more questions, until she shook her head, furiously trying to wrest the thoughts from her mind, putting all of her focus into the room, on what she needed to do now.

Should she call the police?

Tell them she saw him again? Would they believe her? Would he come for her; harm her, kill her for knowing who he was? Logic would say it was possible, but somehow, she didn't think so. He'd rescued her, saved her from being kidnapped or killed; did that make her indebted to him, or to the law?

And there was something else about him, something she couldn't place. When she saw him through the train doors, looked through the blackness that was his eyes, she saw a glimpse of what was inside. Pain and loneliness. A haunted past.

Her mind raced back into the moment, and she decided she needed to do something, take some action of some sort, just to clear her mind ...

Cancel the credit cards. Call a locksmith.

Yes, take care of the basics; the known. Doing that might provide clarity on what to do about the larger issue at hand.

She ran to the phone book and looked up a locksmith.

As she was dialing the phone, her apartment buzzer rang.

17

Asset Two

In the offices above the SRC's Underground Labs, a small band of light shone from underneath a closed door.

The West Wing comprised the public front of the facility; it was the only area of the complex that included floors above ground. Much more like an office than the rest of the complex, it was where the business of SRC dealings was handled. Fluorescent lights hung above a sea of cubicles and offices. The atmosphere was animated during daylight hours with office staff scurrying about, and with the buzz of fax machines, copiers, and routine phone conversations. Though this was where the SRC's money changed hands, the vast majority of the staff did not know the true nature of what went on in the Underground Labs.

On this Friday evening, the office was completely vacant, its lights turned out, the buzz of the day long faded into silence. The only light came from the emergency exit units and from under the closed door of the back conference room.

Behind that door, Nolan Hayes stood at the head of a long oak table, hands cupped back over the edge as he loomed over maps, police reports, news stories, and schematics. Next to him was Argon Clive, his lead investigator. Four of Clive's staff sat at both sides of the table, laptop computers open, poring over files of reports and news clippings.

They'd been compiling reports of mysterious "vigilante" activity on Chicago's north side, and the nature of the reports, including eyewitness accounts, had led Clive to believe the suspect was in fact the man they were in search of.

Hayes was examining a map laid across the table, taking note of the subject's various strike locations, and when the incidents took place.

"You see," Clive had pointed out, "in past cases similar to this one, suspects begin close to their base location and then fan out as they get more confident. They'll go to new places, try new things, based on where they've been and what they've done. If we can establish a pattern, we can attempt to anticipate his next move."

"So," Hayes began, on cue with Clive's next thought, "figure out where he's going next; perpetuate a crime to set the trap, and move in."

"Exactly."

Their labor went on well into the night, until finally, at just before two in the morning, one of Clive's team presented a one-page printout.

Clive took the sheet and read down it. It was a police report filed the previous evening and updated just that afternoon: an aggravated assault at an apartment building on Chicago's far north side; the case pending the victim's decision to press charges.

The updated report provided a detailed account of video footage captured by a building security camera. As the officer had put in the report, the footage exhibited an "almost inhuman swiftness by the accused in response to the complainant's attack."

Clive's eyes shot back to the top of the page, noting the address where the incident occurred: 1615 West Granville Avenue, Chicago.

Hayes, who'd noticed Clive's keen interest in this latest delivery, put down the report he was reading and stepped closer to Clive. "What've you got?"

"*Him*," he said, handing the sheet to Hayes. "We've got him."

18

Unstrung Hero

A flash of lightning in the night sky signaled another incoming storm.

The six-story apartment building at 4670 North Clark Street towered starkly in front of Rage. A second flash of lightning illuminated the building in eerie white light, as if daring him to enter. As he approached the small green awning above its front door, wind whipped at him from every direction, and smatterings of rain licked at his face and hair.

As he stopped at the door, he shifted the large black leather satchel on his left shoulder and looked down at the heavy set of keys in his right hand. There were about ten of them on the ring, along with a few plastic bar-coded grocery-saver tabs, and a worn, golf ball-sized wooden apple as the key chain. He tossed them once in his hand, considering them. He glanced just to the left of the door to see a weathered steel box mounted to the brick wall. On it was the tenant list, an apartment-buzzer button to the left of each name.

Cautiously, he took a step forward to examine the list; sure enough, there it was, plain as day: Givens, apartment 403.

The woman from the bank. She had recognized him as well.

The unfamiliar feeling of indecision spread over him. It thwarted logical thought, debilitating any movement; it was as if he were covered in molasses, his mind and body bereft of direction. He felt his heart rate jump, and his stomach began to knot up.

What was he doing here?

Growling himself into motion, he placed his finger on the buzzer. Before he could stop himself, he had pushed it.

Indecision left him; he suddenly had the overwhelming urge to drop the bag and run away. But his feet would not move.

Seconds passed. Nothing.

Thunder sounded overhead, and the rain began to fall.

He placed his finger on the buzzer again but this time did not press it.

Slowly, he withdrew his finger from the button and took a step backward.

He turned to walk away, then felt the weight of the bag on his shoulder, the keys in his hand, give him pause.

The buzzer's intercom made a clicking sound, but no further noise came from it.

Exhaling hard, Rage turned back to face the door. The tiny awning provided no shelter from the rain and wind, so he turned the bag to his front to keep it dry. Squaring his shoulders on the buzzer, he planted his feet determinedly and once again put his finger on the button. Taking another breath, he gritted his teeth as he pushed it.

The intercom clicked once more. Then once again.

"I … I have your bag," Rage forced himself to say.

Silence from the intercom overpowered the thrash of rain now falling harder around him.

"I'm just … I'm going to leave it inside the door," he managed to add.

He began fumbling with the huge set of keys, trying each one in the deadbolt lock in the door. As he was about to try the fourth key, the intercom clicked yet once more, then buzzed loudly.

Eyebrows raised, Rage hesitated; then pushed the door open slightly. Peering in, he opened it the rest of the way and entered the foyer. Dripping wet, he shook some of the water from his hair, trying not to get any of it inside the satchel. It was just a small vestibule, large enough for only the mailboxes and a thick doormat. Rage looked about him tentatively for a second, then slowly lifted the bag from his shoulder, set it down carefully in a dry corner of the vestibule, and dropped the set of keys in it.

He had just turned to open the vestibule door when he heard the sound of footsteps rapidly coming down the stairwell, coming in his direction. Before the unfamiliar panic had a chance to set in again, the footsteps had stopped on the landing behind him. He turned around.

There she stood at the top of the landing, not ten feet away. She was regarding him with a curious expression; one which he didn't know quite what to make of. He remembered her face in much greater detail than he'd imagined he would. Her aura was immediate to him: there was a warmth that almost radiated from her; it filled the small vestibule, drowning out the darkness outside. Her large, light brown eyes revealed the same thing he had seen, but had largely ignored, during their first encounter weeks back: the thing he could not pinpoint, could not understand, yet it drew him to her unexpectedly, irresistibly; undeniably.

She remained on the landing for a long moment, a moment stretched even further by the silence riveting them both to the spot on which they stood. Her full lips were slightly parted, as if trying to exorcise a word, a sentence, something to shatter the overpowering silence. Rage imagined he was depicting a similar image to her.

Instinctively, he reached behind him without looking and hoisted the heavy black satchel off the vestibule floor. Gripping it by the strap, he took a step forward, then another, and held it out to her as far as his arm would extend, as if timidly offering a meager sacrifice to a divine being.

The young woman hesitated, then approached him slowly, stepping down the small flight of carpeted stairs to the tile floor. Rage noticed she was barefoot. She stopped right in front of his outstretched hand, her gaze still fixed upon his. Placing both her hands to either side of his on the strap, she gently took the satchel.

"Thank you," she said earnestly.

Rage found himself unable to reply. He started to nod as if submitting to her, but then he stopped himself, dropping his eyes to the floor. He blinked, then, turning his head away from her, made his way for the door. He pushed it open, letting the hammering noise of the rain outside fill the vestibule.

"Wait," she said, her tone hesitant but insistent all at once. "You're soaking wet. Please come upstairs. I'll get you a towel."

Rage wavered for a split second, surprised at her offer. "I'll be fine," he said, once again placing his hand on the door handle.

"Please. I have your jacket upstairs, too."

Letting go of the handle, he turned slowly to face her. She had not moved, still holding the satchel with both hands, her bare feet remaining on the cold tile floor. Her eyes showed no fear, no revulsion; only concern. Concern for him, a complete stranger.

Another long moment passed before he nodded, then added quietly, "Okay."

The stairs let out small creaks of welcome as he followed her up to the fourth floor.

From the moment he set foot inside the tiny apartment, Rage could feel the same warmth that he'd seen in the woman's eyes. It was everywhere; it resonated throughout her living space. The walls, painted a friendly yellow, were adorned with family photo collages. Over the long couch to his right were shelves that held welcoming items such as candles, miniature stuffed animals, and other small memorabilia. There was a large framed poster of a tranquil mountain landscape on the far wall, and a small metal cross hung just to the right of the white-draped picture window on the wall to his left. The place had a subtle scent of flowers and spice, which he found oddly pleasant. From his faint and brief memories of childhood, the apartment had the feel of an elementary-school classroom: a happy place.

The woman had his denim jacket and had hung it on the inside of the closet door, which lay slightly ajar just inside the front apartment door.

She brought him a large towel. "Please, sit down. I'll make you some tea," she said, heading back to the kitchenette behind him. Her voice echoed through his mind, gentle yet assured, like a soft, soothing breeze.

He held the towel in his hands. White and extra fluffy. Blotting his face and neck with it, he imagined everything about this woman would be as soft.

Once he'd run the towel through his hair a few times, he carefully draped it over the brown wicker chair next to the couch; then, after another glance around the room, he slowly sat down in the chair. A moment later, the woman came out of the kitchenette with a tray that held two steaming tea cups, and offered it to him. After he took one, she sat down on the couch, set the tray down, and took a cup for herself.

Rage took a sip and then held the warm cup in both hands across his lap, keeping his eyes on the cup for a moment. Not at all sure what to say, he found himself unable to look up. Seconds later he glanced in her direction and could see she was having the same difficulty. When she did finally look over at him, she shrugged her shoulders and said feebly, "I-I'm not sure where to start."

He didn't speak for a moment, then finally responded, "Me either."

"I wondered what had happened to you weeks back. I never thought I'd see you again, and I never got to thank you. And I want to understand, but I don't know ..." her voice trailed off. "I-I want to know ... about you," she tried to explain.

The words weren't coming to Rage either. He shifted in his chair. Though he still couldn't fully understand what he was doing here, he did not feel the same urge to run away as he'd had under the awning.

"What do you want to know?" he finally offered quietly, tentatively.

She shrugged her shoulders uncomfortably once again. "I guess ... *why,* for starters. I mean ... who *are* you?"

Rage stared out in front of him, pondering the question as if it had been written in the air. Then it dawned on him: she had his jacket and had seen what was inside.

She knew who he was. What he was doing.

He looked at the floor again. "Who I am is not important," he finally replied.

She cocked her head, confused. "Why do you say that?"

"I could be anyone. No one. That part doesn't matter."

She took a breath, seeming to gather herself. "Let's start over," she began. "Okay. I never told you my name. It's Mira. But, you've probably figured that out by now," she added, nodding to the satchel.

"My name is Rage," he responded plainly.

"Rage," she repeated, appearing to think it through. "Is that your real name?"

"My only name."

"Is that what your parents named you?"

"No parents."

She leaned forward. "Can I ask how you got that name?"

He paused. "At an orphanage. There was an incident. I was four."

"What happened?"

"I threw a chair through a window."

"Why?"

"Other kids were teasing me. I wanted them to stop."

"Did anyone get hurt?"

"No."

"Who gave you the name?"

"One of the teachers. Yelled out something about 'rage.' The name stuck."

"I see," she said, her eyes seeming to contemplate which direction she wanted to take. "Why are you doing this?" she finally asked.

He understood her meaning. "It's … complicated," he said after a pause.

She leaned forward on the couch. Her body language was still hesitant; he could tell she hadn't decided whether or not to be afraid of him.

"Why do you even want to know," he said.

"I-I know what you're doing," she began hesitantly, confirming what he'd suspected. "And there's a reason behind it, there always is. If you need help—"

"I know you're a shrink. I don't need help," he said, cutting her off.

"Social worker actually," she said. "And I don't mean 'help' in that sense. What I mean is, whatever it is that caused you to do what you're doing, I'm sure it was a terrible thing. And sometimes – sometimes it helps to be able to talk about things like that."

He studied her, thinking about the situation from a broader scope. "You do realize what you're doing, right," he said.

"What do you mean?" she asked, leaning forward.

"You know who I am. Why don't you call the police?"

She dropped her eyes to the floor, then sat back on the couch and ran her hands through her hair. "I – I haven't really thought that part through yet," she admitted.

"Then how do you know I'm not going to hurt you," he asked.

She looked back up at him. "Because I just – I just know."

After a brief silence, she continued: "Do you know what will happen if you get caught?"

"What kind of a question is that?" he asked irritably.

"I'm just saying," she offered. "What you're doing. It *is* against the law, and—"

"Laws are kept to maintain order. They don't apply to all situations. They don't protect everyone."

"So you feel you're above the law?"

"Not above. *Outside.*"

"How so?"

"I do what the law *should* be doing."

"And what is that?" she asked a bit skeptically.

"Taking out the scum who violate the law. Who violate decent people."

"So you're saying," she sat back on the couch again, "that you think you're in parallel with the law. That you complement it?"

Rage scowled, not liking her analytical tone. "Don't try to dissect me."

"No, no ... I'm not here to judge you," she replied, carefully backing off a bit. "Or the things they say you've done. I don't agree with killing, under any circumstance – but what you did at the bank – and tonight for that matter – make me see you in a different way. I just want – I just want to help you. To understand better."

"Don't feel indebted," he said, reading her. "I didn't do it for you."

"I – I understand that," she replied, recoiling somewhat. "I want to help ... for my own reasons."

"And what reasons are those?"

"What you're doing ... you have a conscience," she tried to begin.

"What?" he said, not at all sure what she meant.

"A conscience. I can see it in you ... you're conflicted about what you're doing, whether you realize it or not."

"I'm not," he retorted calmly. "I know what I'm doing."

"I'm not going to lecture you about it—"

"Good," he cut her off sharply. "You'd be wasting your breath."

"But," she pressed, "outside of the law, there are consequences for what you're doing."

"And what would those be," he said uninterestedly.

"Do you sleep at night?" she asked.

"What the hell is that supposed to mean?" he grunted, not expecting such a pointed question.

"When someone is conflicted, consciously or subconsciously, there are consequences. The mind has a way of dealing with what's happening. I can see that in you."

"And?"

"So I want to help you."

"I don't need anyone's help," he said. "Not yours, not anyone's."

"What you did that day at the bank was very heroic," she began. "But what you've done since—"

"I am not a hero," he said, cutting her off again.

"I'm not sure I understand," she countered. "They say you call yourself the 'Protector of the People' – how could you *not* see yourself as a hero?"

"That word has no meaning anymore. It's been overused. Misused. There are only a few true heroes. And I'm not one of them."

"Then why are you doing it?" she asked.

"Because ... it fulfills me," he said quietly.

"Saving people?"

"No."

"Then what?"

"It's complicated."

"You said that before. I'm not buying it."

"What concern is it of yours?" he said, feeling probed.

"I'm trying to understand –"

"What *business* is it of yours?" he interrupted, half-turning back toward her.

"It isn't," she said simply. "I didn't mean to press you."

"Why do you even care?" he asked, turning back toward the window. Confusion came over him. He somehow felt himself wanting to share more with her, even if against his better judgment.

"Because. It's what I do," she replied.

The small room was still once again, then Rage spoke up: "Why do *you* do what you do," he asked quietly.

He turned from the window and examined the woman's expression. He could tell her slight hesitation came from his turning the topic around to her, rather than from the question itself. Nonetheless, she decided to play along. "You mean social work?" she asked.

"Yeah."

"Because I want to help people."

"Why?"

Her expression, while still patient, shifted a bit. "I thought we were talking about you?" she asked.

"We can talk about both, can't we," he said plainly.

"Well— " she began.

"I mean, is this a session ... or a conversation," he interjected subtly.

Pausing for a moment, she sighed. "Okay, fair enough," she acknowledged. "So. You're asking *why* I want to help people."

"Yeah."

"I don't know if I can put an answer to that. It's just something that's in me."

"So, it's in your nature."

"If you want to call it that," she said. "Now what about you?"

He turned back to the window. "It's not about people. It's about justice."

From behind him, Rage could hear the woman shift on the couch.

"I think you have it backward," she finally said.

He turned around and regarded her. "That's up to me, isn't it?"

"How could it *not* be about people?"

"People are cattle. They're stupid. Indecent. Cold and uncaring. And they don't know right from wrong. Saving people doesn't mean you've saved them for good, it just means you've saved them one time. They could still be wronged again, or even do wrong themselves."

His gaze stayed on hers for a moment. She said nothing. He turned back to the window again. "People don't change. You can't fix them. So I don't try."

Still staring out the window, Rage heard her get up behind him; heard the slight creak of her footsteps on the floorboards. He glanced to his left and saw her next to him, looking into his eyes, studying him.

"That isn't true," she began, her tone almost one of pity toward him. "People are inherently good. And I think you know that."

He faced the window once again. For some reason, he was having difficulty looking her in the eye. "What world are you living in," he scoffed.

"The same one you are," she said.

"You don't see the things I see," he retorted.

"I don't?" she challenged. "Do you *know* what a social worker does?"

"Yes," he replied. "You see people trying to *fix* their problems. I see people *causing* them. Big difference."

"Everyone makes mistakes. And everyone deserves a chance to fix them, to make good on them," she said.

"If that's what you believe," he said indifferently.

"It is," she said.

"What *makes* you believe it," he retorted, turning back to the window.

Outside, the rain had intensified, and lightning filled the sky.

"I just told you. Because there's good in everyone."

"You're out of your mind," Rage said bitterly.

"No, I'm not," she argued. "It just needs to be found. You know this too, even if you won't admit it. You don't even embrace the good that's in *you*. But it's there, whether you want it to be or not. *I* see it."

Rage, about to reply, stopped himself cold. He examined the woman's face, now staring right into his eyes with a determination he'd never seen in another. Mouth open, he stared at her, dumbfounded. In that moment, he understood it all: what she meant; why she cared; how he was inexplicably drawn to her.

Light.

The woman embodied it.

It was who she was.

The warmth that emanated from her, the radiance – now he understood.

She was a light, a beacon, cutting through the darkness of the world.

His world.

Even though he barely knew her, the connection was clear to him. Unmistakable.

And he could tell it was clear to her as well.

A wave of confusion rushed over him; his face grew hot. Once again, he felt the urge to run out of the apartment, to get away from the strange feeling he was now experiencing. Whatever it was, it was clouding his mind, hindering his judgment. His eyes dropped to the floor.

"I need to go."

"Why?" she asked.

He made for the door.

"Please," she started after him. "You don't have to leave."

"I do," he said, turning to her briefly, then pulling the door open slightly.

"Here – take this." She grabbed a small card from her bag on the floor and wrote something on the back of it before handing it to him.

He held it in his hand, looking down at it. It was a business card. He flipped it over in his palm; she'd written down two phone numbers on the back.

"If you ever want to talk to me – ever – that's how you can get ahold of me. My office line is on the front. My home and cell phone are on the other side."

He continued to stare at the card in his hand, as if pondering it. After a moment's hesitation, he looked back up at her.

"Why are you doing this?"

"I-I don't know … just please, use it … if you want to," she said.

"Thanks," he said, still unsure.

He could sense she wanted to draw nearer to him, but she could read his obvious discomfort and held back. Looking down, he pulled the door open wider and walked out, pulling it shut behind him without another word spoken.

Once outside, he let the driving rain pour down on him. Although he had been there in the room, the interaction almost seemed an out-of-body experience. He could not match reason to any of it. He could not understand the woman's actions, his own actions, or the unfamiliar emotions she stirred within him. And he was angry with himself for it.

He'd been so engrossed in his thoughts on the woman that he ignored the pounding of the rain on him as he walked northward toward his home. He was now soaked to the bone.

It was only when he'd reached the front door to his building that he realized he'd left his jacket in the woman's apartment.

He growled, cursing himself.

As he slid the key into the front door lock, his stomach rumbled loudly, as if sending him a reminder of its own. At that moment it dawned on him that it had been growling since he'd first left the site, hours before. He was starving.

Stopping at the door, he muttered a few choice words, then slid the key out and once again headed over toward the corner convenience store.

As he rounded the corner to the store entrance, through the window he could see Habib, the same clerk as always, still standing behind the counter. And just as always, a convivial smile appeared on his face when Rage, or any customer for that matter, entered the shop.

Rage pushed open the metal-and-glass door, the familiar clinking of the tiny bells taped to the top of the door signaling his arrival. He strode in a few feet, past the gray mat just inside the door. As the door closed behind him and the sounds of the rain became muted, he glanced down, quickly aware that his soaked clothes were dripping water all over the white tile floor. Looking up, his eyes met Habib's almost guiltily, as if he were a child who'd gotten mud on a freshly cleaned carpet.

"It's okay, sir," the clerk said, reading him. "That is why I have a mop."

Rage grunted in reply, feeling unsure of how else to respond. He stepped back toward the mat for a second and wiped his feet; then, shrugging his shoulders, walked toward the frozen section where he took a vegetable lasagna from a middle shelf.

Seconds later he was back at the front counter. He plopped the small box on the worn countertop and dug for his wallet in his back pocket. As Habib rang up the package at three dollars and twenty-six cents, Rage opened his wallet to see only two singles.

He sighed heavily, keeping his head down, his eyes on the open, nearly empty wallet. "What've you got for two dollars," he said, barely above his breath.

"Excuse me, sir?" Habib asked, leaning forward a bit in order to hear him better.

"I said ... er, nothing," Rage replied after a second's thought. "I'll just take a pack of that beef jerky behind you. The small one."

"It's okay sir," Habib said. "You can have the meal. You just pay me later."

"What?" Rage said, not sure he'd heard the clerk right.

"Please, take the meal," Habib repeated. "Pay me next time you are in. I know you. I know you are good for it."

"Can't do that," Rage retorted. "It's not—"

"Please, I insist," Habib persisted, waving both hands and pushing the small box toward Rage. "I'll be here tomorrow. You have money, you pay me then. I trust you."

"I – uh ... thanks," Rage finally muttered, unsure of why the clerk was doing this. He slowly picked up the box, gesturing with a wave of his hand.

"You are welcome," Habib replied, waving back. "I see you tomorrow."

Rage nodded, and slowly walked to the door. As he reached it, he looked back at Habib one final time, as if to make sure he hadn't changed his mind. Then, after a second's pause, he pulled open the door and walked back out into the rainy night.

19

Warrant

Larry was in the shower when the phone rang.

Marcus picked it up, stepping away from the game of checkers he and Daniel were playing.

"Dad!" he yelled. "It's the station!"

"Tell 'em to hang on ten seconds!" Larry yelled back, rinsing quickly and shutting off the water. He grabbed a towel and dried himself quickly, still dripping a little onto the hardwood floor. Marcus held the phone by the doorway, a sly smirk on his face.

"Hot date, right?" he asked.

"Knock it off," Larry said under his breath, taking the phone. "Parker."

"Parker," the voice from the other end said. Larry recognized the voice as that of his precinct Captain, Robert Engalls, whom everyone in the precinct referred to simply as 'Chief.' "Your warrant came back from the judge about an hour ago. You can come in and pick it up, but I want to talk to you about it first."

"Sure, Chief," Larry said curiously.

"I'm in til about three today, finishing some paperwork, reviews and other crap. So it's your lucky day. Otherwise I'd make you wait til Monday. But you're not getting it til we talk first, understood?"

"Ten-four," Larry replied. "Be there in about twenty minutes."

Five minutes later, Larry came out of the bedroom in uniform. Noticing this, Marcus and Daniel chimed in unison, "Hey! Day off? Cubs game?!"

Larry suddenly remembered: he'd promised to take the boys to the Cubs game, their opening Saturday of the season, and his first weekend day off in a month.

"Sorry guys, I completely forgot."

"Well, are you still taking us or what?" Daniel asked anxiously.

Larry looked at Marcus and back to Daniel. The game had become a tradition over the past three years. Only the past two days' distraction had taken it from the forefront of his mind. "Of course. I'll get changed, and you need to, too. Each of you hop in the shower. Hurry up. And make sure you brush your teeth good this time, Marcus."

The boys got up, Marcus bounding for the shower while Daniel picked up the checkerboard game.

In the car, Larry headed east on Montrose toward Halsted. Marcus and Daniel sat in back, reluctantly as always. Marcus was the only one who still held out enough hope to call shotgun each time.

"Hey Dad," Marcus said, glancing around at the red, almost velvety seats in the car. "This was your first car, right?"

"Yep," Larry answered.

"You should try selling it to the next pimp you bust. Could be some sweet cash."

Larry looked back at him through the rearview mirror. "You're a real barrel of laughs, you know that."

"How about getting a *new* car?" Daniel chimed in.

"Sure," Larry replied with a grin. "We can use your allowances to pay for it."

"Yeah, this car's fine," Daniel decided.

"Hey guys," Larry changed the subject, looking back in the rearview mirror at the boys. "I need to make a quick stop at the station on the way."

"What for?" Marcus asked.

"Just need to pick something up, is all. Should be just a few minutes. You guys can wait outside the Chief's office, all right?"

"Whatever," Marcus replied, looking out the window. "Just don't make us late for the first pitch."

Larry turned off Halsted onto Addison Street. The streets were jammed with cars, cabs, buses, and crossing pedestrians, all trying to make their way to Wrigley Field just a block to the west. Larry pulled the Buick into the small lot behind the station.

The station was abuzz with activity, as plenty of beat officers prepared to begin their day. Weekend Cubs games usually brought an extra twenty thousand people into the neighborhood. The steel desks and scuffed tile floor did nothing but amplify the commotion reverberating throughout the large, open room. The long row of windows on the east and south walls filled the office with natural light during the day. Today was so bright that many of the black plastic roll blinds had been pulled.

Larry told the boys to sit in the row of chairs outside the Captain's office while he went inside. He opened the door and entered the office.

"Hey Chief," Larry said, pulling the heavy, windowless door shut.

Captain Robert Engalls looked up from his paperwork and regarded Larry with a scowl. In the ten years Larry had been on the force, all of them under Engalls' command, he'd never once seen the man smile. Behind his desk Engalls always sat crouched over, poring over whatever paperwork was keeping him there, his broad shoulders hunched, the dark skin of his bald scalp the first thing to greet any visitor.

"Parker," his deep voice acknowledged Larry with a grunt. "Have a seat."

Larry approached the desk and sat down in one of the two worn vinyl-and-wooden chairs facing it. "Thanks. What's up?"

"I think you know. Your warrant came through," he replied, studying Larry's expression. "But before I give it to you, I need to know two things."

"Okay," Larry replied, already knowing the direction this was going.

"First," the Captain began, "you put in for this warrant around me, bypassing my authority. That doesn't sit well with me. Why did you do it?"

"Because I knew you'd have questions. And I wanted it fast," Larry said.

The Captain stared at him hard. "Parker, I don't need to remind you that I can have this warrant quashed right now, making this whole thing a moot point."

"I understand, Chief."

Engalls blew air through his nostrils, then sat back in his chair and placed his hands behind his head. "Listen, Parker," he said. "You're a good cop. One of our best. And you usually have your head in the right place. But this – is not one of those times."

"The trial is proceeding without all the facts. This guy is a key witness."

"Don't play by-the-book with me," Engalls shot back. "This is going to be an open-and-shut case. Prosecution has all it needs. Even the defense knows it. You need to be focusing your time – and the city's resources – on catching that 'Protector' serial killer. You and Urrutia both."

"I understand, Chief, and we are," Larry replied. "But I gotta pursue this."

"Why?" Engalls challenged him. "There's nothing to be gained by going this route, and the city has limited resources to pursue it. I don't understand why you want to chase it."

"Because there's something about this guy, Chief. We need to talk to him more."

Engalls' eyes narrowed on Larry, as if examining him. A long moment of silence passed. Finally, he slid the warrant across the desk to Larry. "Fine, then. But I'm not doing this because I think it's necessary, because it's not. You have three days to get what you need from this character. After that I kill the warrant. You copy?"

"Loud and clear," Larry said plainly, picking up the warrant.

"Now get out of here," Engalls grumbled. "It's your day off. I see your boys out there; don't keep them waiting."

"Thanks," Larry said. Putting the warrant in his pocket, he got up and walked out of the office, closing the door behind him.

20

Deployment

In the alley behind 1615 West Granville, the two black transports rolled to a heavy stop.

Evening had begun to set in across the Midwest, the sun disappearing into the western horizon for the day. After the ninety-minute flight from Reagan International to Chicago's O'Hare airport, Hayes' strike team had quickly boarded the transports and made their way directly to the subject's residence. The next phase of the mission would be done under cover of darkness.

Two of the four black sedans trailing them turned in as well, stopping immediately behind them. The other two sedans continued southbound on the side street. The thirty-two man strike team poured out of the two transports, trailed by Clive's five-man investigative team.

Nolan Hayes and Argon Clive emerged from the front black sedan. Hayes moved to the beginning of the line of troopers. Behind his lead, the group traveled silently on foot down the alley, headed for 1615 West Granville.

From what Clive had shared with Hayes so far, they appeared to be in as much luck with Asset Two as they had been with Asset One – no close relatives or friends; one adoptive mother, deceased eight weeks prior. Any remaining details would be covered upon inspection of the subject's residence. They could then effectively blame his 'death' on a revenge killing at his residence, and would cover their *own* tracks for being there under the guise of national security.

As long as they maintained the element of surprise, it should prove to be a quick – and most importantly, quiet – acquisition.

Hayes ordered his men to remain in the alley while he, Clive, and Lieutenant Charles Hill, his deputy for the mission, approached the edge of the alley that spilled out onto Granville.

Within moments, they would be making first contact with Asset Two.

21

Rage Under Fire

Rage shuffled tiredly into his apartment at just after seven o'clock pm.

It had been an extremely long day at the site, one that at times had begun to sap even his seemingly limitless stamina, but because it was a Saturday -- at double-time pay rates -- he wasn't about to complain.

He'd also gotten his paycheck, so not only was he able to pay Habib for the frozen lasagna, but he had actually bought some groceries to get him through the next couple of days. He lazily dropped the two plastic bags on his kitchen table and pulled open the refrigerator door, loading in packages of ham, turkey, and sliced cheese, a bottle of mustard, and a six-pack of Coke. He tossed a loaf of wheat bread and two bags of chips on the kitchen counter next to the fridge, then switched on the radio. "Moonlight Serenade" by Glenn Miller began to flow gently through the room.

He walked back to the fridge and opened it, one arm leaning on the kitchen counter and the other on the open refrigerator door as he looked in. He grabbed the lunchmeat, cheese and a can of Coke, then on the way to the couch snagged the loaf of bread from the counter. After setting his dinner items on the coffee table, he pulled off his sweaty shirt, kicked off his dirty shoes, and yanked off his soiled socks. He slumped down in the center of the couch and sighed.

Arching his back, he fished out the card the woman had given him from the back pocket of his jeans. He flipped the card over a few times, half-examining it and half-staring past it. He was still puzzled about why she had given it to him. Though he hadn't felt the overpowering impulse to call her just yet, he somehow knew he would at some point.

He thought about what she'd said to him, about being able to sleep at night.

He thought about his nightmares.

This he knew: they'd started right around the time of his first nightly outing.

He wondered if she was onto something.

No.

It was coincidence, nothing more.

He knew what he was doing, and he knew it was right.

Taking two pieces of bread and slapping some meat and cheese between them, he took a ravenous bite, then glanced to his left, out the window. It was a clear, beautiful early April evening. Through the slightly open window, he listened to the sounds of the evening swirling about outside: the faint sounds of traffic on the streets below, the breeze rustling through the trees that lined the streets, the occasional horn of a car in the distance. It was one of his favorite times of the evening, watching the gloriously setting sun, listening to the calm before his storm.

Taking another bite, he glanced down to the coffee table and looked at the card again. Maybe he would call her tonight. Talk to her. No. Maybe.

Sitting back on the couch, Rage was just finishing the third bite of his sandwich when he heard something: a subtle noise in the hallway outside -- nothing more than a faint click, then a tiny creak in the floorboards. Maybe a rodent, maybe that cop again, but definitely something moving.

Just as he began to sense something was wrong, he heard the loud crack of metal deadbolts smashing through wood frame as his front door was violently kicked in, and roaring gunfire filled the room. Without a second's thought he instinctively back-flipped over the couch as the bullets sprayed in his direction, splintering the wood from the couch and sending it flying all about him. On the floor behind the couch, small bits of plaster showered him as bullets punched holes into hundred-year-old walls. But as he looked up at the wall from his brief cover, he saw that they weren't bullets at all – but rather some kind of dart, silver and sleek.

Without being able to see who or where his attackers were, he rolled backward into the open corner closet merely a split second before streams of darts followed him in. Once inside, he slammed a hole in the ceiling and pulled himself up into the closet of the apartment above him, the projectiles filling the closet as he did so, one of them nicking his small toe.

He ran through the apartment above his, and a woman coming out of the bathroom shower screamed at him. Rage yelled at her to stay in the iron tub and not make a noise, then sprinted out of the apartment and up the hall stairs, taking them six at a time, toward the roof. He stepped on something sharp at the top of the stairs and realized he was both barefoot and shirtless. He kicked the old, rusted roof door open and rolled out into the right, anticipating the possibility of someone waiting for him. Someone was. Of the full clip that was fired, only one dart sliced into Rage's left leg as he rolled behind the first brick chimney available. He bought himself about two seconds to think before the man appeared in front of him, an armored trooper all in black, with a helmet and visor obscuring his face. The trooper leveled the automatic rifle point blank in front of him. Ignoring the pain in his leg, he kicked the gun out of the man's hands and pulled him down onto the roof's gravel surface with him.

He knew that someday he would be discovered, and that the police would eventually come after him. But these weren't police: there were no markings anywhere on their body armor, no badges on their shoulder, nothing. He had no idea who he was dealing with, or how dangerous they could be.

He had already begun to feel woozy from the first dart that had hit his leg.

He growled urgently into the trooper's face: *"Who are you? How many?"*

The visored face hadn't yet responded when Rage felt something pierce the back of his right shoulder. He whirled to the side just in time as three more darts were fired in his direction, missing him by mere inches, but finding a home in the chest of the trooper he'd been holding.

Without hesitation, he grabbed now-unconscious trooper by the boots and swung him through the air like a baseball bat, so that the man's body slammed into the two troopers who'd appeared behind him with rifles pointed. The three men tumbled to the roof's gravel surface as Rage suddenly heard footsteps kicking through the gravel from all directions around him.

There are too many of them, he quickly realized.

Making his decision, Rage took off running toward the rooftop's edge, and leapt to the roof adjacent to his, a barrage of darts following him into the air, yet a third dart finding a home in his upper hamstring as he landed.

He fled southbound, crossing rooftop after rooftop, leaping over each alleyway and cross-street with as much power as his beaten legs would muster. After fifteen blocks, on the rooftop of an abandoned building overlooking Montrose Avenue, he collapsed in exhaustion.

Flat on his back on the rooftop, his eyes flitted open and closed; he could see the cloudless, darkening sky above him and hear the evening sounds of the city all around and below him. He could not move; like a massive weight, vertigo was pressing every inch of his body down onto the roof's surface.

Slowly willing himself up, he stumbled across the rooftop to the stairwell door, broke the lock, and clambered down the steps, holding the wall for support. Finding the nearest door he kicked it in, falling backward while doing so. On the floor, legs splayed, he looked himself over to see that bloodstains had spread around each of the dart wounds he'd sustained. The pain had begun to fade, but cold numbness was quickly claiming him.

Picking himself up off the dusty hallway floor, he entered the large empty room, again staggering to the nearest wall. He slithered into a cobweb-ridden corner, covering himself with some old, torn curtains that had been lying on the floor.

Curling up under them, he finally let his consciousness slip away.

22

Revelations

The cool night wind made its way in through the open window.

The radio on the kitchen counter was tuned to the sports talk station, which featured the usual two know-it-alls chattering back and forth about what the Cubs should have done differently to win the day's game. The dishes were piled in the sink, as-yet-undried traces of spaghetti sauce wiped across each of the plates, a crust of garlic bread resting at the edge of the plate on top.

The boys sat at opposite ends of the couch, each playing a worn-out handheld electronic game. They'd reluctantly agreed to put the games on silent mode.

In the far corner, sitting on a steel folding chair, Larry fiddled with the old 19" television set. He had the back plastic panel of the unit removed and was examining the exposed wiring and circuits, not having a clue what he was doing. With a heavy sigh, he stopped for a moment, taking a long swig of Coke from the can on the windowsill.

The constant chatter coming from the radio was the only thing breaking the otherwise calming quiet.

"Hey Dad," Marcus started, "you mind if we change the station or something? These dickheads are starting to piss us off."

"Speak for yourself," Daniel chimed in quietly, his eyes not leaving the game.

"Marcus, what have I told you about using that language?" Larry looked up from behind the TV irritably. "One more and I might have to ground you for a week."

"Sorry," Marcus said quietly, shrinking back into the couch.

"Go ahead and change it," Larry said dully. "I'm about done with that myself."

Marcus got up and walked toward the kitchen.

Larry looked back down into the television's rear panel. Marcus turned the dial to the local news radio station. As Larry examined yet another component within the unit, his mind wandered back to the conversation he'd had with Captain Engalls that morning.

He fished into his pocket and pulled out the warrant. Looking at it, his eyes glazed over as he second-guessed his decision not to go to the man's apartment for further questioning. This was his day with the boys, he kept reminding himself; they needed more of that from him.

He would go to the man's apartment tomorrow, when he was back on duty.

As he folded the warrant back into his pocket, the address ran through his mind: 1615 West Granville.

1615 West Granville.

Why had he suddenly thought of that?

It was at that moment that he realized … he hadn't.

He gazed toward the radio on the kitchen counter.

Getting up, he walked over to the kitchen, leaned onto the counter, and turned up the volume.

"What's up, Dad—" Daniel began.

"Shh," Larry quickly cut him off.

He listened in to the breaking news story:

"*… Chicago Police currently have the building cordoned off, but are not being allowed inside for what is being called reasons of national security. Initial reports indicate that a resident of that building may be a suspected terrorist, but no other details have come in as of yet … Again, breaking news of what appears to be a massive Homeland Security raid of an apartment complex at 1615 West Granville …*"

Larry's heart began to race. That was the address. *His* address.

Suddenly it dawned on him, like a massive piece of a puzzle snapping into place.

The eyewitness accounts of what had happened at each murder scene …

What he'd seen weeks ago in the alley …

How he had moved so blindingly fast in the surveillance video …

Could it be possible?

He turned from the radio. Walking over to the couch, he stooped down in front of the boys. "Marcus. Daniel," he looked them in the eyes. "I need to go out for a bit. I'm taking the cell phone with me, so if for any reason you need to reach me, call it. Okay?"

"Sure," Daniel replied, taken aback by his serious tone. Marcus nodded as well.

He went into his bedroom and came out two minutes later in uniform.

Alerted by this, Daniel got up from the couch. "Dad, what's going on?" he asked, a look of concern on his face. Marcus also got up.

"I can't explain right now," he replied. "Everything's fine, so don't worry."

"Where are you going?"

"I have to go check something out for a case. I'll be back later tonight. Be in bed by ten, understand?"

"But it's a Saturday ni—" Marcus began to protest.

"No arguments, Marcus! You guys understand?" Larry said with finality.

"Yes," Daniel replied. Marcus nodded reluctantly.

Larry closed the apartment door and descended the stairs as fast as he could. Getting out to the street, he ran to the Buick, started it up and, tires screeching, pulled out of its parallel-parked spot. Putting the gas pedal to the floor, he sped northbound on Damen Avenue in the direction of the suspect's apartment.

23

The Other

Back in the Underground Labs, a discovery waited to be made.

Well into her sixteenth hour, Loretta Barnes walked to the kitchen to pour herself another cup of coffee. As she leaned against the white counter, mixing cream and sugar into the small Styrofoam cup, her mind strayed to the previous night's discoveries.

Elias Todd. Too many things simply didn't add up.

Beyond the extraordinary traits she'd already seen from his other samples, she'd also discovered that Todd's DNA had a rigid molecular density which suggested that both his tissue and bone were extremely damage-resistant. The samples also displayed an advanced cell-regeneration factor, implying that damaged cells could repair themselves in a fraction of the time a normal subject's cells could. And finally, she found a limitless, perhaps even scalable supply of adrenaline – or some advanced form of it -- in his bloodstream.

But in addition to those remarkable attributes, there were also signs of other, even more mysterious elements in Todd's genetic makeup. Loretta had had to dig deeper to understand, but once she'd pinpointed them, they were unmistakable.

The subject had a severe chemical imbalance which could produce intense levels of aggression, and perhaps even violent behavior.

She had no idea how this trait was possible, or if the imbalance was related to the other attributes, or how so many anomalies could be present in one individual.

Were there more like him? She wondered.

She dumped the rest of her coffee and returned to her lab, going straight for the cold-storage unit. Her eyes sweeping the shelves, she took vials from four other containers, each marked in the same manner as Todd's had been.

Walking back to her microscrope, she set up each sample for examination. But after inspecting them, she found no significant similarities to what she'd seen in Todd.

She returned to the chamber to return the samples. As she was replacing the last vial to its container, she spotted a familiar name she hadn't noticed the first time around. She pulled over the small foot stool, stepping onto it to get a closer look.

As she had thought, the name read, "Hayes, Nolan P."

The Executive Special Agent.

Why in the world would they have a sample of his blood?

Before she could change her mind, she opened Hayes' container and carefully slid one of the tiny vials out from its holder.

24

Curiosity Killed the Cop

Larry parked the Buick along the east side of Ashland, about a block south of the suspect's address.

Five or six television-news vans were all parked nearby, but it looked as if no press was being allowed near the building. As he walked north on Ashland, a few reporters ran toward him, microphones in hand, but he waved them off.

The scene was oddly subdued, almost controlled, in a way he'd never seen in all his experience as a cop.

As he got closer to the building, he noticed that the police lines and blockades were still up, but the two men just inside the slightly ajar vestibule door were not Chicago Police. They appeared to be in full SWAT gear, and as he got closer, both of them withdrew M-16 rifles from holsters on their backs, pointing them toward the ground.

Larry paused. *What in the world was going on?*

He stopped fifteen feet from the door, holding his arms above his head to indicate himself as no threat. "Chicago Police, request permission to approach," he bellowed.

One of the two held up a hand to halt Larry, while the other seemed to be speaking into a headset. After a few seconds the first one waved Larry forward.

Within a few feet of the front door, he observed the odd-looking magazines clipped into the M-16s. He quickly looked back up, pretending not to have noticed.

The trooper who had waved him forward spoke. "Officer. Please identify yourself," he said through the shaded helmet visor that obscured much of his face.

"Parker, badge 8729, Chicago Police," Larry responded. "What's the situation?"

"For reasons of national security, we're not at liberty to say at this point," the trooper answered. "Chicago Police have been relieved. This is now a Federal situation."

"Relieved?" Larry asked.

"I'm unable to share anything beyond that," he said shortly. "I have orders. I also have orders to inquire about your presence here," he added.

"This is a crime scene in my precinct," Larry replied bluntly. "It's my job to be here."

"As you've been told, officer, the Chicago Police have been relieved of their duties here, and we've assumed control of the scene. It's not clear to me how you managed to miss, or perhaps ignore, the order that should have come from your C.O., but you will need to vacate the premises immediately."

Larry turned to see the other guard, standing a few feet away with the M-16 still pointed to the floor, tighten his grip on the rifle.

"There's no need for that," Larry glared at him, nodding at the firearm. "I'm leaving."

Once outside, Larry began walking back toward the Buick. He'd call the captain once he was in the car, in case the Feds were using wide-band audio surveillance. With all he'd seen thus far, nothing would surprise him at this point.

About twenty feet from the Buick, Larry was approached by yet another reporter. He was about to wave the man off without looking when he was addressed by name.

"Larry. Parker," the deep male voice said.

Wondering how this person knew his name, Larry turned to see the familiar face of Oliver McBride walking anxiously toward him from the right. McBride, or Ollie as everyone had always known him, was a close friend of Larry's from high school. Once the skinniest kid in the class, the fifteen years since graduation had added a few pounds to Ollie's frame, mostly in the healthy, Guinness-fed beer gut he paraded around with. He'd usually wear the same thing: a mostly tucked-in white-collared shirt, sleeves rolled up to the elbows, front pocket always bulging with small note pad, pen, and pack of Marlboros; somewhat-ironed pants; sneakers. For a married guy with four kids, Larry always wondered why Ollie's wife wouldn't just dress the guy for him. The wide green eyes, freckled skin, and thinned curly red hair gave away Ollie's South Side Irish roots almost as much as the ever-present White Sox cap turned backward on his head.

"Ollie," he said curiously, looking around as he continued to walk toward the Buick, "do you know what's going on here?"

Ollie came within a few feet of Larry, then began walking beside him. "S'what I was about to ask you, man. Lotsa weird shit happenin'," he said, almost whispering.

"Come on, get in the car," Larry said quietly back to him. "I'm not sure who might be listening."

Once in the car they swung a u-turn and began heading south on Ashland. Ollie started to light a cigarette.

"No smoking in the car," Larry cut him off.

"What, you kiddin' me? You particular about this piece o'shit?" Ollie protested.

"This 'piece' is all I got," Larry replied. "I gotta take the boys around in it."

"Fine, whatever," Ollie sighed. "So come on, what the hell's goin' on back there? All us media were told to keep at least a hundred feet away from the building – for our own safety, they say -- or face arrest. Even got a call from the high ups at the paper, Editor-in-Chief himself, sayin' to keep back. I've seen stuff like this happen before, where the Feds come in and tell the press to buzz off, but never this quickly. Usually, the bureaucracy itself holds things up, and we're able to get some scoop before we get the boot. Not this time, though. This one apparently came straight from the top. Must be one hell of a secret they're tryin' to keep bottled up in there. What'd they tell you?"

Larry nodded, thinking through everything Ollie had just shared with him. He knew it all had to revolve around this mysterious Rage character; though in his wildest imagination, he would have never guessed anything involving national security. Trying to determine what he should share, he looked over at his longtime friend. "Listen, I don't know much. But before I tell you anything, this all has to be off the record. Agreed?"

"Yeah yeah, of course – I know that," Ollie said. "But you're actin' awful suspicious about this. Can I ask why?"

"I don't know. It just has a weird feeling to it, and I don't think a scoop is worth potentially putting both our lives in danger."

"Whoa, man," Ollie said cautiously, eyes wide at Larry's comment. "What the hell you talkin' about?"

"I'm saying," Larry explained, "that if you print a story with details the Feds don't want the public to know, you might end up in something deep."

"Alright, alright," Ollie said, a bit bothered by Larry's insistence. "Like I already promised you, I'm not gonna print anything. But I think you're being paranoid."

"Call it my cop's instinct," Larry said. "You just develop it after awhile."

"So come on with it," Ollie pressed. "What'd the Feds tell you?"

Larry second-guessed his decision on what to share. "Nothing they didn't tell you, I'm sure," he began. "Subject a suspected terrorist, a matter of national security, whatever that means. CPD's been ordered off the scene since the Feds are here. I was told to ask no questions, and to leave immediately."

Ollie scratched his head, perplexed. "I just don't get it … why wouldn't they want CPD's help apprehending the guy? And why's it a matter of national security? Something just doesn't add up."

Larry's thoughts again went back to Rage. Something in his expression must have given him up, for when he looked back at Ollie, his friend was regarding him curiously.

"You know something else, don't you?" he said slowly, eyes narrowed.

"What makes you think I know anything else?" Larry asked.

"Call it my *reporter's* instinct," Ollie said with a sly grin. "You just develop it after awhile."

Larry sighed. "Listen, I don't," he began. "At least nothing concrete. I'm gonna call my captain and see what's going on. If I hear anything, I'll call you. In the meantime, I'll take you back up to your car."

Turning right onto Foster Avenue, Larry began to make his way back north toward Ashland and Granville.

After dropping Ollie off, Larry drove by the building once more, taking another look at the two troopers in the vestibule door. Their heads followed him as he went by. Exhaling his frustration, he picked up his cell phone and dialed the Captain.

After a few rings, the Captain picked up. "Engalls."

"Chief, it's Parker."

"Parker. How did I know I'd be hearing from you tonight," Engalls grunted.

"Listen, I just left the homicide at 1615 West Granville—"

"You did what? Why?" Engalls barked, interrupting him.

"Why?" Larry asked, perplexed. "Because the key witness from the bank robbery lives in that building, and I think he might also be—"

"Parker," Engalls interrupted him again, exasperated. "If I'd wanted you involved I'd have called you. Now listen closely. The CPD has been dismissed from the case. By the *Feds*. If you've been there you probably know that by now. So that means stay away. There's nothing we can do. It's out of our jurisdiction."

"But chief, I think this guy is—"

"Parker, for the last time," the Captain cut in again, now angry, "it's out of our hands. I don't care if you like it or not. Now you will go home and you will call it a night. Any more arguments, any further mention of this case, I will consider an act of insubordination, and I will *suspend* you for a week. You understand me?"

Larry kept the phone to his ear, staring angrily at the road ahead as he drove. After a few long seconds, he finally responded. "Understood."

"Good," the Captain replied immediately, and then after a few more seconds he continued. "After the smoke clears, and *if* your witness is not at all involved in whatever the Feds are after, I will *consider* extending your warrant."

"Okay, chief," Larry replied, trying to veil his continued ire.

"Now goodnight, Parker."

"Yep. Goodnight chief."

He turned the Buick around once again, heading back south once more on Ashland, passing the building one final time as he went.

He was fuming inside. This was *his* case, *his* suspect, and most importantly, he was *positive* this Rage guy was the "Protector of the People" suspect they wanted. And he couldn't do anything about it whatsoever – until the all-clear was given by the Feds.

He continued southbound on Ashland, heading home.

On the roof of 1615 West Granville, Nolan Hayes paced in the rising moonlight. Overlooking the building's eastern edge, he watched intently as the grey Buick sedan passed the building for a second time, proceeding southbound on Ashland Avenue.

"Hill," he uttered into his headset, watching the vehicle's progress down Ashland.

"Sir," the voice came back in his earpiece.

"Have you heard back from Mobile Command on that cop's information yet."

"Not two seconds ago, sir."

"And?"

"Name's Lawrence Parker. Resides at 4333 North Damen Avenue, third floor; Chicago. We have phone number, tax ID number, records, whatever you need."

"More importantly, I need to know if this is the same officer who filed the police report on the subject the other evening."

"Confirmed," came Hill's reply. "Mobile also noted that this same officer just obtained a warrant for a month-old bank robbery case, involving the subject."

Hayes looked down at his feet, rubbing his chin. He contemplated this unexpected development. The connection was too strong to ignore.

This cop could make things messy.

He had to put a stop to it – right now.

Having made his decision, Hayes spoke into the headset once again. "Send two of your men patrolling the area to the officer's residence, and eliminate him."

"Sir?" came Hill's reply, clearly surprised.

"He poses too large a risk. Clive's team will begin working on a cover. Also send two more for rooftop cover across the street from the residence. Take no chances."

"Sir. Yes, sir," Hill replied.

With that Nolan Hayes disconnected from Hill and placed a call down to Clive to begin working on a cover for the officer's death.

25

In Harm's Way

Rage awoke to the sound of screams.

Throwing the curtains off him with a small cloud of dust, he anxiously looked about him, head darting in all directions, eyes wide, listening closely as the last of the screams' echoes died into the large empty space. It was dark. He looked, listened: nothing. A few seconds passed before he realized that the screams had been his own.

He sat up and eased himself back to rest against the wall. His heart rate began to slow. The room's only light came from the three windows on the far wall. He could see the dust swirling in the wide beams of moonlight that entered the room at an angle and settled to the floor in the shape of large rectangles. There was hardly a sound aside from the faint murmur of traffic from the streets below.

His mind was still dazed. He had no idea how much time had passed. He couldn't yet piece together all that had happened that evening, nor what it meant for him. And he was too mentally exhausted to think about it now.

He got up slowly and walked over toward one of the windows. The pain of his wounds had subsided into a small ache, and he could feel his strength coming back. In the moonlight, he looked himself over. His wounds had mostly healed, the skin coming back together, the holes the darts had torn into his flesh barely evident. Their only remnants were the dried blood stains which had spread across his shoulder and legs.

As his eyes adjusted, he took his first good look around the room he'd holed up in. It was several times larger than his hole-in-the-wall apartment; it seemed more like a large storeroom of some sort. It was mostly empty with the exception of some old curtains which had fallen from a few of the windows, an old folding table beside the main door, and a row of shelving racks toward the far end. There was also a second door just past the shelving racks. Rage walked toward it, hoping it was a bathroom, and hoping the place still had water.

Stepping in the doorway, in the dim light he could just make out the old porcelain pedestal sink, the cracked mirror mounted above it on the mildew-covered tile wall, and the toilet just to the right. He found the light switch and flipped it, then tried it a second time for good measure. No electricity, of course. He stepped forward to the sink and turned the rusted knob to the left. No water either. So much for washing himself off.

Sighing heavily, he walked back toward the windows and lowered himself into a sitting position against the wall where he'd slept.

What would he do now?

He couldn't go back to the apartment; it was no longer safe.

He had the basics on him: his wallet with ID, credit cards, and some money; he was clothed for the most part, but he didn't have shoes.

Still, something was eluding him … he felt as if something he needed was still back in that apartment, but he couldn't figure out what it was. He closed his eyes and tried to picture everything there, everything he'd left behind.

Think.

Then it came to him.

The woman.

He'd left her card on his kitchen table.

If they found it … they could find her and try to get to him through her.

Just by making her acquaintance, he had put her in harm's way.

His heart began hammering.

He had to warn her. Go to her. Now.

Letting adrenaline take over, he got up and ran toward the hallway door. Once up the stairs, he kicked open the roof door, sprinted across the rooftop, and made the leap to the building across the street, in the direction of the woman's apartment.

26

The Window

The clock struck ten o'clock as Mira finished her late dinner.

Sitting back on the couch in an oversized gray sweat suit and thick wool socks, she stretched and let out a big yawn.

She picked up the TV remote and changed the channel to the evening news program, then walked over to close the window. Spring's evening chill had begun to creep into her apartment.

She went into the kitchen to make some tea, and she began thinking about Rage. She still wasn't sure why she'd forced her card on him, imploring him to call her. Was it indebtedness? Sympathy? Professional instinct? Something else? All she knew was that it was out there now, in his hands, up to him to call her. If nothing else, she still had his jacket, so perhaps he would call her for that reason.

While the tea was brewing she went to her front closet. The jacket still hung on the inside of the door. Its torn, faded black denim was a stark contrast with the bright-colored garments which hung behind it. She ran her fingers along its frayed collar. It felt the way she imagined he felt: rough, battered, in need of care, yet at the same time, staunch and protective.

The microwave beeped. She closed the closet door.

Large mug of tea in hand, she sat back down on the couch and tuned in to the evening's lead story. She settled in and took a sip as an on-the-scene reporter described a massive government raid on a suspected terrorist's apartment in the Edgewater neighborhood. The reporter stood with a row of buildings behind him, the furthest of which appeared to be cordoned off by crime-scene tape and barricades.

The voice came from the TV: "You can see behind me the apartment building at 1615 West Granville, and this is as close as we've been allowed to get. A 100-foot perimeter has been set around the building by Federal authorities. Chicago Police aren't sharing any information at this time; but from what we've been able to gather, the building has been completely evacuated, and no one is allowed near it for what's being said are reasons of national security. Again, a massive raid on a suspected terrorist's residence in the Edgewater neighborhood, and that's all the information we have right now. We'll update you as we're able to get more details. Reporting live from the scene at Ashland and Granville, John Garcia, ABC-7 News."

Mira shifted on the couch, pulling a small blanket over her feet, when she heard a loud rattling outside, as if someone had fallen on the fire escape outside her window.

She glanced toward the window to see a shadowy figure peering into her apartment, silhouetted in the moonlight.

Startled, she shrieked. Jumping to her feet, she backed away from the couch and toward the front door, fumbling for the phone as she did so.

The figure tapped on the window urgently and was saying something to her; his muffled voice sounding familiar.

She caught a glimpse of his face in the moonlight. It was him. Rage.

Heart still fluttering, she put a hand to her chest and cautiously walked toward the window. There he stood like some kind of dark sentinel, waiting motionless on the fire escape as she approached to let him in. As the questions flooded her mind, she opened the window, then stepped back to allow him to enter. He was half-naked, only wearing pants, with no shirt or shoes.

He climbed in through the opening and looked around. "Are you all right?"

"Y-yes," she replied with uncertainty, alarmed by his demeanor. "Are *you*?"

"No," he said flatly, and went to her front door, making sure it was locked. "Has anyone called you this evening, or come to your door?"

"No one," she answered. "What's going on?"

"No one else, not even a knock on your door," he persisted.

"*No*," she repeated emphatically. "What's the matter?"

"Listen to me," he said, his dark eyes a reflection of urgency. "It's not safe here. I've put you in danger."

"What are you *talking* about?" she asked. In the back of her mind, she started to worry that he was delusional.

"There's no time," he said, going to the window. He was exhibiting all the signs of clinical paranoia. "I'll explain everything. We need to go, right now."

"I'm not going anywhere," she said firmly. "You need to explain to me what you're doing here. Now just relax for a minute. Tell me what's going on."

At that moment, his head whirled in the direction of the front door. She'd heard it too, an unfamiliar clicking sound.

"Get behind me," he told her.

Before she could react, her front door was kicked in, and two men in what looked like SWAT gear appeared in the doorway. Each of them had a rifle, pointed at Rage.

27

Flight

The woman behind him, Rage rounded on the two men who'd emerged in the doorway.

Before he could process another thought, they fired upon him, the blast of their guns filling the room.

With breakneck speed, he grabbed the woman and pulled her to the floor, as yet another dart stabbed into the back of his neck. An enormous surge of pain shot throughout his head, neck, and shoulders. Grimacing, he looked up and saw several other darts slicing through the air over his head and puncturing the wall with a series of sharp thuds, like arrows piercing a target. Ignoring the intensifying pain, he quickly picked the woman up and pushed her into the bedroom, yelling at her to find cover. A second wave of darts careened in his direction. He dodged them, plucking the dart out of his neck as he did so.

He still didn't understand who they were, or how they could have found him so quickly.

There was little time to ponder. Eliminate the threat; ensure the woman's safety. Those were his only objectives right now.

Somersaulting into the air, he crashed into the two men at full speed, smashing them into the hallway floor before breaking both their necks. Before he got up, he looked to either side of him and saw two more armed troopers, one on each side of him, rapidly closing in, rifles leveled at him. As they fired their weapons, he back-flipped through the doorway back into the apartment. In the hallway he saw the darts intersect paths in the air over the bodies of the first two men, then plunk into the floor.

He got up, anticipating that the two men would round the corner into the doorway. Grabbing hold of an end table to shield himself, he made for cover behind the kitchen counter, when suddenly he staggered.

Like before, he began to feel woozy, his energy again being sucked out of him.

He could hear a low, urgent voice in the hallway. Holding onto the kitchen counter for support, he listened, picking up fragments as he did so:

"Two men down, require immediate backup … 4670 North Clark … repeat, subject has been engaged, package has been delivered, however …

still up, repeat subject is still up and extremely dangerous … repeat, require immediate backup …"

He glanced over at the bedroom door. The woman had closed it and was hopefully barricading it to give herself time to get out if he wasn't able to protect her.

Rage remained behind the kitchen counter, waiting. He could hear the men in the hallway, speaking in whispers to each other. He could feel his strength returning to him; his body was counteracting the dart's effects. He needed to get out of there before their backup arrived, but he was pinned down. He needed a plan.

In the hallway, flanking the bodies of their squad mates, Agents Smith and Rodriguez stood on opposite sides of the door, crouched slightly, rifles primed.

"Do you hear him in there?" Rodriguez whispered.

"Negative," Smith replied. "Possible the tranquilizers have taken him down."

"Can't assume that," Rodriguez countered. "He was hit maybe once, twice at best. Briefing told us it'd likely take three."

"Well, you wanna go in there and check?"

"Negative. Too risky. We wait for backup. Seven minutes. Meantime, we have him trapped. If he makes a move for the door—"

In that split second the wall to Rodriguez' right exploded into the hallway. Amidst the huge chunks of plaster and wood being sent into the air, Rodriguez felt a massive pain in his midsection as he was tackled hard and slammed into the far wall. His neck was snapped before his next breath.

Smith didn't even have time to realize what had happened before the subject had literally flown into him, body-slamming him to the floor, pinning him down. He felt his ears nearly tear from the sides of his head as his helmet was ripped off. He was face-to-face with the subject – the black, hateful eyes boring into his own from inches away, the hot breath upon his face – like a vicious beast. They were so close that Smith could hear what sounded like a snarl. Then came the harsh, deep voice:

"How many of you are there?" the subject demanded with another snarl.

Smith, despite the warnings of his C.O., decided to employ his strength and skill to escape the subject's grip, so he began to push against him with all his might, using any leverage he could. But the subject didn't budge an inch until he pulled Smith up by the collar into a sitting position. Then, like a ball on a tee, the subject struck him hard across the face, sending him back to the floor, where the back of his head slammed down. He screamed in agony; his jaw had been broken. The bitter taste of blood filled his mouth, and he could feel that some of his teeth were missing.

"Wrong answer," the man said coldly. *"How many?"*

Smith struggled to speak, but managed: "Me."

"But backup is coming. *Who are you working for??"*

"Go ahead and kill me, you son of a bitch," Smith spat angrily back at him. "By the time you find out, it'll be too late."

The man picked up Smith's gun from a few feet away, then stood up and planted a foot on Smith's chest. Aiming the gun at his neck, he said with a sneer: "Fine. Let's see how well these darts work, then."

Smith did not scream as he felt the first dart, then a second, pierce his neck on either side of his larynx.

Rage stood over his unconscious attacker for a second, trying to recognize anything on his black armored uniform. There was nothing. Were they CIA? FBI? NSA? Someone else? There wasn't time to figure it out. He needed to get out of the building with the woman before more of them showed up.

At that instant he heard a static-filled sound coming from the helmet he'd thrown several feet away. He picked it up and saw a small earpiece mounted to the inside. He pulled it from its mounting.

Putting the earpiece in his ear, he ran back into the apartment, and noticed his jacket hanging in the front closet. He quickly put it on, then moved toward the bedroom. Opening the door, he saw the woman crouching behind a dresser, a can of mace in one hand, baseball bat in the other.

"We need to get out of here, now," he said.

"What is going on!?" she asked, panicked.

"I don't know," he replied. "But right now we just have to get out of here. Grab anything you immediately need, and then we're leaving."

As he finished his sentence the earpiece crackled the words: "Rodriguez. Smith. Anderson's unit has entered the building; ETA less than two minutes."

He looked at her. "Scratch that. More of them are on their way up."

"Who *are* they?" she demanded.

"I don't know. There's no time. The fire escape. Come on." He pried the bedroom window up. Out in the hallway, he heard the stairwell door slam open.

Helping the woman out onto the fire escape, he looked around for the best escape route. They were too many stories below the roof to try to leap to another building, plus he'd never leapt with anyone else's weight to support before. It was too risky.

Then he spotted the cable-wire extending from just above them, sloping downward steeply to the second-floor fire escape of the building across the alleyway.

It was their best chance.

He pulled one of the thin iron bars out of the fire escape railing, bent it at a ninety-degree angle, and placed it over the cable-wire, holding it with his right hand.

"Grab onto me, and hold tight," he told her.

She did so without hesitation, wrapping an arm over his left shoulder and another under his right arm, interlocking her hands across his chest.

He immediately placed his other hand on the iron bar, gripping it tightly, and pushed off. They began to slide rapidly down the cable-wire toward the building across the alley, picking up speed as they went.

"Hold on!!" he shouted to her as they closed in on the fire escape. Just as they reached the edge, he let go of the iron bar, his momentum carrying him into the building, the woman holding on for dear life. He threw his arms out and crashed into the brick wall. His palms took most of the impact, but the force of his momentum pushed him into the wall so hard that his head carried forward, and he smashed his forehead into the wall's coarse surface. He fell backward, the woman with him, almost off the fire escape, but the iron railing stopped them. The woman regained her balance first; he could feel her soft hand on his chest, holding him tightly, steadying them, her other hand on the railing. His heart was pounding rapidly; and even in the heat of the moment he wondered if it was from the danger they were clearly in, or from the woman being so close to him.

Before he could contemplate that, he heard the loud clang of boots on the fire escape across the alley above them. Not even looking up, he grabbed the woman and, seeing a boarded-up window, backed into it as hard as he could, ramming through it. A cluster of darts plinked onto the fire escape as they went through the window, missing his feet by inches.

Once inside, they landed hard on Rage's back upon the floor, the woman on top of him. He felt her warmth against him, holding tight to her for a moment. He found himself not wanting to let go.

Mira held Rage closely on the floor, her arm extended across his chest. She could feel his heart beating quickly, as was hers. Her whole body ached; the past few moments had been like a stunt in a movie: although she could tell he'd been trying his best to protect her, she'd been tossed around like a rag doll.

She remained on top of him for a moment, just holding on to him, not saying a word. In the brief time this stranger had been in her life, everything had turned upside down. He was at best a tormented soul with a twisted sense of right and wrong – but, despite all of this, she felt a closeness to him; a bond. She wasn't sure why; perhaps it was because he'd saved her, perhaps it was something else. But the feeling was there; there was no sense denying it.

She felt his hand touch her shoulder. "We need to get up, get moving," he said softly, breaking the silence.

She let go of him slowly, allowing him to get up and to help her up. She glanced around in the low light. The room they were in was musty, ridden with cobwebs and trash; a storage room of some sort. Looking at him, she asked, "What do we do now?"

Rage looked around, searching for a door. Finding one, he grabbed her hand and led her toward it. "We get clear of here; get 'em off our tail. I need to get you to safety before I can deal with whoever's chasing us."

"Why are they chasing us?"

"It's me they're after. They only came to you to get to me."

"But why? Because of what you've done?"

"Can't think of any other reason."

"Is it the police?"

"I don't think so," he said leading her down the stairs. "Something else is going on here. Either way, I'm taking you to a police station. Only place you'll be safe."

"The *police* station?! You can't go there, you'll be arrested!"

"Better than being shot. The cops won't catch me."

They exited a side door off the far alley which emptied onto Wilson Avenue. Seeing a cab, Rage hailed it and opened the door for her. "Hurry. Get in."

"A cab?" she asked, hopping into the back seat.

"Can you think of a faster way there?"

"I guess not," she admitted, scooting across the back seat as he got in.

"Halsted just north of Addison," Rage ordered the cab driver. "And step on it."

The cab's tires screeched as it turned southbound on Clark toward the station.

28

Intruder

As Larry approached Damen Avenue, his cell phone rang.

With a sigh he glanced down at the tiny screen. It was Gino.

He flipped the phone open and answered it. "Hey," he said flatly, spotting a parking space on Damen across from his apartment.

"Hey," Gino said. "Guessin' you heard about your guy's apartment building."

"Yeah," Larry said, turning the steering wheel as he began to back into the spot. "And yes, I did go over there."

"Figured," Gino said, huffing. "Listen, I forgot something in my locker, so I gotta drop by the station tonight. If the chief's there, I thought I'd ask, since I *am* such a good partner to you, if you wanted me to say anything to him."

"Like what?"

"I dunno," Gino replied. "I'd ask him for whatever he *might* know. I figure you got questions. I also figure you're probably the *last* person the chief wants to see tonight, so I figure I'd spare him the headache and you the trouble."

"No," Larry said, throwing the car into park. "Think I'm just gonna sleep it off."

"S'what I wanted to hear," Gino said, satisfied. "Best you get your mind off it. We'll see what tomorrow brings. G'night."

"Gino," Larry cut in, changing his mind.

"Yeah?" Gino replied.

"The Feds … ask him about the Feds."

"What about 'em?"

"Ask why they were there."

"He's probably not gonna know that."

"Just ask him."

"Why do you wanna know anyway? Once they clear out, you can go back about your business with this character from the bank weeks back."

"I don't know … something about this guy."

"Whadda you mean?"

"This 'Rage' guy," Larry tried to put it into words. "I think *he's* why the Feds are there."

"What the hell are you talking about?" Gino asked, confused.

"Gino," Larry began. "I think this guy is also the vigilante we've been trying to track down."

"The 'Protector' lunatic?" Gino tried to clarify.

"Yes."

"Ah, you're frickin' nuts," Gino said dismissively. "Listen, go get some sleep. You need it. That and maybe get your head examined."

"I'm serious. You never saw what he did in that alley. It pretty much matches the eyewitness accounts in the vigilante cases. So maybe there's something about him. Something the Feds want, maybe."

"Why would a vigilante case be of interest to the Feds?"

"Maybe that's not what they're interested in. Maybe it's something else."

"Give it up," Gino sighed. "You're grasping at straws."

"You're not looking at everything here," Larry said.

"And you're looking for something that's not there," Gino responded. "Get it out of your mind. Go get a good night's sleep. I'll call you in the morning. Okay?"

"Fine," Larry said irritably, knowing there was no convincing Gino otherwise. "'Night, then," he added, and hung up.

Frustrated, he shut the door of the Buick and walked toward his building.

When he got to the top of the stairs, he slid the key into the lock and quietly pushed open the front door. The apartment was dark, save for the small light above the kitchen stove and the night light in the bathroom. He left the lights off. The digital clock on the microwave read 10:33 P.M. He could hear the boys sleeping in their bedroom.

He opened the fridge and poured himself a glass of orange juice. Taking a sip, he went over to the bay window and stood in the dark, gazing out onto the street below. It was quiet for a Saturday night. He felt the soft breeze through the slightly open window. A black sedan slowly drove southbound on Damen before picking up speed.

He had cooled off since his talk with the Captain, but his talk with Gino had not helped matters. Although he was certain this Rage character was also the 'Protector of the People' vigilante they'd been after, he was also certain that there was something else, something much bigger, about him. He didn't care if Gino believed him. The case itself didn't explain the Feds' involvement; they wouldn't call in a heavy-duty task force like the one he saw for a local case, nor would they dismiss the help of the Chicago Police. Not unless something larger was at stake.

Something they wanted to keep a secret.

That had to be it.

But what? What needed to be kept under wraps?

Shaking his head, he downed the rest of the orange juice and walked back toward the kitchen. He set the glass in the sink and rubbed his eyes slowly, trying to clear his head. The clock read 10:39. The breeze sifted in through the window, slightly billowing out the sheer curtains. Amid the muted sounds of late-night traffic outside, he could hear a dog barking. One of the boys rolled over in bed. A faint click came from the front door.

Larry was suddenly alert. Drawing his gun, he moved toward the door, his back to the wall along the way. He stopped a few feet from the door, watching it intently.

A few seconds passed; nothing happened.

You're being paranoid, he chided himself.

Still, he quietly took two more small steps toward the door, trying his best to keep the floorboards from creaking under his feet, his eyes on the doorknob with each step.

He quickly glanced over to the boys' bedroom. Their door lay slightly ajar, and he could tell the fire-escape window was open a few inches, the incoming breeze rocking the mostly-closed window blinds gently back and forth.

He eyed the apartment door one final time. Still nothing.

Dropping his shoulders, he holstered the pistol and walked to his bedroom. *Must've been hearing things*, he told himself. He leaned against his dresser, palms cupping the front edge. He was exhausted.

He had begun to undo his gun belt when he heard another noise in the hallway, this time a small thumping sound.

Something is wrong.

Keeping the belt on, he moved quickly to the boys' bedroom, shutting their door behind him. He shook them both awake. "Marcus. Daniel," he said quietly.

Marcus and Daniel both grunted. "Whuh … Dad, wuzzup," Daniel said groggily, turning over to squint at his father.

"I need you both to listen to me. I need you to go into your closet and climb up to the opening to the attic. I want you to get up into the attic and hide. Do it quietly, and close the opening behind you. Don't make a sound while you're up there." He unclipped his cell phone from the belt and handed it to Daniel. "If you hear anything at all, anything, dial 911. Don't come out until I say. Understood?"

"Dad, what are you talking — "

"Don't ask questions. Do it NOW," Larry whispered urgently.

Without another word, Marcus and Daniel threw off the covers and headed to the closet, Daniel placing the chair that rested by the closet underneath the small, covered opening that led to the attic.

Larry turned from the boys and watched the closed bedroom door, trying to figure out what was going on, both outside and in his head. There was no logical reason for him to believe there was any danger – the sounds in the hallway could have been anything. But instinct had taken over. He *felt* something was wrong. And with everything he'd seen in the past few days, the past few *hours*, he wasn't about to ignore his instincts.

He kept an eye on the boys as they climbed their way up into the attic, each one hoisting himself from the chair, grabbing on to the top shelf before pulling himself through the small opening. Marcus first, followed by Daniel. Just before pushing off from the chair, Daniel looked over to his father. Larry nodded to him vigorously, imploring him to get up there, waving his hand to the right in signal to close the opening behind him. After a split-second's hesitation, Daniel obeyed.

Once the opening was closed, Larry moved the chair further into the closet, still underneath the opening, then closed the sliding door.

His eye on the door once again as he moved silently toward it, Larry's hand moved to his gun holster. He undid the flap and pulled out his .45, holding it with both hands as he stood next to the bedroom door, his back to the wall. He listened closely, trying to hear any sound whatsoever in the main room just beyond the door.

Hearing nothing after several seconds, holding his gun tightly in his left hand, back still against the wall, he placed his right hand on the doorknob, waiting another few seconds before turning it, anticipating what, if anything, might be on the other side.

Slowly, as quietly as he could, he turned the knob.

Taking a deep breath, he flung the door open and pivoted himself into the doorway, pointing his gun into the main living space in front of him. It was dead silence. Eyes wide, gun pointed, he scanned the room, looking for any signs of disturbance.

At that moment, he noticed the apartment door was open.

29

Tail

The steadily cooling night breeze had picked up; the trees began to rustle more noisily along the nearby streets.

Hayes looked down at his wristwatch: 10:43 P.M. He'd received confirmation that Rodriguez's squad had engaged the subject, and that Anderson's team was moving in to provide backup. The latest report had the subject trapped in the woman's apartment, but there was no confirmation of the tranquilizer having been administered. Anderson or Rodriguez would report in at any moment.

The call came. "Sir," Hayes heard Anderson's voice over the headset. "Rodriguez's squad all down, we found three dead, one unconscious –"

"And the subject?" Hayes cut him off anxiously.

"Negative, sir," Anderson replied. "He escaped just prior to our arrival. Moore and Wallace reached the fire escape and opened fire but were unsuccessful."

Damn it, Hayes thought angrily. *He's better than I'd anticipated.*

Just then a second voice came in from a separate frequency on Hayes' headset. It was Agent Blake, running surveillance from the mobile control room in one of the two transports. "Sir," he began, "I'm currently tracking Smith. He's broken off from the rest of his unit still stationed in the woman's apartment building."

"Copy that," Hayes replied. Suspecting what had happened, he switched frequencies and addressed Anderson. *He might be listening.* "Anderson. Re-route to channel eight."

Anderson changed frequencies. "Yes, sir."

"Now. Switch again to the encoded channel."

A second later, he heard Anderson on the encrypted frequency. "Done."

"Reconfirm visual on Smith's current location."

"Sir," Anderson said, "Smith is currently unconscious, in the hallway outside the woman's apartment at 4670 North Clark Street."

"Where is his *helmet,*" Hayes specified.

A brief pause, then came the reply: "About three yards down the hallway, sir. Retrieving it now."

"Confirm the headset is accounted for, or missing," Hayes pressed.

"Missing," Anderson responded. "Sir, does this mean —"

Hayes switched frequencies, addressing Blake. "Confirm Smith's whereabouts."

Blake pinpointed the signal on the map grid. "Montrose Avenue, heading eastbound. Estimated speed thirty-five miles per hour."

Hayes glanced toward the southeast, then: "The subject has Smith's GPS. Place a tail on him immediately. Send one of the sedans in pursuit, then have the other meet my squadron in front of this building. I'm going to engage the subject myself."

30

The Station

Throughout the entire city, the precinct at Addison and Halsted was no doubt the epicenter of activity on this Saturday night.

Even though the department had beefed up staffing for the Cubs' first weekend home game of the new season, the processing area was packed with all sorts of troublemakers that had been rounded up over the past several hours. Most were the usual cases: drunks who'd gotten into fights in the neighborhood bars, or been caught urinating in public, or intoxicated drivers. Rows upon rows of desks showed a similar scene: a uniformed or plain-clothes officer filling out a series of forms, while the delinquents he or she had brought in sat on the other side of the desk and complained about their rights, protested their arrest, claimed they had nothing to do with "it," or sat silently in their chairs, staring at the floor. Amidst all this were the sounds of shoes shuffling across the tile floor, keyboards tapping, phones ringing, and the crackling intercom, paging officers and administrators here and there.

Gino Urrutia's tall, wide frame eclipsed much of the double-door entrance as he lumbered through the front vestibule. He shook his head as he surveyed the activity that had taken over the large room before him. "Worse every frickin' year," he grumbled, pushing through the second set of windowed doors into the main room.

Crossing the long, fluorescent-lit space toward the back of the building, he nodded and grunted to the many officers who greeted him as he passed.

"What's up Gino."

"How's it hangin' big guy."

"Hey, how're Vera and the kids?"

"Gigantor, what's goin' on?"

"Gino! You on shift tonight? Could sure use ya."

"What's new, big fella?"

Once he made it to the back of the room, he went down the stairs and through the steel door into the locker room. He found his locker, slid the key into the lock, and pulled open the door, grabbing a small plastic bag. He pulled out a tiny, velvet clamshell box, then peeked inside at the pair of ruby earrings. Vera's birthday present. Her birthday was tomorrow, and his locker was the only place she couldn't snoop.

Pleased with himself, he pocketed the box and closed up his locker.

He came back up the stairs and looked to his left to see the familiar scowl of Captain Robert Engalls towering over two rookie officers, finger-pointing from one to the other as he delivered instructions. Gino ambled over toward them. Not taking his eyes off the two rookies, Engalls held a long finger into the air, signaling Gino to wait until he'd finished. Gino rolled his eyes and turned toward the coffee machine, pouring himself a cup. He took a sip: bitter and stale, as usual. As he took another gulp and leaned against the wall next to the machine, one of the younger officers, Billy Jenkins, sidled up to him. One of the guys he and Larry had trained a few years ago, Jenkins was a skinny, bright-faced kid who had a personality more suited for politics than for police work. Always running around with a big-toothed smile that flared his nostrils and eager to start up conversation, he'd gained the reputation of being the precinct clown, whether he'd meant to or not. The guys around the precinct even had a running bet that if ever faced with a bank robbery situation, Billy'd sooner talk the robber into actually giving the money back than getting into a firefight with him.

Gino murmured to himself, looking sideways at Jenkins as he approached.

"Hey Big Gino," he said, the broad smile coming to his face. "Brings you into the circus tonight? Lookin' to make some overtime?"

Gino gave himself the up and down. "I look like I'm comin' into work, kid?"

"Why wouldn't you?" Jenkins countered, his smile converting to a smirk. "Busiest day of the year at this joint. Who'd want to miss out on all this fun?"

"Sane people, that's who," Gino said uninterestedly. "Or old guys like me who know enough to ask for it off."

"So, why you down here then?" Jenkins asked, shrugging his shoulders.

Gino glanced over at Engalls, who was still coaching the two rookies, then boredly set his eyes back on Jenkins. "To check up on young jokers like you. And looking around, I'd say it's pretty busy around here for you to be talkin' to me. I mean, good thing the Chief ain't noticed yet. Capieche?"

"Yeah, yeah," Jenkins' smirk turned wry. "I get the picture. Well, hope the rest of your night off puts you in a better mood," he added, then strutted off.

"It already has," Gino chuckled after him.

A cheery grin still on his face, he turned to his left to see Engalls standing there annoyed, as if he'd been waiting for Gino instead of the other way around.

"What is it, Urrutia," he said impatiently.

"Chief, you gotta lighten up," Gino grinned. "I mean, you're in your element tonight. I've known you too long; crazy nights like this are what you live for."

"Not like this," Engalls muttered. "Too much of the weird stuff happening. First that situation up in Edgewater with the Feds, and now we've got all sorts of oddball cases down here; sexual assaults, robberies, even a homicide. Bad stuff."

"Yeah, about that Edgewater thing," Gino began.

"Don't start with me about that," Engalls cut him off. "I'm sure Parker's been on you about it like he has me, and I'm done discussing it. So drop it, now."

"Actually Chief, there might be something else to it," Gino replied darkly.

"And what would that be?" Engalls asked skeptically.

"What if," Gino began. "The guy Parker's after is actually the guy we've been looking for – the vigilante character."

"I wouldn't call a serial killer a 'character' in any sense of the word, Urrutia," Engalls replied testily.

"You know what I mean, Chief. And you're missing the point," Gino went on. "What Parker saw the guy do in the bank alley weeks back, matches the witness accounts we've got in these cases. Physical description is similar too. In my opinion, we probably should've connected the dots sooner. There's just a lot of things at play here that deserve a second look."

Engalls crossed his arms. "Fine. I'll play along, Urrutia. Why then, did these cases just suddenly start popping up? Nothing; then all this?"

"Who knows?" Gino shrugged. "Maybe something set him off. Had an epiphany. Lost a family member. Got a vendetta on. Could be anything. I'm just saying it's a lead, and we should pursue it."

"It's a conclusion you're drawing," Engalls wagged a finger. "Fed by Parker, no doubt. We'll discuss it in the morning, after all the smoke clears. Plus, as you can see, I've already got my hands full tonight. That enough to get you out of my hair?"

"Good enough for me, Chief," Gino said, satisfied. "See ya tomorrow." And he turned to leave.

After wading through the station's increasingly-crowded main room, Gino pushed through the doors to the outer lobby, waved goodnight to Doreen in Dispatch behind the front desk, and exited out the front doors to Addison Street. Taking a deep breath of the cool night air, he fished out his keys and started toward his car. As he slid the key into the lock, he heard what sounded like feet hitting the sidewalk behind him. He whirled around to see someone, a small man it appeared to be, setting down a woman about twelve feet away from the front door of the precinct, close to a light post. He looked up toward the roof of the three-story building, trying to figure out where exactly they'd come from. He put his hand over his brow, attempting to block out the glare from the street light, straining to get a look at the couple, when suddenly a black sedan came barreling around the corner, tires screeching as it lurched to an abrupt halt. From the vehicle stormed four heavily-armored troopers complete with riot helmets and what appeared to be M-16s, taking position on the two individuals. As they advanced and leveled their weapons, the small man lunged forward toward a public mail drop and, to Gino's amazement, literally tore the steel unit, bolts and all, from the concrete sidewalk. He quickly retreated back toward the woman, holding the mailbox in front of them as if it were some sort of shield.

And in that instant, without warning, the four troopers opened fire.

Using the mailbox as a shield from the incoming barrage of darts, Rage yelled back at Mira to stay directly behind him. "Wait til they reload! Then run for the door!" He growled in pain as one dart sliced past his left forearm, then a second found a home in his outstretched leg.

"Stay low!" he screamed to her as he set down the mailbox and yanked out the dart. *Damn it*, he thought. He hadn't yet fully shaken the effects of the first dart. They were only a few feet away; he had to get her to safety before the second dart kicked in. They were alternating their firing sequences, reloading two at a time, so there was a constant hail of darts keeping them pinned down. Meanwhile, he knew they were fanning out, surrounding them at all angles, so at any moment the makeshift cover he'd bought them would be useless. Feeling the woman behind him, holding him close, his mind worked desperately to find a way out of this situation.

"FREEZE!"

The bellowing voice came from Rage's right. He glanced in that direction to see a large man taking cover behind a police cruiser, pointing a gun in the direction of the four troopers.

"Chicago Police. Drop your weapons, and raise your hands in the air," the large man shouted.

The reply came from the direction of the troopers. "Officer, you are ordered to stand down. This is a matter of national security, and you are obligated under Federal law not to interfere. Should you not comply, I am authorized to use force."

"You have opened fire unprovoked on two unarmed individuals," the large man returned, firearm still pointed at the troopers. "Present your credentials by tossing them on the hood of this vehicle."

"Sir, you are to stand down immediately, or you will be shot where you stand," the lead trooper responded. From behind the mailbox, Rage could see two troopers reaching for their handguns.

He knew this was their only chance. "We're going for the doors. Stay behind me. When I say, you run," he whispered to Mira.

"What about you?" Mira asked.

"I can handle myself. Just get inside."

He slowly began to make his way toward the front door, at which point the troopers once again began firing upon them. As they moved he could hear shouts between the police officer and the squadron leader, then gunfire. *I can't help him*, he thought. Once they were by the door he yelled to her, "Run!" at which point he felt her hands, which had been at his sides, squeeze him gently one final time, then let go.

He heard the door close behind him.

She was safe. Now he could tend to other matters.

The shots had missed Gino by a matter of inches. Ducking behind the cruiser for cover, he held his gun close and glanced to either side of him. He had no idea what was happening, who these people were or why they'd fired without warning at the couple; all he knew now was they were firing at *him*. No time to think about anything else.

They'd be advancing on his position any second now. He didn't have his radio on him, but they must've heard the gunshots inside the precinct. Heart hammering, he double-checked his weapon. He needed backup soon, or he'd be a dead man.

Then, unexpectedly, he heard a bone-chilling scream, cut off by the harsh sound of metal smashing together. Gun still primed, he peered over the top of the cruiser door to see that the mailbox had been flung at two of the troopers, who were now dead, crushed between it and the black sedan they'd arrived in. The entire right side of the car had collapsed inward, as if it had been hit by another vehicle going full speed. His mouth open in amazement, he watched as the small man leapt at least ten feet into the air to land in front of one of the remaining troopers, then abruptly snapped the trooper's neck with the ease of someone turning a knob. The small man then back-flipped over to the fourth trooper, who'd started to run, and grabbed him by the collar. He slapped the rifle out of the man's hands, causing it to clatter on the street surface, then held him high in the air by the neck.

Before Gino could react, the front doors of the precinct flew open, and Captain Robert Engalls and seven other officers emerged with guns pointed. At that same instant, another five officers appeared from around the corner at Addison and Halsted, surrounding the entire section of Addison Street. They immediately spread out behind cover of police cruisers and parked cars, keeping their weapons leveled at the small man, who was still standing in the center of the street.

"Don't move! You are surrounded. Lower the hostage to the ground, and put your hands in the air," Engalls commanded through a megaphone.

Gino glanced around to see that a few small pockets of onlookers had begun to gather around the scene. He stood up to wave them back when he saw a second black sedan, identical to the first, careening around the corner, tires squealing in protest as it came to a sudden halt. From the sedan emerged three more armored troopers and then an extremely large man, who immediately leveled his gun and fired upon the small man.

Surrounded, Rage desperately scanned the area for an escape route. He was too exposed to leap toward cover, even if his movements hadn't been slowed by the tranquilizers in his bloodstream. He'd used a lot of energy taking out these four troopers; there was no way he'd be able to fight through all those surrounding him now.

The second dart had really begun to kick in; he could feel his thoughts start to cloud; his strength begin to fade.

At that moment another car – or maybe there were two of them, his vision was starting to blur – came around the corner, heading straight for him. He stood transfixed as the car slammed on its brakes and stopped twenty feet or so away. Having a second to think, he wondered: *How had they found him so quickly?* Then he realized: *the headset.* He'd been tracked.

The doors opened and four more heavily armored agents came out, pointing their rifles at him. The largest agent, emerging last from the front passenger-side door, came to the front of the squad and immediately fired at him. Rage swiveled, moving the trooper he was holding up between himself and the gunfire, and heard three darts pierce the man's back. He felt the agent immediately go limp in his grasp.

Nolan Hayes was not pleased with how this situation was developing. They had the subject trapped, but in a very public place, and once again it involved the Chicago Police Department. There were too many witnesses. His quarry, even though surrounded, had proven cunning and resourceful enough to potentially escape them once again. He could not take that chance.

"Fan out," he ordered his men. "Surround him from all sides. As soon as you have a clear shot, fire at will."

He then addressed the subject in a commanding voice: "By order of the United States Government, you are hereby ordered to surrender. Stay where you are and place your hands in the air."

Hayes didn't know how many tranquilizers were already in the subject, but he knew the man's metabolism would already be counter-acting them. If they hit the subject more than three times, antidotes were available at mobile command if need be. His main concern was to bring him down, here and now.

Additional officers had arrived on the scene, working to push back the growing crowds of onlookers. Police blockades were being deployed, and somehow, down the street, a TV news van had already arrived and begun setting up its equipment. From behind a police cruiser by the station's front door, handgun still pointed, Gino crouched next to Captain Robert Engalls, looking on as events continued to unfold.

"Aren't we gonna do something?" he asked the captain under his breath.

"Like what," Engalls replied quietly, his eyes not leaving the suspect in the center of the street.

"I don't know," Gino said, "but these guys, they're firing without warning. Did the same when the woman was outside, too. Innocent bystander. Could've killed her. No concern for civilian safety."

"Urrutia," Engalls replied tersely. "Don't you think I know that? But they've got authority here, and we're not in a position to question their methods. We are backup, and backup only, if the situation gets out of hand."

Gino did not reply. In the seconds that followed, he and Engalls could only watch in shocked silence as the standoff erupted to a sudden, violent conclusion.

Rage knew this was the end. He held the unconscious federal agent in front of him as a shield, his only protection from being shot again. His legs buckled; he felt more unsteady by the second. The remaining armored troopers had moved in, taking up positions, surrounding him.

Then he turned to see that the large agent had advanced on him as well. This man was the leader, beyond a doubt. Rage looked into his eyes: cold, murderous, clear and blue, like slicks of ice. A flash of familiarity gripped Rage, elusively – then let go before he could understand. They had known each other somewhere, or sometime, before.

The agent smiled malevolently, nodding at him. As if issuing a challenge. Rage somehow knew that taking him out would present his one chance to escape.

He had to do it now, before his consciousness slipped away completely.

Without hesitation, he dropped the unconscious agent and leapt forward. In a blinding motion, the enormous man reached out, caught him mid-leap by the neck, and swiftly threw him down to the pavement.

Dazed, head pounding, Rage looked up at the night sky, which faded in and out as a blur of darkness and the faint glow of street lamps. He saw the man appear in his view, staring down from above, then promptly had the wind knocked out of him as a massive foot planted itself across his chest.

"I'll gather you're not used to this," the man said smugly, leveling the rifle.

The agent fired, and everything went black.

Nolan Hayes stood over his quarry, looking down at the unconscious body. It was done. He needed to secure the subject, settle matters with the local authorities to keep them from speaking to the press, and then they could depart.

But first he would need to tend to the urge building inside him.

He ordered his men to surround Asset Two until the transport arrived, made his way back into the black sedan he'd arrived in, and closed the door.

Gino lowered his firearm. From the corner of his eye, he saw Engalls follow suit. The two did not say a word to each other. He was still unsure of exactly what he'd just witnessed, and he could tell by the captain's body language that he was thinking the exact same thing. They could not interfere with a Federal case, but in Gino's mind, something seemed very, very wrong about this.

"It's over," the captain finally broke in. "Urrutia," he began. "Help the other officers keep those pockets of people back. Tighten up the perimeter, make sure no one, no damned TV cameras can get through, and then you can go home for the night."

"'Course, Chief," Gino began. "But even after, I plan on stickin' around a bit."

"Fine," Engalls replied. "We could probably use you."

"Good enough," Gino said, turning toward the blockades being set up. "Once I'm done with this I figure I should give Parker a buzz."

"How did I know that was coming," Engalls grumbled. "Just get on that perimeter, will you."

"On it," Gino said as he started toward the blockades.

"NOOOO!"

Gino turned to see a young woman who'd apparently just come out of the station's front doors, running toward the small man's body in the center of the street. He then saw Captain Robert Engalls' long arm reach out and grab her by the arm, corralling her into a bear hug to prevent her from getting any closer to the scene.

"Please keep back, miss," Gino heard him say to her. "It's not safe."

The woman, visibly upset, was struggling in the Captain's arms, straining to look at the body. "No," she said, panicked. "I have to get to him! Please let me go!"

"You can't help him," the Captain told her, holding onto her firmly. "Please miss, you need to stay back." He made eye contact with Gino. "Urrutia," he barked at him. "Please take care of this young lady. Get her back inside, get her a cup of coffee."

"Of course," Gino replied, heading toward them. Nearing the woman, he recognized her: the woman from the bank robbery, weeks back. The same bank robbery from which the mysterious intervener, the man Larry suspected of being the 'Protector' vigilante, had fled. Snapping back into focus, he extended a hand to her reassuringly. "Come with me, miss. We'll get you inside."

Seeming to realize the futility of the situation, the young woman blankly took his hand. She was fighting back tears. Putting an arm around her, he led her back toward the station. As they went through the double doors, he looked back to see that a large black bus had pulled up. Four of the troopers had begun unloading some kind of large metal object from the cargo door, while four more agents remained standing atop the unconscious man, rifles pointed at him.

Meanwhile, he realized, the large agent had disappeared.

Keeps getting weirder by the second, he thought to himself.

For reasons he couldn't quite put a finger on, he was beginning to feel affected, even troubled, by what had just happened moments ago. And, much as he tried, he couldn't shake the feeling.

31

Authority

Inside the station, Gino sat the woman down at one of the desks.

She'd begun to shiver, quite possibly as much from the cold as from shock, so he draped his jacket over her shoulders.

"Miss, I'll be right back," he said. "I'll get you a cup of coffee."

At the coffee machine he was approached by Shane Sullivan, one of the desk jockeys on the night shift. "Gino," Shane said as he walked up to him. "Hey. You processing that one? Yeah. She came in about five, ten minutes ago, asked for someone to come outside and help her friend. Anyway, we hear gunshots right around the same time, so Chief rounds up some officers to go outside. Meantime, I sit her down but she won't say nuthin', just wants me to go out there and help her friend. Then, without sayin' anything, she just goes runnin' back outside. I didn't have nothin' to hold her on, so I just let her go. So I'm just sayin', I ain't sure you're gonna –"

"Thanks," Gino interrupted him. "I think I got it."

Returning to the desk, he handed her a cup of coffee, then sat down across from her. "Miss, I'm Officer Urrutia. We met weeks back – the bank. Are you all right?"

Still shivering, she looked up at him and seemed to recognize him as well. "I-I'm fine," she began, her young, striking features clouded in confusion. "Do you know what's happening? Why can't you *help* him?"

"Unfortunately, I don't know," he replied. "And we can't help him right now. Even if we were so inclined, we wouldn't have the authority."

"*Authority?* But you're the police!"

"I understand that, miss," Gino tried to explain patiently. "But your friend out there appears to be wanted by the Federal Government, for reasons we haven't been told, but that means that we have to step back and let them do their job."

"But they were just *shooting* at us!" she exclaimed, becoming upset. "They didn't even try to talk to us, or ask us any questions, nothing! How could they *do* that?"

"I wish I could explain that," Gino said, feeling conflicted himself. "Listen, miss, I know this may be difficult. But I need to ask you a few questions about tonight."

She wiped away a tear. "What – what do you want to know?" she asked.

"I need to know everything *you* know," he went on. "How you met him, how long you've known him, any details on him that might be helpful to us."

"I thought you just said you couldn't help him," she said derisively.

"I don't know if we can just yet," he replied. "But anything we can piece together just might lead to something we can do. Again, I don't know."

A thought appeared to dawn on her, and her eyes narrowed at him. "You're the ones looking for the vigilante," she said. "You think it's *him*, don't you?"

"Do you?" Gino asked.

"It doesn't matter what I think," she replied. "I'm not the police."

"Miss, please," Gino said. "We need your help. We don't know how he may be involved in that, or anything else for that matter. What I do know is that we need as much information as we can get to try and figure things out. And right now you are our only link to him. So I'm just asking for whatever you can tell us, anything, that might be able to lead us to some answers. Will you do that?"

Across the desk from the burly, gray-haired officer who'd brought her inside, Mira let her eyes drop to the cup of coffee she was holding between her hands. She knew the tactic the officer was using on her; she'd used it herself on many occasions with her own clients. *Adservio mutuus*, or "Help me to help you," as it was commonly termed. And for a police officer, he employed it fairly well.

"What will happen to him?" she asked.

"I can't tell you that. I don't know," he admitted, shaking his head. "But we'll do whatever we can within the bounds of the law."

"Okay," she said, exhaling. "I'll tell you everything I know."

Over the next several minutes Gino asked questions, and the woman provided answers about everything that had transpired from the other evening, all the way up to moments before. It all but confirmed what Larry had come to suspect: this man was, beyond a doubt, the vigilante they'd been seeking.

When they'd finished, Gino reached across the desk and placed a giant hand on her shoulder. "Thank you, miss," he told her. "You've been very helpful."

She looked up at him and nodded uncertainly.

"We're going to send an investigation team to your apartment. They're going to gather evidence. We're also going to make sure it's safe for you to return there before we recommend you do. I assume you have a place to stay while we take care of that?"

She nodded. "And what about Rage?" she asked.

"We're going to do whatever we can for him," he replied reassuringly. "Let me make a quick phone call, then I'll get you another cup of coffee, okay?"

"Thank you," she replied quietly.

He nodded back to her and smiled. Walking away from the desk, Gino unclipped his cell phone from his belt, then hit the speed dial button to Larry's cell phone.

32

Hayes' Secret

With Hayes' blood sample in hand, Loretta walked back toward the examination table.

With an eye dropper she extracted a drop of Hayes' blood from the vial, pressed it between two thin plastic strips, and placed it in the microscope tray.

Upon analyzing the samples, she found Hayes' genetic makeup to be strikingly similar to Todd's: there were matches in the reflexology, adrenaline, molecular density; all of it.

Even a similar chemical imbalance was present.

But there was one significant difference in Hayes: his blood showed much faster cellular repair, with complete regeneration occurring in one-fifth the time of Todd's blood.

But that difference had a flip-side: the very factor that allowed Hayes' cellular makeup to regenerate more quickly was also causing those cells to reproduce and die more quickly, suggesting that Hayes was aging at an extremely rapid rate.

She had no idea how this was possible; how any of it was possible, for that matter; but the deeper she went, the more she needed to understand.

Logging into her workstation, she accessed the electronic archive to see if any of Hayes' history had been kept in the official records. As she'd suspected, upon searching for his name, her access to the system was denied.

That in mind, she searched his name in the main contact directory. To her, Hayes appeared to be at least in his late forties, perhaps early fifties.

His profile popped up on the monitor. As the rancorous blue eyes glared up at her from the small screen, she scanned the profile and found what she was looking for:

DOB: April 21, 1974

He was thirty-seven years old.

She sat back from the screen for a moment.

There had to be a connection: the cell regeneration, Hayes' aged appearance …

This was clearly not a trait in Elias Todd: he was twenty-eight and looked it.

In her mind, Loretta knew without question that something was going on far beyond what she was being told. And the more she learned, the more ominous things seemed to become.

33

Arm of the Law

L arry stood just outside the boys' bedroom, gun drawn and pointed at the door.

He remained still, eyes sweeping across the room. The door lay slightly open, not more than a foot, so it was impossible to tell if whoever had opened it was still on the other side or already inside the unit. He listened.

Then he heard a noise from inside his bedroom.

Gun held close, he inched his way along the wall toward the source of the sound. He had to assume his position was known now; the intruder was in the apartment, had likely seen that the other bedroom door was closed, and almost certainly heard a door opening. They would be expecting someone coming from his direction. But perhaps they didn't expect he was a cop.

He made his decision. With his booming voice, he delivered the command: "Chicago Police. Come out of the bedroom slowly, with your hands above your head."

Nothing.

Suddenly a heavily-armored agent appeared in the front doorway, helmet and visor covering his face, gun drawn and aimed at Larry's head.

Instinctively, Larry dove to his right toward the kitchen counter. As he lunged, he fired three times into the agent's face, sending him crumpling to the floor.

Crouching behind cover of the counter island, Larry checked his weapon. Three shots left. His heart was hammering loudly inside his chest; so loud that he almost wondered if the other intruder could hear it as well.

Then the reality of his situation began to sink in: the Feds. Somehow, they were targeting *him* now. But why? What had he done? What did they think he knew?

There was no time to think about it. There was at least one more of them.

And until he got them in the clear, the boys were in grave danger.

He peered around the counter island toward the front door. The agent who'd appeared in front of him lay dead just inside the doorway, splayed out like some discarded marionette. He had to think: where was the other agent? Had he moved, advanced on Larry's position? Were there more of them?

The boys had to have heard the gunshots; they would be dialing 911 if they hadn't already. Given the present danger, Larry hoped they'd do it without being heard.

Inside the musty, pitch-black crawlspace in the attic, Marcus and Daniel searched in terrified silence for Larry's cell phone. At the sound of the gunshots, Daniel had jolted in surprise, sending the small device flying from his hands and landing somewhere in the blown-in insulation lining the attic floor. Both boys were leaning forward, reaching out in all directions, attempting to grasp the phone but having no luck.

"You got it?" Marcus whispered as quietly as he could.

"Marcus, be quiet," Daniel whispered back. "We can't let them hear us up here."

"What's happening down there?" Marcus worried. "D'you think Dad is okay?"

"He's okay," Daniel said. "He's gotta be. But we gotta stay quiet."

Reaching out one more time, Daniel touched something plastic. The phone. Picking it up, he recoiled back to a sitting position and touched a button on the side, the tiny LED screen revealing the look of relief on his face.

He flipped open the phone and was about to dial when it began to ring loudly, and once again he dropped it in surprise.

Downstairs, Larry peered around the counter island once again toward his bedroom. Then, through the small gap between the hinges of his open bedroom door, he saw what appeared to be movement. He tried to look closer, peering intently into the bedroom, when he heard his cell phone ring.

Momentarily confused, he instinctively reached for his belt clip, then, eyes wide, immediately turned his head toward the ceiling above the boys' bedroom. He was certain the gunman could hear it too. After two rings it stopped, and he could hear Daniel's voice coming through the ceiling, exposed by the sheer silence in the apartment.

No time. I need to move now.

Adrenaline flowing, Larry rushed the bedroom door with gun pointed. As he rounded the corner, he saw the large trooper taking aim at the ceiling. Lunging forward, Larry tackled him with every bit of momentum he could muster. They both fell to the floor, Larry on top; they knocked into his dresser as they went down. Fighting to recover first, Larry went after the man's gun, grabbing his right wrist and pinning it hard to the floor. With his other hand he moved to get his revolver in front of the trooper's visored face when the man reached up with surprising speed and knocked it out of his hands, sending it skidding under the bed.

The two struggled on the floor, Larry's left arm pinning down the agent's right, his right grappling in the air with the man's left. In the skirmish he was able to tear off the man's helmet, exposing his only vulnerable spot. Looking directly into the man's eyes in the dark of the room, Larry pushed down with all his power on the man's right wrist, trying to force the gun from his hand; but the larger man's considerable strength was proving difficult to match, and Larry could feel his arm being pushed upward from the floor. Gritting his teeth, arms shaking with exertion, he fought as hard as he could, but the man's power was too much, and Larry felt the wooden knobs of the dresser press into his back as he was pushed up against the unit, then forced down toward the floor. Still gripping the man's arm that held the silencer pistol, he was focusing all his strength on keeping the gun pointed away from him, when he looked up and saw his wooden gun box teetering at the edge of the dresser, directly above the trooper's head. With all his might he kicked the dresser, forcing it to shake and knocking the heavy gun box over the edge, where it fell and smashed onto the agent's head. To Larry's luck, the rusty lock gave from the impact of the crash, spilling the contents of the box onto the hardwood floor. Moving as quickly as he could, Larry knocked the gun from the stunned agent's hand and sent it flying a few feet away; then pushed upward, forcing the man off of him. Before the agent could recover, Larry sat up and, with arm fully extended, followed through with a crushing roundhouse to the face, sending the agent's head jerking backward and into the dresser with a loud crack.

Larry gathered the spare pistol up from the floor and immediately pointed it at the agent. He looked around for the other gun and found it was past the man's feet, just outside his immediate reach. Standing up slowly, not taking his eyes off his dazed adversary, he put his foot on the man's gun and kicked it back toward the corner of the room. He unclipped his handcuffs from his belt, tossing them into the agent's lap.

"Put your hands where I can see them, and place the handcuffs on. Close them tightly," he ordered the man.

The agent remained on the floor, back up against the dresser, hands at his sides on the floor, not saying a word. It looked like he was staring at the handcuffs, smiling.

This isn't over.

"DO IT NOW!" Larry shouted.

The agent stayed put, silent for a few seconds before he finally said, "You have no idea what you're doing."

"I'm telling you one last time," Larry commanded. "Put the cuffs on now. You're under arrest. If I have to … I *will* shoot you."

"Do you realize I'm a Federal Officer," the man said. "You'll stand down *now*."

At that moment Larry could hear static coming from the man's helmet, which still lay at the foot of his bed. Then it dawned on him: *he's buying time.*

There was a thumping noise in the attic, and for a split second Larry's eyes instinctively darted upward. The agent's right hand moved suddenly as if seizing something. *No choice. Shoot.* Larry fired at the man's right shoulder mostly to debilitate him, but he didn't succeed: the agent produced a small handgun and made to aim at Larry, when Larry fired again, this time into the agent's forehead.

The agent's arm dropped, gun clattering against the wood floor; his bleeding head slumped forward.

Larry exhaled heavily, his heart still pounding at a maddening rate.

The boys.

His head swiveled toward the ceiling, then back to the floor. *Secure the apartment first.*

Rushing over to the front door, he stuffed the spare pistol into his belt holster, then dragged the body of the first agent all the way into his bedroom, next to the other. He didn't want the boys to see this. He then shut the apartment door and dead-bolted it, wedging a chair under the knob for good measure.

He moved to the boys' bedroom and threw the door open. Rounding the corner into the room he called up to them: "Marcus! Daniel! Are you all right?"

"Dad?" came Daniel's muffled voice from above.

"It's me," Larry replied, opening the closet door. "It's all right. Come on down now. We need to leave."

He pulled the chair out of the way as the attic opening's wooden cover slowly shifted. Daniel's head appeared in the opening, a frightened look on his face. "Come on, it's okay," Larry said, holding his arms up. "I'll get you down."

Daniel's head disappeared, replaced seconds later by his feet. As his torso scooted downward through the opening, Larry held him by the waist and gently set him to the floor, then did the same with Marcus a moment later.

Looking them over quickly to make sure they were okay, he squatted in front of them and put a hand on each of their shoulders. "Listen," he began, attempting to calm them. "Everything's going to be okay, but we need to get moving. I'm taking you to the police station. You'll be safe there. Now just listen to what I say and don't ask questions. I need you to wait here for a few seconds. Put some shoes on. When I say so, I need you to move quickly to the door. Keep your eyes forward. We're going straight to the car. Stay close behind me. If I say run, you run. Got it?"

The boys nodded, dazed expressions on both their faces.

"Do you have the phone?"

Daniel blankly reached into his front pocket and produced the cell phone, handing it to Larry.

"Stay here and be ready to move when I say," he said, then turned back toward the living room.

As he moved to the front door, he pulled the spare pistol from his holster and checked the ammo. Four shots left.

At the front door, he removed the chair, then slowly turned the knob before throwing open the door, gun pointed.

He checked the hallway, listening for anything. No one.

He called back to them. "Marcus, Daniel. Let's go!"

The boys hurried out of the bedroom toward the front door, Daniel in front.

"Stay close behind me," Larry whispered, leading them into the hallway.

Moving quickly, they walked down the side corridor toward the back stairs, then descended toward the alley. He checked for movement. Again the coast was clear.

"We're going to the car. Let's move," he said quietly.

Leading the boys through the gangway toward Damen Avenue, Larry paused as he heard a car pulling up out front. Just as he peered around the front steps and recognized the unmarked squad car, his cell phone rang. It was Gino.

He picked it up. "That you out front?"

"Yeah," Gino quickly replied. "Hurry up, get in."

He hung up, then turned and nodded to the boys. "Head right for the squad car, run as fast as you can, and get in back. Let's go."

Turning toward Damen Avenue, Larry ran so the boys could keep up behind him. They reached the squad car, Larry making eye contact with Gino as he opened the door. He got the boys in, then hopped in quickly himself. As he slammed the door shut behind him, two bullets ripped through the roof of the cruiser, one punching a hole into the brown vinyl seat between Larry and the boys.

"Move!" Larry screamed.

He heard Gino's foot slam down on the accelerator as the car lurched forward amid screeching tires and then sped away, the ping of a second bullet sounding on the trunk of the cruiser.

34

Questions

B ehind the closed door of the Police Captain's office, Mira sat in the worn chair facing the desk.

She listened as the Captain spoke in heated tones to someone who, judging by the conversation, was one of his superiors. She could hear the intensity of the deep voice on the other end. The Captain stood behind the desk with his back to her, every few seconds rubbing his bald, dark-skinned head with his left hand.

Not ten minutes ago she was at Officer Urrutia's desk. Then he went to make a call on his cell phone and, while still on the phone, ran out of the police station without warning, leaving her sitting alone at his desk.

Then, seconds after Mira was moved to this office, the Captain's phone had rung, and he'd been on it since that moment.

After another few minutes on the phone, the Captain glanced back in Mira's direction, then motioned toward the window to the main room behind her. Within a few seconds, the office door opened, and a young officer walked in. He was of average height and quite lean, with babyish facial features and freckled skin.

"Uh, miss," he said quietly, "why don't you come with me for a moment?"

The officer walked her to one of the desks along the back wall. "Hi there. I'm Officer Jenkins," he said, almost too happily. "Please, have a seat."

She sat down and looked around. The enormous room was crowded. A rail-thin, creepy looking man with greasy shoulder-length hair and several facial piercings was winking at her, mouthing something slowly. The officer across from him was staring into the tiny computer monitor on his desk, intermittently looking down at his keyboard to type before looking back up at the monitor. Two teenage boys sat at the next desk over, waiting with nervous faces while the officer behind the desk talked on the phone. Every desk appeared to be filled. Looking toward the front of the room, she saw a crowd of reporters and TV cameras crammed into the front vestibule.

Her gaze returned to the officer across from her. He smiled at her pleasantly, his awkward, toothy grin flaring his nostrils. "It should only be a coupla minutes; then I'll take you right back into the Chief's office. Can I get you a cup of coffee, anything?"

"No, thank you," she replied, brushing a wisp of hair back from her face. "Can you tell me what's going on? No one seems to know."

"'Fraid not," he replied, shaking his head and shrugging boyishly. "I haven't even been told about what happened outside yet. There's so much activity tonight, we're just trying to keep up with all the stuff we have going on in here."

"The officer I was with," she began.

"Officer Urrutia," he finished for her.

"Why did he run off?"

"Again, I dunno," he said, shrugging again. "I saw him leave too, and to be honest, I'd never seen the big guy move so fast."

Her shoulders slumped; she was feeling more confused by the minute.

"Listen," he began somewhat awkwardly, "I hear you need a place to stay. Is there anyone you wanna call?"

"Please," she replied.

He pushed the desk phone toward her. "Not a problem. I'll leave you alone for a couple minutes, okay?" he said, then got up and walked toward the coffee machine.

She picked up the worn black office phone and dialed her closest friend, Lora, trying to figure out exactly what to tell her.

As she was dialing, she glanced toward the vestibule again to see the enormous man in black, the man she'd seen standing over Rage's body, striding into the main room, rifle slung over his shoulder, accompanied by two similarly dressed troopers. The man proceeded straight to the Police Captain's office and, without knocking, opened the door and went inside. As he closed the door behind him, the other two men stopped and stood at each side of the doorway, facing the main room, as if standing guard.

After hearing an earful from the Police Superintendent, Captain Robert Engalls hung up the phone angrily. *Complete bullshit,* he thought. First, his precinct is turned away from a potential terrorist situation in the Edgewater neighborhood by the Feds; who then show up at his precinct, shoot at unarmed civilians, supersede his authority, and leave him with a mess of reporters asking questions. And to top it off, he is being blamed for one of his men interfering with a federal manhunt.

As he stood up to retrieve the young woman, his door opened, and a large, scar-faced agent, dressed all in black armored SWAT gear, entered his office. He approached Engalls' desk boldly, a look of menace in his icy blue eyes.

"Officer—"

"Engalls," the Captain responded, nodding curtly and extending a hand. "Captain Robert Engalls, Chicago Police Department."

The large man nodded in reply but did not return Engalls' gesture. "I'm Colonel Nolan Hayes, Executive Special Agent to the NSA. It's my understanding you've been briefed on the nature of this evening's situation."

Engalls let his hand slowly drop back to his side. "'Briefed' is one way to put it, Colonel Hayes," the Captain replied, changing tact in response to the Agent's demeanor. "With all due respect, I'm not understanding why the situation that happened in Edgewater, and now here at my precinct, is even a Federal matter, much less something that should be drawing the attention of the NSA."

"It's a matter of national security," Hayes responded matter-of-factly. "And with that it becomes a Federal situation, and therefore out of your jurisdiction. And it's in everyone's best interest your department remains … unburdened with unnecessary information. Am I making myself clear?"

"Frankly, no," Engalls shot back, standing his ground. "If this situation poses a threat to national security, then it also poses a threat to this city, the city I'm responsible to. As an officer of the law, I cannot step aside and ignore that. I think it would be in everyone's best interest that my department be allowed to assist your team in this matter – whatever the matter may *be*, that is."

"Let me be clear," Hayes spoke quietly. "I don't believe I need to remind you your authority here is limited. And now, your precinct has interfered with a sensitive matter of national security. For that I could have you arrested and locked up for as long as the NSA sees fit."

"Then let *me* be clear," Engalls said, raising his voice. "I did not invite you into my office. Get the hell out."

"Let me explain to you," the large man in black said, leaning forward and putting his hands on Engalls' desk. "You are in way over your head. If you know what's good for you, you'll listen closely and cooperate. What occurred outside your precinct tonight is a matter of national security. You are not to speak of it to the press. You are to simply reply 'no comment.' Not doing so will be treated with the same severity as would an act of treason. You will relay this message to your entire precinct immediately. I will hold you personally responsible for doing so. Am I making myself clear?"

"Go to hell," Engalls growled at him.

"I'm glad we understand each other," he said, and turned to leave.

With the door closed again, Engalls sat down to think. He'd been given the same order from the Superintendent moments before, also with no explanation. Something much bigger was going on, something a lot of people wanted to keep a very tight lid on.

In this particular instance, he thought, it may already be too late. A good number of witnesses, both cops and civilians, had seen what happened on Addison Street, and there would be questions; many questions, including some that a simple "no comment" from his precinct wouldn't satisfy.

With a resigned sigh, he got up from his chair and walked to the door to retrieve the young woman.

Mira had been watching the door of the Captain's office since the moment the giant man in SWAT gear had closed it. Listening to the raised voices inside, she'd barely noticed that Officer Jenkins had sat back down across from her.

"Sure I can't get you anything, miss?" he asked politely.

"What do you think they're saying in there?" she wondered aloud, her eyes still fixed on the Captain's office.

"Not sure," he answered impassively. "Probably something about what happened outside. Beyond that, though, your guess is as good as mine."

Suddenly the Captain's office door opened. The large man emerged, then turned toward the front vestibule and briskly walked out of the main room.

Seconds later the Police Captain appeared in the doorway. Hands at his hips, he looked around the room, then, spotting Mira, walked over to Jenkins' desk.

"Thank you, Jenkins," he first addressed the officer, then looked at Mira. "Miss, would you please follow me back into my office?"

As she sat down, he closed the door behind her. "I apologize for making you wait. It's been an uncharacteristically busy night for us," he said, taking a seat himself.

"I can imagine," she replied, not really sure what else to say.

"I'm not quite sure if I've even introduced myself yet," he continued. "I'm Robert Engalls, Captain of this precinct. From what I understand, you were able to provide Officer Urrutia with some details on what happened to you this evening."

"What did the man in your office have to say?" she asked out of the blue.

The Captain hesitated, clearly taken aback. "I'm … not at liberty to share details."

"Who are those people? What do they want from him?"

"Miss Givens," the Captain leaned forward in his chair, appearing to choose his words carefully, "this has become a matter outside of police jurisdiction. Now as far as I'm concerned, your friend is a person of interest in a serial murder investigation. That is trouble enough. Beyond that, I can't make any comment."

Mira slumped back in the chair, feeling increasingly frustrated and helpless.

As if reading her thoughts, the Captain added, "Now, I don't know everything that's going on in your head, but right now you can't help him. I'm afraid I can't tell you what to do. I understand you share a brief history with him. But at this point, there's nothing you, I, or anyone can do for him. In my mind, you need to walk away."

"No," she said, putting her face in her hands and beginning to cry. "You don't understand any of it."

From behind his desk, Robert Engalls looked on as the young woman across from him began to break down into tears. She was young, no older than one of his daughters; though the troubled, sorrowful look in her eyes made her appear much older than she really was. He was disturbed by what he'd seen tonight; and, while more than anything he felt the obligation to do the right thing – even if he didn't know exactly what that was in this case – there was nothing he could do. He couldn't help the situation.

He couldn't help her.

"Miss," he began solemnly, "if there is anything we can do for you, anything at all, I want you to know –"

She looked up at him, tears streaming down her face. "Yes!" she cried. "You could help him! Get him back here! Why won't – why won't you *help* him?"

"Miss Givens," he replied softly, handing her his handkerchief, "you know we can't do that. It isn't up to us."

They sat in silence for a moment, the young woman just staring at the floor, wiping her eyes with the handkerchief. Engalls was trying to think of anything he could say to help ease her anxiety, but he was coming up empty.

Finally, he broke in. "Listen. I can't promise you anything. But depending on what happens, and if there is a way that we can help, I promise you we will do what we can. Within the bounds of the law, and provided he's not guilty of anything."

"I ... appreciate that," she said, wiping her eyes and looking up at him.

"Now," he started again in a more business-like tone. "Given a few recent developments, I need to speak with a few of my officers. As Officer Urrutia hopefully informed you, we'll need to run an investigation in your apartment, as well as make sure it's safe for you to return there. I assume you've arranged a place to stay?"

"Yes, thank you," the young woman nodded.

"Good," he replied, standing up. "While I'm out there I'll arrange for an officer to take you where you need to go. Please sit tight, and we'll have you on your way."

Clearing his throat, he got up and headed out his office door. He needed to address his men on the nature of what had happened outside.

35

The Curtain

Hundreds of miles to the east, the ticking clock struck midnight.

On weeknights around this time, cleaning crews performed a basic tidying of the labs: sweeping up floors, emptying waste bins, and disposing of hazardous materials. On Saturdays, a different crew was brought in to perform a deep cleaning, which entailed a full disinfecting of the labs in addition to the normal duties performed during the week.

Hector Barretto had begun his shift a bit early this Saturday night, hoping to finish early as well. His annual family picnic was tomorrow, and he wanted to help his wife Gilda and their daughters with the preparations. But when he learned that the other half of his two-man crew, Stanley, had called in sick, he knew there was no chance of wrapping up early. He was in for a long, busy night.

He wheeled the large cleaning cart down the long, wide hallway, one of the rubber wheels wobbling as he pushed it along, almost mimicking Hector himself, who'd walked with a limp ever since his hip surgery last year.

As he came upon the entrance to the lab, he nodded to the heavyset soldier stationed there, then swiped his card through the reader in the wall. When it beeped at him, he stepped forward, placing his face in front of the retinal scan station. A single "blip" sound, followed by a green light just above the scanner screen, signaled he was cleared to enter the lab. Stepping back from the machine, he heard the double door locks and air-tight seal disengage.

Entering the lab, he noticed the night guard seated behind a small desk just to the right of the door. Holstered to his belt was a large pistol. Spread out on the desk was a newspaper and walkie-talkie. In the countless times he'd cleaned the facility, never once had there been *anyone* in the main lab this late, much less an armed guard.

The guard was a tall, powerfully-built man who appeared to be in his late twenties. A flat-top haircut capped his young features, and the small gold badge just outside his right lapel displayed the name: Cpl. Gibson.

"Stop where you are," he said, his hand not reaching for his gun but close enough to it for Hector's taste. "Do you have clearance to enter this lab?"

"Yes, sir," Hector said submissively, his heavy Spanish accent laboring the words. "Every Saturday night I clean this lab, top to bottom."

"I wasn't aware there would be any outsiders allowed in the lab, with …" his voice trailed off. He rubbed his chin. "I'll need to see the work order."

"Yes, sir," Hector replied, digging in his pocket for the work order detail he received each week. Finding it, he unfolded it and handed it to the night guard.

The guard took the printout from him and glanced over it, his eyes moving briefly up to Hector's before setting back down on the piece of paper.

He handed the printout back to Hector. "Fine," he said flatly. "But I advise you to work quickly and keep your eyes on your business and nothing else. Understood?"

"Yes, sir," Hector nodded. "Of course, sir."

As he made his way out onto the main floor of the lab, Hector wore a puzzled look. He wondered what the guard had meant.

And then, as his eyes cast forward, down toward the far end of the lab, he saw it.

It was nothing more than a white curtain, rising about eight feet into the air. It hung from a circular steel rod. It was maybe twelve to fifteen feet in diameter, so whatever was inside of it was fairly big.

He paused for a split second, then continued to push the wobbly cart forward, toward the far end of the room. That was where he always began his cleaning; he didn't see any reason to change up the routine just because something new was in the room.

Hector began the cleaning as he always did, wiping down work areas, supply cabinets, machinery, and equipment. Every few moments he would glance curiously over at the curtain, then again to the guard. A few times he had to remind himself to stay focused on the task at hand. If he meandered, he would finish late. If he finished late, he would miss out on helping Gilda prepare for the picnic.

Moments later, Hector had finished disinfecting the area and was ready to move down toward the next cluster of workstations. As he placed his cleaning brush in its slot on the cart, he heard the sealed door at the lab's entrance disengage. The guard had stood up and was opening the door. He looked over to Hector and pointed a finger into the air, signaling he'd be returning momentarily.

The door seal re-engaged, leaving Hector alone in the lab. Once again he glanced to the desk near the entrance, then back to the curtain.

Just one look. One quick look.

Knowing he had only moments until the guard returned, Hector hobbled up to the curtain.

In the restroom, Corporal Sam "Sonny" Gibson emerged from the stall, casually zipping up his trousers as he made his way to the row of sinks by the bathroom entrance.

Washing his hands, he mulled over how long he'd be stuck doing graveyard shift in the main lab. Other than the old man cleaning the lab tonight, he'd gone hours upon end without so much as seeing another human being.

Too much more of this and he was sure he'd go crazy.

He pushed through the bathroom door into the hallway and strode lazily down to the lab entrance. Nodding to the hallway guard Sgt. Charlie Moses, he swiped his card, went through the retinal scan, and pushed open the doors as the air-tight seal disengaged.

The main lab was filled with a horrible, high-pitched screaming. It echoed loudly off the walls and ceiling. Not understanding what was happening, Gibson looked down to the far end of the lab to see the round curtain flapping fitfully, as if something inside it were trying to punch its way out.

Heart suddenly pounding, he rushed back to the hallway security post and noticed that Moses had already risen from his chair and was moving quickly toward the door.

Gibson grabbed his walkie-talkie. "Code Red! I repeat: Code Red! All security personnel to main lab, stat! Repeat: all security to main lab, immediately!"

He shot an anxious look at Moses, who shared his expression, then nodded and pointed forward. Both drew their sidearms and quickly advanced on the curtain.

The screaming escalated into a horrific crescendo as they drew closer, and Gibson felt his grip tighten on his gun. Suddenly, a dark-skinned hand wrapped around the edge of the curtain and pulled. One of the steel rings along the curtain rod broke with a tight popping sound, followed by a second, then a third, and the curtain began to come down, revealing the terrified visage of the old janitor. The old man's eyes were wide, his mouth trying to form words but only issuing cries of sheer terror. Gibson stepped forward and saw the full, gruesome picture: the janitor's right arm, fully extended, ended in the mouth of the lab subject, who had literally clamped down on the old man's hand with his teeth. The hand itself was indiscernible: it had completely disappeared into the subject's mouth. The subject's face was covered in blood; he gnawed hungrily at the wrist, twisting his head every which way, growling like a rabid animal.

Gibson acted first. Stepping forward, he pointed his firearm at the subject's head and commanded him to let the janitor go. Moses rushed forward to the old man, wrapped his long arms around his midsection, and began to pull, trying to wrest the man's arm from the subject's grip.

Gibson wanted to shoot the subject; *needed* to in order to save the janitor's life; but protocol was strict: the subject was not to be harmed under any circumstances; even, inexplicably to Gibson, in matters of life and death.

At that moment, blood began to spurt from the old man's wrist, spraying high into the air and covering the white curtain with splotches of red. The old man screamed again, a high-pitched, terrible sound that pierced Gibson's ears, chilling his insides. Within seconds, the old man's cries had faded; his body had gone limp. Gibson immediately knew why: the subject had bitten through the man's radial artery. He was rapidly bleeding out. In seconds he would be dead; there would be no saving him.

With a triumphant laugh, the subject released his hold on the old man, causing Moses to stumble backward with the now-flaccid janitor in his arms. He spat out the shredded remains of the old man's hand and wrist; the tiny bits of flesh and bone landed in small red chunks on the tile floor at Gibson's feet.

His indifferent gaze moved from Moses to Gibson. He smiled, revealing large, blood-soaked teeth. "Hmmp," he huffed contentedly. *"That was too long in coming."*

"My God," Gibson said, almost stammering, gazing at the subject's bindings, keeping his gun pointed. "My God, my God, he *killed* him! Jesus – Jesus Christ, *how?"*

"Mmm," the subject groaned happily, spitting another small chunk of bone into the distance. "Funny. I didn't think it would work, really."

Moses set the dead janitor gently down to the floor. He pulled out his walkie-talkie and issued the emergency call to the control room.

"But in the end," the subject said casually, stretching his neck as if to remove a kink. "It was easy. He opened the curtain, shocked to see me in here. Horrified, actually. I asked him to touch my forehead and pray for me. He hesitated, but – you can figure out the rest."

"You son of a bitch," Gibson said. "I'd shoot you dead right here if I could."

Stretching his neck once again, Elias Todd ignored the soldier's comment. He glanced up at the ceiling, feeling content for the first time in days. He'd almost forgotten how *badly* he needed to kill – and how often he needed to do it – just to keep his sanity.

He closed his eyes and smiled, anxiously awaiting his next opportunity.

36

Loose Ends

The crowds had begun to disperse from the scene at Addison and Halsted.

The later evening chill was now sweeping its way through the night air. The Chicago Police had left the barricades in place, along with a few officers to keep foot traffic moving. Vehicle traffic had been rerouted. The media had gathered at the northeast corner of the building along Halsted, waiting for the precinct's Captain to address them on the situation.

Standing in the street, Nolan Hayes surveyed his squad's clean-up progress. The subject had been placed in the secure cage specially designed for transporting him, and had been sedated again. All in all, the subject had been hit five times with the tranquilizer; but his remarkable immune system was fighting off its effects so well, only a small amount of antidote was needed to regulate him.

Over the past few moments the other teams had delivered their updates. Clive's team was wrapping things up in the subject's apartment building. Hill's squadron had remained with them. Other squadrons had already been collected and were in the other transport. Rodriguez's team had been incapacitated at the woman's apartment, and Connelly's squad had been taken down here at the station.

All by the subject.

Unarmed, he'd single-handedly taken out eight of Hayes' men.

All heavily-armed, highly-trained men.

That left Arroyo's team, which had gone to eliminate the nosy cop, as the only squad whose status was still unknown. He'd be getting an update any moment, at which point he'd need to dispatch Clive's team to remove any trace of their presence there.

The cop was one loose end. The woman was the other.

They had no choice but to take her with them. She'd seen too much. She would need to be deprogrammed by hypnosis or an old-fashioned brain-washing. He'd let Clive's team handle the details so she wouldn't be missed while in their custody.

The other option was to eliminate her, but there was a disadvantage to going that route: if they kept her alive, she could be an effective tool at helping to cover up the events of the current evening. During deprogramming they could easily feed her a fabricated account of the night's events, suggesting that Hayes' strike team was in effect protecting her from a dangerous terrorist who had targeted her. The story could easily be contrived.

At that moment his headset sounded. It was Hill.

"Sir," Lieutenant Hill's voice pinged through the tiny speaker, "update from Arroyo's squad: target escaped; both Engram and Wells non-responsive. Target headed northbound on Damen Avenue in an unmarked sedan. Sniper fire success unconfirmed."

Damn it to hell, Hayes thought, getting angrier. *This was getting messier by the minute.*

"Have one of the remaining men maintain lookout status opposite the building. Send the other into the unit to confirm Engram and Wells' status. Dispatch Clive's team and set a perimeter. Mark it a Federal crime scene. Let no Chicago Police in. Once the building is secured, instruct Clive's team to dress the scene properly to guarantee the officer's status as the guilty party. Do you understand?"

"Yes, sir," Hill responded.

"Did Arroyo get a plate on the vehicle, anything to identify it with?" Hayes asked.

"No plate, sir," Hill replied. "Vehicle was moving too quickly. Maroon sedan, standard police issue Ford Crown Victoria, otherwise unmarked. Likely bullet-holes in the roof from the sniper fire."

Hayes thought for a moment. "Mobilize three squadrons. If visual contact is confirmed, shoot to kill." Then he added: "Once I've taken care of some unfinished business here, I'm going after him myself as well."

37

Turnabout

Gino stuck the red police light on the roof as the unmarked squad car sped northbound on Damen Avenue.

"Sniper?" Gino asked, panting slightly.

"Had to've been," Larry responded. "There were two in the building that I saw, and I took them both out. Keep low, boys," he added, looking at Marcus and Daniel, who were crouched on the back seat.

"J-Jeezus," Gino said quietly, his brow lowering with concern. "Once we're in the clear you're gonna have to explain what the hell's going on."

"How did you know to come so quickly?" Larry asked.

"Daniel," Gino replied. "Kid told me what was going on, said you were in the apartment and there was gunfire."

Larry looked down at Daniel. "Good thinking, Daniel."

Daniel's frightened expression changed slightly into a half-hearted smile.

"It's going to be all right, boys," he said, looking over the two of them. "We're going to take you to the police station."

"No, you don't wanna do that," Gino intervened, coughing once.

"What? Why?" Larry asked.

"Feds're ... all over the place there. You don't wanna take 'em there. Somewhere else. Anyplace else."

"Damn it," Larry mused. "Then Aunt Edna's. It's the only option right now," he decided, looking at the boys.

"Just be for the night, 'til all this mess gets cleared up," Gino added.

He turned to Marcus and Daniel. "Boys, we're taking you to Aunt Edna's. Everything'll be okay. But I want you to promise me something. When we get there, you can't tell her anything, okay? She'll just worry more, and we don't want that. I promise I'll tell her everything tomorrow morning. Understood?"

The boys nodded back at him, keeping quiet.

Larry pulled out his cell phone and dialed Aunt Edna.

After a few rings, she picked up, the sharp tone in her voice making clear her displeasure at such a late call: "Hello."

"Aunt Edna," Larry responded.

Her tone immediately shifted to one of concern. "Larry? What is it?"

"I need you to take the boys tonight."

"Well, of course. Is everything all right?"

"Yes and no," he said uncertainly. "Listen, I can't really talk about it. Everything's going to be fine, but I just need you to do this. I'll explain tomorrow."

"Okay, then," she replied. "Bring them over, I'll get their beds ready."

"Thank you," he said gratefully. "We'll be there in about five minutes," he added, and hung up.

Larry, Gino, and the boys drove in silence the rest of the way to Aunt Edna's.

After dropping the boys off and trying to calm an extremely anxious Aunt Edna, Larry and Gino once again sped off in the unmarked cruiser, continuing northbound.

"S-so, now what?" Gino asked, his voice wheezing a bit.

"I don't know … I'm trying to think."

"Well, think out loud then," Gino said, then coughed loudly.

"We need to figure out what's going on," Larry said. "Have you radioed in yet?"

"No," Gino replied. "I figure the Feds're … tapping into all our frequencies."

"What I was thinking too," Larry agreed, sighing in relief.

"You haven't explained anything yet," Gino said sharply. "Who is looking for you, and why? I mean, what the hell happened in your apartment?"

"Two of them. Not including the sniper. Feds, I'm certain, from the suspect's apartment building, because that's where I was just before. Broke in at about 10:30, equipped with silencers, tear gas, maybe more. No questions asked, just started firing."

Gino thought of what had happened at the station, how the four armed men had opened fire on the two civilians without any warning. "Why'd they come after you?"

"Like I said, I have no idea," Larry replied tensely. "They must have somehow tied me to whoever they're after in that building. Like I told you before, it could be the vigilante suspect. Maybe somehow they're tying me to him."

Gino looked over at him, hesitant. "About that," he began cautiously.

"What?" Larry said, reading Gino's expression.

"The 'Rage' guy you wanted the warrant on," Gino began again, coughing again. "He showed up at the station with a woman, and …" his voice trailed off.

"And?" Larry demanded.

"Feds were right on his tail. There was a standoff, and they got him."

"What do you mean, 'they got him?'"

"C-captured him," Gino clarified, his voice wheezing again. "Some kind of tranquilizer dart or something. Whatever the case, he's locked up now."

Larry looked out at the road in front of them for a moment, deep in thought. "What the hell does it all mean," he wondered aloud.

At that Gino coughed and grabbed his chest.

"Are you all right?" Larry asked him tensely.

"Fine. I'm fine," Gino said, waving him off. "Anyway. Means nothin' now," he answered Larry's original question. "They obviously got ... what they wanted. It's over."

"It's not over," Larry said. "There's something else going on. The Feds wouldn't have tried kill me if they didn't want to keep something quiet. Something they somehow must think I'm involved in."

"What would *you* be involved in?" Gino asked.

"Nothing, obviously," Larry replied. "But that doesn't change what's already happened. I had two federal agents break into my apartment tonight and try to kill me. I had to kill them in self-defense –"

"Wait," Gino interrupted, coughing again. "You *killed* 'em?"

"I had to," Larry said, voice raised. "Otherwise I'd be dead and so would the boys, probably."

"Oh, my God," Gino said anxiously. "W-we've gotta go back there."

"Are you kidding? It's too dangerous!"

"You don't get it, do you?" Gino shot back, his words starting to sound labored. "You got ... two federal officers dead in your apartment. If they wanted to cover up *anything* surrounding this 'Rage' character, they'll certainly want to ... cover *this* up. We gotta go back there, report it, m-mark it as a crime scene ... before ... they get there and do who knows what. Hell, they'll probably try and ... frame you."

As Gino's words sunk in, Larry's heart began to race. He'd been so concerned with getting the boys to safety that he'd lost sight of the larger issue: the federal government had sent two people to kill him, both of whom were now lying dead on his bedroom floor. They had targeted him in the first place to keep a lid on something in which they suspected his involvement.

The squad car drifted to the right and almost hit a parked car before Gino swerved back onto the street.

"Hey!" Larry exclaimed. "What the hell's going on?"

"N-nothin," Gino wheezed back at him. He pulled the cruiser to the side of the road, throwing it into Park. "You drive. Let's get ... back there before it's too late."

At that moment, Larry looked down at the seat in front of Gino, noticing the hole in the brown vinyl seat. He then saw the blood on the seat. His eyes traced up to Gino's chest and saw the exit wound, blood soaked through his shirt.

"Jesus!" Larry yelled. "You've been shot!"

"F-flesh wound," Gino said gruffly. "Hell with it."

"We've gotta get you to the hospital," Larry decided, getting out of the car.

"No," Gino argued, his breathing becoming more labored. "Gotta ... get to your ... 'fore the Feds do ..."

Having no choice, Larry pulled Gino's massive frame by the arm across the front seat to the passenger side. "No chance," he said. "Just hold on, I'm gonna get you out of here. Stay upright so you don't lose any more blood."

Gino huffed agonizingly. "You think I don't know that?" he said crankily. "I been shot in the shoulder, not the head."

Good, keep him alert, Larry thought. That would help him stay conscious until they got to the hospital. He just prayed Gino was right about it being a shoulder wound and not a punctured lung. His breathing was extremely labored.

Once in the driver's seat, Larry stuck the siren light onto the roof. The cruiser's tires screeched as they pulled away, headed toward the nearest hospital.

Deciding he had no choice but to risk alerting the Feds to their whereabouts, Larry picked up the cruiser's radio handset and radioed the station. He needed to speak directly with Captain Engalls and figure out what to do.

"Unit seven-oh-nine, please disclose location," dispatch replied over the receiver.

"Negative," Larry replied quickly. "Listen, I need to speak with the chief immediately. Please put him on."

"Roger. Just one moment," dispatch replied.

Seconds later Captain Engalls' voice came over the radio speaker. "Parker," he said abruptly. "What's going on? Where are you?"

"Have a man down, Urrutia's been shot," Larry said urgently. "Need assistance-"

"Parker," the Captain cut him off. "Get off this frequency. Dial my mobile phone, do it now."

Larry understood. Watching the road ahead of him, he hung up the radio mike and fumbled to get his cell phone from his pocket. Without looking at its tiny screen he hit a button to speed dial Captain Engalls' cell phone. The chief picked up immediately.

"Parker. Where are you taking him," the Captain asked quickly.

"Ravenswood Medical, on Broadway," Larry replied.

"I'm going to have two men meet you there," Engalls said. "Hold for a second."

"Copy," Larry said. He looked over at Gino. His head was back against the head rest, a strained look on his face, still clutching his bloodied chest with his right hand. "Just stay with me, partner," Larry told him. "We'll be there in just a few."

Gino swiveled his head over to Larry and frowned at him through his grimaced expression. "H-hell you think I'm gonna go?" he wheezed. "Just drive the damn car."

The Captain came back on. "Tell me what happened," he said.

"Feds. Two of them, in my apartment. Both dead, self defense. I was able to get out with my sons. Urrutia showed, but in the process was shot."

"What's his status?"

"Chest wound, upper left side. Lost blood. Still conscious."

"Get him there, Parker," Engalls responded. "I'll have two men waiting for you at the ER."

"Copy that, chief," Larry replied.

"Once Urrutia is in, get back in contact with me immediately."

"Copy," Larry again replied.

"Over and out," Engalls finished the conversation, then hung up.

Larry closed the cell phone and stuffed it back in his pocket. They were only a few blocks away now.

Gino spoke up. "Hey," he began.

"Yeah?" Larry replied, looking over at him.

"Just make me a promise," Gino continued. "Whatever you do, don't call Vera about this. Not tonight."

"What?" Larry said, surprised. "How come?"

"It'll … just make her worry," Gino said, struggling. "She thinks I'm … out with the guys tonight."

"Partner, she's gonna be worried either way," Larry countered. "You're out way past your bedtime."

"Yeah, but … just do what I tell ya."

"Okay," Larry agreed reluctantly. "Don't worry, you're gonna be okay."

"I ain't worried," Gino said, wheezing a bit. "Quit actin' like that; you're … startin' to piss me off."

Moments later, they arrived at the ER. As they pulled up, a marked police cruiser came screeching up as well, parking about twenty feet to the right of the sliding glass door. Two officers were inside; Larry recognized them as Sullivan and Shoenbeck. Upon seeing the cruiser, Sullivan got out and rushed to the passenger-side door to help Gino out, while Schoenbeck headed toward the ER entrance to alert Triage to their arrival. Seconds later, two medics came out with a wheelchair, gingerly loading Gino into it before wheeling him inside. Gino's voice was wheezy and his eyes had begun to look glazed over, but he still had enough presence of mind to slip in a wisecrack at Sullivan as they rolled him toward the sliding doors.

Larry followed the medics in; then, as they wheeled Gino into one of the open patient bays, he instructed both officers to remain close to Gino while he got back in contact with Engalls.

Larry stepped outside once again into the parking lot, then took a deep breath before gathering his thoughts. He had no idea what to do next; the Feds were surely already in his apartment, doing who-knows-what to manipulate the scene. No, it was too late to go that route; he had too many other concerns: ensuring his family stayed safe, figuring out why the Feds were after him, clearing himself of whatever they'd somehow tied him to, and now, protecting Gino from any threat. Things seemed to be spinning out of control; he couldn't decide whether getting the Chief involved would help his situation or pull even more people into the mess he now found himself in.

Nothing was clear at this point.

Cupping his forehead in his left hand, he rubbed his temples with his thumb and middle finger. He sighed heavily, preparing himself for what he'd say to the chief, then flipped open his cell phone.

The screen lit up, revealing that he'd missed four calls.

He grunted in mild surprise at this, then remembered he'd left the phone on silent since getting back into the cruiser with Gino, after dropping the boys off at Edna's.

He hit the info button to see who had called him.

Aunt Edna's number showed on the screen.

All four calls had been from her.

He looked at the time stamp. All four calls were from inside a two-minute period, just a few minutes before.

"What the hell," he muttered to himself, frowning intently.

Instinctively, he hit the "Call back" button, letting it ring several times. No answer.

He dialed again.

Still no answer.

Something is wrong.

Heart pounding, he opened the phone and stared once again at the missed calls.

Without a second's thought, he ran back toward the parked cruiser, dug the keys from his pocket, and pulled out of the ER loading area. Flooring the gas pedal, he sped out of the hospital parking lot, heading in the direction of Aunt Edna's house.

38

Mobile Command

Assured that the cleanup at the police station was complete, Nolan Hayes could now attend to other matters.

He ordered his remaining men into the transport, then, directing two of his agents to join him, once again headed back toward the front entrance of the police precinct.

They'd completed their main objective, the acquisition of Asset Two, and concealment narratives were in development to address any conflicting reports by the Chicago Police, the local media, or the eyewitness accounts outside the station.

However, a few lingering items remained, and they needed to be sewn up quickly.

He was no longer as concerned with the woman; within moments she would be in their custody and on her way to the SRC for deprogramming. As far as any eyewitness accounts she'd shared with the local police, Hayes already had men in her apartment building to handle the situation.

Hayes' main focus now was the cop.

The cop had proven a far tougher target than he'd originally thought. He had single-handedly taken out two of Hayes' best-trained men in close combat, and somehow he had also escaped the two snipers installed outside the building.

Nonetheless, his team had just completed laying out the perfect trap for him. In moments the cop would play right into it, eliminating any threat he might pose as well.

Pushing open the station's front door, Hayes stepped through the vestibule, once again ignoring the two uniformed officers behind the high front desk, and strode into the main room, looking for the Police Captain.

Finding him, he rounded the corner of the last row of desks and approached the Captain. Upon seeing Hayes, his scowl turned to a grimace. Hayes smiled at this.

"And, how may I help you this time?" the Captain asked petulantly.

"The woman you'd processed earlier," he began. "We need a word with her."

The Captain's eyes narrowed. "And *which* young woman are you referring to?" he said, crossing his arms and cocking his head skeptically.

"You know precisely who," Hayes said crossly. "She arrived at your precinct with the subject we were pursuing. I need to see her, now."

"I'm afraid that's impossible. We released her a short time ago."

Hayes' expression darkened. "Then you'll need to retrieve her immediately."

"And how do you expect me to do that?" the Captain asked.

"Don't play games," Hayes said. "She's under police escort to wherever she's going. Order them to turn around and return her to the station. Immediately. Any delays and I'll have you *swimming* in charges for obstructing a federal investigation."

"Step into my office," the Captain replied callously.

Nodding to his rookie officer to continue booking the two teenagers, Captain Robert Engalls turned and led Hayes into his office for the second time that evening, the two armored goons stopping just outside it. He closed the door.

Seeing that the agent had remained standing across from his desk, Engalls elected not to take a seat either.

"Now, make that call," Hayes repeated.

"What do you want from her, anyway?" Engalls inquired, leaning onto the desk.

"She is a key witness in our investigation," Hayes replied simply. "Beyond that I'm unable to elaborate."

"Humor me, then," Engalls said sardonically.

Hayes leaned forward onto Engalls' desk. "Don't think for one second I don't know what you're doing," he said. "Quit stalling, or I'll make a call to your Superintendent."

Saying nothing, Engalls kept his eyes on Hayes as he pressed down on the large red button marked "Dispatch" on his desk phone. "Doreen," he spoke into the small speaker on top of the phone.

"Yes, Chief," the tinny voice replied through the speaker.

"Contact Officer Jenkins in unit twelve-ninety-six, please," he began. "Find out whether or not he's dropped off Miss Givens. Either way, instruct him to return back to the station with her, ASAP."

"Consider it done, Chief," Doreen responded.

Taking his finger off the red button, Engalls stood upright once again. "There," he said, exhaling. "Good evening, then, Colonel Hayes."

"I'll leave a squad here. They'll contact me if she isn't here in twenty minutes."

"I'd count on no less," Engalls replied derisively.

Without another word, Hayes turned and walked out of the office.

The moment the door closed, Engalls picked up the phone and once again hit the red button. "Doreen," he began quickly. "When you make contact with Officer Jenkins, have him contact me directly on my mobile phone. Give him the number, tell him to call immediately. Tell him *not* to use the police band, understood?"

"Certainly, Chief," Doreen responded. "I've radioed his unit but no response yet."

"Thank you," Engalls replied. "Keep trying. And keep me updated. I need to speak with him as soon as possible."

Letting go of the red button, Captain Robert Engalls sat down in his chair. He didn't know exactly what Hayes had in mind for the woman, but in his gut he knew he had to do whatever he could to keep the man from getting to her.

With his two agents following closely behind him, Nolan Hayes emerged from the police station and strode out to the government transport. At the back of the transport was the closed-off mobile command center. After punching in the three-digit access code, he pulled open the narrow door and entered the command center.

The small, windowless room was filled literally wall-to-wall with flat-panel TV monitors, multiple-band closed frequency listening devices, and highly advanced tracking equipment. Hundreds of LEDs blinked along the multiple panels that were affixed above the small workspace ledge bolted into the back wall of the room. A single fluorescent light ran along the center of the ceiling. In the tiny floor space wrapped by all the high-tech equipment were two rolling chairs. In those chairs were his two top surveillance men, Aaron Rosch and Brian Blake, both busy monitoring a number of different radio and telecommunications frequencies.

As Hayes entered, both arose from their chairs and stood at attention.

"At ease," Hayes said flatly. "I've got something new for you to work on. I need you to keep ears on two lines of communication. The first you're already on top of: the Chicago Police band for this precinct. I need you to monitor any exchanges between dispatch and a Unit twelve-ninety-six, an Officer Jenkins. He radios in to the station or vice versa, alert me immediately. I need to know his whereabouts, as well as where he's headed. Secondly, I need you to obtain the mobile phone number of the precinct's Captain, Robert Engalls. Once you've got it and isolated the phone's signature, lock on to the signal and monitor any and all incoming and outgoing communication. If Engalls establishes contact with either Jenkins *or* Parker, alert me immediately."

"Yes, sir," Blake and Rosch promptly replied.

"Good," Hayes replied. "And continue to monitor the local news media as well. We need to know what's being shared with the public, and by whom."

As Hayes was about to leave, the police scanner sounded: "Unit twelve-ninety-six, calling unit twelve-ninety-six. Officer Jenkins respond."

"Unit twelve-ninety-six responding," the voice replied on the scanner.

"Lock onto that signal," Hayes said quickly.

Rosch rolled to his keyboard, punching in a few commands. Within seconds, he'd pinpointed the signal. "Intersection at Irving Park Road and Damen Avenue. Moving westbound."

"Jam their signal so the unit can't communicate with dispatch. Remain locked to them, and keep me apprised of their progress," Hayes ordered them. "I need to know exactly where they are at all times until we've made visual contact. I'm taking a squad to them immediately."

"Understood, sir," Rosch replied. "Signal locked, jamming frequency now."

Pulling the door shut behind him, Hayes checked his silencer pistol. "Langley," he called out to the agent seated toward the front of the bus. "Get yourself and a man from your squad ready. You'll be accompanying me to an acquisition assignment, departing immediately."

39

Trigger

In the cruiser, Larry sped westbound in the direction of Aunt Edna's house.

He did not have time to put up the siren-light, so he bobbed and weaved through the late-night traffic, zooming past honking horns and expletives shouted angrily from car windows he passed all too closely.

As he was turning onto Western Avenue, his cell phone rang. He frantically plucked it out of his belt clip, hoping it to be Aunt Edna, and peered at the tiny screen to see it was Captain Engalls' mobile.

He picked it up. "Parker," he answered, his heart pounding wildly.

"Parker, you were supposed to call me," the Captain said. "Where are you?"

"Long story Chief," Larry said hurriedly. "I'll explain when I can."

"Parker, I need you to listen to me," Engalls replied sternly. "And listen to every word I say. The Feds have just put an APB out on you, claiming you've killed two federal agents. I don't know what's going on, but I need you to come in immediately."

"No can do, Chief," he replied. Gino's nightmare scenario had come true. "I need to take care of something first."

"Parker, are you *insane?*" the Captain barked in surprise. "You *don't* come in, it'll come across as an admission of guilt!"

"Chief –" Larry started.

"I don't know what's going through your mind, but stop and think for a minute," Engalls implored him. "You come in now, I can help you! You don't, it's gonna make things a lot more difficult! Don't you understand?"

"I wish I had time to explain," Larry replied emphatically, turning onto Edna's block. "But I gotta go."

"Parker –" the Captain began to shout, but Larry snapped the phone shut.

Larry didn't have time to think through the mess he was in. Despite what the Chief may have believed, Larry wasn't certain that the Department could do anything to dig him out of it. Not with what he'd seen thus far tonight.

Parking the cruiser less than a block away from Aunt Edna's bungalow, he jumped out and advanced toward the side street, staying in the shadows. He drew his gun and deftly moved from one house to the next, keeping out of sight, hearing only the soft sound of his feet on the grass and the faint hum of traffic along Western Avenue.

As he reached Edna's bungalow, he noticed that her lights were on at the back of the house, while the front was in complete darkness.

Crouching down next to an air conditioning unit, Larry's mind worked to determine the best way to enter the house. He had keys, but if they had laid a trap, he needed to figure out the fastest way both in and out.

Then he remembered: *the crawlspace.*

When the house was first built just over a century ago, it ran over one of the main sewer lines servicing the city's north side and was the only ground-level access point for several blocks. To accommodate the turn-of-the-century building boom while not disrupting the infrastructure, the house had been the only one in the neighborhood built without a basement. Instead, it had been specially fitted with a crawlspace, with entry under the back steps, to allow the city access to the sewer main without needing to enter the house. The crawlspace was obscured by white lattice paneling placed on the side of the back steps. The three-foot wide pipe stretched about two-and-a-half feet above ground, right up through the crawlspace. The city had installed a side access opening in the crawlspace, just large enough for a full-grown man to fit through it and descend into the sewer using the iron rungs welded to the inside. The original sewer opening was still in the floor at the back of the kitchen, tactfully covered by a wooden bench Edna had placed there when she'd first moved in.

If he could access the opening in the crawlspace by wedging the manhole cover free, it would then only be a matter of quietly pushing up the second manhole cover to gain entry into the kitchen, all without being seen.

Reaching the back steps, he kneeled down and pulled back the lattice paneling. He stuck his head into the crawlspace. By the narrow band of moonlight beaming in from between the houses, he was just able to see the sewer pipe's side access opening only a few feet away. Now, he just needed something to pry open the manhole cover.

Crawling into the cramped crawlspace, ignoring the pain of the sharp gravel stones poking at his knees and palms, he felt around for something he could use. He knew from Edna's past complaints that the city would sometimes leave random spare tools behind, usually on the back steps, which she would promptly throw into the crawlspace. To his luck, he found a small crowbar. Picking it up, he immediately wedged the pointed end under the lip of the manhole cover.

After two tries, he'd successfully wrenched the cover from the opening.

The putrid smell of the sewer hit him like a blow to the face, and he instinctively covered his nose and mouth with his right hand. He unclipped his flashlight from his belt and peered into the opening, first looking up at the sealed opening just above him, then down into the sewer about ten feet below.

He backed into the opening feet first, feeling around with his left foot for one of the iron rungs. When he was in about waist-high, he looked back out at the crawlspace and noticed a pipe wrench lying next to the crowbar he'd just dropped.

Might come in handy.

He reached out, grabbed the pipe wrench, and slipped it into the long cargo pocket in his left pant leg.

Once Larry was inside the massive pipe, the rancid odor of the sewer below seemed to intensify, making his stomach lurch.

If anything's gonna give me away, it's gonna be that damned stench, he thought irritably.

Readying himself, he pressed against the rusty manhole cover with the top of his head and his right palm. The cover slowly gave way, and he saw slivers of light coming from the kitchen through the opening.

Eyes just above floor level, he lifted it upward a few more inches to get a glimpse of the kitchen, searching for any sign of movement.

He waited for a few seconds. Nothing.

He gently set the cover down to the side of the opening. Then he looked up to see the bench above his head. Lifting it just off the floor, he quietly moved it forward until it was clear of the opening. He pulled himself up onto the kitchen floor and drew his gun.

He crouched behind the bench for a second, again surveying the kitchen and the dining room beyond. Once again, no sound or movement.

Then he saw it.

At the center of the kitchen, hanging at eye level by a thread from the ceiling, was a single Polaroid photograph, spinning slowly in the circulating air.

Staying low, he went around the back of the bench and approached the photograph. He clasped it between his thumb and forefinger to get a look.

He gaped in horror.

It was a Polaroid of Edna and the boys, bound and gagged.

Beneath the photo was a handwritten message:

"Say Goodbye"

Heart hammering, he glanced toward the front door to notice the handle had been rigged with some sort of triggering device. Turning, he looked to the back door to see the same device had been fitted there as well. At that moment, his eye caught a small, gray box on Edna's kitchen counter. He could see tiny red numbers blinking in the LED panel. He then saw the motion-detection sensor just to the right of the gray box on the counter, and a second one at the far end of the kitchen, red lights blinking rapidly.

Then it all dawned on him: the triggers, the sensors, the numbers.

Count down.

Pivoting toward the back of the kitchen and shoving the bench out of the way, Larry dove feet-first into the manhole, hitting the back of his head on the top rung as he fell. He plummeted straight down, landing in the sewer main with a splash, just as Edna's house exploded.

40

Retrieval

The soft green glow of the police cruiser's digital clock showed it was exactly midnight.

Sitting back against the dark blue vinyl front seat, Mira gazed out the window at the buildings, parked cars, and tree-lined parkways moving slowly by. On their way to Lora's apartment, it seemed Officer Jenkins had decided to take only the busiest of streets for a Saturday night: Addison, then Halsted, and now Irving Park. The officer was almost moseying in a happy-go-lucky kind of way, as if oblivious to everything that had happened that night.

As they approached Irving Park and Ashland, she saw him look out the window at a small donut shop. The narrow storefront had a neon sign above the open doorway that read "Happy Donuts," a neon donut as the letter "O" blinking on and off.

Looking over at her, he asked, "Hey, can I get you something? Coffee? Donut?"

She glanced back at him, wondering if he was really serious about stopping. She just wanted to get to Lora's. "No, thank you," she replied.

"Uh – okay," he said, with an air of hesitation.

Reading him, she felt a pang of guilt. He'd probably been working all night and was hungry. "But, if you need to get something, go ahead," she said, regretting the offer the second it escaped her lips.

"Really? Okay, thanks. I kinda need a lift. Sure you don't want anything?"

"No, I'm fine," she said, but to make sure he was quick about it, she added: "But I'll go in with you."

"Well, of course," he said. "Can't leave a lovely lady alone out here, um, you know," he trailed off, seeming to realize the awkwardness of the statement.

She smiled at his fumbled attempt at charm. "Let's just go inside," she said.

Moments later, they walked out of the donut shop, Officer Jenkins with a large coffee in one hand, a French cruller in the other, and a pleased look on his face.

As they got in the car, he took a heaping bite of the cruller, set the coffee in the cup holder, and pulled out of the double-parked spot. "Best French crullers in the city of Chicago," he said. "Shoulda gotten another one."

At that moment the police radio sounded: "Unit twelve-ninety-six, calling unit twelve-ninety-six. Officer Jenkins respond."

His expression turning a shade more serious, Jenkins picked up the handset. "Unit twelve-ninety-six responding," he replied.

"Unit twelve-ninety-six, this is dispatch," the voice responded. "I have direct instructions from the chief to contact him on his mobile phone. Stand by for number."

"Unit, standing by," Jenkins confirmed. The serious expression was gone, replaced by an air of self-importance.

At that moment, the faint hiss of the radio frequency went silent.

"Well, that's funny," Jenkins muttered, looking puzzled.

"What is it?" Mira asked.

"Radio just went out," Jenkins said. "Least I think it did."

"Can you try another channel, maybe?" Mira said.

"Frequency?" Jenkins corrected her. "Yeah, sure. There's a couple backup frequencies we use," he said, pressing a button on the radio. Still no sound from the unit. He pressed a second button. Still nothing.

"Awfully odd," he said, perplexed. "We just had new radios installed coupla months ago. Crappy thing's broke already?"

"Can you call them on your cell?" Mira asked.

"Funny thing is, I don't have it on me," Jenkins said, shrugging. "The one night I decide to leave it in my locker. Who'd a thunk it, huh?"

Although she was in her pajamas, he gave her the once over anyway. "Guessing you prob'ly don't have one on you, either, huh?"

Mira glanced at him, half-assuming he was kidding. "No, I don't," she said.

"Okay, then," he sighed. "I'll get you home and whatever they needed I'll take care of once I'm back at the station."

Ten minutes later, they'd turned off Western Avenue onto Lora's street.

"Pull into the alley," Mira explained. "It's a coach house about halfway down."

"All right then," he said, throwing the cruiser into Park as they pulled up alongside the coach house. "Let's get you inside."

Mira opened the passenger door. As Jenkins came around the front of the cruiser to let her out, a black sedan rounded the corner at the far end of the alley ahead of them. It headed straight for them before stopping about twenty feet away, the alley dust swirling in the beams of its bright headlights.

Jenkins stopped in front of the cruiser, holding a hand in front of his face to shield his eyes from the extremely bright light. She could hear him calling out to the sedan: "Hello? Hello! Turn down your headlights!"

The high beams went off, and the doors of the sedan opened. For a second she couldn't make out much, but then she recognized the large man in black with the long facial scar, and she shrunk back in the seat.

He was after *her* now.

Petrified, she listened as Jenkins spoke to them. "Oh, hey," he said assuredly. "I recognize you guys from the station. Everything okay?"

Nolan Hayes approached the police cruiser calmly. He was able to see the woman in the front seat, clearly shrunk back in fear. He grinned at this.

He stopped in front of the officer who stood between him and the vehicle and surveyed him without saying a word. He was a frail-looking kid, likely not two years out of the academy, and probably stupid enough to not realize what he was up against.

"Stand aside," he dismissed him. "We need to collect the woman."

The young officer's head popped backward in surprise. "Collect the woman ... I – I'm not sure I understand," he said simply, a confused look on his face.

"No explanation is owed," Hayes replied sternly. "We have reason to believe she is tied to a terrorist sleeper cell. We need to take her into custody. Now stand aside."

The cop's surprised expression turned to astonishment. "*This* girl?" he said, gesturing to her. "All due respect, you gotta have it all wrong. There's no way she's –"

"I am done speaking with you," Hayes interrupted, growing tired of the conversation. "If you don't comply, we will be obliged to use force."

At this statement, Agents Langley and Caruso took positions at either side of Hayes, each pointing their semiautomatic rifles at the ground.

"Now, stand aside," Hayes ordered him one final time.

Jenkins stood across from the three armed men, trying to figure out what to do. Something was unmistakably wrong here; there was just no way the woman was involved in any terrorist cell; the idea itself was crazy.

He had to decide what to do: step out of their way, or intervene.

In the end, his instinct told him what to do.

As quickly as his trembling hands would move, he unclipped his holster and drew his pistol, pointing it at the large Federal agent facing him.

Half-turning to the cruiser but not taking his eyes off the three armed troopers, he screamed: "Mira! *Run!*"

In the front seat of the cruiser, Mira looked on in terror as the three men faced Officer Jenkins. The two men flanking the large, gray-haired one stepped forward, pulling their rifles out and pointing them to the ground in front of them.

Suddenly, Officer Jenkins pulled his gun and pointed it right at the leader's chest. Turning his head in her direction, he bellowed: "Mira! *Run!*"

Mira hesitated for a split second, frozen in indecision. "But what about *you??*" she screamed to him, panicked.

"Just go! *Now!!*" he shouted back at her.

Heart pounding uncontrollably, she threw open the passenger-side door and began to run down the alley as fast as her legs could carry her.

Hayes watched as the woman sprinted away from them, the padding of her feet sounding throughout the otherwise quiet alley. He had no doubt he would catch her, but he needed to dispose of the cop in short time just to be certain.

His eyes returned to stare down the barrel of the .38-caliber pistol pointed at him, then lifted to meet the eyes of the young cop holding it.

"Do you have any idea what you're doing?" he said calmly.

The cop said nothing. From behind the gun, Hayes could see his rapid, panicked breathing misting in the cool, damp night air.

Suddenly Hayes felt it, swelling up inside him like a wave. It was as if the cop were low-hanging fruit, dangling the temptation in front of him, the gun providing all the reason in the world. He then realized why: in all the evening's activity, he'd missed a dosage; the syringe was packed inside a pocket on his belt, unused.

But there was no time; the woman was getting away.

That was all the reason he needed.

"For your sake," he said with enthusiasm. "This will be quick, but I wish I could say it will be painless."

As the last word escaped his lips, Hayes reached out with both massive, powerful arms and, in one swift motion, slapped the gun out of the cop's hands and broke both his arms just below the shoulders. Wrapping his right arm around both limp, flailing arms, he pulled the screaming cop toward him. With his left hand he grabbed the cop's lower jaw by the chin and pulled it down hard, breaking it so it hung open.

As the cop continued to scream, Hayes punched him hard in the stomach, knocking the wind out of him, so that all that continued to escape his lips were a series of terrified wheezes.

"You," he said irascibly into the cop's disjointed face, "and your department have been a thorn in my side all evening." Pulling the silencer pistol from its side holster, he slowly slipped it into the cop's open, wheezing mouth. "So as the saying goes, you get to take one for the team."

With a malicious smile, he pulled the trigger, blowing a hole through the back of the officer's head.

The cop's body fell backward onto the cruiser's hood with a loud bang; his wide-eyed, slack-jawed face gazed up blankly at the moon amidst a backdrop of blood sprayed across the windshield.

Satisfied, Hayes tucked the silencer back into its side holster. Before he changed his focus to pursuing the woman, he turned to see the shocked, gaping faces of Langley and Caruso.

He cursed to himself. But in the end, the urge overtook him.

Trying to hide the gleeful grin fighting to reveal itself, he retrieved the cop's gun from the pavement and addressed them. "Langley, Caruso. I need you to impound this weapon as evidence."

As Langley stepped forward to retrieve the pistol, a stunned look still on his face, Hayes leveled the .45 and shot him through the forehead, then immediately turned the gun on Caruso and shot him as well. Both men dropped to the ground in a heap.

He laughed viciously; the urge was building upon itself.

He needed to get himself under control, or the entire mission would be jeopardized.

Reaching into the pouch on his belt, he retrieved a syringe and quickly pushed the needle into his arm. Instantly, the urge subsided, and Nolan Hayes exhaled.

He surveyed the bodies of Langley and Caruso.

"Waste," he muttered to himself.

Moving quickly, he pulled the bodies into the police cruiser, setting the cop in the driver's seat and Langley and Caruso in the back. Then, hopping into the sedan he'd arrived in, he drove to the end of the alley to pursue the woman.

He'd taken too long on the damned cop; the urge had struck at precisely the wrong time.

Still, he thought, she can't have gotten far.

She'd go for help first. A busy street.

Throwing it into Park, Hayes got out of the vehicle and began to run toward Western Avenue, reaching the corner of Western and Sunnyside in a matter of seconds.

He stopped at the intersection and looked around intently.

Nothing.

She had eluded him.

Frustration getting the better of him, he slammed his fist into a nearby lightpost, causing it to shake violently and shattering the glass light cover at the top.

Activating his headset, he spoke to Mobile Command: "Send a collection unit to GPS point two-three, require immediate removal of three bodies – two agents, one police officer. Marking GPS point in five seconds."

"Yes, sir," came the tinny voice through the earpiece.

He headed back to the cruiser to mark the point of collection. They would need to depart soon. He would have to leave a few squadrons behind to deal with the woman.

From behind cover of bushes at the alley's edge, Mira watched anxiously as the giant man climbed back into his car and drove off. The cold, murderous look she'd seen in his eyes all evening had intensified, as if he were nearing the point of madness.

She'd heard the gunshots and knew Officer Jenkins had died saving her life.

She couldn't go to Lora now; it would only put her close friend in danger as well.

And now, she was alone.

Sadness and fear overcoming her, she leaned back against the wooden siding of the garage behind her. She began to shiver uncontrollably, fighting to hold back tears.

41

Delirium

Darkness enveloped Rage as he felt consciousness slowly coming back to him.

He felt weak, as if something was draining the energy right out of his body. Lying still, he couldn't even open his eyes.

Where was he?

Sifting through his thoughts, he strained to recall anything that had happened in his recent memory.

Slowly and sporadically, the events trickled back into his mind.

The attack in his apartment.

The woman.

The heavily armed troopers pursuing him.

The police station.

And now, the voices, coming in and out of focus inside his head.

"… coming to …"

"… unbelievable … bastard already … off the tranquilizers …"

"… 'nother twenty CCs ought to …"

Then he felt it, entering his veins with a numbing coolness, flowing into him like a soft tide on a beachfront. The voices faded, he could feel his breathing slow, and the blackness of sleep claimed him once again.

42

Resurfacing

Larry was forced awake by the sensation of something crawling up his leg.

Consciousness filling him, he realized he was lying flat on his back. He looked out into the complete darkness but saw nothing; instead he only felt the digging of tiny claws into his uniform trousers, working their way up toward his torso. Instinctively he struck out at the source with a swift backhand, sending it flying with a squeal into the echoing tunnel.

He kept still for a moment, gaining his bearings. The pitch-blackness of the cramped, dank sewer pipe was accompanied by the constant sound of trickling water.

Larry moved his fingers and toes, then elbows, knees, hips, and shoulders. Nothing broken. He couldn't tell if he was bleeding, but his body ached all over. He'd hit his head on one of the metal rungs on the way down, and then landed hard. He considered himself lucky; it was probably a twelve-foot drop, maybe more.

He rubbed the back of his head and worked his way up into a sitting position, only to hit his forehead on the pipe's inner wall. Cursing as he did so, he sat back a bit, fumbling for his flashlight. He pulled it from his belt clip and switched it on.

The pipe could not have been more than three feet in diameter. The bright beam swept down the stream of water and sewage, all flowing away from him. The powerful odor was everywhere. He was soaked to the bone and could feel that his uniform and skin were covered in sewage.

He then looked up through the pipe to the opening he'd fallen through. He could see the light, feel the heat pouring down from the fires burning hot up on the surface.

Edna's house.

Then it all came back to him: *they'd taken Edna and the boys.*

He needed to get moving, find his way out of the sewer. Find *them.*

They couldn't have been taken too long ago; he still had a chance of getting to them before they were taken to who-knows-where.

Impulsively, he reached for his gun. Grabbing hold of it he realized it had been exposed to the water and was now useless. He tossed it carelessly behind his back.

He began to follow the flow of water in search of another way out.

As he moved down the pipe, he began to piece together what had happened: the Feds, still believing he was some sort of threat, had come to Aunt Edna's looking for him and had instead found Edna and the boys. They'd taken them into custody and booby-trapped the house with motion detectors and door-triggers, so that when he entered, it would set off the timed explosives which had been laid throughout the house.

They wanted him dead. There was no question.

He thought about calling the chief to get help.

No. If he reached out to the station, the Feds would catch wind of it.

The more he thought about it, the more he realized it was to his advantage that the Feds believe he was out of the picture.

He crawled along for several long moments, for what felt like miles. After covering what he assumed were a good eight to ten blocks, Larry shone the flashlight in search of a way out. Another fifty yards down, he saw an opening at the top of the pipe. Making his way to it, he reached upward, grabbed hold of the bottom rung, and pulled himself up the passageway. Upon reaching the top he carefully pushed upward on the manhole cover. The cover lifted, its heavy, rusted rim scraping the lip of the opening.

Larry rotated the manhole cover to the side and peered around. He was in a side alley, the faint yellow lights which hung from power line and telephone poles dimly illuminating the rows of garages, trash cans and dumpsters that lined each side of the paved surface around him. Hoisting up out of the opening, he shook himself off.

He noticed a police cruiser at the far end of the alley, its roof-mounted lights catching but a trace of the soft glow coming from the alley lights. He could also see movement and hear the muted sound of low voices. He moved out of view and watched.

As he looked on he noticed a second car, a dark sedan, parked some twenty feet behind the cruiser. It was blocking the far end of the alley. In the foreground of the sedan were two men carrying something large, something he couldn't make out.

He then saw more movement about halfway between himself and the cruiser. As the figure walked out of the shadows, he recognized the uniform immediately: all black, with visored helmet and riot armor.

Another federal agent.

What were they doing with a police cruiser?

None of that mattered right now. He needed to find his sons. He needed answers.

And he would get his answers from *them*.

Keeping still in the deep shadows, he waited a few moments, making sure there were no more than three of them. As he waited, he was able to better make out what they were doing: it appeared as if they were actually laying a crime scene, making things appear as if they'd happened a certain way.

Likely what they'd done in his apartment as well, he assumed.

The armed trooper was the biggest threat. He needed to be taken out first.

Then Larry could focus on squeezing answers from the other two.

Keeping from view, Larry quietly moved down the alley, toward the three men.

Behind the thick bushes lining the side of the corner garage, Mira did not take a breath. She'd seen the man emerge from a sewer opening in the side alley, standing in the open not twenty feet from her.

She didn't know exactly how long she'd been here; maybe an hour, maybe longer. She'd heard a loud bang several minutes before. It sounded like an explosion, which caused her to stir; but otherwise she'd remained frozen, rooted to the same spot.

She knew he was out there: the giant, scar-faced man, searching for her; and with every sound, every movement, came the fear that he would reappear, and find her.

She could hear voices along with faint noises down the alley. She couldn't decipher any of it, but she hadn't dared move to get a look.

She looked up again to see the man from the sewer moving, crossing into the back alley. In the brief light, she was able to make out that he was wearing a police uniform.

Another police officer? Coming out of the sewer?

Her eyes followed him into the shadows, behind another garage at the other side of the alley. In the darkness she could barely see him, but she could tell that he was watching whatever was going on down the alley.

A few seconds passed. Then, cautiously, the figure began to move forward, clearly headed in the direction of whatever he'd been observing.

Unexpectedly, Mira wanted to call out to him, warn him about what had happened to Officer Jenkins. Her mouth opened; she leaned forward, reaching out a hand toward him, trying to lift the words, any words of warning, from the depths of her throat.

But the figure continued to move determinedly down the alley.

Mira remained there, still frozen, left to ponder her indecision, fearing the officer was headed toward certain death.

Larry was only about ten feet from the armed agent now, silence his only ally. His plan was to get in close and quickly take the agent out, capture his firearm, then move in on the others before they had time to react.

Slipping his hand into the long pocket, he carefully withdrew the pipe wrench. He suddenly wished he'd kept the gun, if for nothing else than a decoy.

The agent stood motionless, facing the other two men from about twenty feet away. He was a large man, as they all seemed to be. And of course he had a semiautomatic rifle in hand, not to mention what looked to be a silencer pistol buckled into his side holster.

His grip tightened on the pipe wrench.

Lunging forward, Larry cocked the wrench with both hands and swung. A loud pop could be heard from its impact with the man's helmet.

The agent fell to the ground.

Dropping the wrench, Larry pulled the agent's sidearm from the holster and quickly advanced on the other two. Both men had turned in his direction, alerted by the sound. Weapon pointed out in front of him, he ordered them: "Chicago Police. Stand up straight, get your hands where I can see them."

The two agents, dressed in what appeared to be white jump suits, dropped what they'd been carrying. Larry quickly realized it was a body. He glanced down briefly and noticed the dead man's police uniform. He fought back a gasp, keeping focus. Gritting his teeth, he turned his gaze back on the two men.

He unclipped the handcuffs from his belt and tossed it to the agent on his left. "Put these on, one on each of you. Do it, now."

Sliding his wrist into one of the cuffs, the first agent began to speak. "I'm afraid you're making –"

"Shut up, now," Larry said angrily, extending his arm, pointing the gun directly at the agent's forehead. "You'll talk when I say. Until then, you say another word, and I'll put a bullet in your goddamned head. Got me?"

The man nodded, stepping back slightly. The younger agent hastily placed the other handcuff around his wrist, looking around anxiously, as if trying to find some kind of angle to escape.

"Don't get any ideas," Larry warned him.

He motioned with the pistol for them to turn around. "Keep your hands up high and move to the back of the vehicle. Put your hands on the trunk, spread your arms and legs. No sudden moves. That was your last warning."

The two agents obeyed, spreading arms across the trunk of the cruiser.

Holding the silencer pistol in his right hand, Larry began to search the two men briskly with his left.

Down the alley, Mira looked on in silence as the events continued to unfold. Angry with herself for her indecision, she'd finally gathered the nerve to move from her hiding spot, and get a closer look at what was happening.

She could see a man about thirty feet away, lying face-down on the pavement. He was wearing riot gear and a helmet, the same as those who had been in her apartment and in the alley earlier. A large wrench lay a few feet behind him. Another twenty feet further, she could see the officer holding two men at gunpoint. They were both wearing white jumpsuits and were being frisked by the officer. Several feet beyond that, she could see what she thought was Officer Jenkins' body.

As the officer began to search the two men, she saw the armed guard, now about fifteen feet away from her, begin to stir.

Larry was patting down the older agent's coat when he felt something flat and firm in the inside upper left pocket. Reaching inside, he pulled out a square-shaped, zip-sealed packet about the size of a compact disc case. He tore it open to find a folded document and two small flash memory drives.

"Hmph," he muttered. Moving to the agent's side, he said, "What's this?"

"Nothing you would find useful," the agent coolly replied.

"I'll bet," Larry said. "Where's your identification?"

"I can get it for you –" the agent began, lifting a hand from the trunk.

"Tell me where," Larry ordered him, pointing the gun into the man's left temple.

"Trousers. Front right pocket," the agent said.

Keeping the silencer pistol pointed at his head, Larry moved behind the agent and retrieved a billfold-style wallet. He flipped it open to see the clearance card of Special Investigator Argon Clive of the National Security Agency, the tiny photograph of the man's face staring back at him. A silver badge adorned the panel opposite the ID card, once again confirming the man's employment with the NSA.

"A woman and two boys. Where have you taken them?" Larry said.

The agent was about to respond when, suddenly, a tiny, vibrating sound arose from inside his coat.

Larry recognized the sound immediately. He plucked the small paging device from Clive's belt, holding it up to view the message.

"Hayes. Frequency 13," Larry read it aloud. He stepped back, keeping the silencer pistol pointed at Clive's head. "Respond. Everything is going to plan. Anything else and you die. Any code words I don't understand, you die. And any sudden movements, you die. That simple. Understood?"

Clive nodded.

Larry watched as Clive switched on his earpiece and spoke the word, "Thirteen." He stepped closer, keeping the silencer muzzle against the back of Clive's neck. Less than two seconds later he could hear the faint, tinny voice coming from the other end.

"Hayes."

"Clive, reporting in."

"Status?"

"Alley clear-out almost complete."

"ETD?"

"Ten minutes," Clive replied.

"Unacceptable. It should have been completed by now."

"Complications arose. A witness needed to be disposed of."

"Wrap it up quickly," the voice ordered him. "Transport one has departed. Asset Two and three witnesses on board. Transport two will be arriving at the designated pickup point shortly. You will be there to await other retrieval teams."

"Understood," Clive replied. "What is status of outstanding items?"

"Only the woman," the voice responded. "Police officer has been eliminated."

"Read you," Clive said.

"Hayes, over and out."

"Out," Clive replied, and switched off the earpiece.

Larry stared at him. "Hand me the earpiece."

Clive pulled it out and gave it to Larry. "They seem to think you're out of the picture," he said, still staring straight ahead of him.

"I heard that," Larry replied before throwing the earpiece into a yard across the alley. "That's the way I intend to keep it."

"You're not going to get away with this," the other agent piped in.

Larry stepped over to the second agent, pressing the silencer muzzle into the back of his head. "I don't think I'm talking to you right now," he said threateningly.

Suddenly, a cry came from behind him, followed by a loud thud and the sound of scuffling footsteps. Larry turned to see the large trooper he'd previously knocked out, stumbling forward and once again falling to the pavement, his rifle clacking against the asphalt surface. In the shadows beyond, he saw the figure of a woman, both hands holding onto the pipe wrench he'd dropped moment ago. She appeared to be struggling to keep her balance, as if just having swung the wrench with all her might.

Then out of the corner of his eye, Larry caught the younger agent swiftly reaching into his coat with his free hand. Turning back toward him, Larry saw the small pistol just in time and, having no choice, shot the agent twice through the chest. Eyes wide and mouth open, his cuffed left arm sticking up bizarrely like a marionette, the young agent slid down the trunk of the cruiser, killed by the shots.

Kicking away the dead agent's gun, Larry turned the silencer on Clive as a warning. "Make a move and I'll shoot, right through the head. Understood?"

Clive, head still facing forward and otherwise not moving, nodded his head.

Keeping his eyes on Clive as he stepped back, Larry moved toward the unconscious trooper. "Please stay where you are, miss," he said to the woman, holding a hand out toward her. "Everything's going to be okay now."

He could see the woman, barely more than a silhouette and still holding the pipe wrench in both hands, nodding in reply. He could see she was trembling.

He flipped the trooper over with his boot, keeping the silencer on him. The eyes were closed, and the body was limp. He slid the rifle from under the trooper's gloved fingers and picked it up.

He kept an eye on Clive, who had continued to remain still and facing the other way, his palms spread across the trunk of the cruiser. The dead agent's body leaned against Clive's right leg, his limp left hand poking out of the handcuff next to Clive's right hand, his left arm sticking oddly upward, raised over his head like a child who knew the answer to some unspoken question.

Larry needed to somehow secure the trooper, but didn't have another set of handcuffs. He spotted some loose cabling spooled up near the garage behind him. Again continuing to glance toward Clive every few seconds, Larry began to wrap the cable tightly around the trooper's wrists, ankles, and neck. Less than a moment later the man was hog tied, so if he struggled with the bindings around his arms or legs, they would tighten around his neck.

Satisfied, Larry stuffed his handkerchief into the trooper's mouth as a gag, then wrapped another few feet of cable around his jaw to secure it.

He looked over to the woman, who was still trembling. Though he couldn't see her face in the darkness of the alley, he could see that she appeared to be in her pajamas.

What was she doing out in an alley at this hour? he wondered.

"We're almost done here, miss," he told her. "Then I'll get you to safety."

Heading back to Clive, Larry's face hardened. Shoving the pistol against the small of his back, he once again began patting him down. "Looks like your muscle won't be helping you out, after all," he said. "Now, talk. Where are the woman and the boys?"

Clive said nothing for a moment, then simply replied: "I can't tell you that."

Without warning, Larry spun Clive around roughly. Grabbing him by the collar, he thrust the pistol under Clive's chin, pressing it hard into the top of his throat.

"Now you listen to me," he spat into his face. "I'm through messing around. You're going to tell me what I need to know, or I'm going to kill you. Simple as that. Now talk. Where are my *sons?*"

Pushing the muzzle further into Clive's neck, Larry stared hard into his eyes. There was clearly genuine fear in them. The man believed Larry was going to kill him.

"I ... I can't," he struggled, the muzzle pressed against his larynx.

Larry did not break his stare, his face only inches from Clive's. He tightened his grip around Clive's collar and pushed him backward an inch, gritting his teeth in a mix of rage and frustration.

"Have it your way, then."

Larry pulled the silencer away from Clive's throat.

Reaching down, Larry unlocked the cuff from the other agent's body, then, pulling his arms behind him, turned Clive back around to place the second cuff on his free hand. He grabbed Clive by the arm and pulled him over toward the spool of cable, hog-tying him as he'd done the trooper. At one point Clive tottered and could do nothing but fall backward, hitting the ground with a dull crash. Larry let him fall. He finally grabbed Clive by the collar and dragged him over to the black sedan. Pulling the back door open, he hoisted him up and dropped him face-up across the back seat.

Noticing the trunk was slightly ajar, he strode around to the back and pulled it open. Looking in, he could see two bodies laying askew across the trunk floor. He shone his flashlight into the trunk and saw the black body armor, the visored helmets. Two more NSA agents. Both shot execution-style, in the center of the forehead.

"Jesus," he muttered to himself.

He clicked off the flashlight and headed back toward the cruiser. As he did so, he came across the body of the fallen officer.

He turned on the flashlight to see who it was.

It was Billy Jenkins.

"Damn it," he said softly, cupping his forehead in his palm.

Kneeling down, he shone the light over his dead colleague. Like the troopers in the trunk of the sedan, he, too, had been shot execution-style; but there was no entry wound in the forehead, and the exit wound in the back of his head was much larger than the others'. And there was something else strange about him: his jaw was clearly broken, almost detached from the rest of his head; it had etched an eerie grin onto his otherwise blank face, making him look like some kind of macabre jester.

Furthermore, both of his arms lay in odd, unnatural positions: his right was pinned under his torso, whereas his left lolled out above his head, palm facing downward.

Almost as if they'd both been broken at the shoulder.

A wave of remorse hit Larry like a hard gust of wind. He staggered a step backward. He was responsible for this. Somehow Jenkins had gotten pulled into this mess, *Larry's* mess, and had paid the ultimate price for it.

Then the realization came to him: *if they'd done this to Jenkins, they wouldn't hesitate to do it to Edna and the boys, too.*

At this thought, he moved unsteadily to the nearest garage and became sick.

Leaning against the garage door for support, Larry tried to gather his thoughts. First, they needed to get out of there, and quickly. He would get the woman to safety, then figure out how to get to his family.

He looked over at Jenkins' still body.

He wanted to alert the Chief, but as he already knew, it was too dangerous to contact him. The Feds had ears there. And Larry needed to appear out of the picture.

He looked for the young woman and noticed she'd retreated to a sitting position, tucked against one of the garage doors in shadow, knees pulled up to her chin, arms wrapped around her legs. She was still holding the pipe wrench in her left hand. She looked up at him as he approached.

He stopped before her and extended his hand. "Please miss; let me help you up."

After a second's hesitation, she set down the pipe wrench and took his hand with both of hers.

As he pulled her up, her face came into the dim light, and he immediately recognized her.

It was Mira Givens, the witness from the bank robbery, from weeks before.

43

En Route

The mammoth black transport sped down the expressway, passing the scant wee-hour traffic, highway billboards, and unlit homes.

The seventeen-hour journey back to the SRC finally underway, Hayes strode to the back of the transport into the holding area. He looked down to his immediate right to see the three members of the policeman's family: an old woman and two young boys, bound tightly against the back of the wide bench seat they sat on, all three heads dropped forward, under heavy sedation.

He'd decided to use them as bait in order to trap the cop, and, in the event the trap failed, as leverage to force him to come forward. Having received confirmation that the trap had indeed succeeded, they were now nothing more than useless collateral to him.

The easiest decision would be to simply eliminate and dispose of all three of them: all reports fed out to local authorities and media would state they'd died in the house explosion, and the NSA could easily delay any local investigations into the fire until they'd planted the necessary evidence.

However, if he were to kill them now, he couldn't properly dispose of the bodies. So it would need to wait until their return to the SRC.

Moving to the narrow door at the very back of the transport, he punched in a three-digit code and opened the door to a small room. His eyes swept to the back wall, to the reason they'd made this journey. Flanked by two armed troopers as well as one of Clive's assistants, Asset Two lay on his back within the makeshift cell: a coffin-sized titanium container, solid in the back with latticed front and sides.

The subject was hooked up to an IV, which fed the tranquilizer into his bloodstream at a steady rate. But his incredible immune system had become increasingly resistant to the drug's effects, forcing Hayes' team to increase its flow over the past two hours and, ultimately, expedite their departure to the SRC.

His alert pager began to vibrate. It was Hill's thirty-minute update; Clive's would be next.

"Hayes," he answered, activating the headset. "What've you got?"

"Female remains at large," Hill reported. "Squads four, seven, nine, and ten fanned out across designated quadrants. Wolf's squad remains at precinct in case the woman turns up there. No updates from APB."

"Read," Hayes replied. "Continue your search, report back to me in thirty minutes unless something breaks sooner."

"Understood," Hill responded. "Over and out."

Hayes switched off the headset.

Things were almost sewn up. The woman would not be difficult to track down.

Moments passed. Clive's report was late.

He pulled the alert pager from his belt, staring at it, expecting it to go off with Clive's call. Any second now.

Holding up the alert pager, he punched in the code for Mobile Command.

Within seconds came the reply. "Blake," came the voice through the earpiece.

"Need you to triangulate the signal for Agent Clive's headset," Hayes instructed. "Pick it up on satellite, track its movements over the past ninety minutes."

About ten seconds later came the response. "Satellite shows signal at the same coordinates for the past forty-seven minutes. Do you need the coordinates, sir."

"No," Hayes replied, thinking it through. "But send the closest squadron to that location on the double, and have them report back to me directly upon their arrival."

"Copy that," Blake acknowledged.

"Over and out," Hayes finished, and switched off the headset.

Glancing out the large tinted window into the night, Hayes took a breath. He would worry about the inconveniences on the ground here later. Right now, they needed to get Asset Two back to the compound as soon as possible.

44

Fugitives

Larry drove the cruiser out of the alley and headed westbound on Berteau Street.

He needed to find a place to stop so they could figure out what to do next.

He glanced to his right at the young woman. He had many, many questions he wanted to ask her, but he had no idea where to start. Reading her expression, he could tell she was about two shades away from shock.

"Miss Givens," he began, "It's okay now; you're safe. I'm going to get you to safety, okay?"

She said nothing.

"What were you doing in that alley?"

She appeared ready to cry, but then she seemed to pull herself together. "I – I was being taken home, to a friend's apartment," she began.

"And what happened?"

"I was with Officer Jenkins … and – and they killed – and they killed him," she struggled, fighting back tears.

"They … the people in the alley?"

"Yes."

Larry strained to think. Jenkins had been killed by the Feds, that much was clear. But the two bodies in the trunk, who had killed *them*? Maybe Jenkins had shot one of them during a struggle, but there was no way he'd have killed both of them before being killed himself, especially not the way it had been done. Even if forced, Jenkins simply wasn't capable of killing in such a manner.

None of it made sense …

Needing answers, he pressed on. "Where was Officer Jenkins taking you from?"

"The police station," she replied quietly.

He stopped on that question. He remembered Gino telling him about the standoff earlier that evening at the precinct, specifically recalling the part he'd mentioned about the vigilante suspect, Rage, showing up at the precinct with a young woman.

Was *she* the young woman he was talking about?

A flood of new questions entered his mind.

Was she somehow *involved* with the suspect?

And were the Feds pursuing her, as they were Larry?

Did they think she had ties to the suspect, as they assumed Larry had?

What else did she know?

His first priority was finding the boys. But if she had answers, maybe he could piece together where they'd taken them.

"Miss Givens. I need you to tell me everything that's happened to you tonight."

The woman sighed heavily. He imagined she'd already shared her story at least once while back at the station, and the prospect of reliving it yet again was a lot to bear.

"If you can, it should help us figure things out," he explained. "And take your time, try to remember everything for me."

She sighed once again, then seemed to gather herself and her thoughts. She slowly recalled the series of events over the course of the evening, as well as her encounter with the suspect on the train and his visit to her apartment, the night before.

When she had finished, she took another deep breath and added, "I don't know what any of it means. I don't know what they'll do to him. I don't know why they're after me now."

Larry remained silent, still absorbing everything she'd told him. Her situation was now clear to him: she was in as much danger as he was.

Finally he spoke. "They think you know something," he said quietly.

"What?"

"They think you know something about him," he explained. "There's something about him they want to keep a secret. That's why they came after him. They think you know what it is, and they're afraid you'll go public with it."

"But I don't know anything!" she exclaimed.

"They won't take chances. And that means *we* can't take any chances."

"What do you mean?"

"I mean," Larry began, choosing his words carefully as he spoke. "That you're in more danger than I'd thought. It's no longer just the Feds who're after you. They put out an APB on me, which means the local and state authorities are now being ordered to bring me in as well. The media has also more than likely been notified. And if they have one out on me, they probably have one out on you, too. Who knows on what grounds, but I've no doubt they've made something up. That's why we need to keep out of sight."

"How do you know this?"

"Because they came after me, too," he said.

"What? *You?*"

Larry took a deep breath himself. "They think I know something about him, too."

"What do you know?"

"Nothing. It's a long story," he said, changing his mind mid-sentence. "I was on a case involving him. They think I know something more."

"But how could they have an APB out on you? You're a policeman!"

Larry glanced at her, deciding they were beyond the stage of deciding what and what not to share. "I was set up," he explained. "They sent two men into my apartment; I killed them in self-defense …" his voice trailed off. "Anyway," he said suddenly, waving his hand brusquely. "That's not what's important. What's important is they've taken my family, and I need to get to them."

"Your family … ?" she said, barely more than a whisper.

"So I need to figure out where they are," he said.

Larry pulled off Berteau Street, turning right onto a side street. He immediately turned left into another side alley, driving about halfway down before pulling the cruiser into an open parking space, nestled between two minivans.

Throwing the car into Park, he flipped open the cruiser's onboard notebook computer, which was mounted in front of the dash, centered between the driver and passenger sides. He then fished around in his pocket, locating the zip-sealed packet he'd taken from Clive. Opening it, he slid out the plastic backing, popped out one of the two tiny memory cards, and pushed it into a slot on the side of the notebook.

"What's that?" she asked, the young, smooth lines of her face illuminated softly by the bluish glow of the computer screen.

"Something I'd gotten off one of the Feds in the alley back there," Larry said, entering his passwords to access the computer. "I don't know if it contains anything we could use, but it's worth a try."

As the machine loaded the contents of the memory card, Larry remembered the folded document he'd also found in the envelope. Pulling it out, he opened it and began scanning it. Just under the header at the top was stamped the word "Classified" in bold red, followed by what looked to be some kind of chronology.

"DOD Operation Code: 15-2883," Larry read the header aloud. "Phase I – Acquisition; Stage II – Asset Two … this looks like an itinerary of some kind. Lot of timelines, but most of it's been encrypted or something. I don't know what to make of it," he added, handing it to her.

She took the document and began examining it carefully.

Looking back at the computer screen, Larry saw that the contents of the card had loaded. There looked to be about ten files in all. He double-clicked the first file, hoping he wouldn't need a password to access it. To his luck, it opened right away.

"Have you got something?" Mira asked, glancing up from the document.

"Yep," Larry replied, keeping his eyes on the screen. "I think it's some kind of procedure manual; there's a lot of contingency protocol in here."

"A lot of what?"

"Contingency protocol," he said. "It's basically a law-enforcement term. Murphy's Code we call it, you know, as in Murphy's Law. For every plan there's always stuff you expect can go wrong, so you work up a contingency plan for each potential problem. Most contingency protocols just cover a few common things; maybe one to two pages deep. But I've never seen anything *this* detailed. Thing's 386 pages long."

"Does it say anything in there about witnesses, bystanders? How they plan to handle them, I mean?"

"Good question," Larry replied, typing in a search of the document for the keyword 'eyewitness.' "But based on my experience with them tonight, I'm pretty sure I know how they plan to deal with us."

Seconds later, the results showed on the screen: the word 'eyewitness' appeared 214 times throughout the text. The first occurrence was a section header about one-third of the way through, to which Larry quickly scrolled and read from the beginning.

"It's what I'd assumed," he said as he finished scanning through it. "Any material witnesses are to be eliminated, or deprogrammed at the SRC."

"Deprogrammed ..." Mira thought about it for a moment. "As in brainwashed?"

"Looks like it," he said, still scanning the text. A wave of hope ran through him: perhaps they weren't planning to kill Edna and the boys after all.

Mira seemed to have the same thought. "Maybe your family is safe then," she said.

"I wouldn't go that far," Larry countered. "They're still in custody. And even though these people operate under the guise of Federal law, they've killed before and will very likely do so again. I'm not going to take any chances."

"I'm going with you," Mira said, seeming to decide in that moment.

"Don't be ridiculous," Larry replied dismissively. "It's too dangerous."

"Like you said, I'm in enough danger already," Mira argued. "I'm safer with you. They have Rage. And, I think I can help you; help you figure things out."

He glanced at her. He was worried about having someone else to look after while searching for his family. "We'll decide once we know where to go."

Then it dawned on Larry; he remembered the end of the passage they'd just read: 'deprogrammed at the SRC.' He'd been so focused on the first portion of that sentence, thinking about Edna and the boys' safety, that he'd glossed over the last part. From the way the sentence had been worded, the SRC was likely where their operations were based. If he could find it, he could likely find Edna and the boys.

Leaning forward once again, he did a search on the key word 'SRC,' looking for any possible definition on what the acronym stood for and where the place might be located. Although 'SRC' was mentioned over fifty times in the document, they could not find a definition of the acronym.

He opened the second file, which appeared to be centered around the vigilante, or "Asset Two" as he was repeatedly named. It seemed to be mostly cautionary information on how to approach, subdue, and contain the subject. Though Larry didn't have time to pore over the details, from what he was able to see, they had a great deal more information on the subject than the Chicago Police had.

After searching the second file and finding nothing, he opened the third file. Scanning through it, he found similar information on what looked to be another individual they were seeking, referred to as "Asset One."

Not finding anything in that file, he opened a fourth. The file contained more information on "Asset One." However, in this file, most everything he scanned through made it clear that "Asset One" had already been brought into custody. It covered in great detail a series of testing procedures, sedation schedules, sample acquisition techniques, and other procedural items Larry couldn't quite make sense of. It went on to document tests that had already been done on the subject, including a series of viral injections to analyze the subject's immune system, as well as the introduction of various flesh wounds, both superficial and deep, to assess his 'cell-regeneration capacity,' as they referred to it. Larry could barely comprehend the details, but he understood well enough: somehow this "Asset One" had an unnatural ability to heal himself, and the Feds were using nothing short of torturous methods to test its limits.

Was this also what they had in mind for the vigilante?

No wonder they wanted to keep their whole operation under wraps, he thought.

"I think I may have found something," he heard Mira say.

"What?"

"Here," she said, holding out the document she'd been studying. "Some of the lines on this schedule or whatever it is, have numbers at the end."

"Okay," he replied curiously, taking the sheet. "What do you think they are?"

"Well, I don't really know for sure," she said uncertainly. "But maybe there's some kind of pattern. What if they're some kind of codes for places or something?"

He glanced over the document once again. It was as she'd said; to the right of about two-thirds of the lines was a numeric code. There appeared to be consistency among the codes: each was comprised exclusively of numbers, and all were eight digits long. Another thing he hadn't noticed the first time he'd looked it over: each of the numeric sequences only appeared at the end of a line of text containing the name of a specific location, whether it be an airport, an entire city, or even a specific address. It even noted the vigilante's address. If no location was included in the text line item, no corresponding numeric code appeared at the end. Continuing to scour over the sheet, he then saw it: both the first and last line of text included the acronym "SRC"; and at the end of both lines was the exact same numeric code: 32306529.

Those were the only two places that number appeared on the document.

In his mind he pieced it together: this was in fact an itinerary, and these two entries were its origin and destination points.

And this "SRC" had to be their base of operations. Larry was sure of it now.

"I think you're right," he finally said.

"So how do we figure out what it means?" she asked.

Larry thought it over for a moment. "We know it's government, and that these guys are NSA. So it's more than likely some kind of location code the military uses."

"Can you just Google it?" she asked.

"That won't help us," Larry said. "It's not information that's accessible to the public. You can only find stuff like it if you have access to –" he stopped abruptly.

"What? What is it?" she asked.

"The Niss," he said.

"The what?"

"The Niss," Larry explained. "N.I.S.S. Stands for National Information Sharing System. A new system we're supposed to be learning. Stems from the Patriot Act. It's designed to let government agencies share information down to the local law enforcement level, and vice versa. I don't know a ton about how to use it, but it's our only shot."

With Mira looking on, Larry logged into the N.I.S.S. interface.

The computer screen popped, and the FBI logo appeared. Below it were the large block letters N.I.S.S., and two entry lines for a username and password.

Larry typed in his information and tapped the "Enter" key. The screen refreshed again. A series of command lines appeared, with a simple box that read "Search."

He decided to try the operation code first, feeling that was the bigger fish. He typed in "DOD Operation Code: 15-2883, Phase I – Acquisition; Stage II – Asset Two," and clicked the "Search" button.

The screen returned no results.

Deciding to scale back a bit, he typed in "DOD Operation Code: 15-2883."

Again getting no results, he merely keyed in "DOD Operation Codes" into the search box, thinking he might be able to locate the number from a catalog or list.

As before, his search came up empty. *Access denied*, he assumed.

"Hmmph," he muttered under his breath. Whatever it is, he assumed, it's either very new or very, very top secret.

Larry decided to move on to the second clue. He keyed in "location code 32306529 src," and once again clicked the "Search" button.

Less than a second later, a series of results appeared. He scanned each one carefully, looking for anything that might connect the number with the acronym "SRC."

On the third page of results, he found something of interest. The title read, "Glossary of Aeronautical Location Codes, Department of Defense Archive."

He clicked on the listing, which brought up another prompt requesting a username and password.

"Well, here goes," he said to himself, unsure if his access included Pentagon data. Crossing his fingers, he once again typed in his information.

To his surprise, the Department of Defense logo appeared, accompanied by the words "Glossary of Aeronautical Location Codes, Department of Defense Archive" and another "Search" box.

It can't be this easy, he thought.

He entered the eight-digit number once again.

The screen refreshed, more slowly this time, revealing a map of the state of Virginia. Toward the north edge of the map was a small marking in the shape of a star.

"X marks the spot," he said to Mira.

Not wasting any time, he clicked on the star which represented the location code he'd entered, and the screen refreshed once again to reveal a more detailed map, once again with a star at the center. It appeared to be some kind of industrial park.

When his eyes moved to the top left of the screen, he immediately forgot everything else.

In the first line of text were the words "Strategic Research Complex."

SRC.

He looked down at the following line of text, noticing the address: 1501 Federal Parkway, Timberville, Virginia.

That was it; he had what he needed.

"I think we know where were going now," he said to Mira.

45

Disturbance

The banging and screaming began just after three o'clock A.M.

After only about twenty minutes' rest, Hayes vaulted up from the reclined seat and raced to the rear of the transport, his gun drawn. He threw open the door to see the two technicians huddled over Asset Two, one of them struggling to reinforce his bindings, the other feverishly preparing another heavy dose of tranquilizer. The trooper on duty stood a few feet back, his weapon drawn on the subject.

"What's the situation, Sergeant," Hayes addressed the trooper urgently.

"Unclear, sir," the trooper responded. "A moment ago, subject was still. And then *bam*, he began thrashing around, screaming at the top of his lungs."

Hayes turned to the technician preparing the sedative. "Cause?"

"Unknown," the tech replied, filling the syringe with the clear fluid. "We had him on an aggressive dosage schedule. Everything normal until a moment ago. There's no logical reason; subject has been and continues to be out. I don't believe he could be dreaming, but just in case –"

"Increase the dosage of strength inhibitor in the sedative," Hayes told him.

"Sir," the tech countered. "The inhibitor is already at a high enough level to potentially compromise the tranquilizer portion. There's a chance –"

"Do it," Hayes demanded. "We have no idea what's happening in his head right now, but despite his unconscious state, we cannot risk him tearing free of those bindings. Keep his vitals in mind, but even if it knocks him into next Tuesday, we need to ensure his strength is kept in check."

"Sir," the tech again retorted, "his bindings are pure titanium, one half-inch thick. I don't think –"

Hayes stepped into him. "Even after all the debriefings, are you telling me you don't have any idea what we're dealing with?" he said in a low voice. "At full strength he can snap that titanium as if it were paper. Within seconds all three of you would be dead, and then we'll have a full containment breach on our hands. Now tell me you understand that."

"Sir, I do, sir," the tech replied, no argument this time.

"Get it done, and quickly," Hayes ordered him. "Do whatever you need short of killing him to ensure he remains unconscious and still. Understood?"

"Yes, sir," the technician said, then immediately turned to the supply cabinet to reformulate the tranquilizer.

As Hayes made his way back toward the front of the bus, he stepped past the older woman and the two boys. All three were awake now and, having clearly heard the screaming, wore looks of pure terror on their faces.

46

The Cave

Rage lay on his back, staring up into a white, cloudless sky.

He had no idea where he was or how he'd gotten there. He didn't know what day or what time it was. Or how long he'd been lying there.

Thoughts began to reassemble. Memories returned. First came distant memories: Georgia Fay, his childhood, growing up. Then, more recent events: his nightly outings, the woman, the attack in his apartment, the police station ...

He searched for his most recent memory, but he could not pinpoint it.

As thoughts continued to trickle into his mind, he became aware that his entire body ached. He tried to move, but every joint felt stiff; every muscle reluctant.

His fingers felt around at the ground beneath him. At first it seemed like soft soil, but he decided whatever it was, was not natural.

He then became aware that there was no sound coming from anywhere around him. He grunted instinctively to make sure he hadn't lost his hearing. The brief noise echoed softly away into nothingness.

He felt disoriented, confused, perhaps even afraid.

What is this place?

Am I dead?

Slowly, he pulled himself up into a sitting position, every limb and muscle providing a painful reminder of the ache that resonated throughout his entire body. Once he was up he leaned forward a bit, emptying his lungs in a deep exhale.

He looked around him. There seemed to be nothing in view, neither near him nor far away. Wherever he was, was pure nothingness – just whiteness in every direction. The ground below him was some kind of soft material that gave way at his touch, though still a solid substance. Looking upward, he now understood that it was not sky he was looking at, but rather just more whiteness, a space with no ceiling, seemingly infinite.

After a few moments, he stood up. He didn't think he was dead; but there was no explaining exactly where he was, the immateriality of this place.

He called out, softly at first and then loudly.

Seconds passed, and a figure appeared in the distance in front of him. No more than a silhouette at first, it began to draw closer, and as it did so, it became clearer. It was the woman. Mira. She was walking, almost floating, toward him, dressed in a flowing white gown that made her appear even more like an angel to him than he'd remembered.

She came before him, her long gown continuing to flow about her hidden feet as if on some soft wind. She said nothing but merely stared at him, a detached, curious expression on her face.

"What are you doing here?" he finally asked.

Her head tilted sideways, more curious. "You brought me here," she said.

"I did?"

"Yes."

"Where are we?"

"You haven't decided yet," she said, looking around.

"*I* haven't?"

"Clearly not," she responded matter-of-factly.

"So … are we dead?"

"No," she said. "I don't believe so."

"So," he began, trying to piece things together, "this is inside my mind?"

"Yes," she said. "Where else *could* it be?"

"Nothing makes sense," he said to himself, looking down at the white ground.

"Do you remember where you just were?" she asked.

"No," he said. "Do you mean here … or out there?" he pointed outward, indicating the reality outside his mind.

"Here, in your head," she said. "Where you just were, before now."

"No," he said. "I don't remember anything."

"Do you want to see?" she asked in an encouraging tone.

"I don't know," he replied.

"Here," she said, and with a broad, flowing wave of her gown, their surroundings changed, the white room shifting into a dark, massive cavern, the sound from the movements of her long gown echoing away into the distance of the immense space.

There was just enough light to see, so Rage looked around.

"Do you recognize where we are?" she said.

"No," Rage replied. "Should I?"

"This is where you go afterward," she said.

"After what?"

"After," she began evenly. "The Lesson."

"What?" he said, not understanding.

"This is where you go after the Lesson. This is where you take yourself."

"For what?"

"You'll see," she said indifferently.

Suddenly there came a sound, from off in the distance. Rage was unable to discern what it was, but he could tell it was drawing closer. The ground beneath him began to tremble; it shook lightly at first but gained strength with each passing second.

He looked at Mira, searching her eyes for answers. She simply returned his gaze, her expression offering nothing back to him.

The sound drew closer. The ground continued to hammer even harder beneath his feet, almost knocking him off balance. Rage thought he'd heard screams in the thick of the ever-strengthening sound.

"What's happening?" he said.

She said nothing but instead took a few steps backward, slowly, her gaze still fixed upon his. Her feet were still hidden by the long, flowing gown; its whiteness was a stark contrast to the dark cavern floor.

And suddenly, it dawned on him. He *had* been here before.

He never saw it coming. It hit him at full speed, throwing him hard into the far wall of the cavern. Jagged, fossilized rock cut hard into his back as he smashed into its surface and then fell forward, face-first onto the cavern floor.

Before he could react, a large, powerful hand grabbed his wrist, hoisting him high into the air, then shook him violently before throwing him down once again onto the rock floor. His face was bleeding; small, sharp points of rock had stuck into his back.

He could hear the noise above him: a terrible medley of screaming and laughter, as if several voices were coming from one single being, each saying different things.

Face down, he could not see the creature that stood over him, but he could feel its presence, smell its breath as it leaned in close.

He remained still on the cavern floor. He absolutely did not want to come face-to-face with the creature above him. Not at any cost.

The figure continued to breathe hard into the back of his neck, as if challenging him to move. Rage remained motionless, clinging to the floor, locked in abject fear. It was a feeling unfamiliar to him, and one he knew he had only felt – *could* only have felt – in this place within his mind, in the presence of that which he couldn't face.

Then, the being screamed at him, and everything went black.

47

Departure

"No!" Mira protested. "We've been through this; I'm going with you."

"You can't," Larry argued, pulling the cruiser out of the alleyway. "Like I said before, it is *way* too dangerous. I don't know what's going to happen once I get there, but I can't be looking after someone else."

"But they're looking for me, too," Mira said anxiously. "It's not safe for me here, either. Not even at the police station. And I told you before, I can help you."

Larry glanced at her. He couldn't be responsible for the woman's safety, but as she'd said, there was nowhere else for her to go. He couldn't just leave her …

"Okay," he began. "But I need you to do as I say every step of the way. Even if you completely disagree with it," he added.

"Like what?"

"I don't know," he replied, turning onto a main street. "I don't know what might happen. But you'll need to trust me."

"Okay."

Moments later Larry took a right onto a side street. About halfway down the block he slowed down, looking at the parked cars.

"Bingo," he whispered, seeing an old rust-pocked silver Volkswagen Rabbit parked on the right-hand side of the road.

He drove to the next alleyway entrance, then turned in, parking the cruiser next to a garage, hidden from the street.

"What are we doing?" Mira inquired.

"We need to ditch this car," he explained. "Just follow me."

Larry took the two memory cards and stuffed them into his pocket, then grabbed the document he'd taken from Clive, folded it up, and handed it to Mira.

"Move quickly and quietly," he whispered to her, opening the door.

When he got to the Rabbit, Larry dropped to his knees and began feeling around underneath the rear bumper. Finding the small plastic box, he pulled down, detaching the magnet that held the box to the inside of the bumper, and slid it open to reveal a key. He waved Mira toward the car and unlocked and opened the passenger-side door for her, then went around the front and got in himself.

He put the key in the ignition, depressed the clutch, and started the car. The engine came to life on the second try, accompanied by a strange grating noise coming from under the hood, as well as what smelled like something burning.

The car's deep maroon interior was badly worn. The cloth material covering the seats and ceiling was torn or had come apart in several places, and the tiny bucket seats creaked under their weight. The dash was covered in dust, and the clear plastic covering on the speedometer and gauges had a straight crack down the center.

"What do you want me to do with this?" Mira asked, flapping the folded sheet of paper in her hand.

"I don't know," Larry said, distracted by the car's decrepit interior. "Hide it somewhere. Put it under the seat for now."

He threw the shifter into first gear and revved the engine, making the car lurch forward out of the parking space and almost killing the engine as he let off the clutch.

"Damn stick shifts," he muttered in annoyance, yanking the shifter backward into second as the tiny car staggered its way down the street.

Out of the corner of his eye, he saw Mira turn to look at him.

"Why did we have to get rid of the police car again?" she asked curiously.

"Because they're going to be looking for that car. We stay in that, we might as well be wearing a target," he answered.

"So ... this isn't *your* car, is it?" she asked in a dubious tone.

"Of course not," he answered. "But just like the cruiser, they'll be *looking* for my car. This one they won't be."

"But, what made you choose *this* car?"

"I've seen this car before; we're close to where I live," he replied, understanding why she was questioning his choice of vehicles. "I once saw the owner hide the key, so I knew where to find it. I also know it rarely goes anyplace, so by the time it gets reported as stolen, we'll be long gone. And we need to buy time to get to where we're going."

"If we make it there," she added skeptically.

"It'll be fine," he replied, the car sputtering as they neared a stop sign.

She glanced down at the storage bin behind the shifter, seeing a small plastic milk container. "How long do you think it's been since this car's been used?"

"I don't know, a while."

"I'd say," she retorted, disgusted. "The date on this milk is from last August."

"We have to stop at a gas station," he said, ignoring her comment. "This thing's on empty and we need cash. If my ATM card still works, that is. And, we need a map."

They pulled onto Clark Street and saw a 24-hour gas station.

Larry pulled up to the mini-mart entrance. "Stay here," he told Mira.

"Take that with you," Mira said sourly, pointing to the milk container.

"Sure," he said, grabbing the container, then closed the door and went inside.

Mira sat back in the grimy passenger seat, taking another look around the interior of the car. She thought about her situation: she was on the run, with someone she did not know, heading toward a place she'd never been, with both the government and the police on their tail, not to mention someone trying to kill them.

Her eyes rested on the center of the dash, and she noticed there was an AM radio just below the air vents. It was an old-style radio, the kind she hadn't seen in a car since she was a child, with a quarter-sized silver plastic knob at each end. She turned the left-side knob to the right, and with a click, the radio switched on. Getting nothing but static, she turned the other knob to the right a few turns and finally got an all-news station.

The news update came through the tinny-sounding speaker in the dash:

"Details continue to come in from the bizarre string of events happening overnight on the city's north side. Federal authorities confirm one person is in custody while at least one remains at large; all are alleged members of a terrorist sleeper cell which had been holed up in the Edgewater neighborhood. Though Chicago Police have not confirmed this, it is believed that the head of this sleeper cell is also the key suspect in the "Protector of the People" vigilante case Chicago Police have been investigating.

"What began with a 911 call in the Edgewater neighborhood quickly became a national security concern, and federal agents were brought to the scene. At that point, several related 911 calls were received from surrounding neighborhoods, which led to a violent standoff involving police, federal agents, and the alleged leader of the terrorist cell himself, who has reportedly been apprehended by Federal authorities.

"We'll have more details as they come in. In other news, a house explosion in..."

Turning down the volume, she sat back in the seat, trying to take in everything she'd just heard. She saw movement and lights in front of her, and she looked up to see a police car pulling into the gas station.

She felt her heart stop as she saw the two officers get out of the car and walk into the mini-mart. There was no place for Larry to hide in the small shop; no way he could avoid being noticed, much less recognized, in his police uniform.

A moment passed, each second seeming its own eternity. Frozen in the seat, leaning forward with her hand on the door handle, she furiously tried to think of what to do to help him, when the driver-side door opened, and Larry quickly got in next to her, head bowed low.

"Oh my God," she said, startled by his sudden entrance. "There are two—"

"Saw 'em coming," he cut in, tossing the map onto the dash before starting the engine and throwing the shifter into reverse.

"Then how did you—"

"Back door," Larry said matter-of-factly. "Come on, oldest trick in the book. My ATM card worked, but we'll have to get gas somewhere else."

Once they had backed the Rabbit out of immediate view, he eagerly jammed the shifter back into first gear, again almost killing the engine as he let off the clutch, and they started down the street, once again in the direction of the lake and out of the city.

48

Expendable

The sun had yet to rise when Ingramov returned to the Underground Labs.

Sitting in his tiny, windowless office, he pored over plans and schematics, preparing for a new phase of testing scheduled for Asset One as of that morning.

The testing procedures had been sequenced into two groups: Level One and Level Two. Level One consisted of basic blood tests, small-scale biopsies, the introduction of bacteria and viruses. Level Two entailed more dangerous, invasive tests. They posed much greater risk, potentially resulting in permanent damage, or even death, to the subject.

To begin Level Two testing, all Level One testing would need to be completed, producing enough samples to model the genome for reproduction.

In addition, the subject needed be deemed fully expendable.

And for that, there needed to be a second subject, ready and waiting for testing.

Enter: Asset Two.

Ingramov knew that the moment Asset Two had been secured by Hayes' strike team, they would be able to move Asset One into Level Two testing.

Hours ago, this had been confirmed: Asset Two was now en route to the SRC.

And not a moment too soon.

In the past twenty-four hours, Asset One's incredible biology had begun to adapt faster than they could reformulate the tranquilizer. There had already been two close calls, forcing them to administer new mixes of the serum ahead of plan.

And then there had been the incident with the night janitor.

Despite all the safeguards they'd put in place, somehow, unimaginably, the subject had still found a way to kill. The fact that his jaws possessed the strength to do what they did to the janitor's hand exposed the limitations of the serum.

Since then, they'd taken steps both to cover the janitor's death and to ensure the subject would not be able to repeat what he'd done.

All things considered, Ingramov figured they had about sixteen hours before the only alternative would be a lethal dose of the formula. And given what he'd seen in the past twelve hours, despite even the additional tranquilizers, even *that* window of time could shrink.

Glancing down at the schematics on the desk in front of him, Ingramov once again began scribbling onto his notepad, completing plans for the final round of testing on Asset One.

49

Failed Trappings

As the black transport made its way eastbound across northern Indiana, Hayes' alert pager began to vibrate.

Looking down as he plucked it from his belt clip, he saw it was Hill.

He switched on his headset, inserting it in his ear. "Hayes," he answered.

"Hill," came the voice in his ear. "Status on Clive's team."

"Go ahead," Hayes replied.

"Willhelm, Caruso and Langley all confirmed dead," he began. "Clive and Samuels both alive. Found Clive bound and gagged in the back of the sedan, Samuels on the alley floor, also bound and gagged. Both appear unharmed."

"Clear the scene immediately," Hayes ordered him. "Leave nothing behind, including any traces of blood, anything. A cold trail is imperative, understood?"

"Yes, sir," Hill replied. "Estimate three minutes til departure."

"Good," Hayes responded. "Advise Clive I expect a full report. Over and out."

Not fifteen seconds later, the alert pager began to vibrate once again. This time it was Blake. Other than Clive and Hill's thirty-minute updates, he'd given everyone strict orders for radio silence except for emergencies. He activated the headset.

"Hayes. Go ahead," he said immediately.

"Blake, Mobile Command," the voice replied. "I have a development, sir."

"Out with it," Hayes said impatiently.

"Security network reports bank card usage of a Lawrence J. Parker at a gas station not thirty minutes ago," Blake stated.

"The police officer," Hayes mused.

"Affirmative," Blake replied. "Location of –"

"Isn't important," Hayes interrupted. "He's certainly no longer there. What *is* important is where he is now. Work to pinpoint his location, however necessary. Over and out," he said flatly, and disconnected.

Clipping the alert pager back into its cradle, Hayes sat back in the seat and closed his eyes, assembling plans around this change of events involving the cop.

Clive's trap had failed.

Somehow, almost inexplicably, the cop had *survived.*

And if he was able to figure out where his family was being held, he would without a doubt be coming for them.

It appeared that they would need to keep the three captives alive a bit longer after all, to use as bait yet once more.

50

Torturous Methods

Elias Todd lay motionless on the examination table.

His half-open eyes stared into the pitch blackness of the massive laboratory, his ears tuned to the complete silence floating around him.

Stretched across the table, he was covered only by the loose, thin smock that extended out to his knees and elbows. His arms and legs remained locked in place, cuffed and bolted in the same position they'd been since he'd awoke days before.

Then, from across the room came a clack and hissing sound. The pressurized lab door was disengaged. The overhead lights flickered to life.

Seconds later, the sound of footsteps resonated through the lab. The examination table began to hum, slowly tilting upward. Within seconds he was vertical, the curtain surrounding him was drawn, and the hateful visage of Dr. Ingramov stood before him.

"Good morning, Mr. Todd," he said, his rueful tone clearly reflective of the events of the previous night. "I trust you slept well last night?"

Todd said nothing, staring blankly back at Ingramov.

"Always the talkative one, aren't you," Ingramov said, chuckling at his own remark. "I have to say you've caused us more than your share of headaches."

"But," he added brightly, "I am pleased to say, your time here is coming close to an end. Beginning today you will be part of some groundbreaking tests. Tests not approved until now, nor outside of this room. You have the honor of being *first*.

"Now, as before, there *will* be some pain and discomfort. In fact probably much more than what you've experienced thus far. And once again, no pain inhibitors will be used, as we continue to measure your pain thresholds. We'll begin momentarily."

Ingramov walked to a portable workstation and began typing on a keyboard, glancing up at Todd intermittently as he did so.

Again the lab door disengaged. Todd could see Polosky walking toward them.

Seconds later the examination table once again began to hum. It started to move slowly back to a horizontal position, until Todd was looking directly at the ceiling again.

Behind his head he could hear a series of clicks, followed by a whirring noise.

Todd immediately recognized what it was: *A saw.*

Ingramov's head appeared in his view, his surgeon's cap and mask on, oversized protective glasses covering the remainder of his face.

He could feel something blunt and round poke at his lower thigh.

The whirring noise filled the room once again, a higher pitch this time. It was close. Todd felt the instrument pierce his skin, slicing through flesh and into bone.

The incredible pain surged throughout his body, tearing through his nerve endings, overpowering the sedatives.

And for the first time, Todd screamed.

51

Grisly Findings

Loretta was into her third model analysis when she heard the lab door disengage.

Her mind mulled over what she'd learned the past evening. Her first thoughts revolved around the DNA strand itself. Based on what she'd found, they simply could not replicate the strand as it was – the chemical imbalance posed too great a danger to introduce to another human subject.

But how was she supposed to explain how she'd discovered it?

And, was it something they already knew about?

As the door clacked open, she looked up to see Dr. Polosky walk in and briskly approach the large examination table behind her. He set down a blue tray. "Level Two testing sample results," he said plainly, keeping his eyes on the table. The tray was full of small, covered containers. He plucked a small Ziploc bag from the tray and set it on the table, then carried the tray into the refrigeration chamber at the far end of the room.

He returned and motioned to the Ziploc bag. "Dr. Ingramov asks that you begin working on these immediately." He then made for the door, exiting the lab.

She strode over to the table and picked up the small plastic bag. Two memory cards were inside, the same format in which the sample data had come to her thus far.

She was anxious to analyze this latest round of findings. All she knew about "Level Two" testing was that it was highly classified, and that it had never been performed on *live* human subjects before.

Loading the memory cards onto her workstation, she clicked open the first file.

"Bone marrow," she muttered in a puzzled tone, her eyes scanning the screen.

Clicking from image to image and graph to graph, her first realization was that this was far too much data to be from just one sample. There had to have been at least six or seven samples taken to produce the amount she was looking at.

The retrieval of bone marrow was an extremely difficult and invasive process; she wondered exactly how Ingramov was able to get so many samples without causing a great deal of damage to the subject.

Rubbing her temples, she decided to view another section of data. She opened the second file, watching as the images popped onto the display panel.

It took her a second to figure out what she was looking at.

She frowned, taking a closer look to make sure her eyes weren't playing tricks on her. The image was taken from the sample marked "No. 10."

Getting up from the chair, she marched to the refrigeration chamber. She reached up and carefully took the blue tray down from the shelf.

Covering the tray were various clear plastic jars, each a different size. Each was sealed with a red plastic lid and a white label stuck onto the top, identifying its contents.

She pulled the container marked "No. 10" from the tray, looking inside it.

In the jar was a human finger, severed and cauterized at the knuckle.

She screamed loudly, dropping the container on the floor, where it shattered.

Forcing back waves of nausea, Loretta stormed out of the lab, in search of Ingramov.

52

Reckoning

When Rage next awoke, he was sitting at the foot of a bed, facing a narrow door.

He looked himself over. Although his body still ached, the wounds from his encounter with the creature were gone.

He found himself in a tiny, darkened room. There was a vague familiarity to it. As his eyes adjusted, he scanned the small space. Peeled brown patterned wallpaper stretched up to the ceiling. To his right was a small black nightstand with a child-sized metal lamp in the center, its aged, yellowed lampshade hiding the dim, flickering bulb inside it. There was a dresser to his left, against the wall; an aged picture of a clown in front of a circus tent hung crookedly above it. The bed on which he sat was stiff and falling apart: pressing down with his fingers, he could feel what was left of the mattress crumbling beneath him, its innards dried to dust with age. The air was considerably stale, as if no one had opened the door in years.

He knew, somehow, this small, dark room had significance to him; though he couldn't quite place how.

But its gloom, as well as something else about it, gave him an unsettled feeling.

He didn't want to be here.

The doorknob began to turn. Rage watched, finding himself unable to move. The door slowly creaked open, revealing nothing but utter blackness beyond it.

Gradually, a slender, fair-skinned hand cut through the blackness. The hand of a woman. As it slowly extended toward him, the rest of the arm followed, accompanied by the face and body of the one he'd already suspected it was: Mira.

She stood before him, once again in the white flowing gown.

"Come," she said, waving him toward her. "It's all right."

Slowly, he rose from the bed and stepped forward, taking her hand. She gently led him through the opening and into the blackness beyond.

The darkness reformed around them, becoming a larger, more open space than the tiny room Rage had just been in. He recognized it immediately: Mira's apartment.

She sat down on the couch against the wall, the same spot she'd sat when he was first in her apartment. She gestured to the brown wicker chair he'd sat in. "Please, sit down."

He sat, having to remind himself that all of this was in his own mind.

"What's happening?" he asked her.

She tilted her head slightly, pondering. "You're still deciding."

"What was that last place? The small room?"

"You don't remember," she responded. "From when you were a child."

It was, he suddenly realized. In his mind's eye, he glanced around the room they'd just left. His first foster home. The young religious couple. The father coming into his room each night, after the mother had gone to bed. Telling him he didn't deserve the food on their table, the roof over their head. The backhand to his face. Covering his mouth. The bruises, the cuts. Curling up on the floor, crying silently to himself, his wounds healing before his eyes. Plotting to escape, to never be found by them again.

"Why was I there?"

She sighed quietly, as if trying to find a way to explain. "Your mind," she began, "is reckoning with you right now. You're going to places you don't want to go but feel you need to, to understand."

"Understand what?"

"You'll know. It will all be clear to you soon enough."

"Why did you take me out of that room and lead me here?"

"You sent for me. Just like last time."

"Why here?"

"This is where you wanted to go."

"Why?"

"Don't ask. Just let your mind lead you."

In all the uncertainty he was feeling, Rage felt a pang of frustration. Mira, on behalf of his own mind, was speaking in riddles to him. He wanted to understand, but his own mind was playing with him, talking to him in circles.

"Why can't I just stop this?"

She looked back at him, understanding his meaning. "To stop this, you would need to awaken."

"What?"

"You would need to end the dream."

"And how do I do that?"

"You can't."

"If it's my own mind, why not?"

"You know the answer to that question."

Then it dawned on him, and he understood.

Awaken ...

End the dream ...

He was unable to end the dream because ... he was unable to wake up.

And he understood why, over the past several weeks, he hadn't been able to sleep.

As he slept, his mind had been trying to reckon with him, to tell him something.

But whenever it took him to a place he didn't want to go, he would wake up, pulling himself out of it, away from the nightmares.

But now ... he was unable to wake up; trapped in a drug-induced sleep.

There was no escape for him now.

Which was why, for the first time, he was unable to escape the being in the cave.

He looked back up at Mira.

"What was ... in the cave?"

She shifted on the couch. "You know, don't you?"

"I want to hear you say it."

"It's a collective."

"A collective of what?"

"All the lives ended."

"People that I –"

"Yes," she finished for him.

"You needed to face them," she began again. "To understand what you'd done."

"Why *couldn't* I face them?"

"Because," she said simply. "Your fear of the truth pulled you out."

"Why?"

"You weren't ready to come to terms with what you'd done. Which is why you couldn't face them this time, either."

"I know what I've done," he said. "I don't lose sleep over them."

"But you do," she countered. "And your mind understands that. That's why it's been trying to make you understand."

"Understand what?"

"That what you're doing," came a sudden, stern voice from behind him, "is not your place."

Rage turned around, instantly recognizing the voice.

Standing in the small kitchen toward the front door, her austere gaze focused solely on him, was Georgia Fay.

53

Into the Fire

Loretta marched down the hallway, in the direction of the main lab.

As she rounded the corner toward the north wing, she almost collided with Dr. Polosky, who was just about to head into the elevator. His lab coat was unbuttoned.

"Excuse me, Dr. Barnes," he said coldly, all but putting up an elbow to avoid further contact with her.

"I need to speak to Dr. Ingramov," she demanded. "Where is he?"

"He's gone home for a few hours' rest," Polosky replied matter-of-factly as the elevator doors opened. "As am I. Now good –"

"When will he be back?" she said, throwing out an arm to hold open the doors.

"I don't know," Polosky said. "That's up to him. If you need to speak with him urgently, I suggest you try his mobile phone. Now good afternoon," he added irritably, and stepped to the back of the elevator.

Loretta stood outside the elevator as the doors closed. She would confront Ingramov in person. While deciding what to do next, she stopped cold.

The subject; Elias Todd ... she needed to see him for herself.

She turned back around toward the main lab. As she approached the double doors, she saw Anderson, one of the younger security guards, standing to the right. She acknowledged him with a short wave as she swiped her access card, underwent the retinal scan, and pushed open the heavy doors to enter the lab.

The air felt immediately cooler than it had been in the hallway. She'd been in the main lab twice before, yet this time the atmosphere was starkly different: the smell of disinfectant hung heavily in the air.

Her eyes moved to the back of the room, and she saw the curtain. It had not been there the last time she'd been in the lab.

Loretta walked toward it and drew back the curtain.

The circular examination table lay at a 45-degree angle. Shackled to it with arms and legs spread, lay the grim figure of Elias Todd.

He was heavily bandaged in several areas. Splayed on the large table, he looked like some kind of nightmarish crucifixion. He lay completely still.

Loretta approached the table. She could see his chest rising and falling slowly. Still alive. There were a number of wounds all over his body. His left thigh. His right calf muscle. Upper left arm. Right forearm. His right hand, where they'd severed his small finger. Right side of his neck. Several places along both his upper and lower torso. And finally a long, deep cut just above the hip.

By rights he shouldn't even be alive. They had cut him in so many places and bandaged him so carelessly, a normal man would have bled to death.

She checked his vitals. His condition appeared to be stable.

She needed to tend to his wounds. She went to the medical supply closet, keying in her access code to enter. She pulled the necessary supplies down off the shelves, dropping a few in her haste, and hurried back to the examination table.

She tended to each wound, clipping off the existing dressing, then cleaning and treating the opening as thoroughly as she could, all the while uncertain whether there was still time to prevent infection. She didn't rest until all of his wounds – she counted twenty-two of them – had been taken care of.

Once done, she went back to the supply cabinet a final time. Retrieving two plasma bags, she wheeled a nearby IV stand over to the examination table, slipped each bag through the hooks at the top, and connected each IV line to a sequential drip line. Finally, she removed the IV line from the subject's arm and replaced it with a new line, connecting him to the IV stand.

Loretta blotted her perspiring forehead.

As she rested, the immediacy of seeing to Todd's wounds began to abate, replaced by thoughts of what she needed to do next.

She was still unable to comprehend what had been done to him, or why.

The methods they'd been using had been cause for concern from the very beginning. But through all of the questions, she was convinced of the importance of the greater goal behind the project, and had thus put those concerns to the back of her mind.

But this had changed things.

What was being done to him now was nothing short of barbaric.

And even if it was somehow necessary to advance the project, she could not sit idly by and allow it to happen this way.

She turned back to Todd, then glanced at the monitor. His vitals remained constant; he continued to sleep. For now, she'd done all she could for him.

Loretta turned toward the door. She would check on Todd again shortly.

In the meantime, she decided to pay a visit to Ingramov's office.

54

The Road

The rolling hills of western Pennsylvania were a welcome change to the never-ending flatness that had been northern Ohio and Indiana.

They had been on the road just over six hours now, and Larry was beginning to feel the exhaustion creeping into his body. Adrenaline had been his only source of energy during the past several hours, and lack of sleep had begun to take its toll.

Donning a black baseball cap and gray t-shirt with a Purdue logo emblazoned across the chest, Larry held the steering wheel with his left hand while clutching a stale, cold cup of coffee in his right. Mira lay back in the passenger seat; a navy blue cap rested upside down in her lap. Now fugitives, they had to change their appearance as much as they could; especially Larry, who had still been in his police uniform. No clothing stores were to be found in the wee hours, so they'd pulled into a truck stop in northern Indiana and bought what few wearable items adorned the shelves.

As he stole a glance in Mira's direction, he studied the lines on her otherwise youthful face. Despite her obvious beauty, her face carried a sadness that went beyond the anxiety of the previous night. He recalled her line of work – a social worker. He thought back to when he took the boys to see the social worker off Diversey and Western. He remembered the office setting: the brightly-colored walls, the flowers and plants, the light of day coming in from the large open windows. All things meant to keep everyone's spirits high. Nonetheless, whenever he set foot into that office, he could never escape the feelings of grief, of loss, of sadness throughout the room. Despite the measures taken to expel them, those sentiments hung heavily in the air like a shroud, dimming the light.

He thought of the toll that situation had to take on someone.

She stirred, and he set his eyes back on the road ahead.

In the early hours of their journey, they'd tuned in to the local news radio stations, listening to the breaking news updates coming in every ten to fifteen minutes. Sometimes there would be new developments, sometimes not; but every time Larry heard an update, he became infuriated with how the story was being twisted: the vigilante was the leader of a terrorist sleeper cell, Mira was his accomplice, and now Larry himself had been implicated: they'd even tied him to setting the explosion at Edna's house.

The news outlets even had reports that the "occupants of the house," Edna and the boys, had been trapped inside when the explosion occurred, and were believed dead.

Larry understood the Feds had created the perfect cover for eliminating his family, and that if he didn't get to them quickly, the Feds would be able to put good use to that cover.

Moreover, now that they knew he was alive, he understood they were anticipating his next move. He had to assume that they'd recovered Clive in the alley by now, and thus learned that Larry was now in possession of enough hard evidence to bury not only whatever project they were working on, but to shake up the entire Defense Department.

He assumed that State Police had set up roadblocks under the pretense that their "terrorist cell" was planning a move on Washington, so he and Mira had taken to the side roads since entering Indiana.

And finally, he assumed that they knew he was still in possession of the evidence, or at least knew of its whereabouts. Thus, they would not kill him on sight, but rather they would leverage the lives of Edna and the boys in order to recover the evidence from him. Once they had what they wanted, he and his entire family would immediately become expendable.

Considering these factors, Larry had decided to hedge his bets.

Stopping at a 24-hour convenience store just as they'd left the city, Larry purchased a photo-mailer envelope, marker pen, heavy-duty mailing tape, and a book of stamps. He dropped the zip-sealed packet with the two memory cards into the photo envelope, then wrote out a quick note detailing the evening's events, instructing the recipient to make copies of the memory card's contents for safekeeping. Taping it up heavily, he scribbled down Ollie's address at the *Chicago Tribune*, adding the words "urgent" and "personal & confidential" across both the front and back. Finally, he slapped the entire book of stamps on the front of the envelope, placing it in the mail drop around the side of the convenience store.

Ollie would likely receive it on Tuesday; by then, this would already be over, and Edna and the boys would be safe. Or dead.

He gritted his teeth and shook his head at the thought of anything happening to his sons. He would not allow it to happen.

And to keep it from happening, *he* now had leverage as well.

Larry kept his eyes on the road ahead, guiding the tiny car eastbound toward their destination.

55

Project Safeguard

After swiping her card through the reader in the door, Loretta entered Ingramov's office.

She clicked on the overhead fluorescent lights, their dull hum filling the otherwise silent space as they illuminated the small room before her.

The only furniture was a desk butted up against the left-hand wall, a credenza off to its side, and a row of three black filing cabinets along the right-hand wall. The desk was littered with paperwork. A large-screen computer monitor was on the back right corner of the desk, a keyboard pushed underneath. Along the far wall were two blackboards, filled with formulas scrawled in hurried handwriting.

She sat at the desk and switched on the computer. She assumed that Ingramov kept a log of his work on the project somewhere on his workstation.

As the machine began to boot up, she glanced around at the papers scattered along the cluttered desktop. She shuffled through them. There was nothing that struck her.

Beneath the right-front of the desk was a drawer. She pulled it open. Inside was a DVD in a clear plastic case. The case was labeled "Debrief – Project Safeguard."

She picked up the case and flipped it to the back side. On it was a small white label that read, "Classified. Official Department of Defense Record."

The workstation had booted up and was showing the login screen.

She didn't have Ingramov's access information, but it was no matter – she'd hacked her way into more complex systems than this one. Within seconds she was in.

She slid the disc into the open tray. Perhaps whatever was on this disc would give her the answers that had been kept from her thus far.

The video began to play. As Loretta watched, she was transported to a dimly-lit room. Four men were taking their seats at a long table, all facing away from her. They were seated before an older man in a dark suit whom she recognized as Dr. Klaus Johannsen, the chief scientist who'd hired her. He was standing at a podium; a second man, considerably larger, stood in shadow behind him …

As the four men settled into their seats at the table, the smaller man by the podium turned on an overhead projector, bathing the far wall in blue light.

The Department of Defense logo appeared on the wall, underneath which read the words in massive black type:

PROJECT SAFEGUARD

Phase I – PROJECT CHIEF ASSET RECOVERY

Johannsen stepped in front of the image to address the small group. The second man remained several feet behind the podium, his hulking silhouette remaining still.

"Mr. Secretary, everyone, good morning," he began in his familiar German accent. "My name is Dr. Klaus Johannsen, Chief Scientist of the Special Projects Division's Advanced Sciences Group, here within the Department of Defense. As some of you know, you're here today because you've been selected to represent the Defense Department or NSA's interest in this joint initiative between our two entities. The importance of this project to our national security, as I'll explain throughout the briefing, cannot be overstated.

"The purpose of this morning's initial briefing is threefold: first, I'll overlay the concept behind the initiative, and why both Defense and NSA have been chosen for involvement. Second, we'll outline our plan to complete the mission. Third and finally, we'll detail the resources needed to carry it out.

"Now. Does anyone have any initial questions before we get started?"

The room was silent.

"Very well," Johannsen said, clicking to the next slide. "Then let us begin."

"I'm going to start us off with a few basic facts, most of which are common knowledge. First, the most important truth: our country is at war. We have been at war since shortly after the terrorist attacks on our soil years ago, and we are now embroiled in an increasingly unstable region of the world. And, despite the claims that the Executive and Legislative branches make to pacify the American public, the fact of the matter exists that there is no clear near-term solution, and things will likely continue to escalate, leading to several years of further deployments to the region.

"In addition to what is happening in the Middle East, tensions continue to rise in other sectors of the world. Rogue nations are gaining influence on their neighbors, and still others are close to gaining nuclear capabilities.

"The United States has always led the way toward world peace, be it through diplomacy or military authority. However, we have entered an age where in many cases diplomacy is no longer a viable option, which has increased the need for additional resources within our Strategic and Armed Forces.

"However, as we are all aware, recruitment for our armed forces is at an all-time low. And with continued deployments to an increasing number of regions, combined with an aging pool of available soldiers, our armed resources will continue to wear thin until the breaking point. And we're closer to that point than we'd like to think.

"All that being said, we have entered an age where the need for a mass armed force, similar to what we've built in the past, is somewhat diminished."

Before Johannsen could continue, the man at the far left of the table cut in. "And exactly how do you arrive at that logic?" he said bluntly.

"Mr. Secretary, Sir," Johannsen identified the man Loretta assumed was the Secretary of Defense, "it's because the nature of our enemy dictates it. In most cases, we are no longer facing large nations whose governments and populace oppose us. Nations with which we can solve for differences through diplomacy, sanctions, or straight military buildup. Rather, our enemy is a faceless one, both in hiding and blending in with the general population all at once, shifting forms with the wind. In those cases, a straightforward military presence does less to preserve the peace than it does to present our soldiers as targets.

"And in countries where the governing body *has* opposed us, we have proven the ability to supplant those regimes with a pro-American rule. The downside to those instatements is the fact they have come at the cost of many American soldiers' lives.

"These are but two examples of how our strategic needs have changed, and why in such cases, rather than a direct military buildup, something else is needed altogether."

"And what do you suggest that is?" the Defense Secretary cut in again.

"A smaller, more precise, *specialized* force. A group of highly trained, highly *capable* troops, created to perform surgical strikes on our enemies. If I may take a step back. It is no secret that we've had challenges capturing our enemies and dealing with rogue nations over the past few years. The widely-held perception has been that the intelligence just isn't there. That perception is wrong. We have the intelligence as you all know; but what we haven't had is the means to be able to quickly punch a hole through the enemies' defenses, debilitate them at the top, and withdraw with minimal collateral damage. You all remember 'Shock and Awe.'"

The room didn't respond; two of the men seated shifted in their chairs.

"Get to the point," the Defense Secretary said impatiently.

"This would be the opposite," Johannsen continued. "A team assembled to perform precision strikes such as these would devastate the enemy and minimize loss of American lives."

"This is nothing new," the man just to the right of the Secretary declared. "We've performed these kinds of operations before. And with minimal success."

"Mr. Armstrong, sir," Johannsen addressed the second man. "That's exactly the reason for this project. As I'd previously suggested, we've historically had two alternatives when making a significant move on our enemy: we either perform a massive strike, which creates significant collateral damage and costs numerous American lives, or we attempt a pinpoint strike with a limited number of soldiers, which in more cases than not has failed. This solution would remedy both of those shortcomings."

"How?" the Defense Secretary once again demanded, his palm slapping the table.

"By creating a new kind of soldier. A better one." Johannsen responded.

"Creating?" Armstrong came in.

"Let me take you through a brief history. In the late 1960s, during the Vietnam War, the Special Projects Division began testing alternative methods to help improve our soldiers' health as well as their performance on the battlefield. Their most groundbreaking research involved altering the DNA code on a collection of frozen embryos, to determine the effects of their formulas.

"In the summer of 1973, they made a significant breakthrough. Scientists were able to successfully adapt a genome, which in effect changed the genetic code of one of the embryos. Upon delivery in April of 1974, the subject showed no outward signs of being any different than a normal infant, but his immune system was quite unique. Our physicians recorded that the child never acquired any kind of virus; not even influenza or the common cold. Bacteria, viral infections, disease; his unique immune system appeared to be impervious to all of them."

"Are you implying you *tried* to infect the subject?" the Secretary said.

"With his permission, of course," Johannsen said.

"How long did this go on for?" Armstrong asked.

"Testing continued for several years; that is, until the fall of 1981, when the largest Defense budget shift in government history effectively shut down the Special Projects Division's workload and eliminated the project altogether.

"However," Johannsen replied matter-of-factly, "although the ability to further our research had been taken away, we continued with our limited funding to test the subject into his adolescent years. And ultimately, it paid off."

With a gesture to the room, Johannsen stepped aside. "Gentlemen, I'd like to introduce you to Colonel Nolan Hayes, U.S. Marine Corps."

At this the enormous shadow stepped forward, the projector's blue light revealing the familiar visage of the Executive Special Agent. Dressed in full Marine garb with numerous medals decorating both his lapels, and even in the video, it was clear he was regarding the group with an intense, penetrating glare.

"Sirs," he addressed the four men seated, standing at attention.

"At ease, soldier," the Defense Secretary regarded him. "I'm well aware of your exploits, Col. Hayes. It's an honor to meet you."

"Mr. Secretary, everyone, as some of you already know," Johannsen resumed. "Col. Hayes is a decorated veteran, a war hero, serving in numerous campaigns including Somalia, Afghanistan, and Iraq. He has led or been involved in several successful missions, many of them covert –"

"We could use more soldiers like him," the Secretary cut in.

"That," Johannsen returned pointedly. "Is *precisely* why we are here today."

"Please continue," the Secretary said.

"Thank you, Mr. Secretary," Johannsen replied. "Col. Hayes' numerous achievements can be attributed to his many unique abilities. Abilities at first undetectable to us, but which over time developed and became quite apparent."

"What *kind* of abilities?" Armstrong asked.

"Many that I'd suggested before," Johannsen replied. "Speed, strength, stamina; but in far greater proportions than we could have ever imagined. Over time, we've tested their limits, and the results have been astounding."

"Can you provide examples?" Armstrong inquired.

"Certainly," Johannsen said, stepping back to the podium. "What you are about to see is unaltered video, captured live during testing. No 'special effects,' if you will."

The slide display on the far wall went dark. In its place a title screen appeared, showing the words "Field Tests, Hayes, USMC, Archive 1-129."

The video began rolling. Over the next six minutes, the video cut to several scenes of Hayes performing physical tests, including lifting a small passenger vehicle from the ground to above his head, performing a standing leap over a semi-truck trailer, sprinting past a running greyhound dog on a track, kicking a hole through a brick wall, and running a series of battlefield simulations, exhibiting his prowess in combat.

The video ended, and the dim lights went back up in the room.

"Very well, then," the Secretary acknowledged. "I'll admit I'm impressed. But I'm afraid my mind still isn't quite framing this properly. What else can you do?"

At this Johannsen cut in. "Perhaps after our presentation we can take you over to our testing facility? That setting will allow the group to witness several examples of Col. Hayes' abilities live and in person. Would that suffice?"

"That would," the Secretary replied. "My assistant will arrange my schedule to accommodate. Gentlemen, I'll assume you'll do the same?"

"Certainly, sir," Armstrong answered. The two men down the table also nodded.

"So, enough background," Armstrong cut in. "What are we doing, and how are we going about it?"

One of the two men seated far to the right of the Secretary, who'd been silent thus far, finally chimed in. "Are we able to replicate Col. Hayes' DNA strand?"

"Undersecretary Millett, is it?" Johannsen acknowledged him. "Yes, we are, and *have* been able to for some time," Johannsen replied. "However, we've determined it is not the solution. The genome within Hayes' DNA code is unique to his genetic makeup. Every attempt thus far to introduce the strand into a foreign body has resulted in terminal failure within moments of introduction to his system."

"*Died?* How many?" Armstrong pressed.

"Seven volunteers to date."

"Jesus," the Secretary commented. "Are we covered on this?"

"Yes," Johannsen answered, understanding his meaning. "All subjects had previously signed off on complete non-disclosure to the project. Next of kin for each subject was notified as per protocol. All records reflect standard KIA at the location of their scheduled deployment."

"Is the strand toxic?" the other man seated down to the right inquired.

"Undersecretary Tolson, correct?" Johannsen responded as the fourth seated man nodded. "Not toxic, per se. However, its complex attributes are more than a normal human system can handle. In other words, the subjects' bodies were simply incapable of processing and containing the adapted genome."

"So what *is* the solution?" the Secretary asked.

"The solution is to replicate the genome, or a clone of it, in a manner that will not terminate its host," Johannsen explained. "The genome itself will need to be altered to adapt to its host's biological structure.

"*How* we will do that is still under development," he continued. "However, we've also pinpointed a second alternative, which may speed up our progress. It's the main reason we're gathered here this morning."

"Do tell," the Secretary urged.

Johannsen clicked the remote once, and the image projected on the wall changed to a photograph of two newborn infants lying on an examination table.

"As I mentioned before," he began. "Col. Hayes was the first successful subject of our research. Over the next eight years, attempts were made to build on that success, but none were successful. That is, until the autumn of 1982, when two subjects with the adapted genome were artificially conceived, and carried through to delivery in June of 1983. However, similar to Col. Hayes, neither subject exhibited anomalies once born. Nonetheless, our research on Hayes and the two new subjects continued for another fifteen months, at which point the project was shut down."

"So, what happened to the other two subjects?" Millett inquired.

"Due to the project being shut down shortly after, and the two infants exhibiting no real signs of physical enhancement, their early age enabled us to outplace them into separate children's homes," Johannsen replied.

"And why again was the decision made to maintain custody of Hayes, when the project had already ended?" Armstrong asked.

"Given his age," Johannsen explained, "we couldn't place him without risk of knowledge of the project being shared. And, fortunately, enough funding was located to continue his testing and development under our control."

"And at what point did his abilities become apparent?" Tolson came in.

"We began to notice them when he was ten years of age, three years after we'd released the other two subjects," Johannsen answered. "They continued to develop over the next several years and appeared to plateau shortly after his eighteenth birthday."

"And then what?" Armstrong asked.

"At which point he enrolled in the Marine Corps. And I believe most of you know the rest of his story from there," Johannsen concluded. "However, the reason we're here today is to discuss the other two subjects pictured here. If we're able to acquire and test them, we will likely triple our chances of replicating a new, non-lethal adapted genome. Plain and simple."

"And what do you know about these two?" the Secretary asked.

"At this time, nothing," Johannsen answered. "We don't know if they've developed the same abilities as Col. Hayes. And, unfortunately, we don't know where they are. Both children's homes have since closed, and records difficult to obtain. We have a team tracking their histories, and believe we're close to finding one of them."

"This begs the question, however," Armstrong posed, "once you do make contact, what's to say they'll agree to go along with your plans for them?"

"Naturally, we all want to assume that, like Col. Hayes, they would understand the benefit to their country and readily volunteer." Johannsen said simply.

"And if not?" the Secretary cut in.

"Then," Johannsen said, "we have a backup plan to ensure their participation."

"One more question," Armstrong stated. "Though I think I know the answer. Why now?"

"Of course," Johannsen began, understanding Armstrong's meaning. "Aside from the increasing demand for soldiers, I assume you're asking?"

"Yes," Armstrong confirmed.

"Then as you said, you do know the answer," Johannsen replied. "Thanks to the recent increases in the Defense budget, we once again have the funding to continue our research."

"And one more," the Secretary added. "What makes you believe your research will work this time? That you'll be able to duplicate this DNA strand?"

"A fair question," Johannsen concurred. "As I suggested before, the first time around, we didn't have the technology to consistently replicate the genome. Now, however, we do. It's simply a matter of constructing the ideal strand itself."

"One that won't kill the subject, you mean," Armstrong clarified.

"Correct," Johannsen replied.

"Where will this project be housed?" Millett asked.

"After researching our options," Johannsen began, "it's been decided that the best facility to serve our needs for the project would be the Strategic Research Complex, just outside Timberville, Virginia."

"The weapons-development facility?" the Secretary asked, sounding surprised.

"Exactly," Johannsen answered. "It's not only the Department of Defense's most advanced research facility; its excess capacity will afford us all the resources and square footage we need to properly perform our research."

"And you're not at all concerned about the potential risks of housing such a sensitive project, and any outsiders brought in, with everything else that's in that facility?" the Secretary pressed.

"Mr. Secretary, sir," Johannsen replied, "we're fully aware of what else is housed in the subterranean labs. But we've also factored in additional security measures to ensure that no 'outsiders' gain knowledge of that weapons cache."

"Because as I'm sure you're aware," the Secretary continued, "many of the stocks, especially the chemical and biological ones, within that area of the facility are as-yet not fully tested and are highly classified. Not even the President knows of their existence. It is imperative that it remains that way."

"Please consider it duly noted," Johannsen said. "It's been factored into our decision. We can ensure there will be no breach of security."

"All right," the Secretary finally stated. "I think everyone understands what's behind this project as well as the reasons for it. Now fill us in on what needs to be done."

"Thank you, Mr. Secretary," Johannsen responded. "Once we've located the subjects, the plan is to acquire them as quickly as possible. The goal is minimal resistance, with no public knowledge or involvement. In order to do this, we need a team of trained men who specialize in covert, civilian operations such as these. Naturally, this is where the NSA enters the picture," he said, gesturing to Millett and Tolson.

"However, in the event that one of the acquisitions does not go cleanly, our investigative team has worked up a thorough contingency plan to cover several possible scenarios. This is another area where the NSA's involvement can benefit the project.

"The centerpoint of the contingency plan is this: Both subjects are to be apprehended under the pretense of national security. In the event of any resistance, public knowledge, or collateral damage during the course of either encounter, the event will go on record as a response to an imminent terrorist threat. As the NSA is central to most every counter-terrorism effort within our borders, its involvement plays into our story very well. Moreover, the press – and more importantly the public – tends not to question government action whenever the term 'terrorist threat' is brought into play. In the end, this story should suffice to cover any collateral issues which may arise."

"I'll assume this makes sense to everyone," the Secretary surmised, looking around to Armstrong, Millett, and Tolson. "Have you chosen who will head up this phase of the project?"

"That would be me, sir," came Hayes' voice from behind Johannsen.

"No one is as qualified to lead this effort as Col. Hayes," Johannsen explained. "His high-level military experience in covert missions is but one reason. Most importantly, if these two other subjects have in fact developed abilities similar to what we've seen in Col. Hayes, there is no one who understands such abilities, or how to deal with them, as well as he does."

"All right, then," Armstrong stated. "So when does this begin?"

But before the next line was spoken, Loretta's attention darted to her left as she heard the door lock disengage. As she stood up from the chair, the door swung open.

In the open doorway stood Dr. Ingramov, a look of keen surprise upon his face.

56

Confrontation

"Dr. Barnes," Ingramov exclaimed, stepping into the doorway. "What do you think you're doing?"

Loretta almost staggered as she jumped from the chair. Her eyes darted back to the screen, then again to Ingramov.

"What are you people really doing here?" she demanded.

Ingramov glanced over at his workstation, then back to Loretta. "I'm afraid I don't understand your meaning," he said.

"You know damn well what I'm talking about," Loretta shot back. "I went into the lab. I saw the subject; I saw what you did to him. And unless you give me a damned good reason not to, I'm going to blow the whistle on this whole operation."

Ingramov stepped inside the office, closing the door behind him. "I'm … disappointed in you, Dr. Barnes," he said. "Although you and I have had our differences, I'd always hoped that ultimately, if shared with you, you would see –"

"TELL ME!" Loretta shouted.

Ingramov did not move, leaning against the office door. "You have seen the briefing, I see?" he said, gesturing to the DVD case on his desk.

"I've seen enough," she said. "I know what you want to do. I was lied to about this project. But I don't even care about that. The subject … how could you do such … such … *despicable* things to another human being? Where's the gain in that??"

"We needed to test his limits," Ingramov said plainly. "To understand his threshold for physical damage, and the extent of his regenerative capabilities."

"Regenerative?" Loretta repeated.

"You saw it at a cellular level," Ingramov answered. "It's noted in your reports. However, the project dictated that it be taken several levels further."

"By severing one of his fingers?" Loretta exclaimed.

"The full extent of testing entailed the extraction of both limb and internal organ. As you may or may not have noticed, the subject's right kidney had also been removed."

Loretta had no response; she found herself beginning to feel sick.

"As – outlandish as these experiments may seem," he went on, "they are of the utmost necessity toward the success of our operation. Imagine, Dr. Barnes, the ability of a human being to heal wounds more quickly, even to re-grow a limb, or a vital organ. Think of the possibilities – it could change the course of human medicine!"

"But what you're doing to him," she countered, "is inhumane – it's not right."

"Dr. Barnes, what you saw this morning was the result of but one segment of the trials we've undertaken on him," Ingramov said. "As you now know, our goal is to thoroughly understand such things so that we may effectively replicate his DNA for the development of more like him."

"Cloning?" she asked.

"In a manner of speaking," he replied.

"To build some kind of ... of 'super soldier?' To *weaponize* human *beings?"*

"Dr. Barnes," Ingramov explained. "Do you not realize what you're a part of? This is a chance to unlock the very potential of the human genetic code. To create something superior to what we currently are, something that can change the world. A being who is impervious to disease; who possesses extraordinary physical gifts; who can recover from bodily damage in a milli-fraction of the time it takes a normal human to do so. And that is only the beginning."

"But to what end? To wage wars more effectively? This was supposed to be about curing disease, about putting an end to epidemics! Not about making the human body into a killing machine!"

"Again, Dr. Barnes," Ingramov said, "I'm not here to get your approval. I can only hope that you will understand the bigger picture and will continue to perform your assigned duties toward our end goal. Do you understand what I'm saying?"

"This can't continue," Loretta said. "You almost killed him."

"I can assure you we didn't," Ingramov said flatly. "But had that been the case, we are at a stage where the subject is indeed expendable."

"What?" she exclaimed.

"You heard me correctly. There is a second subject, on his way here now," Ingramov explained. "Having him in-house enables us to push our testing of Asset One to its limits, and ultimately, understand exactly at what point termination will occur."

"What? You're *planning* on killing him?"

"It is the only way to fully understand his limits," he said.

"How – how did the Pentagon *approve* this?" she said, stunned.

"They didn't," Ingramov replied coolly. "Not exactly, at least. One of the stipulations of this project is *plausible deniability.* Our superiors know the nature of the research we are undertaking, but they don't know the details of it. We have full sign-off that whatever happens within this lab, they do not need to know. The *results* are all that matter to them."

Without hesitation, Loretta charged forward toward the door. "Let me by," she said, pushing against Ingramov to move him out of the way.

Ingramov pushed back against her, shoving her roughly to the floor. "I'm afraid that's no longer an option," he retorted. "You won't be going anywhere."

Loretta started to get up, but Ingramov moved quickly on top of her, backhanded her across the face, then pulled a taser gun from his lab coat and lunged at her, hitting her in the neck with it. She dropped to the floor, stunned.

"Now," he said heatedly, moving toward the file cabinets on the right-hand wall. "You've given me no choice, Dr. Barnes. I regret what is about to happen."

Reaching into the top drawer of the first cabinet, he removed a clear plastic jar filled with syringes. He pulled one out, reached into a second cabinet, and withdrew a vial. He plunged the syringe into it, filling it with clear fluid.

"This is a triple dose of cyanide," he said, moving back over her. "But it has been altered in a way so as to not be detected in an autopsy."

Loretta stirred but could not move. He grabbed her left arm, moving the needle into position. "This won't take but a moment."

As Ingramov set the needle upon her skin, the door smashed open behind them with a loud bang, sending small bits of steel into the air above their heads.

Dropping the needle as he ducked instinctively, Ingramov turned fully around to the open doorway. His mouth fell open in abject surprise.

In the doorway, fists clenched and eyes afire, stood Elias Todd.

57

Escape

He stood wearing only a bloodied hospital gown, his bare feet planted at shoulder width in the smashed-open doorway.

The broken steel door tottered on one hinge, revealing the two massive indents that Todd's fists had made into it not a second before. His hands were soaked with blood, and his vengeful, hate-filled glare centered directly on Ingramov.

Without a word, Ingramov got up and pulled the taser from his lab coat, but before he could make another move, Todd stepped forward and ripped it from his hands. Turning the taser on himself, he hit the trigger again and again as he pushed it into his chest, his smile exploding into a bizarre, maniacal snarl.

"My ... threshold ... for ... pain," he roared, continuing to tase himself. "What ... about ... yours?" As the words were spoken, he grabbed Ingramov by the collar, pulled him forward, and forced the taser into his open mouth.

When the instrument touched his tongue, Ingramov jolted backward with a horrible scream, toppling over the waist-high filing cabinets before crashing to the floor behind them. His feet hung over the far edge of the cabinet as he lay on the floor, groaning in incredible pain.

Tossing the taser aside, Todd approached Loretta. Placing his blood-soaked hands on her lab coat, he lifted her up from the floor and shook her, trying to rouse her. He spoke urgently, angrily, only inches from her face. "Leave. Now."

Still recovering from the taser's blow, Loretta gazed bleary-eyed back into Todd's menacing glare. Abject fear filled her: he was going to kill Ingramov, she knew this; and if she was still in the room when he'd finished with him, she would undoubtedly be next.

He released her, letting her fall to the floor. He was moving toward Ingramov.

The icy flow of terror coursing through her veins motivated her; she forced herself up, placing a hand on the desktop to her right in an attempt to steady herself. Willing herself to her feet, she heard the first scream from behind her, a chilling, falsetto howl that preceded an awful *crunch*. She did not look back, *could* not look back, at what was happening to Ingramov.

There was a cry, a ripping noise, and another horrible scream. Terrible, high-pitched laughter. She stumbled forward, grabbing onto the smashed door for balance as she reached the doorway. Self-preservation had taken over: *get out before he dies ... get out before he dies.*

She was in the hallway now. Her strength returning with every step, she made her way toward the elevator. As she rounded the corner, she saw the first body: it was Anderson, the young trooper who'd been stationed at the main lab entrance. He was lying flat on his back, a few feet in front of the demolished doors to the lab. Blood had collected in a pool around him. His head was turned cockeyed toward Loretta, his wide, empty eyes staring at nothing. She could see three gaping holes in his forehead.

Choking back a gasp, she averted her eyes and continued to move down the hallway, determined to get to the elevators before it was too late. Before she could remove that first gruesome image from her mind, she looked ahead to where the main hallway intersected with the corridor that led to the elevators, and she saw another pool of blood. Crying out, she staggered, leaning against the wall to keep her feet beneath her.

"God," she whispered, tears streaming down her face. "Oh, God."

Unable to take another step, she shrank back against the wall, clutching desperately to its flat surface, beginning to cry harder.

Why was this happening?

How had he gotten free?

Then suddenly, it dawned on her, like a horrible, surreal nightmare come true.

The serum they'd installed to sap his strength.

She'd removed it when she'd swapped the plasma fluid into his IV.

In her haste to tend to his wounds, she had overlooked the one thing keeping him in check.

He must have regained his strength ... and somehow been able to break out of his titanium bindings.

She had traded the murder of one for the murder of many.

She let out a cry of anguish and guilt.

Elias Todd had turned out to be exactly what Ingramov had been trying to create.

A cold-blooded, murderous, human killing machine.

A monster.

Suddenly, from down the hallway behind her, she heard another, familiar voice. It was Polosky. He had entered Ingramov's office. It was too late to warn him. Though she couldn't make out the words, she could hear his cries of surprise turn to utter terror before descending into screams of pain.

With a feeble moan, Loretta forced herself back up, clutching the wall for support, trying to prepare herself for what she was about to see. Arriving at the intersection, she concentrated on the white areas of the floor, trying her best to avoid the splayed arms, legs, and heads protruding from the giant mass of red that seemed to have spread everywhere. There were at least six bodies. He had killed everyone in his path for the sole reason that they were there.

As she walked, she heard a tiny crackling noise coming from the floor below her. She looked down to see a small earpiece, just beyond the outstretched hand of a soldier in heavy gear similar to Anderson's. Instinctively, she picked it up, keeping her eyes averted from the dead body which lay next to it.

She reached the elevators. She frantically pressed the call button, not wanting to look back at the collection of Todd's victims, not ready to acknowledge the horrific acts he'd just done; acts which, without a doubt, her unknowing actions not one hour before had enabled him to do.

She fought the urge to be sick. But the moment offered no time for remorse; she looked behind her, expecting Todd to be there. He was not.

The elevator doors opened. She stepped inside, so close to escape, hitting the ground floor button once before repeatedly slapping the button below it to close the doors. As they began to slide together, she glanced one more time back into the hallway. Only the bodies appeared in her view, no sign of Todd himself. The doors finally shut.

The elevator began to make its way slowly upward. Then, suddenly, with a deep rumbling noise, the entire building seemed to shake, the elevator walls around Loretta making a clacking noise as it happened.

The elevator came to a shuddering halt as the lights flickered and then went out, leaving Loretta frozen, trapped in absolute darkness.

58

The Lesson

Hers were the eyes he'd longed to see again.

She was wearing a long dark skirt suit; the ruffled collar of her white blouse came halfway up the neck. It was the very same outfit she had been buried in.

She walked to the couch on which Mira had sat. He realized Mira was gone.

"I know what you're about to say," she began. "So out with it, young man."

"I … I *have* to do it," he said.

"Why do you think that?"

"Because examples need to be made. *Someone* has to do this. Why *not* me?"

"Because you're doing it for the wrong reasons."

"Why do you say that?" he said.

"It's not your sense of right and wrong that's behind this, but a *need*. One you've held in check your entire life. And it's a much bigger part of you than you want to admit.

"But there's another reason," she went on. "Something you've never really been able to acknowledge. The world has been unfair to *you*."

"I don't –"

"And in many ways, it's true," she interrupted him. "Your life has never been easy. You were always an outsider. This was sometimes your own fault. But in the end, your life has had its share of unfairness.

"On top of all that," she continued, "you think that, now that I'm gone, you don't feel as compelled to play by the rules anymore. As if you no longer have anyone to be good *for*. All this, combined with the raw *anger* built up inside you, has created what you've become. Giving justice to some, at the expense of others," she said. "All decided by you.

"But your *conscience* knows differently," she went on. "It understands that judgment wasn't meant to be placed into one person's hands. And that killing is wrong."

"That's not true," Rage said. "Those *scum* didn't deserve to live."

"You don't know that. Nor do you know whether they deserved to die."

"I –" he began, then paused, mulling over her words.

Deserve to die.

He'd never doubted himself before this moment. Certainly, the people he'd killed had been guilty of their crimes.

But did they deserve to die?

And what about those—

"You'd let live versus those who you'd killed?" she finished his thought for him.

"Yes," he said.

"In each case, what made you choose who would live or die?" she asked.

He knew the answer: *whichever one he got his hands on first.*

Knowing this, she finished this thought for him as well. "You would kill to satisfy your *own* urges. Once that was done, you'd force your 'Lesson' on the other, feeling that if you let that person live, you'd fulfill your obligation to justice.

"But who's to say," she continued, "that the ones you'd let live deserved to live more than the others?"

Rage had no reply.

"The last time you were in this room, you said that when you save someone, you only save that person once. Do you remember?"

Rage nodded.

"That the victim could still be dealt further injustices – or even commit one themselves. And that's why you don't try to save people.

"But it works both ways," she said.

"It's true that people may continue to suffer, or perhaps even do bad things themselves. But by that same token, if given the chance, they may fix their lives. Yes, there are some people who can't be saved. But there are a lot who can be."

"But how do I –"

"You don't," she finished the thought for him. "You don't know. You don't *ever* know who can be and who can't be. And that's why it's not for you to decide.

"And all this has had its effects on you. The nightmares are only the beginning."

He thought about the nightmares. His own conscience had brought him to the cave, where the creature waited for him. But every time he'd awoken and pulled himself from the nightmare, and every time he'd killed, the being in the cave continued to grow, an expanding, swelling chronicle of those whose lives he had taken.

"You can't deny what's inside of you; the deep-welled anger," she said. "But you *can* decide whether you'll allow it to rule you."

"I know," he said quietly, understanding only now that she was right.

"I remember what you were like when I first met you, when I first brought you into my home," she said. "And you remember too."

He nodded.

"All I ask of you," she continued. "Is that you not forget the *good* in you."

He understood what she meant. Though he couldn't deny what he was, he could control what he would *become.*

There was justice, and there was what he had been doing. There was a difference; he understood that now.

But, he would also need to come to terms with what he had done so far.

"What do I need to do," he asked her quietly.

"You already know," she said. "You need to face them."

It was as she'd said. He already knew this.

But for one of the few times in his life, he was afraid.

"Don't be," she said, reading his thoughts. "You're very brave. You'll do what needs to be done. There's no other way."

She stood up from where she'd been sitting, and he followed. She extended her hand to him, and he took it. The moment their hands touched, the room was transformed, and Rage found himself back in the cave.

It was dark and silent. Exactly as he'd remembered it from every time before.

Georgia Fay stared at him meaningfully before stepping backward, leaving him standing at the center of the cave. Before he knew it she had faded into the cavern wall, leaving him alone without another word spoken.

Within seconds, the rumbling in the distance began.

Rage stood still and waited, anticipating what was coming for him.

As it had done before, the beast hit him across the midsection, harder than he remembered ever being hit. He was thrown straight upward, his arms and legs flailing through the air, before his body came crashing down to the cave's damp, rocky surface.

Once again, he found himself pinned face-down upon the floor, his every breath quick and shallow, clutching at the cold rock surface in unrelenting fear.

The being screamed at him; its horrible roar stabbed into his ears, echoing loudly and angrily throughout the enormous space.

Taking a deep breath, he fought against his beaten muscles, his aching limbs, and pulled himself up, keeping his eyes on the floor the entire time. Finally, he raised his head to look at the thing before him.

It was even larger than he'd imagined.

As he looked upon it, this amalgamation of souls before him, he recognized many of the faces staring back at him, some of them fearful, some of them vengeful, all of them fixed upon him.

Stepping toward him, it let out another heart-rending roar, its forceful breath a hot wind that blew against his face, his hair, burning into his eyes, his nostrils, blasting against his skin.

Rage stood there, arms at his sides, as the creature moved in on him.

He was ready to accept the Lesson that only he had created, and that, in the end, only he could receive.

59

Lost Contact

Dark storm clouds had begun to gather off to the west.

What was still a bright mid-day sun shone down on the roof of the black transport as it sped east on Pennsylvania Interstate, casting a moving glare back into the sky.

Hayes checked his watch; it was just past one o'clock P.M. They were only a few hours away now. He'd just heard updates from both Clive and Hill, who were now en route to the SRC; he was expecting Ingramov's next scheduled update to come across his alert pager at any moment.

With the acquisition of Asset Two, Ingramov's team had begun Level Two testing of Asset One, a series of unprecedented experiments that would likely push the subject to the point of termination.

Hayes was quite eager to hear the results.

Moments passed. No contact from Ingramov.

Becoming impatient, he dialed up Ingramov's alert pager.

Another moment passed; still no response.

With a grunt, he dialed up the SRC's Central Command. He would have them page Ingramov within the building or send someone to retrieve him.

The line rang several times. No answer.

Someone was assigned to the CentCom post 24 hours a day, without exception.

Outside the building, at the front access gate, was the main security guard post. He dialed the remote pager number designated for that post. After three rings, the guard on duty responded.

"Point one access," the guard answered, a note of exasperation in his voice. "Corporal Aaron speaking."

"Colonel Hayes," he identified himself. "Need status on comms inside the SRC; no response from within the complex. Send someone in to investigate immediately and report back."

"Ten-four," replied the guard. "Sir, not sure if this is related, but just a minute ago, the ground shook pretty heavily, like an earthquake. Again might or might not be related, but we'll have two men go in immediately."

"Earthquake? What exactly happened?" Hayes pressed.

"Don't know, sir," Aaron said. "But it rattled the windows in the shack here."

"Bring your comm with you into the complex and report in to me as soon as you see anything out of place. And find Dr. Ingramov; he needs to contact me immediately."

"Yes, sir," the guard replied. "Corporal Bataille and myself going in now."

"Out," Hayes responded, clipping the alert pager back into his belt.

Moments later, the pager began to vibrate. Hayes picked it up.

"What've you got?" he demanded.

"Colonel Hayes, sir," Aaron's voice came into the headset, his tone severe. "Situation is code red. We are going to need immediate backup, sir."

"What?" Hayes exclaimed. "Corporal, where are you? What do you see?"

"Underground Labs, north end. There are bodies everywhere, sir," Aaron explained, his voice shaken. "No survivors that we've found. Facility has lost power, only emergency lighting. Corporal Bataille and myself are in the main hallway. Will continue to look for survivors but request –"

"No," Hayes interrupted. "Lock down the facility immediately. No one gets in or out. Enable emergency protocol measures, place all outside security detail on high alert. Put a soldier at every exit possible. Call in every off-duty trooper. Once you've done that, report back in to me."

"Yes, sir," Aaron replied.

Todd. He must have escaped, thought Hayes.

Then the worst-case scenario dawned on him: *the weapons cache.*

If Todd were to find it, he could launch an outward assault on any surrounding forces, perhaps even destroy the entire facility.

As he was deep in thought, a small burst of static emitted from the earpiece, then went silent.

He would need to debrief the inner circle.

But first he needed to put every soldier he had between Todd and that weapons stockpile.

He spoke into the earpiece: "Aaron. New orders. You and Bataille head immediately to the south end of the labs, to the security checkpoint leading to the storehouse. Call ten more on-duty troopers to that location. Need to cover all possible angles. The weapons cache needs to be secured. Do not let anyone by, and shoot to kill. Repeat: weapons cache must be protected at all costs. Do you read?"

Hayes' earpiece remained silent for a moment. Then came the words, in a low, deliberate tone:

"Weapons cache?"

And then silence.

Hayes did not have to presume whom the voice belonged to. He switched off his alert pager. There was no communicating, no negotiating, with the subject. It was clear he'd killed Aaron and Bataille and was now aware of the weapons cache within the facility. The nightmare scenario had come true.

The SRC had been compromised.

Activating his alert pager once again, he initiated the emergency protocol procedure. Hitting a six-digit code into the keypad, he simultaneously dialed up Johannsen, the Secretary of Defense, and the others.

Given this new development, they needed to decide upon the rules of engagement for dealing with Chief Asset Number One.

60

Bloodpath

Elias Todd stood over the bodies of the two armored troopers, the dark red pool of blood slowly spreading on the floor beneath his bare, blood-covered feet.

He rolled the tiny earpiece between his thumb and forefinger for a moment, considering it, before tossing it carelessly onto the body of the trooper he'd pulled it from.

Turning his head, he looked back down the darkened hallway. The dead glow of the emergency lighting system illuminated the bare white brick walls and the passageway to the facility's south end.

Weapons cache.

The smile spread broadly across his face.

He had no idea how many he'd killed in the past hour or so, but his hunger for it had not nearly abated. There would be more.

And the best part was, they would come to *him.*

Now that they knew he was loose in their prized, multi-billion-dollar facility, they would soon be setting up a perimeter, making plans to storm the complex.

And he would need to make plans of his own.

Step one had been to kill everyone in the facility. Not one had been left alive, other than the woman who had been in Ingramov's office.

He wasn't sure why he'd let her go. Nor did he have time to dwell on it.

The next step had been to cut off all power to the facility.

This move would prevent any survivors from communicating with the outside, and it would neutralize any surveillance and motion-tracking devices. There would be no way of knowing where he was in the complex, or what he was doing.

He knew a facility like this one would have its own power generator, and, being a military installation, an armory. It did not take him long to find both.

In the armory, he found a rocket-propelled grenade launcher along with semiautomatic pistols, rifles, sniper rifles, and hand grenades. Slinging the RPG launcher over his shoulder, he made his way to the generator room, where he promptly smashed through the locking mechanism. Once inside, he rigged two RPGs to the generator along with an improvised fuse. He then lit it and ran away.

The ensuing explosion shook the entire complex. Todd had given himself enough time to make it to the northwest end of the building, but the shock of the blast still knocked him off his feet. All lighting in the complex immediately went out; the faint hum of the facility's numerous machines and equipment spooled down to a halt.

A brief second later, the emergency lighting activated, providing just enough light to illuminate a path along the complex's vast maze of hallways.

Now that he'd taken those necessary steps, it was time to find the weapons stockpile.

Stepping over the bodies of the two troopers, he headed toward the facility's south end.

61

Rules of Engagement

"*Compromised?*" came the voice over Hayes' headset, the panic in its tone clear.

"Affirmative, Mr. Secretary," Hayes replied. "The SRC has been compromised. Contact made with the subject himself moments ago. Exact whereabouts within the complex unknown."

"How could this happen?" the Secretary demanded.

"Unknown at this point, sir," Hayes responded. "First priority is to neutralize the threat immediately; upon completion of that, we'll conduct a full investigation and undertake recovery efforts of any damages."

"My God," the Secretary said. "Everyone in the complex –"

"Dead. Almost certainly, sir," Hayes said. "As everyone is already aware, we are dealing with an extremely dangerous individual."

"And the weapons cache?" Armstrong came in. "Is that at risk?"

"I don't believe so, at this point," Hayes lied. "But it reaffirms the need to deploy troops to the compound immediately, to secure it and neutralize the threat."

"What is your ETA at the compound again, Colonel?" Millett chimed in.

"Approximately four o'clock P.M., local time," Hayes replied. "Well over two hours. It's too large a window."

"Who knows what he could be doing in there," Armstrong said.

"He's likely escaped by now," Tolson added.

"An escape attempt hasn't been made as of yet," Hayes replied. "Although he's cut the power inside the complex, external motion trackers and cameras have spotted no sign of him leaving the building."

"What could he be doing in there?" Armstrong said.

"I don't believe we want to afford him the time for us to find out," Johannsen finally commented. "I stand behind Col. Hayes on the need to move in now."

"What's your plan, Colonel," the Secretary said.

"Standard surround-and-penetrate approach," Hayes began. "I'll need fifty men, Class 2 soldiers or above. Five armed transports, .50-caliber mounts on each. Begin with tear gas through strategic openings; smoke him out. Twenty-five will surround the complex, twenty-five will go in, five into each of the entrances, covering all sides."

"Tranquilize?" Tolson asked.

"Orders will be shoot to kill, immediately upon sight," Hayes replied. "We can't afford to take any chances."

"What are the odds he's discovered the armory?" Armstrong inquired.

"Very likely," Hayes said. "But despite the danger he poses, he's only one man. That gives him one shot before his position is compromised, and we're on him. That's why we need to go in big, and from all angles. We'll lose a few men, without a doubt. But it will be over, and quickly."

"Unless he gets into that weapons cache," the Secretary said darkly.

"Mr. Secretary, sir, even if he was –"

"Col. Hayes," the Secretary cut across him, knowing where he was going. "Even *you* haven't been briefed on the magnitude of what's in there. But let me assure you of this: if *one* individual gets his hands on certain weapons in that room, even a battalion of a *thousand* men would be at risk. Instantly.

"What is in that room, as we've suggested before," he went on, "are several stocks of experimental conventional, chemical, and biological weapons, many of them not fully tested, some of them likely too dangerous to ever be put into production. When combined with the vast amount of advanced conventional munitions in there, the amount of explosive power contained in that room could easily wipe a good chunk of the state of Virginia off the map ... killing everyone within a hundred-plus-mile radius. That is no exaggeration, not in the least.

"And then there's the hardware," he continued. "There are several prototypes designed for dispensing those chem and bio mixtures, many of which can cover the area the size of a football field or more in about two seconds.

"If he gets ahold of them," the Secretary concluded, "we will be sending those men into a death trap. It will, as you say, be over, and quickly."

"But," Tolson interjected, "even if he does find the stockpile, what are the chances he'll know how to use any of it?"

"Undersecretary Tolson, if you'd read the file on him," Armstrong answered testily, "then you'd know the subject is a weapons expert well beyond what we classify as 'specialist' level. Searches of his estate uncovered a huge collection of weapons, an underground firing range, even designs of firearms that had never been seen before. We have to assume that he will know, or quickly figure out, how to deploy them."

"All the more reason, sir," Hayes added determinedly, "to move in now."

Silence came over Hayes' headset, as the Secretary was clearly mulling over all possible options.

"Gentlemen," the Secretary said, "what we have effectively done here is swallow our own grenade. We have taken presumably one of the most dangerous men in the world and locked him in with the deadliest store of weapons imaginable. We will without a doubt need to understand exactly how this happened. But for the matter at hand, we have no choice; we have to extract him now before any further damage is done.

"Mission approved," he said firmly. "But Col. Hayes, get this done right, and quickly. The more soldiers die, the more we have to cover. And the more we have to cover, the messier this entire operation becomes."

"Sir, it will be done, sir," Hayes said quickly.

"And Colonel," the Secretary added.

"Sir," Hayes replied.

"Do not let him near that weapons cache," he said. "He breaches that, and he's as dangerous as the intel suggests, we could have a damned catastrophe on our hands."

62

Buried Treasure

Todd stepped inside the storeroom, glancing around in all directions.

After blowing his way through two vault-like doors at opposite ends of a long hallway, then descending down several flights of stairs, he was in.

The storeroom was separated from the rest of the facility, and at least one hundred feet below ground. The cool chamber was enormous inside, perhaps the length of a football field. It had a concrete floor and a twenty-five-foot ceiling. Rows of high, wide storage racks ran the length of the cavernous room. A forklift sat alone at the far wall.

Overhead, rows of hanging lights shone dimly. The storeroom clearly had its own, separate power generator.

Turning, Todd made his way toward the racks lining the center of the warehouse.

As he walked along them, he noticed a wide range of conventional, chemical, and biological compounds, most of which he'd never heard of. Each was stored in a separate, air-tight, stainless steel container. All had markings with similar information: date of manufacture, capabilities, Haz-Mat level, and other numeric codes he couldn't decipher.

Several of them were marked "EXPERIMENTAL ONLY." Perhaps they weren't stable enough; perhaps their power was too destructive; perhaps there were other reasons.

He came upon a row marked "EXPERIMENTAL FIREARMS."

The firearms were marked in a similar manner to the stocks, including which conventional, chemical, or biological discharges were compatible for use with each shooter. Also similar to the discharges, each firearm had been stored in its own, separate steel container, roughly the size of a large suitcase. Every casing had a large steel handle centered on the end facing Todd.

He pulled out the casing closest to him. It was marked "Dev. Weapon 26.2, Range Thrower class, for use with liquid compounds 231.28 and 517.65 ONLY."

He set it upon the floor. The carton itself had been heavier than he'd anticipated; he imagined the weapon itself inside it would be as substantial.

He opened the case. Inside were two jet-black, intricately detailed, snub-nosed rifles, no greater than a foot in length. Jutting out from the underpinnings of each butt end were two half-inch long nozzles. Attachment points for feeder tubes, he assumed.

Leaving the firearm casing on the floor, Todd proceeded back into the previous rows, in search of chemical compounds 231.28 and 517.65.

Two rows down, he located stock 231.28, stacked about twelve feet up.

Todd scaled the rack and pulled the top carton from its slot. It weighed at least three hundred pounds. Holding the crate under his left arm, he scaled back down with his right, grabbing the steel rack every few feet as he repelled back down to the floor.

He opened the casing and counted ten three-liter containers. In a slot in the upper compartment was the carrying apparatus. It had a simple backpack design, complete with clear, detachable tubes that connected to the nozzles on each firearm.

Also in the upper compartment was a clear sleeve with a folded document inside. He pulled it out. A specification sheet for the compound. It read:

231.28 DIOBENZATE URIDIUM SULFATE

DATE OF MANUFACTURE: 11-Mar-2011

DAMAGE CLASS 9.2

CODE 56-344: EXTREME CAUTION HANDLING, STORE AT 62 DEGREES F

FOR USE WITH ADVANCED RANGE CLASS CHEM THROWERS ONLY

WARNING: EXPOSURE TO OPEN AIR IS FATAL TO 20-METER RANGE, USE EXTREME CAUTION WHEN AFFIXING TO DISPENSING UNIT

Todd scanned down the spec sheet, scouring page after page. The compound was a combustible acidic mixture, ignitable within seconds' exposure to open air. Capable of eating through most any material including advanced body armor, it was also highly flammable and would instantly set its target aflame upon contact.

He glanced around him, his eyes moving along the racks.

He imagined exactly how much destructive power was in this room.

And that's when it came to him.

If he were to rig the entire room to blow … there was no telling how far its effects would reach.

His mind working again, Todd stood up, beginning to assemble the elements that would make up his ultimate plan.

63

Deathtrap

The rain had begun to fall on the rolling hills of northwestern Virginia; lightning flickered in the far-off sky.

The five armored transports rumbled along old Route 74, the narrow, winding country road that fed into the massive industrial park. Dust and gravel kicked up in the vehicles' wake as they approached the entrance, the lead vehicle slowing as it neared the turn into the compound.

The park itself was an expansive, twenty-square mile spread of landscape that housed twelve separate low-lying complexes, most of them distribution facilities or R&D centers of public companies.

Inside the lead transport, Lieutenant Thomas Oberlin pored over the schematics of the SRC itself, reviewing the penetration strategy outlined by his superiors. Only one hour ago he had been at home, celebrating his daughter's sixth birthday.

He glanced through the debrief. He hadn't been given much intel on the situation inside the SRC, only that an armed and dangerous fugitive had holed himself up in there, killing several inside. Basic description: white male around thirty years old, about six feet tall with normal build and dark hair. Not much else to go on. Orders were to surround and penetrate the facility, engage the fugitive on sight, shoot to kill.

The primary goal of the operation was to salvage the facility and the enormous amount of classified data inside. Collateral damage, meaning the lives of any surviving hostages inside, was secondary. These orders did not sit well with Oberlin, but they were his orders to follow, not question.

With all the men and firepower under his command, he understood the severity of the situation: the NSA wouldn't throw fifty Class 2 troops and five armored transports with .50-caliber mounts at a minor threat. Whoever was in there posed a significant danger and needed to be put down immediately.

The first bout of thunder boomed overhead, and lightning lit up the sky.

The execution plan was straightforward: launch tear gas capsules through twelve strategic access points in the complex to disorient the subject, then send a five-man squad into each of the five entrances. The remaining troops would surround the facility, each at a predetermined checkpoint, including four at designated sniper posts.

Each of the soldiers was equipped with standard-issue gas masks and special visors, complete with night vision, motion tracking, and heat-signature-detection settings, to ensure that his men would see the target before he saw them.

They would arrive within moments. He radioed to his squadron leaders:

"Miller, Saunders, Benjamin. Wright, Carruthers, Thomas. Nelson, Andrews."

"Copy," the eight men replied almost in unison.

"One last run-through. Miller, Saunders, Benjamin, Wright, Carruthers: ten seconds after gas modules have been launched, proceed immediately to marked entry points. Shoot to kill upon sight; no exceptions. Collateral damage second priority.

"Thomas, Nelson: take up surround positions at designated spots around facility. Thomas, three in your squad and Nelson, two in yours will man the mounts on each transport. Anyone you see exiting the facility even remotely matching the suspect's description, shoot to kill immediately.

"Andrews, proceed to sniping posts, then activate visors. Penetration teams are equipped with jamming equipment for motion-trackers. If you see anything on your motion trackers, again, shoot to kill."

"Sir, copy, sir," each responded.

Oberlin was to remain in the lead vehicle to relay progress reports back to Central Command. He would have rather been in there with his men, but orders required moment-by-moment progress updates.

The rain outside had intensified, tapping loudly on the transport's canvas roof.

He pulled a notebook computer off the dash and switched it on. Each squadron leader was equipped with a helmet-mounted camera that would relay the video feed directly back to the notebook's wireless receiver, allowing Oberlin to see what they were seeing, as well as recording the feeds directly onto the notebook's hard drive.

As the lead transport approached the SRC's security gate, the driver informed Oberlin of its status. "Gate is unmanned, sir," he said.

"Run through," Oberlin ordered.

The driver stepped on the gas, and the transport rammed through the reinforced-steel gate, onto the perimeter access road surrounding the complex.

"Head to the first parking lot. Park in the center of the lot, facing outward."

He spoke into the headset: "Transports two, three, remain here. Park twenty yards apart. Four, five, proceed to opposite lot."

Moments later, after confirming that all were in position, he gave the order. "On my mark, deploy tear gas charges. Ready, deploy."

Almost in unison, a series of popping and hissing noises signaled the launch of the twelve tear gas charges, deployed from each transport. In the distance, the sound of windows shattering could be heard. The capsules were inside and had begun to dispense the disruptive vapors. Oberlin began his stopwatch to count down to the time of attack.

"On my word," he said. "Attack squadrons: deploy. Go, go, go!"

At those words, Oberlin watched as groups of soldiers emptied from the rear of the vehicles.

Seconds later: "Thomas. Nelson. Deploy surround teams. Go!"

Finally: "Andrews. On my word, deploy to sniping posts. Go!"

Oberlin addressed his attack squadrons: "Penetrate teams: confirm in position."

"Alpha: in position," came Miller's voice.

"Beta: in position," came Saunders.

"Charlie: in position," came Benjamin.

"Delta: in position," came Wright.

"Eagle: in position," came Carruthers.

Oberlin issued the command: "Move in."

As the order was made, Oberlin's eyes moved to the eight images being broadcast on his notebook computer screen. Images one through five were being issued from each penetrate squadron leader's helmet, six and seven from the surround teams, and eight from Andrews, from his sniping post off to the northeast. The rainfall had slightly clouded the signal, but he was able to make out most of what they were seeing.

Suddenly, there was an explosion. Followed almost instantly by a second, third, and fourth. Oberlin instinctively whirled around to see a fireball erupting from the entrance nearest to them, and another fireball swelling at the southern entrance. He glanced down at his computer screen to see that images one, two, three, and four had all gone blank, replaced only by static.

Oberlin addressed his men urgently: "Surround and sniper teams, hold your positions! Teams Alpha, Beta, Charlie, Delta, Eagle, what is your status? Respond!"

"Eagle, we are inside the compound," came Carruthers' voice crackling through the headset. "Sir, we heard explosions around the building. Investigate?"

"No," Oberlin responded. "Remain on plan with the mission. Find the target and take him down. I repeat: locate target and take him down.

"Thomas. Nelson," he barked to his surround team leaders. "Send two of your men in; Thomas, send one each to entry points one and two, Nelson, yours to three and four. Confirm status of teams and report."

"Yes, sir," replied both Thomas and Nelson.

His mind working frantically to figure out what had happened, Oberlin attempted to contact the four squadron leaders one more time. "Miller. Saunders. Benjamin. Wright. Respond."

Seconds passed. No reply.

The target must have booby-trapped all the entrances but one. He could think of no other explanation.

"Carruthers," he addressed the Eagle squadron leader. "We have reason to believe Alpha, Beta, Charlie, and Delta teams are all down. Repeat: teams one through four out. Only your squad made it in. Use extreme caution. Stay per contingency plan: remain in formation with your men, do not separate. I repeat: do not separate. Read?"

"Read, sir," Carruthers responded. "Eagle, out."

"Thomas. Nelson. Tell your men to be alert out there. Target has—"

Before he could finish that statement Oberlin heard a series of screams from outside, sounding from all directions. He looked out the transport's side mirror to see someone running, completely engulfed in flame. Then, to his horror, he saw the others: at least eight of his men were in view, their bodies ablaze from head to toe, each of them running and stumbling in different directions before falling to the ground in heaps of flame, burning brightly and strongly even in the heavy downpour.

"Disperse and fall back!" he shouted into his earpiece, realizing what was happening. "I repeat: fall back! Move away from the building, head for cover beyond the grounds. Regroup –"

With an ear-shattering roar, the transport to their left exploded, sending bits of burning shrapnel into the cabin, the force of the blast rocking the vehicle hard to the right. The burning transport had launched into the air, landing several yards forward from where it had parked. He could hear the return fire of the .50-caliber mount begin to issue from the rear of his transport.

"Move, now!" Oberlin screamed at the driver.

As the driver pulled the vehicle forward and stepped on the gas, a single bullet sliced its way through the cabin, punching a hole through the windshield. The driver's head slumped forward onto the wheel, and the transport swung abruptly to the left, almost toppling upon its two right wheels. Oberlin unfastened his harness and threw the door open, diving out and rolling toward the lawn at the parking lot's edge. Bullets sliced the air on either side of him as he zig-zagged toward the cover of trees, one of them grazing his leg, another hitting him in the center of the back, his Kevlar vest stopping it just short of his skin. He did not turn around but was blown into the air as his transport exploded, followed quickly by the one next to it. Arms flailing, he was thrown into the first line of trees, crashing into a giant maple before tumbling to the ground.

Realizing he had no time to shake off the impact, Oberlin scrambled behind the tree for cover. Waves of pain extended across his body like rippling water. His head was throbbing, and he could taste fresh blood on his tongue.

There was more than one target in the complex; there had to be.

Clutching at his ear to cover it from the roar behind him, he barked hoarsely into the headset: "Carruthers. Thomas. Nelson. Andrews. Report!"

"Thomas," replied the panicked, heaving voice in his headset.

"Andrews," came the second.

"Carruthers," came the third.

"Nelson? Report!" Oberlin urged.

There was no reply.

Christ, he thought. *I've got to get them out of there and to a rallying point, now.*

"Andrews," he shouted. "Keep your men in position in the trees, and stay low. Shoot at anything coming out of that building that's not ours. Thomas, gather all your remaining men and anyone who can respond from Nelson's squad, and scatter for the trees. Carruthers, get your men out of there, stat. Anything or anyone gets in your way, blow it sky high. And stay alert; there are likely more than one of them in there. Thomas, Carruthers: rally at point oh-oh-one on your GPS units, transmitting code now. Andrews, your men stay put til I give word. Read?"

"Read, sir," their voices responded.

"Go! Out." he commanded.

Pulling out his GPS unit, Oberlin punched in the rally coordinates, then radioed Central Command. "Oberlin to CentCom," he issued. "CentCom, do you read?"

"CentCom," replied the tinny voice through his earpiece. "What's your sta —"

"Code Red. I repeat, Code Red," Oberlin interrupted. "More than half my men are down, at least three transports taken out, maybe all. Target is using unknown tech and remains loose in the complex. Maybe at least three or four of them in there. Issued orders to fall back and regroup at rally point oh-oh-one. We are going to need backup, stat. Also require extraction for any injured or dead. Copy?"

"Copy that," came the voice. "Orders are to patch any updates through to Head of Operation first before issuance of changes to plan. Will respond momentarily. Out."

"Repeat?" Oberlin shot back, not sure he'd heard correctly. "This is not a change of plan, my men are getting slaughtered! I need backup *now!*"

But the relay was gone.

"Damn it!" he shouted, throwing down his helmet in disgust.

Wincing as his aching joints cracked into motion, he began moving through cover of trees toward the rallying point.

In the depths of the SRC, Sergeant Antonio Carruthers clicked his headset to standby. They'd only been inside the complex three minutes, and in that small span of time, all hell had broken loose: apparently the operation had lost four squadrons to God-knows-what, and they were already being ordered to retreat. He still felt they could take down the target, but he had to follow their C.O.'s orders, like it or not.

He addressed his men, the beam of his helmet-mounted light illuminating their young faces. "Hart, Snell, Roth, DeFranco, we're moving out," he ordered. "Remain in Eagle Flank formation. Shoot at anything, I mean *anything* that moves. Now let's go."

Carruthers leading, the five men quickly made their way back toward the entry point. He didn't need to tell his men to watch for bodies: the corridors were littered with them. At least fifteen he'd counted. Blood lined the floorways; there were even a few limbs scattered about, as if the target had literally torn his victims apart. The facility had been turned into a slaughterhouse.

At the intersection of two of the main hallways, Hart called out in a low voice. "Sergeant Carruthers, sir, I think you need to see this."

Carruthers moved over toward him. "What is it, Corporal?" he said, pointing his helmet light in the direction Hart's had been aimed.

Hart had yet to reply when Carruthers' light revealed the small device that had been mounted to a low point on the wall. He recognized the C-4 compound affixed to it, enough to flatten a good section of the building.

"It looks like a detonation unit, sir," Hart finally said. "But I swear I don't remember seeing it on the way in."

Carruthers looked more closely at the device. On it was a small timer, its red LED display blocked out from view by what appeared to be black marker.

As if whoever had put it there didn't want it to be seen in the dark.

He moved within inches of the timer, his light shining directly on the display, trying to get a look at what it read.

Eight hours, fifty-three minutes. The seconds counted down as he looked on.

He checked his watch. Seven minutes past fifteen hundred hours.

It was set to detonate at midnight.

"Sir," DeFranco exclaimed several feet away, "another one around the corner!"

"And another one here by the elevator shafts," Snell added. "And I see more of them down the hallway, at least five or six."

Carruthers plucked his alert pager from his belt, punching in the code for his C.O.

"Oberlin," came the voice, choppy and short of breath.

"Carruthers, reporting in," he replied. "Sir, we have a situation here."

"Go ahead," Oberlin responded.

"Found several detonation devices in lower level corridors," he said. "Appears target has wired complex to blow at Oh-twenty-four-hundred-hours."

"Jesus," Oberlin replied. "I'll report it in immediately, get an anti-bomb unit inside, stat. In the meantime, get out of there. Out."

"Out," Carruthers replied, replacing his headset. "Let's keep moving, men."

As they neared the narrow vestibule that led to the exit stairs, a small clinking sound echoed once throughout the otherwise deathly quiet corridor.

Carruthers held up his men. "Outward formation," he said in a low voice, and the men moved into position facing outward from one another, their M-16s at the ready.

"Do not move til I say," he murmured.

The five soldiers remained in position, helmet lights illuminating the space around them, listening for any sound in the dark space, hearing only their own shallow breathing.

Suddenly from somewhere in the darkness came a tiny, sharp whoosh, as if a small valve had been opened. There was a brief noise that sounded like spraying water, and from behind him Carruthers could hear Snell make a surprised noise. Then he burst into flame, screaming.

"Jesus!" Carruthers yelled. "Open fire, all directions!"

The sound of automatic gunfire filled the corridor, hammering through the space like an explosion. Snell, consumed completely in flame, had grabbed onto DeFranco in terror, who in turn was fighting him off in order to keep from going ablaze himself. In the madness that ensued, Carruthers could hear screaming and yelling all around him, the flash of bullets lighting up the small area. He saw DeFranco kick the burning mass that was Snell into the far wall, where Snell promptly collapsed to the floor, then fight to keep the flames from spreading up his arm and leg, the sound of his shrieking voice partially drowned out by the unrelenting roar of gunfire. He turned to his left to see Roth's head blow apart, his body crumpling straight to the ground amidst a shower of blood. Through the din, Carruthers thought he'd almost heard the sound of high-pitched laughter. He continued to fire blindly in every direction, unable to track the target, yelling into his headset: "Team Eagle! We are pinned down in the building! Lost Snell, lost Roth! Need backup immediately! I repeat, need backup, now!"

At that moment, he looked over to see DeFranco, unable to quell the flames that had quickly spread across his body, fall to the floor in a blazing heap.

He grabbed Hart by the shoulder. "Let's move," he ordered, and the two men ran directly for the door, the flash of gunfire from their M-16s leading the way. About ten feet from the exit, Carruthers felt a strong tug from Hart, whose legs seemed to buckle, so he pulled him harder. "Come on, move," he urged, before looking to his right to see Hart's head turned awkwardly to the side, his neck having been broken.

"Jesus Christ!" Carruthers exclaimed in terror, then looked around behind him, dropping Hart and pointing the gun in all directions, firing off rounds. "Where are you, you son of a bitch!" he screamed. "Come out and fight like a man!"

The room went silent for a moment, Carruthers looking around, trying to get a glimpse of the target.

A low, gurgling, almost childish laughter came from behind him.

Carruthers whirled around.

There, standing just inside the exit door, his shape illuminated by the fiery glow of DeFranco's and Snell's burning corpses, stood the target.

"You want me ... here I am," the silhouette said softly.

Carruthers' helmet light flashed upon the target's taut face. The orange, crackling glow of fire in the room gave him the appearance of some sort of perverse demon.

Roaring at the top of his lungs, Carruthers charged forward toward the target, firing the M-16 in rapid succession. Before he'd taken two steps, the target ducked low beneath the line of fire, coming up underneath with a blinding quickness he'd never seen the likes of before. In one swift motion, the target had jettisoned the M-16 from his grip before landing a crushing uppercut to his jaw. Carruthers flew backward into the air, landing with a crash against the far brick wall. Before he could fall to the floor the target was once again upon him, holding him up by the neck, a fiendish smile upon his face.

Despite the intense pain, Carruthers grasped at the target's forearm, his fingernails digging into the man's skin, trying to rip the tremendous grip away from his neck. In response the target merely grabbed onto Carruthers' grasp with his free hand, pulling the hand away and crushing it with horrific ease. He laughed as Carruthers screamed.

"Sergeant ... Carruthers," the target said upon finding Carruthers' badge, "you probably had *no idea* what you were heading into, did you."

Struggling for air, Carruthers did not reply, fighting the pain in his jaw and hand.

"The funny thing is," he continued, "I'll bet your superiors knew. Not a good feeling being put up for slaughter, is it? Like some kind of animal."

Carruthers squinted, choking and gasping for air beneath the target's unyielding hold around his neck.

"But now," he said, searching Carruthers' equipment belt. A second later he found the combat blade, "comes the *real* fun part."

The terrible, piercing laughter began once again, quickly overpowered by Carruthers' horrific screams.

Outside, Oberlin arrived at the rallying point to see Thomas and two of his men there, waiting for others to arrive.

"Thomas," he addressed the squad leader. "Eyes open. The three of you form a perimeter around this spot. Who do we have?"

"Myself, Phillips and Ramirez here," Thomas replied. "George, Danvers, Lau and Forde on their way."

Only eight of us, Oberlin thought. *Carruthers' and Andrews' units leave seventeen total. I've lost two-thirds of my men.*

He forced the thought from his mind. The target was still out there, and if what Carruthers had found was legitimate, the danger had just become far greater.

Once again, he punched in the code for CentCom. The relay picked up.

"Oberlin, reporting in from fallback position," he began quickly. "Lost at least two-thirds of my men. Target or targets are still at large, have wired SRC complex. Eagle unit found multiple C-4 pods in lower level corridors. Again, will need heavy backup and anti-bomb unit to location immediately. Copy?"

"Copy, Lieutenant," the voice came back. "Patching through to Head of Ops."

Seconds later a deep voice came through the line: "Hayes. Report."

"Oberlin, reporting in," he began, then repeated: "Code Red situation. Two-thirds of my men are down, target is still inside complex; has wired several C-4 pods in basement. Set to blow at Oh-twenty-four-hundred hours."

"Copy. Unit en route to arrive within the hour. Will assemble bomb unit immediately. In the meantime, ready your men for second offensive."

"Sir," Oberlin replied, stunned. "Likely multiple targets in there; dug in and using unknown tech. Wiped out over thirty men and all five transports in a matter of seconds. Going back in without the proper plan would be suicide."

"There is only *one* of them in there, Lieutenant," the voice said tersely. "You will follow orders. Assemble at new rallying point, stat. Sending coordinates now."

"Sir," Oberlin countered angrily. "I *cannot* send these men back in without –"

"You WILL follow orders or I will have you court-martialed, Lieutenant!" Hayes shouted back at him. "Assemble at the rallying point and move in. Maintain radio silence; break silence only with *major* updates. Out."

The line was gone.

Oberlin was at a loss. What they were being ordered to do was nothing short of suicide. The target had set up a goddamned firing squad in there, and all he had done was line his men up as target practice.

He turned to see that Danvers and George had joined the group, with Lau and Forde coming into view through the trees. Lau and George were limping severely.

He dialed up the sniper unit. "Andrews," he began. "Any movement by the target inside the complex?"

The other end was silent.

"Andrews, Sniper Unit," he addressed the squad. "Do you copy? Over."

Seconds passed; still nothing.

"Carruthers. Eagle unit," he addressed Carruthers' unit. Desperation entered his voice. "Do you copy?"

"Eagle unit, respond!" he barked after a second's silence.

The faint hiss coming from the earpiece signaled that they were all alone.

Oberlin stood in disbelief. In the moments when he and his men had fallen back, the target had taken out the rest of his men, including, inexplicably, the sniping unit that had been behind cover. He and the seven men in his view were all that remained.

Gathering himself, he turned to address his remaining troops. "Men," he began with a long breath, "here's our situation. Our target has turned out to be far more dangerous than our superiors had planned. And as a result we're all that's left."

The men stared back at him, stunned.

"Jesus!" Danvers exclaimed. "Who in God's name is in there, Lieutenant?"

"I don't know," Oberlin said. "But we need to get ready. We're going back in."

"What?!" Danvers again interjected. "All respect aside, sir, you might as well just shoot us all right here!"

"Not another word, Corporal," Oberlin shot back. "Now the Op Head has a unit en route to provide backup within the hour. The facility has also been wired to blow, and an anti-bomb unit has been deployed."

"Sir," George finally came in. "What's our plan?"

"Ops has just sent us a new rallying point. We're going to proceed to it as a unit, sticking together and watching each others' backs. There is a remote chance the target may have exited the facility, so we need eyes open. Once at the rally point we'll divide into four two-man units and push forward into the facility in search of the target."

"Sir, does Ops know how many of them are in there?" Forde asked.

"One," Oberlin said. "Now let's move out. And be ready for anything."

64

Enclosed Spaces

In the pitch blackness of the elevator, Loretta Barnes remained completely still, not making a sound.

The elevator itself felt like some sort of unintended panic room - confining, suffocating, yet protective from the chaos that had ensued outside. The screams had mostly stopped, but every few minutes the walls rattled from the explosions, which, although fewer in number, were still going off sporadically.

Loretta had been trapped for nearly three hours now, her only connection to the outside world was the tiny, crackling sound of voices coming through the earpiece she held in her right hand.

Though its tiny speaker could issue sound, it had been damaged when its previous owner had died. It did not work when she tried to use it to call for help.

At the first sound of those tinny, crackling voices, she held out hope that they were coming for her; that she would soon be safe.

But in the past few moments, many of those voices had devolved into screams.

They wouldn't be coming for her. She would die in here.

As she held the small earpiece in her hand, her eyes gazing blankly into the small black space, a familiar voice came over the earpiece.

"I want to speak to Lt. Oberlin," the voice said. It was Elias Todd.

Seconds later another voice responded. "This is Oberlin. Who is this?"

"This is the man you're trying to kill."

"What do you want?"

"What do *I* want? I'm only trying to stay alive."

"You've killed forty-two of my men."

"Then I suggest you and your small band of leftovers leave before the *real* fireworks start."

"What do you want!" Oberlin shouted.

"It's not *what* I want, but who," he continued. "And I'm certain he's on his way. His name is Hayes."

"Hayes," Oberlin repeated, in a tone suggesting that he understood. "Yes, he is on his way. And he'll bring an army of men in there to take you down."

"He can bring them," Todd said. "And I'll be glad to kill them. But in the end, all I want is him. And I *will* get him, with or without any others getting in my way."

"So you want him alone," Oberlin clarified.

"Yes."

"Why? Why him?"

"That's not your concern."

"What gives you the idea he'll play by your rules?"

"Because I hold the trump card. You see, I've wired this entire building to blow, with enough explosives to wipe it off the face of the earth, along with everything around it for miles. Everything he's been working for, gone in a cloud of dust. But that won't happen 'til midnight tonight. If Hayes can take me out, that would leave plenty of time for a bomb squad to come in and defuse all the charges I've set. Do you follow?"

"Crystal clear," Oberlin replied. "So what if my men and I come in there and kill you right now?"

Todd laughed. "Of course, be my guest. But there's *one* more wrinkle. I have in my hand a short-range remote detonator. Like the others, it's bonded to a pack of C4 compound. I let go of the button I'm holding down, and it will begin a countdown to simultaneously detonate all fifty-seven charges in the building. If you or one of your men gets a lucky shot, you'd have thirty seconds to get far enough away from the building to prevent the chain reaction from happening. You get it outside the radius and that detonator will still blow, but the others won't. Inside the radius, they all blow."

"What's the radius?" Oberlin asked.

"One thousand meters; roughly a quarter-mile. You'd never make it."

"And if Hayes shows?"

"It's simple. I deactivate the remote."

"How?"

"A simple code. But that's not important. What is important is that you pass this information along to Colonel Hayes. Tell him I'm in the main lab. Waiting for him."

There was a click, and the line went silent.

Loretta, who'd been listening to the entire exchange, pondered the terror of what Elias Todd was planning to do.

She needed to get out of there; to warn the authorities to evacuate nearby towns, and then get as far from the facility as she could.

But how?

Thinking through her options, she began to jump as high as she could to try to reach the access hatch in the ceiling. She tried again and again, but she couldn't reach it. She then tried for several minutes to pry open the doors, using every utensil available in her lab coat, again to no avail.

There was no escape. She was trapped.

And she dared not call for help, for fear that the only ears she would attract would be Elias Todd's.

Her only hope was that, at some point, an opportunity would present itself.

But it had better happen soon, she thought.

The clock was ticking.

65

Approach

The falling rain had strengthened.

The clock read 3:30 P.M. as Larry and Mira crossed into Shenandoah County, Virginia, having driven in silence for the past forty-five minutes. The air in the tiny car had a thickness to it, a still tension that each of them could feel. The AM radio buzzed softly, the Christian news station little more than background noise in the small cabin.

"Listen," Mira said softly, cutting into the silence. She turned up the radio.

"... national news, the federal manhunt continues for two suspects believed to be involved in planning a terrorist attack on our nation's capital. A thirty-three year old man and a twenty-seven year old woman were last seen in their home city of Chicago early this morning, and are now believed to be traveling together in a silver 1983 Volkswagen Rabbit. The vehicle was reported stolen after the owner, a Chicago man, heard the news reports and noticed his car was missing. It is an Illinois license plate, number WAN 236. Again, that's license plate number William-Andrew-Nancy, two-three-six. If you see this vehicle, you are asked to contact the authorities immediately. A report obtained by the Associated Press reveals that federal authorities may have actually had the two suspects cornered early this morning, but the fugitives were able to avoid capture. Stay tuned to WPPX for more on this story as details come in ..."

Mira turned down the volume. "Now what do we do?"

Larry kept his eyes on the road, considering what he'd just heard. "We're almost there," he started. "And it's not like we can get a different car out here," he added, gesturing to the countryside around them. "We're on back roads, so we're less likely to be seen. We just have to keep going, and hope we don't come across anyone."

"What about changing the license plates?"

"Again," Larry said. "Change with what car. And, plates are less of a concern; we're going too fast for anyone we pass to read them. They'll either notice the car, or they won't. We'll have to make do as is from here."

They drove on, drawing nearer to their destination, the heavy rains continuing to fall from the black storm clouds above.

66

Arrival

The transport neared the SRC, the driving rain hammering upon its heavy steel roof.

Nolan Hayes switched off his earpiece. The details of Lt. Oberlin's latest report still echoed in his mind. In the last thirty minutes, the situation involving Asset One had taken yet another, even deadlier turn. Not only had the subject discerned how to use the weapons found in the cache, but he had used them on the initial wave of soldiers with a level of skill even Hayes had not imagined.

He'd ordered Oberlin to carry out their previous directives: to penetrate the facility by whatever means possible and wait for further orders. They were to lay low and, most importantly, not engage with the target under any circumstances. If anything, judging by all that had happened thus far, he was certain the target would find them first and deal with them.

That battalion had served its purpose. They were now expendable in his mind.

His alert pager rang. It was Armstrong, rounding up the inner circle.

"Hayes," he said into the earpiece.

"Armstrong," came the voice. The Defense Secretary, Millett, Tolson, and Johanssen followed.

"Hayes, what's the situation?" Armstrong began.

"Target still live in the complex," Hayes responded. "All but a handful of wave one offensive are KIA. Second offensive underway with remaining troops."

"My God," the Secretary of Defense came in. "How many dead?"

"At last count, forty-two," Hayes replied.

"How could this have happened?" Armstrong said.

"As I've said before, subject is extremely dangerous," Hayes said flatly. "Successful or no, initial offensive was necessary to prevent target from digging in further."

"What's your ETA, Colonel," the Secretary of Defense asked.

"Five to six minutes," Hayes replied. "Mr. Secretary, there's more."

"Go ahead," the Secretary replied.

"Sir, it appears that the subject has wired the facility with numerous C4 charges and has set timers to detonate at Oh-twenty-four hundred hours."

"Christ," Armstrong said, exasperated. "How *many* charges?"

"Fifty-seven, according to the C.O.'s report."

"That will blow the entire facility, and cause a chain reaction to take a considerable land mass with it," Armstrong said urgently. "We are talking a hundred square miles, at minimum. That means neighboring towns. We'll need a census report for the surrounding area, immediately, to understand all that we're dealing with."

"On it," Tolson chimed in. "Will have the data momentarily."

"C4 could have only been found in the weapons cache, which means he has in fact been down there," Armstrong went on. "Our worst fears have been realized. We need to extract the target from the facility and get anti-bomb units in there to begin deactivating those detonators immediately."

"Col. Hayes," the Secretary came in, "what's your plan for taking out the target."

"That's where another piece of the puzzle comes in," Hayes replied. "I believe we've been given an 'in' to engage the target directly."

"Meaning?" Armstrong cut in.

"Target is holding an additional, remote detonator," Hayes went on. "He activates it and a thirty-second countdown ensues which will synchronize with all other detonators in the facility."

"And this is good news how?" Armstrong demanded.

"If I may, sir," Hayes continued. "Target is demanding a direct confrontation with me inside the facility. He's using the remote as leverage. When I show myself, he has stated that he will deactivate the remote, at which point I will take him down."

"You know this as fact?" Armstrong inquired.

"The demand was made by the target to the first-wave C.O. a short time ago."

"And you trust he'll do it?"

"All respect sir, at this stage I see us having very little choice."

Tolson came in: "Census bureau data shows fourteen villages and municipalities within the radius. Total population seventy-six thousand, five hundred twenty."

Millett chimed in. "Should we order an evac?"

"I advise against it," Hayes countered. "I'll have the target down inside the first few moments of contact. The anti-bomb units can take it from there. Ordering an evac will accomplish little other than to create a region-wide panic, and raise a great deal of unwanted awareness and scrutiny upon our operation."

"Col. Hayes," the Secretary began, "we're talking about seventy-plus thousand lives here. Are you certain you can neutralize the threat? Because if not, we're talking about consequences that are beyond catastrophic – for our entire nation. This would dwarf any previous attacks we've had on American soil; no one would feel safe, anywhere, anytime. I am not comfortable having that on our heads."

"Sir," Hayes responded, "I will neutralize the threat. Of that I am certain."

The line was silent; then, the Secretary addressed the group.

"We'll hold the evac order until eight o'clock P.M. Col. Hayes, you have until then. I expect an update as soon as you have one. Are we clear?"

"Yes, sir."

"In the meantime we'll issue calls to Langley and Quantico to assemble the anti-bomb units. We'll need every able body we can get on those detonators."

One by one, the parties disconnected. The line went silent.

Hayes sat back in the seat, still facing the window.

He called over his four squadron leaders. It was time to lay the final plans for their second wave offensive on the facility.

He once again unfolded the schematic of the SRC, spreading it across the small table before him. It was 4:15 P.M.; they were moments away from reaching the complex.

He glanced up at Sgts. Garza, Heath, Temple, and Perillo. He surveyed their faces, expecting perhaps only one of them, if they were lucky, to survive the mission.

"Men," he began, "you've all been briefed on the situation going on within the SRC. Not two minutes ago, I received an update from the C.O. on site. Target is still holed up and has planted enough charges to level the facility along with a considerable amount of land surrounding it. Charges set to detonate at midnight. Anti-bomb units coming in from Washington, Quantico, and Langley, but target has also fitted himself with a remote detonator. If activated, remote will simultaneously detonate all other charges. Our mission is to take him out so that the bomb units can go in and do their job.

"This is, without question," he continued, "the most important, and the most dangerous, mission you will ever be a part of. It is imperative that we neutralize the threat; that we do not lose that facility. Am I making myself clear?"

"Yes, sir," the four men responded.

"Now," he began again, taking a marker to the schematic, "we're going to run a surround-and-penetrate offensive to storm the complex. Three paths in. Garza. Your men will approach from the west. Perillo, yours from the south. Temple, your men will come with me. Heath. Your men will remain on the bus, keeping watch on Asset Two. You will remain out of the target's line of sight, just beyond the lot in cover of trees."

"Sir," Heath inquired, "what about any remaining men from the first wave?"

Hayes glanced up at Heath, pondering the relevance of the question. He was certain none of Oberlin's men would still be alive by the time they arrived. "I'll coordinate a rendezvous with that squad once everyone is in position," he lied. "The most important thing is that each team carries out its assigned task. Understood?"

"Yes, sir," they responded again.

At that moment, the driver called to Hayes. "Approaching south lot of complex."

"On my word," Hayes told his men. "Let's move out."

Miles away, in a darkened meeting room deep within the halls of the Pentagon, Edward Armstrong sat across from his superior, eyes still set on the speakerphone at the center of the table.

The call had ended moments before, but Armstrong still found himself absorbing the ramifications of the situation they were now facing.

Their plan to develop a new, more effective soldier, meant to save thousands of American lives, had free-fallen into chaos, putting thousands of American lives in peril.

"Armstrong," the Secretary of Defense said, his tone resigned.

"Sir," Armstrong replied. "I'll begin working on a Contingency Protocol immediately."

"Like hell," the Secretary growled. "There *is* no Contingency Protocol for *this*. Civilian witnesses, soldiers KIA on American soil, entire *towns* in jeopardy. *Damage control* is all that can be done now.

"Ensuring *no more lives* are lost is priority one," he continued. "And that means taking down that son-of-a-bitch holed up in our building, then locating and diffusing every charge in there, and any other threats we may not even *know* of yet. Then, and only then, can we set a cover plan into play."

"Sir," Armstrong said, "once Hayes has taken out the target, the greatest part of the threat will be neutralized."

"Yes. But by doing that we are betting the lives of thousands on one man," Armstrong replied. "I'm not comfortable with that. As little choice as we have, I'm going to send another offensive unit in with the anti-bomb squads.

"If we lose contact with Hayes," he concluded, "or if for any other reason I feel it necessary … I will order them to move in."

"And if the target decides to blow the facility as a result?" Armstrong asked.

"Again," the Secretary mused, "if Hayes fails, what other options do we have."

67

Incoming

Edna Parker noticed that the bus had stopped.

The rain came down in sheets outside. Banging loudly and constantly on the roof over their heads. From her view out the window they were nowhere near any building.

She looked down one shoulder at Marcus, then down the other at Daniel. Both had their heads down, their eyes fixed upon the floor. Each had grown restless at different times. She had done her best to keep them calm, not wanting to attract the soldiers' attention.

From beyond the partial wall to her left, she could hear the mens' voices, especially the booming voice of the enormous man with the scar. In the past several moments, their voices had sounded urgent, as if something had gone wrong, had altered whatever plans they'd made … and they were readying themselves to deal with it.

She heard the hiss of the hydraulic door opening, then the sound of footsteps. The bus' engine remained on, its low hum reverberating throughout the floor beneath her feet. It was as if all of their captors had left. Then came a voice she hadn't heard before.

"Forrest," the voice said. "Check on the subject in the holding room."

"Yes, sir," a second voice called back.

As the words hit the air, a young soldier with a slight build came into her view, crossing the open space toward the locked room at the very back of the bus. He glanced in her direction momentarily but then quickly averted his eyes. When he reached the narrow door to her right, he punched in a code, then disappeared from view.

Edna sat there in silence, staring out the window at the rain coming down outside.

A moment later, the narrow door opened. The young soldier emerged and shut the door behind him. As he turned to walk back toward the front of the bus, his eyes once again caught Edna's briefly, but again he quickly looked away. He took several steps before he slowed, his body language uncertain. He stopped and turned to look at them curiously, almost guiltily, before glancing away and finally disappearing from view.

The rain softened. Edna began to hear an exchange of voices from beyond her view. Though she was unable to pick up complete sentences, it didn't take her long to realize the voices were discussing her and the boys.

"... sir ... just an old lady and two kids ..."

"... strict orders from the Executive Special Agent ... need to follow protocol ... too much at stake ... can't alter the plan ..."

Edna breathed as deeply as the gag would allow. If nothing else, her spirits felt a lift; perhaps not all the men who'd taken them hostage were monsters, after all.

And for a brief moment, she felt what she thought was a glimmer of hope. She couldn't explain it, but in that moment, something in her told her that, somehow, perhaps they had a chance to get out of this; that everything would be all right.

That thought was catastrophically interrupted as a tremendous jolt sent Edna and the boys high into the air, then suddenly crashing down with such force that her teeth bit through the gag, and her restraints broke the surface of her skin. The entire world seemed to have turned upside down. A deafening roar had taken her hearing, the sound of the outside world replaced by a high-pitched whine that she was certain were her eardrums screaming in terrible pain. Intense heat burned her face. Fear had forced her eyes shut tight. Fighting to open them, she saw flames burning brightly. Licking their way along the wall to her left. Terrible heat pressing forward. She breathed rapidly, shallowly. Her hearing began to return. She glanced to either side of her to the boys. Both were screaming through their gags. She knew she was also screaming. Marcus had a cut above his right eye, and both of their faces were covered in dark soot. Through the smoke, she could see that all of the windows were heavily cracked but still intact. Beyond them were dark clouds; raindrops pelting the fractured surface.

It then dawned on her that the entire bus had been thrown into the air and had landed on its side.

There was a loud bang to her right. She looked over to see that the narrow door had been smashed partially outward. A large dent protruded out from its center, and one of the door hinges had separated from the frame. Suddenly, the door flew across the area, cutting a swath through the smoke and landing with a dull crash somewhere to Edna's left.

From the opening, a hand appeared, then a face. A young man. There was no soot, but the face was bloodied. As if on the receiving end of a battering ram. The man pulled himself over the threshold, then fell sloppily onto the floor, only a few feet away. His wrists and ankles bore cuts. He'd been bound also. He gathered himself up slowly. He was disoriented, trying to get his bearings.

She continued to yell through the gag at him. He finally appeared to hear, turning so quickly toward her that he once again almost lost his balance. He staggered toward them, grabbed onto the end of the bench. From up close his eyes were bleary, dazed. The awareness, then the alarm, spread across his eyes as he realized the situation they were in. He shook his head vigorously to rouse himself from his stupor, then quickly looked around them, surveying their surroundings.

Then, without warning, he wedged himself between the floor and the bench. With a loud, pained yell he began to push, as if trying to tear the bench from the floor. She began to scream louder at him, panicking. He was obviously delusional, thinking he could rip the entire bench out of the floor. He needed to find keys to their bindings. It was the only way they would be able to escape.

There was a drawn out, metallic creaking noise. The bench began to move. Then a loud snap. She and the boys jolted in their seats; one end of the bench had been freed from the floor. The man continued to push the end of the bench in the same direction, and before Edna knew it, the bench was perpendicular to the floor. Another loud wrenching sound and the other end of the bench had been torn free as well. He picked up the bench and set it, Edna and the boys still on it, against the rear wall from which he'd just emerged, facing away from where he stood.

Then he spoke, his raspy voice cutting through the din: "Heads down, eyes closed. Do it now."

As Edna closed her eyes, from behind them came a grunt and a loud thud, then what sounded like crunching glass, and finally the clamor of falling rain. He'd dislodged the window to use as their escape route.

"I'm getting you out of here," he shouted above the din. "Fuel tank's gonna blow any second. It's gonna be bumpy."

The bench was then picked up and stood upright, so that one end of it was leaning against the window opening. Out of the corner of her eye she saw the man leap upward to the opening. The rain fell onto them; its cool wetness washed the soot on her face into her eyes and mouth. Suddenly, her head jerked hard to the right as the bench was yanked upward through the opening, then swiveled around so that the man was carrying them lengthwise across his back, his arms hooked through the seat back so that they were facing backward, away from him.

He leapt off the top of the bus, and Edna and the boys jostled in the seat as they hit the ground with a numbing crash. They wobbled for a moment as the man briefly lost his balance upon landing and then, once he'd regained it, began moving quickly, away from the burning bus, each impact of his running feet jarring them in the bench seat.

They were moving along so rapidly Edna felt the steady wind blowing against the back of her head. She didn't understand how someone could be running so fast with all that he was carrying on his back; but she didn't question it; rather, her only hope was that he was moving fast *enough*.

Just as that thought crossed her mind, Edna instinctively closed her eyes as the explosion blasted a hot wind against her face. Its force pushed them all forward, again almost knocking the man off his feet, but he kept his balance; kept running. Fearfully, she opened her eyes to see the expanding fireball which had been the bus only seconds before, stretching its way toward the sky.

68

Passage

The explosions had been less than a minute apart, the second much larger than the first.

From the thicket of trees to the east, Nolan Hayes turned toward the source of the blasts. Both had come from the main parking lot area.

The transport carrying Asset Two.

The target must have somehow seen the transport and hit it with an RPG.

Hayes couldn't be concerned with that now; taking down Asset One had taken priority over all else. Once the threat was eliminated, he could focus on whether or not the other subject had survived.

Garza's and Perillo's squads were moving toward the building from the west and south. Per Hayes' plan, they would easily be seen as they approached, keeping the target busy for the necessary moments it would take for Hayes to make his way in.

Hayes pushed through the brush, leading Temple and his men to the spot of which he and only a few others had any knowledge.

When the SRC was built, it had been equipped with an emergency escape tunnel, in the event that any staff in the Underground Labs were trapped down there by fire or other danger. The 300-meter-long tunnel led straight out the back of a supply closet at the complex's far eastern end, ending at a one-meter wide, forty-foot high silo where escapees could climb to the surface.

Arriving at the spot, Hayes halted his men. The access point was both concealed and secured. Any entry would alert the SRC's security system of a breach.

Ironically, thanks to the target's efforts, the grid was down, meaning they could slip in undetected.

He reached down to the ground, his large hands feeling around the soft, wet earth. The small, open area was about twelve feet in diameter and appeared as just a normal plot of land, with green grass and soil covering the ground below them. But hidden in the grass were two grip handles. Finding both, Hayes pulled and began to twist clockwise. With a lift, he removed the small patch of earth from the ground, tossing it aside.

Six inches below the surface lay a smooth titanium-alloy cover. Hayes knew the release trigger was only on the inside: there was no access from above. He slammed his boot down onto the cover with tremendous force, repeating this three more times, until the cover had finally bent enough so he could rip it from the hinges holding it in place.

He switched on his helmet light and looked down the silo. Iron rungs protruded down one side, disappearing into blackness beyond the halogen's glow.

He motioned to Maldonado, the most junior of Temple's squad, and therefore the most expendable. If anything waited for them at the bottom, he would be the litmus test.

"Private," he addressed him, "proceed down the silo, scout ahead fifty meters and report back up. Confirm area secure by clicking on your helmet light twice."

"Sir," the soldier nodded, then descended down the rungs, disappearing from view.

A moment later came two tiny flashes of light from below. It was clear.

Hayes motioned to the rest of his men to descend. Within moments, they were all at the floor of the silo, and Hayes gathered them once more.

"The plan is this," he began. "Inside the complex, you four will remain behind me, out of sight. Upon visual contact with me in the main lab, target will deactivate the remote detonator, at which point I will say target's full name, 'Elias Masters Todd.' That will be the signal for you to move in. Maintain radio silence, no exceptions.

"Shoot upon sight," he continued. "And shoot to kill. Empty the clip. Take no chances. If he survives he will re-activate the remote. We cannot allow that to happen.

"Now, switch to night vision," he said, nodding. "Let's move out."

With a click, Hayes turned off his helmet light. He then activated his infrared sensors, pulling the crimson visor down over his eyes. The others followed suit.

Without another word, Hayes and the four troopers began moving down the long, black tunnel.

69

Dodging Bullets

The violent explosion seemed to vaporize everything around them.

The long bench seat stretched across his back like a massive wing, Rage continued to run through the high, wet grass of the field, headed toward a far-off group of trees. His wrists, gripping the bottom of the long, metal seat-back, felt as if they would tear off from his arms at any second. His legs rippled with pain from the weight of the steel bench and the three people still tied to it. He was still groggy, and he could feel his strength only beginning to return to his body; but it had been adrenaline that had forced him from his drug-induced slumber, and it was adrenaline that was carrying him now.

Finally satisfied that they were far enough away, he set down the bench seat behind a large oak tree. He staggered backward for a split second before regaining his balance, then stepped forward to undo their shackles, placing a finger at the end of each cuff, snapping them apart.

He observed that all of their wrists and ankles were bruised and bloodied, especially the old woman's. She would likely need medical attention, as soon as he got them out of wherever they were.

He stood up and took in their surroundings. There was no one in sight. Nothing moving. Then he saw the building in the distance, in the direction from which they'd just come. That seemed to be the only shelter as far as he could see, and likely the only place they could get, or call for, help.

"W-what happened?" the woman's voice came from behind him, breaking through the din of the heavy rain. She was clutching at her wrists, as were the two boys. "What … what *was* that?"

He turned toward her. "We got hit. Something big. Small missle or rocket-propelled grenade."

"W-we were tied up," she said, the shock still spread across her face. She was having trouble speaking. "We c-couldn't move, couldn't get out."

"Probably the only reason you're still alive," he said. "Otherwise, you'd have been thrown, broken your necks, like the two bastards in that small room with me."

"Do … do you know what's happening?" she asked. "Why did they take us?"

"No," he said flatly. "But I'm going to get us all out of here."

Again he looked over at the building, then back to the woman and the two boys. "Do you think you can walk?"

"Yes," she nodded, acknowledging the boys as well.

"What about run, if need be."

"Yes," she repeated. "As fast as my legs will carry me."

"Good," he said. "We need to head toward that building over there. Once we're in, we can call for help. But we're going to stay with as much cover as we can get. Whoever hit us before is still out there somewhere. Now follow me."

Turning to once again survey the land around them, Rage headed toward the nearest thicket of trees, the woman and the two boys right behind him.

70

Search and Rescue

The transport had arrived at just the right time, giving Oberlin's squad a brief window with which to enter the complex unnoticed.

As Oberlin's squadron reached the front entrance at the complex's west end, they walked through the enormous blast opening where the target had booby-trapped the entry point. Among the debris lay the charred remains of Wright's squadron.

As they walked through what appeared to be a front office, the soft emergency lights inside and blackened sky outside did little to illuminate their progress.

About twenty feet in, he motioned to his men to gather up.

"Men," he began in a low voice, "again, we're not to engage with target until the C.O. has removed the detonator from the equation. Maintain strict radio silence until we hear otherwise. At which point we will move in per new orders.

"In the meantime," he said after a pause, "this just became a search-and-rescue mission. We're going to look for survivors."

"Sir," Thomas came in, "are we really to believe that anyone survived this?"

"We won't know until we try, Sergeant," Oberlin answered him.

"And what if the target finds *us*?" Danvers asked uncertainly.

"You know the orders, Corporal," Oberlin said, understanding where he was going. "We are not to engage. You do, and get a lucky hit, we're all dead."

"So we're all just sitting ducks?" Danvers said.

"Let's just hope to God we don't come across him," Oberlin said. "Now. We're going to split up. Four groups of two. Thomas, take Danvers and head to the top floor. Phillips and Ramirez, second floor. Forde, Lau, you stay on this floor. George, you and I will head down below. Report back here in thirty minutes, unless you hear otherwise."

"Now move out," he said, pulling down his visor. "Use night vision, maintain silence unless you see something. Do not shoot at anything, or anyone, under any circumstances. I'll see you back here in thirty minutes."

Turning away, Oberlin and George headed to the stairs, making their way toward the basement.

71

The Elevator

Reaching the bottom of the stairs, Oberlin scanned the area for signs of movement.

As he rounded the corner, night vision on the open hallway ahead, he saw them.

Twenty feet before him were scattered bodies resting atop a massive pool of blood. The blood glimmered in the emergency lighting, giving an almost icy appearance.

"Stay alert," he ordered George quietly, and moved toward the intersection.

They were about five feet from the blood-soaked junction when Oberlin thought he'd heard something. A subtle *bump*.

He stopped in his tracks, signaling for George to follow suit.

Seconds later, he heard it again. Once. Twice.

"You hear that," he asked George.

"Sounds like it's coming ..." George began.

"From inside the elevator," Oberlin finished for him.

He inched closer to the elevator, motioning to George to keep watch around them.

Carefully stepping over the blood and bodies, he came close to the door itself and placed his ear against the cold steel surface.

Inside the elevator, Loretta slumped back against the far wall. For what seemed like hours, she'd been trying to find the ceiling escape hatch, to no avail.

Knowing the hatch was her only way out but not tall enough to reach it herself, she had improvised, using one of the instruments in her lab coat pocket to unscrew the metal handrail in the elevator wall. It had taken long moments to remove the rail in the elevator's pitch blackness, but she had done it. She'd been hoisting the handrail upward, tapping against the ceiling in an attempt to find the hatch.

As she sat and caught her breath, she thought she'd heard something.

She remained still, listening; hoping for anyone in the world but Elias Todd.

It happened again. A knocking on the elevator door, and a voice.

Unsure what to do, she called out. "H-hello?"

The voice came more clearly now: "Is someone in there?" it said.

Loretta dropped the metal handrail with a clang and instinctively began banging on the door, calling back to them. "Yes! In here! In here! I'm trapped!"

The voice began speaking again, and she quieted down, trying to hear.

"—going to get you out of there. Again, just sit tight, back away from the door."

As relief began to wash over her, she suddenly remembered the situation. The noise could attract Todd, putting whoever was out there in grave danger.

Overtaken by panic, she banged on the elevator door again, calling to them. "Stop! Please listen to me! He-he's out there somewhere! Please, please be careful!"

"Just sit tight," the voice called back. "Remain calm. We're coming for you."

Loretta didn't respond, obeying the voice's instructions and stepping back toward the elevator's far wall. She waited in anxious silence as the next few harrowing moments unfolded.

72

Gunpoint

The rain had begun to slow as Larry and Mira neared their destination.

The black clouds above had stirred a deepening darkness; mists had begun to rise, specters in the low fields surrounding the narrow asphalt road. They came upon a hill. Larry switched the Rabbit's lights off, beginning to drive very slowly.

"What are we doing?" Mira asked.

"We're getting close to it, I'm almost positive," Larry explained. "We need to be quiet; blend in with the dark. We'll probably need to go on foot in a few minutes."

They crested the hill, and in the valley beyond, they could see the vast industrial park, a series of massive, low buildings that branched off along both sides of the main roadway. All of the buildings had outside lights on, along with illuminated parking lots.

All of the buildings except one.

As Larry peered out the windshield to look more closely at the enormous, three-story building far off to the right side, set furthest apart from the rest of the buildings in the industrial complex, he knew right away that was the place.

"That's it," he said. "Right side, off in the distance. The only one in the dark."

"Of course," Mira said, exasperated. "Why *wouldn't* it be that one?"

Larry picked up on her irony. "Just be ready to go on foot in a minute," he said.

As the Rabbit continued along slowly, Larry began to get a fuller picture not only of the building, but also of the area surrounding it. Despite the heavy rains, there was a haze in the air, as if something had been burning.

But there was something odd about the haze; though there had been no wind to disperse it, it was scattered all around the building, instead of in just one area.

Almost as if *several* things had been burning.

As that notion crossed Larry's mind, they turned onto the perimeter drive and could see the security gate. It had been smashed in.

"What in the world," Larry muttered to himself.

Seconds later, the south parking lots came into view. Larry's attention was drawn to a massive smoldering heap near a group of trees just beyond the parking lot's edge.

"What is that?" Mira asked warily.

Larry took a closer look. One half of the mass was completely gone, turned to nothing more than scattered shrapnel and debris. Along the remaining half, patches of tiny fires still burned among sporadic plumes of wafting smoke. Through the smoke, toward the rear of the blackened mass, Larry could make out what looked like a wheel.

"It's a ... bus," he said. "Or was."

"Look over there," she said, pointing to the parking lot beyond.

Larry followed her gaze. In the parking lot in front of them were three more blackened husks, each the size of a delivery truck. Though no smoke emanated from them, it was clear that whatever had hit the bus had also hit them.

What had happened out here, he wondered.

And most importantly, what was happening inside?

"If you're going inside," she read his thoughts, "I'm going with you."

Larry turned toward her. "Listen to me," he began. "I have no idea what's happening in there. If you go in with me, I don't know if I can protect you."

"Don't you think I know that?" she said. "But right now, no place is safe for me. We've come this far; I'm not leaving you now."

"Fine," he said, knowing there was no convincing her otherwise. "But stay close to me. From here on out, we're gonna need to go on foot. From the looks of what's happened so far, staying in the car will only put a bigger target on our heads."

Larry yanked the parking brake upward and shut the engine off, then reached under the driver's seat to pull out the handgun he'd taken from the alley those many hours ago.

"We're going to run toward the building, to that covering on the left," he told her. "Stay behind me. Go as fast as you can. If something happens to me, I want you to run back to the car and drive out of here. Don't hesitate. Okay?"

"Okay," she agreed.

They got out of the car.

"Let's go," he said, beginning to run toward the complex, Mira right behind him.

A minute later they reached what appeared to be the building's main entrance. The large overhang provided them shelter from the rain, which had picked up again.

Larry immediately saw the blast hole which had been the doors, then looked down to see the bodies among the blackened debris.

"Jesus," he gasped, then quickly reached to Mira to put his hand over her mouth. She had just noticed as well, her eyes wide in horror.

"Don't scream," he told her. "Look away. Keep your eyes up."

They went inside, Larry keeping an eye on the floor in front of them.

"Now we need to move quietly," he whispered. "I don't know what's waiting –"

"Freeze," a low voice boomed behind them. "Hands above your head."

As Larry froze in his tracks, a beam of light suddenly washed over them. In the relative darkness of the room, the light was blinding.

Larry's mind worked, trying to figure out what to do. They couldn't have come this far, only to be trapped at gunpoint less than twenty feet inside the entrance.

"I said, hands above your head," the voice commanded.

Larry complied, nodding to Mira. Still shaken by the sight of the bodies, she blankly followed suit.

Larry tried to make out who was in front of them. He heard two sets of footsteps.

Finally, the first man came into view, followed by the second. Both were pointing M-16 rifles at him. Larry recognized the heavy, black armor of the Federal agents who'd been pursuing him.

The soldier closest to them spoke. "This is a restricted Federal facility. Trespassing on these grounds is a punishable offense. State your reason for being here."

Confused, Larry's mouth opened slightly, but no words came out.

Trespassing?

Did they not recognize who he was?

"State your reason now, or I am obliged to use force," the soldier commanded.

"Your men kidnapped my family," he responded before he could think it through. "A woman and two young boys. I'm here for *them*."

The first soldier paused, then quickly moved his eyes to the second. The two exchanged a brief glance, keeping their rifles pointed at Larry the entire time.

"Kidnapped?" the first soldier repeated Larry's words, bemused. "I don't know what you're talking about. This is an extremely restricted area. I'm afraid we're going to have to take you into custody until we can figure out what to do with you."

"What's happened here?" Mira blurted out suddenly.

"That's classified," the second soldier came in. "But there is an imminent danger here; civilians shouldn't be anywhere near this facility."

"But –" Mira began.

"Mira. It's okay," Larry cut her off, catching her eye. He decided they needed to play along, at least until he understood what was going on and what to do.

"Radio down to the C.O.," the first soldier told the second. "Figure out if there's a holding cell, somewhere we can lock them up 'til there's an all-clear."

"Orders are radio silence unless we see something," the second soldier said.

"And this doesn't qualify as 'something?'" the first said.

"Not in my mind," the second answered. "We've completed the sweep of this level anyway. The Lieutenant is below. Let's take them to him; let him decide."

The first soldier led the way across the large office space, with the second behind Larry and Mira, keeping his rifle trained on them.

As they approached the stairwell, Larry's mind continued to assemble all the pieces of the puzzle in his mind. He knew in his gut that Edna and the boys were here, somewhere. So how was it possible that these two soldiers didn't know about them?

And what exactly was happening right now? What was the imminent danger?

Could they be talking about Rage?

Just as with Edna and the boys, Larry assumed *he'd* been taken here as well.

Had he escaped, now somewhere in the building, on a murderous rampage?

Somehow ... Larry didn't believe that.

But if *he* wasn't the danger ... what else could it be?

As they reached the bottom of the stairwell, the glow of the emergency lights illuminated sections of the wide hallways, leaving others in darkness. Larry glanced around as they passed the first hallway junction.

"Eyes front," the soldier behind him said tersely.

As they rounded the corner to a considerably larger hallway, Larry could see movement up ahead. Two lights, similar to those mounted to these soldiers' helmets, were moving around near what looked like an elevator. As they got closer, Larry could make out that someone, a woman, it appeared, was being pulled from the elevator.

"Jesus Christ," Larry heard the soldier in front of him utter.

As the lights moved around, they illuminated the floor around the elevator area, and Larry understood the soldier's reaction. He prayed Mira wouldn't scream when she saw the bodies strewn about there, atop the pool of blood.

"Lieutenant Oberlin, sir," the soldier in front of Larry called out.

As they reached the intersection with the larger hallway, the light turned in their direction; Larry felt it train first on Mira, then on himself.

"Corporal Forde," the voice came from the helmet light. "You found survivors?"

"Trespassers, more like, sir," Forde replied. "Picked them up by the entrance."

"Trespassers?" Lt. Oberlin replied incredulously.

As the lights trained on Oberlin, Larry could see the man's visor was up, revealing a man about ten years his senior. His face seemed to be covered in dried blood.

As Oberlin approached them, Larry caught a glimpse of the two people standing behind him. A man about Larry's age, African-American, wearing the same gear as Oberlin, his visor also up. The woman standing next to him appeared to be in her early forties and was exceptionally tall and slender, with tousled blonde hair and an alarmed gaze in her eyes. There was a considerable amount of blood on her lab coat. She was feverishly trying to explain something to the second soldier, who in turn was trying to calm her down.

"Yes, sir," Forde replied to Oberlin. "We saw them walk *in* to the building."

Lt. Oberlin walked up to them, looking first at Mira, then to Larry. "Do you people have *any idea* on what you've walked into?"

Before Larry could respond, there was a scuffling of feet behind them.

At that moment, another light switched on, bathing Oberlin's face in its beam.

Oberlin took notice and shone his light beyond Larry. He drew his gun.

Suddenly, shouting began from all directions. He saw Mira whirl around. As she looked behind them, she gasped, the look on her face more amazement than fear.

As Larry turned to see who was approaching, the shouting grew louder, more vehement, and he saw both Oberlin and George point their guns in that direction.

His gaze fixed upon the figure who was illuminated by Oberlin's light. His eyes widened in disbelief.

Not ten feet from him stood Rage, holding a gun to the head of yet another black-armor-clad trooper.

And several feet behind them, crouching low, their faces petrified with terror, were Edna, Marcus, and Daniel.

73

Down Below

Moments earlier, Rage had led Edna, Marcus, and Daniel into the complex, entering undetected from the south.

His plan was to call for help and get the woman and the boys to safety.

Once inside the building, he spotted a stairwell. On a hunch, he decided to follow it to the upper floors.

"Up," he whispered, motioning with his hand. "Follow me."

They proceeded silently up the stairs, the dull glow of the emergency lighting units barely illuminating their progress.

As they reached the landing to the second floor, Rage thought he heard voices on the other side of the stairwell door.

He turned to the woman and two boys. "Someone's in there," he explained. "But I don't know who. Might not be safe. Stay here. If you need me, call out."

"But what if it's not safe for –" Edna whispered anxiously.

"I can take care of myself," Rage assured her. "I'll be right back."

Edna Parker pulled Marcus and Daniel toward the left wall of the landing, where she huddled close with them. The boys had been nearly silent since their narrow escape from the bus; she was doing her best to keep them calm and focused, but it was all she could do to keep herself from slipping into shock at times.

She watched as Rage silently opened the door. In the dim light, she could see two figures in black just inside the room. As the door began to swing shut once again, the two figures raised their guns at him. She gasped in horror, and the door swung shut.

Then through the door came a series of loud bangs and crashes; voices yelled.

Then silence.

Keeping her eyes on the door, she began to tremble, instinctively placing her hands over her two young nephews' eyes.

The door began to open, slowly swinging out toward them.

Her heart sank as she saw the soldier, clad in the all-too-familiar black armored uniform, emerge. But something seemed odd about him. Then she saw why: as he came more into view, she saw the thick forearm around his neck, partially hidden from view, wedged between his helmet and chest-plate. Rage was behind him, keeping him in a tight stranglehold. As Rage turned him to the side so he could face her, she saw the pistol being held to the back of his head.

"You're not going to shoot him!" Edna exclaimed, horrified.

"Only if he makes me," Rage replied, giving the soldier a forceful shake.

"There were two of them," she said. "Where's —" she began, then peered through the still-open doorway to see a second armor-clad trooper, sprawled out on the floor.

"You didn't –!" she gasped.

"No," Rage said. "But he'll be out for a while. We need to get moving."

"Where are we going?" Edna asked, the two boys helping her up.

"Basement," he replied. "According to this one, the leader's down there. They were about to radio him the heads up, til I decided we should pay him a personal visit."

Marcus and Daniel at her sides, Edna followed Rage down the stairwell.

Moments later they were descending the final flight of stairs into the subterranean level, Rage leading the way. The soldier in front of him maintained his struggles, murmuring senseless comments to Rage as they made their way down.

"It doesn't matter that you have me, or hostages," he said angrily. "As soon as they see you don't have that detonator, they will shoot you on sight."

Rage had no idea what he was talking about, but he wasn't about to engage in any discussion. He needed to get to whoever was in charge. He would fight his way out of here if need be, but most importantly, he needed to get the woman and boys to safety. Only then would he get answers on why they had wanted *him*.

Once they'd reached the lower level, they turned a corner into a large hallway. Up ahead, Rage could see several figures in an open area, next to an elevator. Sharp beams of light jutted forward from three or four of the figures' heads. As they moved, they illuminated small sections of the area. Even so, Rage was unable to make out much of anything from the distance they held.

Rage turned his head back toward Edna. "Stay low and keep back," he instructed her in a low voice. "But watch your back. If this gets hairy, run back upstairs."

Out of the corner of his eye, he saw Edna nod in acknowledgement.

"You got one of those headlights," Rage said to the soldier. "Switch it on."

Without a word the soldier slowly put his right hand to the base of his helmet and pressed a small switch. A shaft of light carried forward, illuminating the scene up ahead.

Rage instantly recognized Mira and the cop, then saw the bodies and pool of blood on the floor. A mad rush of thoughts entered his head, but he had no time to process them, because as the four soldiers surrounding Mira and the cop immediately turned in Rage's direction, the trooper in Rage's grasp began shouting:

"He has no detonator but there are hostages!" the soldier called out. "Repeat: no detonator but three hostages behind!"

"Drop the gun!" shouted one of the troopers ahead. "Release the hostages now!"

As Rage took another step forward, all four troopers drew their weapons; the two further back in the hallway took up firing positions, aiming at Rage.

"Aim high, for the head!" the trooper in Rage's grip yelled. "Hostages are down low behind me!"

"Hold all fire!" the soldier closest to Rage ordered the others, his pistol also pointed at Rage. "You! Drop the gun now, and release the hostages!"

"Shoot the bastard, now!" screamed the soldier in Rage's headlock.

"Get to cover!" Rage called back to the woman. "Get the kids away from here!"

At that moment, the cop, who had just turned around and made eye contact with Rage, began yelling to the woman and the boys behind him. The soldier next to him interpreted his sudden motion as hostile, and he struck the cop across the back of the head with his rifle. The cop fell to the ground, and the soldier pinned him face-down to the ground with his boot, the firearm pointed at the back of his head.

Both Mira and the old woman screamed. The lead soldier repeated his hold-fire order, louder this time. Events escalated all around Rage: guns were pointed, the shouting and screaming intensified; the entire world seemed to be on the verge of complete chaos.

Then out of nowhere came a loud burst of automatic fire; its clear, ripping blare overpowered the shouting that had filled the room. The two soldiers immediately ahead of Rage crouched low, swiveling their heads in all directions in an attempt to determine the source of the gunfire, but Rage had seen: in the open intersection further ahead, the other two soldiers who'd taken up firing positions dropped to the floor, one of their guns hitting the blood-soaked surface with a flat clack just as the cascade of bullets ceased.

The soldier who'd pinned down the cop turned and headed toward the intersection, taking cover against the wall for a split second before turning the corner and aiming his gun in the direction from which the gunfire had come.

"Forde!" the lead soldier screamed to him. "Fall back and take cover! We don't know what's down there!"

But it was too late. As Forde turned the corner, he was instantly struck by something blindingly fast, which lifted him into the air and pinned him against the wall. Without a second's notice, his neck was snapped, and he was dropped to the floor in a lifeless heap.

In the spot where the soldier had died, a solitary figure now stood over the body.

It was at that moment, with the figure illuminated by the soldier's helmet light, that Rage got his first look at him.

It was as if he was looking at a mirror image of himself.

74

Convergence

As the black eyes settled on him, Rage stood thunderstruck.

Before him was a man roughly his age, with jet-black hair and eyes as dark as his own. His face was beaming, a twisted pride known only to madmen. He was wearing a blood-stained hospital gown, an enormous belt wrapped his waist, supported by a large shoulder strap, both of which carried several pouches, large and small. At least five that Rage could see appeared to be large enough to carry a handgun. His bare feet were covered in the blood that was spread across the floor. His right hand tightly clutched some kind of small device Rage couldn't recognize; at its top was a tiny red light that blinked once every second. In his left hand was an automatic pistol.

Despite all those around him, the man's eyes had locked onto Rage, as if he were the only one in the room. The vicious smile spread wide across his face.

And in that deathly stare, without knowing how or why, Rage understood: somehow, the two of them shared a history.

And he knew that he was all that stood between this man and the lives of the others around him.

He abruptly released the soldier he'd been holding. "Get. Everyone. Out of here," he said to the soldier in a low voice.

Without hesitation, the soldier obeyed, first moving toward Mira, who had pulled the unconscious cop to the side and was huddled down low over him. The soldier had taken only two steps when the black-eyed man leveled his pistol and shot the man twice through the head. He dropped to the floor. Mira and the old woman screamed again.

"Leaving so soon?" the man said, amused. He waved the gun carelessly. "The party's just begun!"

"Leave them be," Rage said, stepping toward him. "It's *me* you want."

"No," the man said blandly. "I don't even want you." And in that split second he pointed the pistol at Rage's head, again firing twice. Rage darted to one side, both bullets missing him cleanly, then lunged forward at his attacker, hitting him across the midsection, ramming him hard into the far wall. As they slid to the floor, Rage began landing heavy blows to the man's head, hitting as hard and as fast as he could. He needed to buy enough time to allow everyone to escape, which he hoped was happening behind him at that very moment.

Twenty feet behind them, Larry shook his head, trying to bring himself back into focus. He was sitting upright, his back against a brick wall in the narrow corridor.

The blow from the soldier's rifle had knocked him cold; for how long, he didn't know. As he collected himself, he saw Mira huddled close in front of him, her hand to his forehead, rubbing it gently with her thumb. His vision clearing, he was able to see Edna in front of him, to Mira's immediate right. He felt a tug at each of his arms; Marcus and Daniel were at either side of him, holding him tight. They had surrounded him, as if shielding him from whatever was going on outside the protective circle they'd formed.

Just behind them he could see the lead soldier, standing vigilant toward the edge of the opposite wall, his M-16 rifle pointed at the hallway intersection just beyond. The woman who'd been pulled from the elevator stood nervously behind him, glancing from him to Larry every few seconds.

"Let me up," he said to Mira. "We need to get you all out of here."

"Larry," Edna said worriedly. "Can you stand up?"

"Yeah," Larry responded, feeling woozy as the boys helped him up.

He looked at the woman in the lab coat. "Can you lead them out?"

The woman nodded. "Yes," she replied.

Mira, Edna, and the boys seemed to protest all at once.

"Listen to me," Larry told them urgently. "I'm going to buy you more time to get away. I *will* see you once I'm out. Now go!" he ordered them.

The woman in the lab coat hurried Mira, Edna, Marcus, and Daniel toward the stairs, all of their eyes staying on Larry until they were around the corner, out of his view.

As Rage continued to hammer at his enemy's face, he felt something slice through his left shoulder. Excruciating pain began to spread across his upper back. He jolted backward for a split second, overcome by the intensifying sting.

In the low light he saw the exit wound in his right shoulder.

Gunshot ... from down the hall ... but ... who ...?

His opponent seized the opening, his foot hitting Rage square in the midsection, and Rage felt himself launched into the air. He crashed against the opposing wall with such force that his vision blurred. He tasted blood on his tongue.

He looked up. His adversary stood before him, a gun pointed at his head.

Suddenly a voice shouted from Rage's right: "Drop the gun!"

Rage turned to see the lead soldier and the cop leveling their rifles at his attacker.

The dark-eyed man looked over at the two and laughed. "*You* know you can't shoot me," he said derisively, shaking the device in his hand slightly. "But *I*, on the other hand ..." and in one swift move he pointed the gun at the lead soldier and pulled the trigger, shooting him square in the upper chest.

"TODD!" bellowed a voice from Rage's left.

The entire room seemed to turn, its focus now upon the enormous silhouette approaching them in the dim, patchy light of the wide corridor, the heavy footsteps drawing closer in the suddenly silent space.

"Disable the remote, now," the voice commanded.

The man named Todd gazed to his right down the hallway as the massive silhouette approached. His gun was still pointed in the direction of the fallen soldier, who was now being feverishly tended to by the cop.

At that moment, the silhouette came into the nearest light, and Rage immediately recognized the colossal figure standing mere feet away from him.

Pieces of the puzzle began to come together in his mind; he understood now who had shot him just seconds ago.

In front of Rage, his icy, murderous gaze fixed solely on Todd, stood the black-armored Agent who'd captured Rage at the police station only the night before.

75

Face Off

"Disable the remote," Hayes ordered Todd once again. "You wanted me. So let's finish this."

Turning his head toward Hayes, Todd stood upright. He smiled knowingly.

"Order your men to come forward," he said.

Hayes paused, then ordered his men: "Temple. Approach my position."

Four additional armored agents came into view, appearing at either side of Hayes.

With fierce precision, Todd shot them all in the head, killing them instantly. They dropped to the floor, their bodies splayed about Hayes' feet.

"Now," Todd said, "we can finish this. But first ..." and he aimed the gun back to the spot on the floor, where the other man lay waiting to die.

But the man was gone.

At the stairwell's first landing, Rage set the soldier he'd been carrying down upon the steps. Though he was still reeling in pain from the gunshot wound, his strength was quickly returning. Larry stood just behind them, M-16 pointed back down the stairwell.

"Is everyone out safely?" he asked, turning to Larry.

"Yes," Larry replied. "They should be out of the building by now. We need to get right behind them, get him to a hospital, and call for help."

"No," the soldier cut in, his breathing heavy, his voice hoarse. "There's – still a danger here. The detonator –"

"What detonator?" Rage asked, remembering what the other soldier had said to him in the stairwell.

"The target – Todd," he began, forcing his words out quickly. "He's set the facility to blow – multiple charges – all over the place. That remote he's holding – if he activates it – will blow them all – in 30 seconds. Blast radius – for miles. You – can't allow him to."

"If he does," Rage asked, "how do I stop it?"

"*If* he activates it," the soldier repeated, his breathing becoming more labored, "the remote has a range – one quarter-mile. Get it outside the range – the remote will still blow – but the others – won't."

Rage turned back toward the underground corridor, then back to Larry. "Get him to a hospital," Rage told him. "I'm going back down there."

"Wait," Larry cut in, grabbing his arm. "I can help you."

"No," Rage said. "Take care of the others. Your family, they need you alive. Mira; keep her safe. I'll handle this on my own. Now go."

And without another word, Rage descended the steps and disappeared from view.

With the woman in the white lab coat leading the way, Mira, Edna, and the two young boys made their way from the stairwell across the first-floor office space.

The woman ahead of Mira was walking as quickly as she could. She called back to them: "Once we're outside, I'll call for help," she said. "No cell phones allowed inside, so I have mine in my car."

"And then what?" Edna asked, panting, as they hurried through the blasted opening that had been the front entry way, amidst the charred bodies that still lay upon the ground. It had stopped raining, but black clouds still loomed in the sky above.

"And then we get as far away from here as we can," the woman replied.

"No," Mira interjected. "We can't. Rage and Larry are still in there."

"There's no time to explain this," the woman said quickly, still calling back to Mira as they began crossing the parking lot. "There's a bomb in there big enough to wipe out the entire area, and it could go off at any minute. We've got to get out of here."

"No!" Edna cried out. "Larry is still down there. We can't – we can't *leave* him."

The woman turned toward Edna, who was struggling to catch up. As the two met, the woman gripped both her arms and looked her in the eye. "Please understand," she implored, "if we don't leave now, we could all die. It could be too late as it is."

As those words were spoken, a noise arose in the distance. Mira turned toward the source. It was to the south of the complex, beyond the trees. It rapidly grew louder, and within seconds, a small convoy of armored vehicles could be seen through the trees. There were at least six or seven of them, all of them roughly the size of a motor home; all of them had large guns mounted to the top above the front cabin. Two black sedans followed closely behind. Three of the vehicles continued on the perimeter drive to the north; the remainder sped directly toward Mira and the others.

As the vehicles came to a screeching halt some fifty feet from where they stood, Mira could hear the woman in the lab coat say in a hushed voice: "Looks like we won't be going anywhere after all."

Before Mira could question that statement, armored troopers began spilling out of the vehicles in droves, and from the black sedans emerged six men dressed in similar SWAT gear to the agents who had killed Officer Jenkins. As they approached, four of the agents drew their weapons and pointed them at the group.

"By order of the United States Government," the agent in front commanded, "I order you to remain where you are and put your hands above your heads."

From the shadows behind the building's blasted entrance, Larry watched the unfolding scene. He'd carried the soldier, Lt. Oberlin was his name he'd learned, up to that spot when he saw the convoy approaching and the soldiers taking up positions outside the complex.

"Now what the hell do we do?" Larry said quietly.

"Simple," Oberlin said, still struggling to speak. Based on his labored breathing, Larry assumed he had a partially collapsed lung. "You – leave me here. I radio to their C.O. – and explain – the situation inside. They need to – evac the area."

"And what about the guns pointed at my family?"

"I'll – handle that," Oberlin said. "You go back in – and help your friend – get that detonator away from the target. If he fails – we're all gonna die."

Larry glanced back toward the dark office space behind him, then back out toward Edna, the boys, and Mira. There was no time to decide.

"All right," he finally said. "Just take care of my family."

"Get going," Oberlin replied. "Don't have – much time."

Carefully setting Oberlin down against a torched cubicle wall, Larry turned and headed across the dark office space, down toward the basement once again.

Inside the lead transport, General Jack Dunlap surveyed the grounds of the Strategic Research Complex through an array of wall monitors. The images streamed from the other transports taking positions around the facility.

An hour ago, he'd been debriefed on the situation happening inside the SRC: an extremely dangerous terrorist had holed himself up inside and had single-handedly taken out a battalion of fifty armed special-forces agents. At last count, there were no survivors.

The terrorist had wired the facility to blow, all the way down to the top-secret developmental weapons stockpile in the subterranean level. Based on the intel he'd received, any detonation within the facility would cause a chain reaction that would take out a hundred-square-mile land mass, at minimum.

His orders were to accompany the eight anti-bomb units that had been dispatched from Washington, Langley, and Quantico, take positions around the building, and await further orders.

According to the debriefing, none other than Colonel Nolan Hayes, formerly under Dunlap's own command, was inside the complex right now, engaging the target. Dunlap wondered if this situation had anything to do with Hayes' deployment to the civilian mission he'd caught wind of days ago. He hoped it did not.

If contact was lost with Hayes, the Pentagon would issue the 'go' order, sending Dunlap's men in to provide cover for the anti-bomb units, or to engage the target directly.

When the convoy approached moments earlier, the lead driver had spotted a small group of survivors emerging from the building's front entrance. Three women and two children. Dunlap ordered a squadron out to pick them up for questioning.

"Sir," a trooper's voice came through his headset, "survivors unharmed. Three others still inside with Col. Hayes and target. One of them is ours."

"Copy," Dunlap responded. "Have Medical set up a station to examine them. Once complete, your team will take up position at your set point."

"Copy, sir," the trooper replied. "Over and out."

Dunlap then addressed all of his squadron leaders. "All squadrons confirm when in position," he commanded. "Be ready to move in on my order."

Dunlap switched off his headset and turned back to the monitors. He sat quietly in his command chair, awaiting the order from the Pentagon.

76

Death Duel

Todd turned back down the hallway toward Hayes. He would deal with the interloper later.

"Disable the remote," Hayes ordered him a third time, stepping over the bodies of Temple's squadron. "I want your finger *off* that button when I finish you."

"Of course," Todd replied matter-of-factly. "I'd given my word."

He punched in a three-digit code upon the device's keypad. The blinking red light went out. He set it on the floor near the wall.

Without hesitation, Hayes charged forward, drawing both automatics from his belt and firing upon Todd, emptying the clips.

Todd moved to evade the incoming barrage of bullets, but Hayes had spread the fire in a way that made it impossible to dodge them all. As Todd dropped to the floor with flesh wounds in his right arm and both legs, Hayes was upon him.

"Lesson number one," Hayes snarled, kneeling over him and pulling a third pistol from a holster in his right boot, "never drop your leverage til your demands are met."

"Lesson number two," Todd countered, "never give your opponent such an opening up close." And before Hayes could react, he pulled two small knives from a pouch on his belt and shoved one through Hayes' right Achilles tendon, the other into the femoral artery at the top of his left leg.

Hayes staggered backward, screaming. Blood began to spurt from his left leg, spraying against the white brick wall next to him, drenching it in splotches of red as he stumbled. Steadying himself, he yanked the knife from the artery just as two more knives flew into his chest, punching through layers of Kevlar, flesh, and bone before finding a home in each of his lungs.

Choking for air, Hayes fell backward, tripping over the bodies of two of Temple's men before crashing hard to the floor. He gasped horribly, struggling to pull the knives from his punctured lungs.

Todd moved in and stood over him.

"Armor-piercing knives," he said in a smooth tone. "Special alloy. Just one of so many wonderful *toys* in this place. Like *this* one," and at that he pulled a blunt-nosed, four-barreled pistol from another compartment on the belt. From about eight inches away, he fired it into Hayes' right arm. Hayes jerked backward, roaring in pain.

"Burrowing rounds, they call these," he said, admiring the gun with a sickening grin. "They break apart under the skin, then the microscopic particles latch onto the bloodstream, clotting the arteries, killing the victim in minutes. Sounds painful. Is it?"

Recoiling in agonizing pain, Hayes snarled at Todd, spittle flying from his mouth.

"Cruel device; horrible way to die," he said flatly. "But then I guess that's why it's still in here, and not approved for the field, eh?"

Hayes said nothing. He'd pulled the first knife from his chest and was now laboring on the floor to remove the second one as well.

"Which brings me to a question," Todd continued. "Do you know why I wanted this? You and me, that is?" He gestured from himself to Hayes with the gun.

"It won't matter," Hayes wheezed viciously. "Once – you're dead."

"I wanted this," Todd continued, ignoring the comment. "Because I, just like you, want to learn something. About us. I figured out early on that you and I, we're alike. Since I've been here, they've done all sorts of tests, pushing me to the limits. Maybe it was all meant to kill me, maybe not. But either way, here I stand, still alive, plain as day.

"So it got me to wondering," he continued, picking up the remote detonator and clipping it to the belt. "What *would* it take to kill us? Bullets don't do it. Knives don't. Poisons don't. I'll bet even what I've done to *you* so far won't.

"So," he concluded, "now I'm just plain curious. I was your guinea pig, now you'll be *mine*. The result? You die, and I'll find out what it takes."

"Too bad for you," Hayes grimaced, "that I don't *care* how you die." And with a blinding movement, he grasped the pistol that had fallen to the floor and fired six times at point blank range, emptying the clip.

Todd maneuvered to dodge the bullets, but the range was too close. Two of the rounds hit him square in the midsection, the exit wounds punching out massive holes across the center of his back.

As Todd reeled backward, Hayes corralled his strength, standing up slowly as air once again began to collect in his lungs. He pulled the knife from his Achilles tendon and slapped another magazine into the pistol. When he looked up, Todd was gone.

It was then that he noticed a small, round object, roughly the size of a golf ball, had appeared from around the corner and was now rolling in his direction.

Bomb.

Without hesitation, Hayes leapt backward away from the object, but it was too late: the force of the blast carried him several feet into the air and down the hall, smashing his face against the ceiling before he careened into the pile of twisted metal and concrete rubble that had been the main lab entrance.

His skin felt hot, charred from the explosion; his bones seemed to crumble in spots as he tried to move; he'd likely broken a few in colliding with the wreckage.

He hadn't taken a breath when Todd was upon him once again, hurtling into him with ferocious velocity, his body a blunt instrument. Both men crashed into the main lab itself, tumbling to the center of its expansive floor, and immediately began exchanging blows. As they fought, the sound of each impact echoed throughout the complex; the sheer force shook the emergency lighting fixtures on the walls around them.

Out in the hallway, Rage had arrived in time to hear the explosion, and he saw Todd slip around the corner toward the source of the blast.

This much he knew: the two men, Todd and Hayes, seemed solely bent on killing one another. And the one left standing would control the detonator Todd was holding.

He needed to somehow get the detonator away from them, and outside the building's range.

As he began to move toward the fray, he heard footsteps behind him.

He whirled around and recognized the cop immediately. "Hell are you doing back down here?" he whispered harshly.

"You're gonna need help," Larry said in a low voice.

"No," Rage urged him. "Get all of them away from here. Now, before it's –"

"Already too late," Larry said, cutting him off. "They'll never get far enough away in time. We don't have a choice. *We* need to stop it from happening. You and I."

Rage eyed him skeptically but knew there was no time to argue.

"Fine," he finally said. "Can you hit him from a distance?" he asked, nodding to the pistol Larry was holding.

"If I get a clear shot," Larry answered. "Even while he's moving."

"Then follow my lead," Rage said.

Without another word, the two made their way toward the main lab.

Outside, General Jack Dunlap received the call he'd been waiting for.

"Sir," he answered, taking the call from Armstrong on his headset.

"General Dunlap," Armstrong replied. "Moments ago, the signal from Col. Hayes' GPS unit was terminated. This could mean anything, but we're taking no chances. Prepare your men for insertion per contingency plan."

"Copy that," Dunlap replied. "Over and out."

Once again, Dunlap switched his frequency to broadcast and issued the order: "All units," he directed them, "prepare to insert on my command."

At the center of the lab's sprawling floor, Todd remained on top of Hayes, the two continuing to pummel one another, neither uttering a word, each using all the brute force he could muster in every blow.

Amid the exchange, Todd removed another golf ball-sized explosive from his belt. Hayes knocked it from his grip, sending it flying across the room. It hit the floor and rolled to a wall, detonating under a chemical workstation table.

As the chemicals ignited, tiny flames began to dance beneath the large table, rapidly stretching their way upward.

Hayes jammed two fingers into Todd's larynx, jolting him backward. Using the opening, he wedged a foot between himself and Todd and pushed off. Todd was launched high into the air, soaring across the room before plummeting into an array of machines along the far wall with a deafening crash.

Hayes leapt to the spot where Todd had landed, grabbed hold of Todd's wrist and ankle, and threw him again across the enormous room. Todd's body once again smashed full force into rows of heavy machinery before spilling to the floor.

Again wasting no time, Hayes moved to where Todd lay amidst the splintered, metallic debris of the machines he'd collided with, his body sprawled awkwardly like a broken doll.

Hayes towered over him. It was time to finish this.

As Larry and Rage came upon the spot of the last explosion, small flames still flickering among the debris, something else caught Larry's eye.

Not ten feet from the flames, mounted to the wall about eighteen inches off the floor, was a small device.

Taking a closer look at it, he noticed the blacked out LED display and what looked like gray putty packed to the side of the unit.

C4 compound.

One of Todd's detonators.

His eyes met Rage's, who nodded back to him, clearly thinking the same thing. If any of those detonators caught fire and went off, a chain reaction with the other units would still occur, regardless of what happened with the remote Todd was holding.

Spotting a fire extinguisher on the near wall, Larry pulled it from its mounting and hastily doused the debris until the sparse flames went out.

"Now we got two jobs," Rage told him. "Take out the bomber, and keep all the other charges from blowing, too. No fire, no ricocheted bullets, nothing."

Seconds later, they arrived at the demolished entrance to the main lab.

The opening to the room itself glowed and flickered a bright hue of orange; its heat emanated out toward them menacingly. An opening straight into hell itself. The entire room looked like it had caught fire. From beyond, thunderous crashes echoed throughout the space.

Rage turned toward Larry. "Change of plans. We gotta get that fire out."

"No," Larry said. "I'll handle the fire. You take him out. No time to waste."

Without another word, they moved toward the entrance.

Looming mere feet away from where Todd had landed, Hayes pulled the combat blade from its sheathe in his left boot.

"Did you really believe for one second," he said, "that you stood a chance toe-to-toe with me? Even with all you can do, you're nothing but a high-priced gun. A *terrorist*. We brought you here for a purpose, and you served it."

Several yards behind Hayes, near the room's destroyed entrance, flames had spread quickly to other workstations, igniting chemical compounds on shelves.

"But the time's come to end this," Hayes concluded. "Stand up."

Todd, who'd begun to stir amidst the wreckage of the machines, slowly pulled himself together and stood up to face Hayes.

As his gaze met Hayes' cold stare, a smile spread widely across his face.

"Your arrogance," Hayes said derisively, tossing the knife in his hand, "is what's going to make this all the more satisfying."

"And yours," Todd replied, "will be the reason you die."

With a flick of his wrist, Todd threw two pea-sized capsules at Hayes. They landed on his blood-stained uniform, sticking to the front of each shoulder. Then, without warning both capsules detonated, blowing both of Hayes' arms off clean at the shoulder.

Screaming in agony, Hayes fell forward onto his knees. The flashpoint of the two tiny blasts had mostly cauterized the wounds, but small amounts of blood still spurted and flowed from the two stumps of charred flesh where Hayes' arms had been.

"Micro-grenades," Todd told him. "Coated with a combustible adhesive that activates on impact, igniting the charges inside. Pure genius."

Hayes did not respond; his eyes glazed over in shock as he remained kneeling on the floor, his body twitching spasmodically.

Back across the room, the flames had now begun to spread across the floor. Chemicals on tables and shelves burst in their containers from the heat, spraying up onto the wall and floor, adding fuel to the blaze. Most of the room flickered and glowed a bright orange, intensifying with every second.

"Where in all your training," Todd said, beginning to circle Hayes, "did you learn to underestimate your opponent? Give him a chance to recover? To think for one *second* that, even if 'just' a hired gun, that he wasn't every bit the killer *you* were?"

Bending down, he grasped Hayes by the hair, pulling his face close to his own.

"You think that, just because you kill in the name of country," Todd snarled, "that you're free of consequence. That the end justifies the means. You call it duty. I call it necessity. But in the end, it doesn't matter why. We do it because we *can*. It's one of our gifts.

"But *this,*" he exclaimed, placing his three-fingered hand in front of Hayes' face, "is one of our *limits*. All the things we can do, there are breaking points. Just like now, with you," he said, gesturing to Hayes' missing arms.

"*Now* we know," Todd continued, "there are things that can't be healed. A severed limb. A lost organ. Both were done to me. But for all that *was* done, one question remains: what will *kill* us?"

As the words left his lips, Todd withdrew yet another weapon from the belt: a small, black and silver device that looked like a miniature crossbow. An oversized trigger curled outward from its side. Protruding out from the center was a pointed, two-inch spike.

Tightening his grip on Hayes' hair, Todd pointed the spike into his forehead, the tip touching his skin. "It's time we found out," he said.

Suddenly he was struck hard from the side, tackled at the waist by some unseen force. As he was hit, Todd watched the device fly from his hand, sliding across the floor until it disappeared beneath one of the large machines at the far wall.

Gaining his bearings, Todd glanced around to see who had hit him.

"You," he said, the vicious smile flashing across his face. "I'd almost forgotten."

Outside, Dunlap watched as the array of monitors on the wall began to relay visuals from each of his squad leaders' helmet cams. The eight squadrons had begun to make their way into the facility, entering from multiple points. Orders were for radio silence unless visual contact with the target was made. If visual contact *was* made, the order had been issued: fire upon the target at first sight, no hesitation, shooting to kill. At this stage, collateral damage was inconsequential.

After ramming into Todd with as much force as he could muster, Rage tumbled to the floor, gathering himself for Todd's next move.

Todd, who had flown several feet from the impact, now stood up, his black eyes settling on Rage intently.

"This ends now," Rage said. "Where's the remote."

"This, you mean?" Todd asked, patting the detonator with his left hand, the device clipped to his belt.

"No. I'm not quite finished here yet," Todd said musingly. "If you want it, you'll just have to take it from me."

"Have it your way." And with a roar Rage leapt forward, striking Todd across the face before pinning him to the floor, pummeling him with his bare fists. Todd countered with an uppercut to Rage's chin, then kicked him off, throwing Rage back into a rolling workstation, which he took crashing to the floor with him.

Not twenty yards away, Larry quickly realized that the paltry fire extinguisher he'd brought to battle the flames wouldn't even come close to doing the job. Within seconds he'd emptied it, to no effect on the flames that had continued to slither up the wall.

A beaker on a nearby table exploded, forcing Larry to shield his eyes.

He glanced around through the expanding haze, in search of another extinguisher. It then dawned on him that a place like this would have to have some kind of alarm, or –

Sprinkler system.

He looked desperately up to the ceiling, hoping for what he might find. Through the veil of smoke, he saw it plain as day: the network of narrow pipes running a checkerboard pattern along the high ceiling, the sprinkler units themselves every ten or so feet apart.

So why hadn't they activated?

Despite the power having been cut, no sprinkler system was powered by electricity, in case of the very event of a power outage.

Unless … the bastard had outright disabled it.

There had to be a manual override. But where *that* was, was anyone's guess.

Using his sleeve as a shield from the billowing smoke, he began searching for it.

Todd got up and strode forward, standing in front of Rage.

"Felt good to do that, didn't it," he said, wiping blood from his lip. "Always feels good. Striking someone, hard as you can. Over and over. I know. I have it in me, too."

"No," Rage said, slowly getting up. "I'm not like you."

Todd laughed. "The only difference between you and me," he said. "is that you don't admit it. Like just now: you didn't even *try* for the remote. You just wanted *me*. No; you and I, we're *exactly* the same."

"Only one of us is gonna walk out of here tonight," Rage said.

"A shame," Todd replied wistfully. "Because I have no quarrel with you. Maybe you're even here for the same reasons I am. Against your will. But once I'm done with Hayes, I see now that you're the only one who might stand in my way. So you'll need to be dealt with, too."

As the words left Todd's lips, he drew the blunt-nosed, four-barreled pistol once again. Pointing it inches from Rage's face, he pulled the trigger. Rage ducked underneath it by a hair, then followed through with a devastating uppercut, striking Todd hard below the chin before following again with a roundhouse kick to the side of the head. As Todd reeled backward, Rage stayed on the offensive, straight-leg kicking Todd square in the chest once, twice, until finally pinning him against the wall, slapping the gun from his grip. He thrust a hand around Todd's neck, pushing him upward against the wall.

"Goddamned guns," Rage snarled, squeezing Todd's throat. "Never a fair fight." With that, his free hand grasped the remote, ripping it from its clip on the belt.

Suddenly, ice-cold water began showering down upon them. As Rage instinctively glanced upward, Todd pulled another pistol from the belt, shoving the nozzle into Rage's stomach before firing twice. Rage roared in pain as his grasp on Todd's neck loosened. Todd immediately straight-armed him in the chin, forcing Rage backward, falling to the floor.

Todd quickly advanced on him, planting a forceful kick into Rage's stomach.

"In a fair fight, on pure brawn alone," he began, picking up the remote from the floor, "it would seem you have me beaten.

"But then, as you say," he smiled, tapping the tip of the gun to the side of his head, "when is there *ever* a fair fight?"

Grabbing Rage by the hair, he pulled his head up, pointing the gun into his mouth. "Now," he said simply. "Time to say goodbye."

As Todd set his finger on the trigger, a bullet sliced through his chest.

Todd faltered, losing his grip on the gun. His wide, unblinking eyes flickered in the fading, orange-hued light of the room.

Letting go of Rage, Todd stumbled forward, gasping horribly. He frantically looked around, in search of who had shot him.

Another bullet punched through his chest. A third. A fourth.

Todd's vision blurred. Through the sprinklers' deluge, the room came in and out.

Gaining his focus, it was then that he saw him. A lone figure with a handgun, pointed directly at him.

Todd staggered, almost falling. Then, reclaiming his balance, clawing at the very air in front of him, he sprinted forward at the man.

Twenty yards away, the towering flames had begun to wane as the sprinkler system continued to douse the massive room.

Not one minute before, Larry had found the manual override box toward the center of the lab's back wall, broken the glass, and pulled the heavy steel lever. The main valve opened, immediately activating the network of sprinklers overhead. Larry watched as the downpour began to quell the inferno on the wall opposite him.

Suddenly, amid the din, Larry heard the loud pop of gunfire. He turned to see Rage falling backward onto the floor and Todd quickly stepping over him. Through the shower, he could make out the gun being drawn, forced into Rage's face.

No time. Need to act now.

Aiming at Todd's chest, the largest and easiest target amid the deluge, Larry drew his pistol and fired.

He saw Todd stagger backward but remain standing; not taking cover, but rather searching for who had shot him.

Without hesitating, Larry fired a second time, again connecting with Todd's chest.

Todd faltered once again but as before did not fall.

Larry fired twice more.

He watched as Todd stumbled, clutching his chest. After almost falling to the floor; Todd once again recaptured his footing, desperately glancing around the room.

Todd's gaze locked in Larry's direction. He'd been spotted.

With a savage roar, Todd raced toward Larry, launching himself into the air as he bore down upon him.

Backpedaling toward the wall, Larry pulled the trigger once, twice, but no bullets fired. Either the pistol had jammed, or the magazine was empty.

In an instant, Todd was upon him, face contorted, the maniacal snarl filling Larry's ears. With a blinding quickness, he thrust his fist at Larry, striking him in the side of the head. Even though Larry instinctively rolled with the punch, its sheer force knocked him hard to the floor.

But as Todd's bare feet made contact with the tile floor, he slipped on the wet surface. Losing his footing, he fell forward, face first, head smashing into the sprinkler system's manual override box with a loud crash. The already-broken glass splintered into hundreds of smaller shards, raining down upon Larry as he lay dazed on the floor.

Larry covered his face as the tiny shards cascaded around him. Seconds later, he glanced up to see Todd, facing away from him, slowly slipping down to the flooded tile floor, his body twitching spasmodically. As Todd struggled to turn toward him, Larry saw the large shard of glass that had lodged itself deep in the center of his throat.

Bleeding uncontrollably from the jugular, Todd's horrific gaze settled on Larry. Death had begun to creep into his jet black eyes. He tried to speak, but only gargled blood spilled from his mouth. The glass had severed both his jugular and windpipe.

Hands shaking, he withdrew the remote detonator from under his gown, and, with a wayward glint in his emptying eyes, placed his left hand on the activation key.

"NO!" Larry screamed out, realizing what Todd was about to do. Still on his back, he kicked off against the wall, lunging at Todd in a desperate, frantic attempt to pull the remote from the dying man's hands.

But it was too late. As the final, rasped breath left his lips, Todd's trembling hand firmed its grip on the key, and turned it.

Heart pounding, Larry reached Todd, tearing the remote from his flaccid hands. Glaring at the tiny display, he saw that the countdown had begun.

00:30.

He quickly turned the key back, in the hope it would stop the counter's progress.

00:29.

00:28.

"God," he said, his voice cracking. He searched the small device for any button that might halt the countdown, then desperately looked around, as if an answer lie nearby.

Suddenly, a voice called out to him: *"Here!"*

Larry glanced to his left to see Rage, moving quickly toward the door.

Understanding, he heaved the detonator to him. "It's live! Go!" he shouted.

But as the remote landed in Rage's hands, another voice bellowed out: *"HALT!"*

Larry whirled around.

At the entrance stood ten soldiers in full SWAT gear, rifles all pointed at Rage.

"By order of the United States Government," the voice called out, "I hereby order you to stay where you are, placing your hands in the air!"

77

Timebomb

The glass exploded outward as Rage launched through the first-story window, his bare feet hitting the soft, wet earth as he landed.

Bleeding heavily from multiple gunshot wounds, he began sprinting through the clearing, toward the wooded area beyond.

Nine seconds earlier, the cop had screamed out to Rage that the bomber had activated the remote detonator. They had thirty seconds to get it at least a quarter-mile away from the building, or they would all be dead.

But as he made for the exit, several soldiers appeared, guns pointed at him, ordering him to surrender the remote.

There was no time. Rage ran at them, smashing through, spilling them about like bowling pins. But in the brief seconds before impact, they had begun to open fire on him, their shots connecting numerous times in his legs, arms, and torso.

The pain was excruciating; he could feel his insides, his muscles bleeding.

One quarter mile.

Once he'd reached it, he could allow himself to die; but not before.

About midway across the clearing he could hear a voice shouting. More gunfire. Bullets ripped through him, slicing his flesh. He felt one of his lungs puncture. His legs came close to giving way as he felt the tendons around his right knee tear apart.

He was near the end. Another shot, two at most, and his body would give out.

As he neared the end of the clearing, he could hear screaming, then more shouting; and suddenly the gunfire ceased.

He raced through the wooded area, chest heaving, trying to take in more air; his bullet-riddled legs churned beneath him.

As he ran, he caught the remote's LED timer out of the corner of his eye.

00:13.

He forced himself to run harder. He had no idea how fast he was moving or how far from the building he actually was.

As he cleared the wooded area, a large, open space lay before him. At that moment, it dawned on him: running alone would not carry him far enough.

From a full sprint, gasping desperately for air, Rage pushed off against the ground, leaping into the sky with as much power as his legs could muster.

00:10.

When it reached 00:02, he would hurl the device as far away as he could.

Coming down to earth with a hard landing, Rage coughed up blood. The world around him blurred. Ignoring both, he regained his stride and, pushing off once more, launched into the air to the fullest extent of his legs' remaining power.

High in mid air, Rage gave the timer one final glance.

00:03.

Rage cocked his arm and made to throw the device.

As the remote left his fingertips it exploded, consuming Rage in a flash of blinding fire.

78

Tragic Ally

Pinned down against the grassy knoll just beyond the parking lot, Mira's head jerked upward when she heard the explosion.

Less than a minute ago, she had watched as the window shattered outward on the near side of the building, and the lone figure dashed toward the wooded area in a blur. When she saw, she knew exactly who it was, and exactly what he was doing.

Then, to her horror, the soldiers around her began firing at him. Though he tried to dodge the barrage of bullets, she could see several of them strike him, almost knocking him off his feet.

But he kept running.

Instinctively she ran toward him, directly into the line of fire, screaming for them to stop. She heard Edna shriek at her. A deep voice called over a megaphone, and the gunfire ceased. Seconds later, two soldiers caught up to her, pinning her face down to the soft, wet ground, holding her by the arms to restrain her.

Now, as the soldiers helped her to her feet, she witnessed the flash of orange light from over the tree line, and a wave of emotion came over her.

He had done it. He had saved them all.

And she believed, she *knew*, he'd gotten away from the bomb safely. She knew that any moment, he'd reappear through the woods and return to them, would return to her, having saved them all. He would be a hero, vindicated from anything in his past, ready for a future entirely different than everything his old life had been.

Suddenly, from behind her, delighted screams reached her ears.

Eyes full of hope, she turned toward their source.

A guilt-ridden mix of relief and disappointment came over her as she saw Larry appear in the blown-out front entrance, accompanied by four soldiers, and begin walking toward them.

Edna and the two young boys ran to him. Mira pulled free of the soldier who'd been holding her, who did not restrain her. As she ran to Larry, she glanced back at the woods every few seconds, expecting to see Rage emerge from the trees.

As Larry's family embraced him, Mira did as well, and his arms reached out further to include her, his left hand clutching her shoulder tightly.

As Larry and his family held her, she began to cry, her eyes staying on the woods.

Larry had emerged from the building beaten and scarred, but alive.

Only a moment ago, he'd stared death in the face not once, but twice: first, the demonic face of Elias Todd; then the detonator that would kill everyone he cared about.

It happened all too quickly from there: Rage; the soldiers; the gunfire; Larry surrendering; the soldiers' discovery of Todd's body.

From there, they discovered the body of Col. Hayes, who'd been fighting with Todd before they'd arrived. Larry didn't know if Hayes was alive or dead.

He was more concerned with Rage.

When he heard the blast from inside the building, he braced himself for the worst.

When seconds had passed, and nothing happened, he knew.

The son of a bitch had done it.

But had *he* survived?

Gotten *himself* far enough away from the blast in time?

As he saw Edna, Marcus, and Daniel amid the pockets of federal agents in the parking lot, they began running toward him, and he pulled them all into a bear hug, which Mira joined seconds later. Exhaustion began to wash over him. His entire body ached; his limbs felt locked up; but holding them was all he wanted to do. Letting loose his emotions, he pulled them all closer to him, exhaling a long, choked breath.

Seconds later, two soldiers approached him. "Officer Parker," one said, "we have questions for you about what happened inside. Can you follow me, please."

Glancing up at the soldier and nodding, Larry pulled his family and Mira tighter.

"Oh, Larry," Edna said, her voice shaking. "Is it ... is it over?"

"Yes," Larry told her. "It's over."

Moments later, the two soldiers led Larry into the lead transport, where a tall, barrel-chested officer waited for him. He'd been sitting in a command chair next to several flat monitors mounted to the wall, but he stood up when he saw Larry approach. Judging by the numerous pins and medals crowded across his lapels, Larry assumed he was of high rank. The two soldiers who'd accompanied Larry onto the bus stopped about ten feet away, saluted the officer, then remained behind, standing at attention.

"Officer Parker, is it," the officer addressed him, extending a hand. "General Jack Dunlap, USMC. I head up the Pentagon's special task forces unit. Please, have a seat." He gestured to a second chair facing the command chair.

"How do you know my name?" Larry asked curiously, sitting down.

"Well, aside from watching CNN," Dunlap answered with a slight huff, "given everything that's happened over these past twenty-four hours, I've received a full debriefing on you, your companion, Miss Givens, and the situation you're both in."

"So you understand that we're innocent," he said, cutting right to the chase.

Dunlap paused.

"Without revealing more than I am allowed to," he began carefully, "it's come to the Pentagon's attention that ... certain people involved with this project had made some ... rogue decisions while carrying out the mission. Decisions unbeknownst to, and unauthorized by, the Department of Defense.

"During the mission," Dunlap continued, "the assertion was made that you and Miss Givens were involved in a terrorist cell. Until proven otherwise, we were inclined to pursue you."

"So I assume that, since I'm here and not in a cell or a bodybag," Larry assessed, "it's been proven otherwise."

"Correct," Dunlap confirmed. "So that being said, you, Miss Givens, and the others will need to go through a full debriefing process. As this entire matter is one of national security, the public can never know the details of what happened here. I'm sure you can understand that."

"So what does that mean for us?" Larry said.

"It means that," Dunlap explained, "after the debriefing process, we'll need to maintain close surveillance on all of you for a specified time period. This includes certain members of your police precinct, who as a matter of course are also being debriefed in the exact same manner as you will be."

"*Spying* on us," Larry said derisively.

"Officer Parker," Dunlap replied, a quiet laugh under his breath, "as I'm sure you already know, there's no such thing as 'off the grid' anymore. This happens every day, to more people than you'd ever guess."

Larry paused, allowing himself to absorb Dunlap's last statement. "And if we cooperate?" he finally asked, not wanting to even ask about the alternative.

"If all goes as we expect with the debriefing," Dunlap stated, "you, Miss Givens, and everyone will be granted a full pardon. Your names will be cleared immediately, and there will even be compensation provided to you, for your suffering and inconvenience."

"Hush money," Larry said, again a disapproving tone to his voice.

"Call it what you will," Dunlap said with a frown. "And know that you may always refuse it. The details will be in your debriefing. Now. The Pentagon is already working on an explanation for the 'misunderstanding' of circumstances that you, Miss Givens, and your family found yourselves wrapped up in."

Larry exhaled. "All right," he said.

"But if something comes out – from anyone – during the surveillance period, or even after," Dunlap warned, "that can change very quickly."

"Is that supposed to be a threat?" Larry said.

"No, just the truth, Mr. Parker," Dunlap replied matter-of-factly. "The nature of the operation in which you found yourself entangled, the public can never know. Your government will go to great lengths to ensure it remains that way. The important thing for you to remember is, no one was hurt."

"Not true," Larry argued. "An officer in my precinct was murdered last night."

"Yes," Dunlap agreed grimly. "By a rogue agent acting *alone*, not on behalf of the Pentagon. And for that he *will* be tried in a special court of law."

"But it was because of your 'operation' that it happened in the first place," Larry challenged.

"Officer Parker, I am not here to debate with you," Dunlap stated, keeping his voice even. "I am empowered to offer you amnesty. You are in a terrible mess. I don't need to remind you that you've killed three Federal agents."

"In self-defense!" Larry exclaimed, becoming angry.

"*That* can be decided in a court of law, if need be," Dunlap countered. He paused, then went on: "On both sides, there are truths we need to accept in order to move on. This – what I'm offering you now – is a chance for you, Miss Givens, your family, everyone – to move on, relatively unscathed, from the situation you're in. It's not a blank check; yes, it has conditions, but it's the best we can do, given the circumstances. Do you understand?"

Larry sat in silence for a moment, keeping his glance at first on Dunlap, then turning to regard the monitors. He understood; there really was no choice in the matter.

"So what's next," he said flatly.

"Very shortly, a transport will be arriving to take you to the Pentagon," Dunlap explained. "There you'll be debriefed and instructed on what to do next."

At that moment, Larry remembered the one remaining loose end: the two memory cards he'd dropped in the mail to Ollie. If not retrieved, they would jeopardize his end of the bargain.

"There is something," he began. "Last night, in a mail drop just south –"

"Ah, the data cards," Dunlap said, as if it had appeared to dawn on him as well.

"Yes," Larry said, bewildered at how Dunlap had guessed what he was thinking.

"Don't worry," he said. "We have them. Once it was discovered they were missing, it didn't take long to locate and retrieve them."

"But how did you ...?"

"How did we find them?" Dunlap finished for him, a wry smirk on his face. "You're a man of the law. Surely you didn't think we'd have information of that nature out there without some kind of tracking beacon, did you?"

Larry stared at him in disbelief.

"And, quite frankly, I might add," he went on, "good thing for you that you'd left them when you did. About an hour longer and we'd have had *you*, too."

"May I go now," Larry said, suddenly deflated from fatigue. "I'd like to be with my family."

"Of course," Dunlap said, gesturing to the door with his hands. "Morgan, Onorato," he addressed the two soldiers behind Larry. "Please escort Officer Parker outside. Have one of the EMTs take a look at him and dress his wounds."

"Yes sir," one of the soldiers behind Larry replied.

Outside, the sun had broken through the clouds and was beginning to settle peacefully into the treetops off to the west. Four more transports had arrived, and Larry watched as the bomb squads rushed into the building in search of the remaining detonators.

He glanced ahead of him to Edna, Mira, and the boys, each of whom was being looked over by one of the EMTs on scene. The boys suddenly looked older to him; more mature, as if they weren't children anymore. Edna was fussing with one of the medics; reading her lips, he saw her telling him 'not to fret so much' over her. Mira sat quietly, staring off into the distance, a lonely look in her eyes.

Larry knew whom she was waiting for.

He looked beyond the scene ahead of him, first to the enormous SRC building, then to the green landscape surrounding it, and finally to the line of trees that thickened into the forest beyond. He watched the trees closely, their vibrant, colorful foliage in the setting sun, hoping that, among their stillness, there would come a sign of him.

There was none.

79

One Week Later

Daybreak came over Washington, D.C.

General Jack Dunlap strode down the hallways of the Pentagon's fourth floor. It was Sunday morning, just before seven o'clock, one week after the events that had transpired at the SRC. He was headed to a post-briefing, his presence requested due to his involvement in the project's "late stages," as they'd called it.

Dunlap likened himself more to a "clean-up crew" than anything else.

Upon entering the briefing room, he saw Edward Armstrong, the Secretary of Defense, and three men he didn't recognize. After a brief round of introductions, he learned they were Undersecretaries Ferguson Millett and Ronald Tolson of the NSA; and Dr. Klaus Johannsen, Chief Scientist of the Pentagon's Advanced Sciences Group.

Dunlap took a seat next to Armstrong.

"What do you know," Dunlap said quietly, leaning toward him.

"Most of what you will, too, in about ten minutes," Armstrong answered.

At that moment, Johannsen stepped forward and took the podium.

"Gentlemen," he began. "Thank you all for joining. In the days following the terrible events at the Strategic Research Complex, my teams have been working around the clock to determine the causes behind the security breach that resulted in the deaths of twenty-three SRC employees and forty-nine NSA special-class troopers.

"As you know, our official story was parceled out to the media immediately after the event: a terrorist cell seized the SRC, resulting in a hostage situation and firefight with NSA troopers. The media has taken this story and run with it, so communication with them on this ongoing investigation is our key priority.

"Yesterday we concluded the debrief of the civilian witnesses who survived the event, and we have all measures in place to ensure the situation will be contained.

"And as for our potential whistle-blower," he continued, "I'm pleased to report that an agreement has been reached with Dr. Barnes to ensure her cooperation as well. Because the Inner Circle had plausible deniability on all tests performed on Asset One, she is now of the understanding that Dr. Ingramov acted of his own accord, *without* authorization from the Department of Defense. Further, her participation within our team will continue, however in a somewhat different capacity.

"As for the operation itself, however," he continued. "Due to the high death toll from the incident, some congressional leaders have demanded an official inquiry.

"It is Mr. Secretary's and my opinion," he said, gesturing to the Secretary of Defense, "that this will force the President's hand to authorize an external investigation. Therefore, in order to protect the long-term viability of the operation, all activities surrounding the project will be put on hold."

"For how long?" Tolson inquired.

"At least until the investigation has completed," Johannsen answered. "In the meantime, all samples and records will be moved to an undisclosed location."

"What about Hayes?" Dunlap cut in.

Johannsen paused, clearly taken out of rhythm by the General's interjection. Without speaking a word, he clicked a button, and the Department of Defense logo on the far wall disappeared, replaced by an image Dunlap would not soon forget.

"This," Johannsen said solemnly, "is the current state of Col. Hayes."

The image was of a white, windowless room. At the center of the far wall was some kind of steel-and-glass enclosure. Johannsen advanced the image again, revealing a close-up of the enclosure itself. Inside it was a hospital bed, and on the bed lay a man. Both of his arms were missing at the shoulder, replaced by tightly taped stumps that jutted out only a few inches from his protruding collarbone.

He was horribly emaciated; his wrinkled, loose skin was ghost-pale; his closed eyelids bulged from recessed sockets. He appeared to be nothing more than a shell. Several tubes fed into his nose, mouth, and chest.

The silence in the room only amplified the shock Dunlap was feeling.

"As you all know," Johannsen began, "Col. Hayes was in many ways the prototype for the research that also produced Assets One and Two. In fact, his DNA is nearly identical to the others. However, there is one key difference, and it's the main reason we couldn't use him as the basis of our operation."

He advanced the slide one more time. It now displayed a different picture of Hayes: a recent close-up of his face, prior to the events at the SRC.

"You see," he went on, "a key trait in all three subjects is rapid cell regeneration. It enables them to recover more quickly from fatigue and injury, at roughly a milli-fraction of the time it takes in a normal human subject. It also all but prevents them from being susceptible to illness or disease. In Assets One and Two, there appear to be no downsides to this trait.

"However, in Col. Hayes' case," he concluded, "this regeneration factor resulted in his aging at one-point-three times the rate of a normal human subject."

Across the room, Dunlap leaned back in his chair. He pondered this fact, recalling the changes in Hayes' appearance in the years under his command.

"You see, despite his mature appearance," Johannsen began again, gesturing to Hayes' image on the screen, "Col. Hayes is in his mid-thirties."

"So how is it," Armstrong began, "that he looks like he's at death's door now?"

"Because, quite frankly, he *is*," Johannsen replied somberly. "In Col. Hayes' case, physical damage requires additional cell regeneration for the body to repair itself, which in turn *accelerates* the degenerative process of *existing* cells, thus making him age even *more* rapidly. He sustained extensive injuries while engaging with Asset One. Further confounding things, what his body can't repair, it nonetheless continues to *attempt* to repair, keeping the cycle going … likely, until the point of termination."

"And there's nothing you can do?" Dunlap asked.

"Unfortunately, no," Johannsen said. "Ironically, another objective of this project was to find a way to slow Col. Hayes' aging process. It was a key reason behind his motivation to bring the subjects in. But at this stage, I'm afraid we're almost out of time."

"How long does he have?" the Secretary inquired.

"We estimate it's a matter of days," Johannsen answered.

Silence fell over the room.

"Gentlemen," the Secretary finally broke in, "let me summarize where we are. Forty-nine servicemen and twenty-three civilians have lost their lives due to what amounts to botched security measures at the SRC. Even more of our fine servicemen died in the field under Col. Hayes' command. Our operation has been put on hiatus, and in the process, we've lost the country's best soldier.

"It is clear that we have taken a step *backward*, not forward," he concluded. "And right now, our best move is to adjourn all talks among us until I deem otherwise.

"Do I hear any objections," he added grimly.

There was no response from the room.

"Then this meeting is adjourned," he finally said.

Moments later, Dunlap was walking alone down the Pentagon's outer hallway when Armstrong strode up next to him.

Dunlap looked over at his longtime colleague. "What is it, Edward."

"Jack," Armstrong said, "what did you think about all that, in the briefing room?"

"About *what*, exactly?" Dunlap glanced sideways at him as he continued to walk.

"About what you *learned*," Armstrong answered. "About what you now know about Hayes. What you think about the operation. About … getting involved."

Dunlap stopped and glared at Armstrong. "I think a *lot* of things, Edward," he said, his voice deep with anger. "I think what you knew about Hayes should have been shared with me a long time ago. I think you should bury this 'project' as deep into the ground as you can, lock it up, and throw away the key.

"And lastly," he said, "I don't know what conversation you heard back there, but as of five minutes ago, there is nothing *to* get involved in. It's over, Edward."

"In its current state, yes," Armstrong said, a curious tone to his voice. "But … why don't you come to my office with me, and we'll talk."

80

Beginnings

Compared with its normal buzz of activity, the precinct at Addison and Halsted was relatively quiet that Sunday morning.

Larry pushed open the front double doors, taking in the stale but familiar air inside. It was a welcome breath. His first time back in the precinct since the events from the prior weekend, he didn't know what to expect coming back through those doors.

Somehow, he'd expected the place to have changed during his absence. Or at least *feel* changed. It hadn't. He felt an odd sense of comfort from this.

It was only a few minutes after eight o'clock, so most of the officers had either just departed from their shift or were down in the locker room suiting up for the day.

He thought about the last several days in the Pentagon: he, the boys, Mira, and Edna all separated, meeting with counselors, psychologists, profilers, and others. In lieu of the truth, the week was spent 'learning' the story he'd now memorized: the federal manhunt leading to Chicago, the military task force secretly dispatched to kill or capture the leader of a new terrorist cell. While the strike team was on the ground, a high-ranking agent went rogue, falsely identifying a Chicago police officer and his female companion as members of the terrorist cell. A chase ensued, and members of the officer's family were taken into protective custody. During the manhunt, the rogue agent killed a Chicago police officer, along with several federal agents under his own command.

A standoff with the terrorist ensued at a north-side Chicago police precinct, where he was eventually captured, but in the process, killed eight federal agents.

In the meantime, federal authorities continued their search for the officer and the woman, who had fled after witnessing the rogue agent execute another police officer before gunning down two of his own men.

During the manhunt, the Chicago Police Department remained in full cooperation with federal authorities and assisted in bringing down the terrorist leader.

Larry had learned that members of the precinct, along with a few top officials within the Department, had all been debriefed in the exact same manner.

They were to maintain the official story, no exceptions. No comment to either the public or the press. They could only speak about the incident amongst themselves, or Pentagon counselors if needed, but never over the telephone or electronic communication. Nothing that could ever be recorded or traced.

An unrelated story was created for Elias Todd: a professional hit man arrested on charges of murder and illegal arms trade, he'd committed suicide while in federal custody.

All of them would be subject to one year of surveillance by the Pentagon, by wiretap, GPS, satellite, long- and short-range recording equipment, and other means.

Larry hated this part most of all. Even though he understood that *everyone* lived in a glass house in this day and age, Larry found it unsettling that there was no such thing as true privacy anymore.

And he had his misgivings about the truth.

The official story was in many ways true, or at least close to the truth. He did, in fact, believe that the agent pursuing them had gone rogue; there was little question to that. And, never understanding what actually went on in that federal compound known as the SRC, Larry had no basis to wonder why it had been left out of the official story.

But the vigilante, Rage, was a different case altogether.

To cover up the truth, he'd been made a scapegoat of convenience.

Though Larry was convinced he was guilty of the crimes he'd committed in recent weeks, this was not the form of justice he deserved.

Not one to whom so many owed their lives.

He had no surviving family; no one to hold memorial services for him, no one to claim what meager possessions he must have had, no one to settle his affairs.

No one to identify what little remains of him had been found.

And no one to know the truth on his behalf.

No one but Larry and the others, who were not even allowed to speak of it.

And in the end, Rage would never know why they'd wanted him in the first place.

"Larry?" a familiar voice said, cutting into his thoughts.

Doreen, who was just wrapping up her shift, stood not ten feet from him. Her normally abrasive demeanor quickly gave way to the almost motherly hug she lunged forward to quickly wrap him up in, squeezing the breath out of him.

"H-hi Doreen," he managed as the air was forced from his lungs.

"We didn't – I mean we didn't know –" she began blubbering, pulling back so she could see him, her wide face soaked with relief.

"If I was alive?" he asked, smiling. "You mean that wasn't in the briefing?"

"Not funny," she scolded him, shaking her finger once. "You're probably here to see the chief," she added.

"I am," Larry answered. "He in his office?"

"Where else," she said, her exuberance quickly fading back to her usual demeanor. "I'll see you." She waved and headed for the door.

Larry shook his head, grinning. Even Doreen had gone back to normal.

He walked up to Captain Engalls' office and paused at the closed door, taking a breath before putting his hand on the knob.

"Come in, Parker," the gruff voice barked from the other side.

Larry opened the door to see Engalls sitting behind his desk, the familiar scowl upon his face, his expression impatient, as if he'd been waiting for Larry longer than he'd expected.

"Hey Chief," Larry said after a moment's hesitation.

"Parker," Engalls growled, barely nodding. "Close the door and sit down.

"Everyone all right," he asked as Larry sat. "Your aunt, sons?"

"All fine," Larry answered. "Some emotional trauma, but otherwise okay."

"You got back yesterday, I hear," he asked.

"Late in the day," Larry replied. "A full week. All under sequester."

"I suppose you're wondering, then," Engalls began, "what's gone on in the real world since you've been the guest of Uncle Sam."

"Nope," Larry answered. "I got caught up on the news last night."

Engalls grumbled a laugh. "Straight from the reporters outside your door?"

"Yeah, there were a few of them," Larry said. "But Sullivan and Schoenbeck cleared a path to the door for us. Thanks," he added.

"Don't mention it," Engalls said. "So, the story on TV the same they fed you?"

"Every word, far as I could tell," Larry said. "What they told you, too?"

"Vigilante was a terrorist, agent went rogue, you and the woman falsely ID'd, so on and so forth," Engalls inquired.

"About the gist of it," Larry confirmed.

"You notice the spooks yet," Engalls asked.

"Surveillance guys?" Larry said. "Yeah. Just a couple. I think it's more hardware than feet on the street."

"Cameras and mikes everywhere," Engalls commented. "Not much we can do."

"You think anyone will talk?" Larry asked.

"About what?" Engalls inquired. "Except for the two of us and Urrutia, no one has any details outside of the rogue agent. Official story's really all they know."

"I suppose you're right," Larry admitted.

"Of course I am."

"What about Billy," Larry asked hesitantly.

"Officer Jenkins," Engalls said with a deep exhale. "Services were Wednesday."

"I'm sorry I wasn't here."

"Not much you could've done," Engalls told him. "Listen, Parker, I don't want you to feel responsible for everything that happened. It was bigger than what you got yourself wrapped up in."

A brief silence passed before Larry spoke up: "What about the 'protector' guy?"

Engalls' eyes narrowed. "How did I know you'd bring that up," he growled.

"The only question left," Larry said.

"Parker," Engalls addressed him in a serious tone, "I told you this before we all got into this hot water. Let it go. The case is closed. *Really* closed, now. The vigilante is dead. There's no point in pursuing it."

"Wasn't gonna," Larry said, leaning back in the creaky wooden chair, folding his hands behind his head. "But you gotta admit, the whole thing's curious."

"Then we let the mystery die unsolved," Engalls said in a deliberate tone.

"I know, Chief," Larry said, nodding slowly. "I know."

At that moment, a knock came at the door.

"About time," Engalls called out, checking his watch. "Come in."

The door swung open, and Larry turned to see the large frame of Gino Urrutia filling the open doorway. He was moving slowly, clearly still dealing with some pain from the gunshot wound, but a hint of a smile appeared on his face.

"Gino," Larry said, standing up. "Where were you, I called you last night."

"Yeah, figured," Gino replied, sitting down gingerly. "Vera. All shook up still. Got us staying up at her sister's in the burbs. I'll have her back home by week's end; they can't handle my snoring."

"Or much else about you, I'd guess," Engalls grunted.

"Chief, I gotta admit," Gino said, "that was almost *funny*. Maybe this whole episode was a good thing for you. You seem like a changed man."

"Sit down, Urrutia," the Chief replied flatly.

"So chief," Gino said, "now that you got us both here at the crack-ass of dawn, on my day off I might add, what's this all about?"

"Aside from the obvious, Urrutia," Engalls grunted, "the three of us are the only ones that *really* know what happened a week ago. I want to discuss it with both of you, *before* you return to active duty and the other officers start asking questions."

"Fair enough," Larry acknowledged. "What do you need from us?"

"You can probably guess," Engalls responded. "Under no circumstances whatsoever, can either of you breathe a word about what really happened. Got me?"

"Chief, all due respect," Gino said, "who we gonna tell?"

"Don't give me that, Urrutia," Engalls snapped. "I'm not worried about wives or lady friends. Both of you have friends on the force; guys you're close to aside from each other. I know the Code of Silence doesn't apply to fellow cops. But no matter what, you need to keep quiet about this. Period.

"There're a lot of eyes on us right now," he went on. "Will be for a long time. After awhile, you might get a false sense of security and let something slip. Well, don't.

"The son-of-a-bitch that created this whole mess, who killed Jenkins, went rogue," he concluded. "He's behind bars, awaiting punishment. We leave it at that, and all this gets put behind us. Simple as that. Got it?"

"I might not agree with all of it, Chief," Gino spoke up. "But I got no desire to relive all that went down last weekend. Case closed far as I'm concerned."

"Parker?"

Larry paused for a moment, then finally spoke. "Good enough for me, Chief."

"It's settled, then," Engalls said. "Now I'm trusting you. And Parker, make sure your family —"

"They're covered, Chief," Larry said. "Don't worry."

"The woman, too," Engalls added.

"Yep," Larry nodded.

"All right," Engalls got up, motioning them to the door. "Now I've got work to do. See you back on shift."

Gino behind him, Larry made for the door and exited the Captain's office.

Hours later, Larry was back at the apartment. The boys were excitedly hauling up a video-game system and a bagful of games, while Larry directed the two delivery men up the stairs with their new big-screen TV.

The Feds had given the apartment a thorough cleaning, leaving no details to chance. There were no signs of altercation anywhere, not even a drop of dried blood.

Edna had been placed in temporary housing while her bungalow was being rebuilt. Larry had offered for her to stay with him and the boys, but she'd politely said no, explaining that it was already a bit too cramped in his small, two-bedroom apartment.

"And besides," he remembered her adding, "since those Pentagon people are picking up the whole tab, why shouldn't I live it up for a little bit?"

The boys were soon settled in, playing one of their new video games.

Larry walked into his room and took off his shoes, kicking them toward the open closet door. He glanced upward. Even the bullet hole in the ceiling was gone.

He took off his jacket, setting it on the bed; then he undid his shoulder holster. He removed his revolver from the holster and placed it on the dresser next to the gun box, which had also been repaired and put back in its place. He pushed the key into the old, rusty lock and removed it from the box. He tossed the lock into the trash can, set his revolver in the box, and slapped a brand new lock onto the clasp.

He sat down on the bed, pulled off his socks, and thought about the boys; about how proud he was of them. Not only had they survived a traumatic, near-death experience, but they had adjusted to it better than he imagined anyone could have, especially two teenage boys. Perhaps what they'd been through with their mother's death years ago had hardened them more than he'd thought; but no child should ever have to go through *one* experience like the one they'd been through, much less two.

Aunt Edna would need some more adjustment time, he understood; but deep down he knew she would be okay. In addition to the counselors, she had him and the boys to talk to, anytime she wanted.

And then there was Mira.

From what he'd learned about her in the week they'd been acquainted, she was extremely resilient; but still, he knew she had no family near her. She had friends, but he wasn't sure how much she could share her feelings with them.

No: in the end, she had Larry, Edna, and the boys.

And perhaps he could see her again soon.

He glanced to the phone on his nightstand. Right next to Janna's portrait.

Feeling a sudden pang of guilt, he stood up, uncertain.

It had been four years. But when was long enough?

He suddenly felt light-headed.

Rubbing his temples, he walked out to the kitchen to pour a glass of orange juice.

"S'matter with you, Dad?" Marcus called back, turning back to notice Larry's uncertain demeanor as he sat down on the recliner behind them.

Larry took a large gulp of orange juice. "Nothing. I'm fine."

"You sure?" Daniel said, half-turning back to him also.

"Yeah, guys, I'm okay," he said, taking a breath. "Just keep playing your 'arrow,' or whatever that game is."

"It's called *Halo*, Dad," Marcus corrected him. "We're gonna play all the way through the fifth one."

"Or 'til dinner, whichever comes first," Larry said. "Remember, your first day back at school tomorrow. Then the counselor's at four."

"Yeah, yeah," Daniel groaned. "Don't remind us. Tomorrow's not today."

Larry looked out the window. He thought about Daniel's words.

Tomorrow's not today.

How long was long enough …

He would never know until he tried.

He got up from the chair.

"Guys, keep the volume down," he called back, walking into his bedroom again.

He sat down on the bed and picked up the portrait of Janna. He held it to his chest, as he'd done every day since she'd died. He kept it there for long moments.

"Always," he said quietly.

He set the portrait down.

Leaning back and taking a breath, he once again looked over at the phone.

The brightness of the day had begun to fade into the horizon.

Even though it was only six o'clock, Mira felt the slow creep of exhaustion begin to overtake her. Despite what she'd been through in the past ten days, she found her first day back at home to be no less taxing.

Her answering machine had been full for days. She spent much of the day returning phone calls, texts, and emails, letting everyone know she had made it home. Friends had stopped over during the day, wanting to hear everything. Her mother called, insisting she would be coming to stay for the week, arriving sometime the next day.

But despite all the activity, throughout the day, throughout much of the past week, for that matter, her thoughts often wandered to Rage.

They'd found his remains in a field just under a half-mile from the building site; though she'd been told there wasn't much left of him to find.

In her brief time with him, she had found herself understanding perhaps the most *misunderstood* person she'd ever known.

Despite being persecuted, hunted, imprisoned, and mortally wounded, he had gotten the bomb far enough away from the building, and saved thousands of lives.

Despite his anger towards people, he had, in the end, given his life for them.

And despite his desire for justice … when all was over, it had never found its way back to him.

The truth would never be known.

They had labeled him a murdering criminal and decided that, for the sake of public interest, it was best for all parties that the record stand per the 'official' story.

The story they'd *fabricated.*

It was better this way, they had told her.

It was better this way.

They had even offered her a substantial sum of money as 'compensation' for her pain and suffering. She had refused it.

She would not take blood money. Not in his name.

She stepped away from the steaming pot of noodles on the stove and pulled her hair back into a ponytail.

She suddenly found herself feeling alone. A quiet desperation came over her, making her knees weak for a split second. She moved to the sofa to sit down.

Everything would be all right, she told herself. *You just need to talk to someone; it doesn't matter who. Just call the first person that comes to mind.*

Wiping her eyes, she stood up and walked toward the phone.

As she placed her fingers on the handset, she paused.

Who should she call? Who *could* she call?

Then, to her surprise, the phone began to ring.

She paused once again, uncertain that whoever was calling her, would be someone she'd want to talk to.

In the end, she decided to let fate be the judge.

Taking a breath, she lifted the handset from its cradle and answered.

Epilogue

On the third floor of the brownstone at 4426 North Damen Avenue, the blinds were drawn closed, as they had been for the past several months.

A windowless stairwell led from the tiny rear courtyard up to the third floor, where a barely-used black doormat with the words "Go Away" printed in large white text greeted the less-than-occasional visitor. A loose, rusty doorknob hung sullenly on the shabbily-painted dark gray door.

Inside the murky studio apartment was barely enough light to cast a shadow. The only sources were two oversized computer monitors in the corner and an old set of Tiki lights strewn loosely around the bathroom doorframe, mounted there years earlier with tiny squares of duct tape.

The room carried the stench of rotted food; the odors so diverse and pervasive that it was impossible to discern whether the origin was produce, poultry, a combination, or something much worse. Tiny fruit flies floated silently above a cracked fruit bowl filled with blackened bananas and shriveled oranges, next to which lay a mold-covered loaf of Wonder Bread.

Facing the corner farthest from the windows and door was a massive desk cluttered with stacks of CDs and DVDs, boxes full of memory sticks and cards, programming magazines, crumpled sheets of paper, food wrappers, and other random debris. At the center of the desk were the two monitors, flanked by thin speaker towers with a printer shoved in the corner. Hanging in brackets underneath the desk were two computers, resting only inches above more piles of food wrappers and debris. Behind the desk on the wall was a frayed poster of a dark-haired supermodel, next to which hung a bulletin board overcrowded with Post-Its and other random scraps of paper. A plastic sign hung by a chain at the bottom of the board, which simply read, "Hackers Rule."

His unshaven face bathed in the blue glow of the giant monitor screens in front of him, Richard Ray Stevens wiped the back of his hand across his mouth, taking much of the excess powdered sugar with it. The box of donuts lay open on the stool next to his chair. Before he'd finished chewing his last bite of donut, he reached down into the box to take another; his hand felt around inside, forcing him to take his eyes off the monitors for a second. It was empty.

He muttered something inaudibly, then bent down, forward in the chair, eyes level with the underside of his desk, hunting around for something. Despite being burdened only by his wire-thin frame, the chair underneath him creaked as he leaned even further.

Finally, he found the open bag of potato chips back near the wall. Lunging forward, he grabbed the bag and dropped it into the empty donut box, pulling out a few stale chips and shoving them into his mouth before turning back to his monitors.

He was simultaneously wrapping up three projects: a spam email push for a Canadian pharmaceuticals distributor, an algorithm for a local start-up, and an under-the-table mainframe hack job for an undisclosed third party client.

Richard, or Ricky Ray as his mother always called him, was the best hacker he knew. He'd never met a code or security setup he couldn't crack, undetected.

He'd built a life where he rarely needed to leave his home. Everything he needed to do, he did through his computers – ordering groceries, paying bills, anything – he didn't need to get up from his programmer's chair to accomplish whatever he needed. The most rewarding part of this setup was that he rarely had to see another human face. He saw only his mother and the few contacts at the freelance agency.

Having just turned twenty-five, he realized he was getting bored. He needed to keep freelancing to pay the bills, but he needed something new. A new hobby to master; a new conspiracy to chase; a new code to crack. Exactly what, he didn't yet know.

He rubbed his eyes. He needed a break.

Maybe he'd take the afternoon off.

Then he glanced to his left, to the stack of work orders in his inbox.

No break today, he told himself. There was too much to do.

Shrugging off his straying thoughts, he stuffed another handful of chips into his mouth and was about to return to his coding, when the phone rang.

Grumbling, he looked at the clock. A few minutes past eleven o'clock a.m.

He picked up the receiver. "Hello?"

"Richard Stevens?" came the voice from the other end of the line.

"Yeah, that's me."

"Williams Freight calling," the voice replied. "I have a vehicle, just arrived in our facility, registered in your name."

"Vehicle," he began, then realized: his car, which had been stolen by a cop they'd thought was a terrorist.

"It's been almost two weeks," he complained. "What took them so long?"

"Sir, we don't ask questions," the voice replied. "We just take 'em in and store 'em. So right now we just need you to schedule a pickup time."

"Pickup time?" Ricky Ray scoffed. "No, no. The people who called me said it would be delivered. *Here.* Nothing about a pickup time."

"All right, let me put you on hold for a moment," the voice said.

He waited on hold for a few long moments, pacing back and forth.

"Sir?" the voice returned. "It does say delivery on the slip. We'll have it delivered to your address in about an hour."

Two hours later, he was bounding down the rear stairwell. As he got to the bottom, the light of day hit him, and he shielded his eyes in a vampire-like protest.

As he reached Damen Avenue, he saw the flat-bed tow truck, double parked, lowering his Rabbit onto the street. The driver stood near the back of the truck: a short but burly man with dark sunglasses and a bald head that shone in the mid-day sun as if it had just been polished. He did not look up as Ricky Ray approached.

"Hey!" Ricky Ray called out to him. "Be careful with that car."

The driver glanced up briefly, then shook his head slightly before turning his attention back to the hydraulic controls.

When the driver finished lowering the car, Ricky Ray walked around it, giving it a close look over. He tried opening the driver-side door, but it was locked.

At that moment, the driver, having finished raising the flat-bed, was now walking toward him, keys in one hand, clipboard in the other.

He handed Ricky Ray the clipboard but kept the keys in his other hand.

"Sign here, please," he said plainly.

Ricky Ray's eyes darted from the driver's face to the keys, then back up to the man's face. "How do I know it's not damaged?" he said suspiciously.

"Welcome to inspect it, if ya want," the driver said with a shrug. "Not sure yer gonna be able to tell what'd be new or old."

Ricky Ray didn't like the driver's tone; he felt like he wasn't being taken seriously. "How do I know nothing inside was stolen?"

"Heh," the driver snickered. He tossed him the keys. "Fine. Here. Yer welcome ta look. Don't know why anyone'd wanna touch anythin' in there anyway. Now willya just sign the friggin' paper, please, sir."

Ricky Ray glanced back at the car, then finally stepped forward and took the clipboard, signing the document. He didn't have time to play games with this dimwit; he'd check the car and file a report if anything had gone missing.

He handed the clipboard back to the driver, who took a quick look at the form to make sure it had been signed. "Have a nice day, sir," he said, stepping into the truck cab and closing the door behind him.

As the tow truck pulled away, Ricky Ray unlocked the Rabbit, climbed in, and started the sluggish engine. He looked around the cabin intently.

Nothing appeared to be out of place. It even seemed to have been cleaned thoroughly: all the dust was gone, replaced by the dull shine of his dashboard and gauges.

He tried to think of any valuables he'd kept in the car.

He then remembered: in case of emergency, he kept an envelope with fifty dollars inside, taped to the underside of the passenger seat.

If they'd stolen anything, that would be it.

Leaning over, he extended his long, skinny arm under the seat, feeling around. He cupped his hand upward and first felt the smooth surface of the tape, followed by the envelope itself. He pressed his fingertips against it, making sure it felt padded, a sign that the fifty singles were still inside. They appeared to be.

As he began to retrieve his hand from under the seat, the tip of his finger brushed something close to, but definitely separate from, the envelope.

A curious look on his face, he extended his arm once again, feeling the area around the envelope. Sure enough, there was something, it felt like a folded piece of paper, wedged between the envelope and the bottom of the seat, as if it had been shoved through one of the sides Ricky Ray hadn't taped.

Closing his fingers on one end of the piece of paper, he pulled, removing it from where it had been. With it in hand, he sat back up in the seat.

"Hell is this," he muttered to himself.

It was just a plain white piece of paper, folded into thirds. He knew he hadn't put anything else down there, so where could it have come from?

Not wasting any time, he unfolded the sheet, turning it in his hand so he could see the front side. The first thing that caught his eye was the word "Classified," stamped in bold red, at the top.

Ricky Ray's eyebrows went up.

He scanned the header at the top of the sheet: "D.O.D. Operation Code: 15-2883," he read out loud, becoming more intrigued by the second. "Phase I – Acquisition; Stage II – Asset Two."

D.O.D. …

Department of Defense?

He rubbed his chin, now beginning to wonder more about the circumstances surrounding his stolen car.

He scanned the sheet, taking in line after line of the encrypted message.

Maybe he would take the afternoon off, after all.

It was better this way.

The sun had gone down along the east African coastline, giving the transport boat the cover of night as it cut silently through the calm waters of the Indian Ocean, heading westbound toward the shore.

Strapped into one of the jump seats near the head of the vessel, he stared vacantly toward the land mass ahead, watching the shadows of twilight grow larger and form more intricate, detailed shapes as they drew closer. He took in a breath of the salty ocean air.

It had been six months since that fateful day, the day on which one life had ended and the other had begun; the day he had shed his old identity and begun the path to becoming something more.

His burning body had been thrown several hundred feet from the force of the blast. He'd come crashing down to earth through the thick of trees. It would be quite some time before they found him. The next several weeks were spent repairing his body: reconnecting limbs, grafting skin, resetting shattered bones.

The first face he would see was a woman's. Lying in his recovery bed, he remembered the hope that rose within him as his vision began to return, as his eyes set upon the figure at his bedside, tending to him. He thought it would be Mira. Instead, it was the doctor he'd seen in the hallway, mere seconds before his deadly encounter with the killer whose eyes were as black as his own. He recognized her tall frame, her striking features, her sandy blonde hair. He would learn she'd been leading the efforts to bring him to recovery. She'd been at his side the entire time, and once he had fully healed, she left the facility, never to return, saying she'd accomplished all she'd set out to do. He was grateful to her, and he would not soon forget all she'd done for him.

Though his skin had healed, the intense heat of the blast had altered his appearance. There were no deformities, but his new face no longer resembled the one he'd known his entire life thus far.

He thought he would miss his face. Miss his old life.

Instead, he embraced his new life with a surprising vigor.

Project Safeguard.

A small, covert elite force, revolving around him, assigned by the Pentagon exclusively to top-secret, perilous missions, targeting the greatest threats to the world.

They were the arm, holding the sword of justice.

And *he* was the edge of the blade.

They understood him; understood his needs, understood all that made him tick.

And he understood they were using him; his unique abilities, his talents, to carry out their agendas.

But in truth, *he* was using them as well.

To fulfill *his* needs.

To answer *his* calling.

The Unit he was a part of was clandestine: outside the public eye, outside the law.

The missions were clear, unadulterated: Intel would identify and pinpoint the whereabouts of a prime target. He would go in, punch a hole through their defenses, and retrieve the target.

Plain and simple.

In doing it this way, there was little to no collateral damage; few to no innocents killed in the process. He would only kill if there was no other choice.

Also, in doing this, they removed the burden of judgment from his shoulders.

He needed only to execute the mission.

He understood his role; what he was doing for the world.

And there were no more nightmares.

Tonight's mission was a Somalian warlord who funded terrorist operations by channeling opium into Africa. They were to take the operation down and bring the warlord into custody.

As the vessel drew upon the secluded, rocky shoreline, the fifteen soldiers around him silently began performing their last-minute checks before disembarking. They were Navy SEALs, Team Six Class all of them, any of whom could hold their own in battle with the worst the world had to offer.

And their sole responsibility was to protect him at all costs; to watch his back throughout all phases of the mission.

He glanced around at them, then back toward the SEAL Commander. He had begun to understand the camaraderie, their bond with one another, the brotherhood that made them as one. It was as close to being a part of something as he'd ever felt.

But he knew the truth.

He was an outsider.

As he would always be.

He set his eyes forward again, toward the approaching shoreline.

The boat met the jagged rocks of the coast. The SEALs began to move ashore, establishing their positions to scout the terrain ahead.

He leapt from the boat onto land, scaling the rocky wall to the cliff edge above.

The Unit began the two-mile trek toward the target warehouse.

As he moved ahead silently, through the dark of night, his thoughts involuntarily traced back to her.

He had barely known her, but in their brief time together, he felt a connection he'd never known possible with another. He was exposed to feelings he never knew existed within him.

He remembered her warmth; her light. He longed for it even now.

But he knew he could never give in return; could never provide her with the light, the warmth she had so easily provided him; could never give her all that she deserved.

Her life would be better for not having the burden of him in it.

His darkness would always offset her light.

It was better this way.

For the both of them.

The ancient, dilapidated warehouse was within view. The barely-visible lights shone through soiled, cracked windows. They were within one hundred feet now. Fifty.

He made note of the watchmen at the roof corners; the two armed guards on the loading dock, flanking the twelve-foot-high door that would be their insertion point.

From cover, the Unit snipers quickly did their part, and the path was clear.

He smiled broadly. It was time.

Launching himself into a full sprint, he closed in rapidly on the warehouse.

At full speed, he lowered his right shoulder, smashing through the massive, inches-thick wooden door.

As splinters large and small exploded into the enormous room, he peered beyond them, to the twenty or so dark-skinned men scattered about, some sitting on chairs and at tables, some keeping watch out the windows, others standing guard around the target himself – all of them glancing up in surprise.

Eyes blazing, he scanned the room. They were evildoers, all of them: filling their coffers with the earth's forbidden wares, then expending them with hate and violence against the innocent.

Clearly none of them had expected a frontal assault such as this.

And none would be ready for what would happen to them next.

As they made for their guns, he let out a vengeful roar.

Clenching his fists, blood surging through his veins, he charged forward.

It was time to go to work.

About the Author

Chris Lindberg was born and raised outside Chicago. After college he lived on the West Coast for a few years before settling back down in the Chicago area, where he now lives with his wife, Jenny, and their two children, Luke and Emma. *Code of Darkness* is his first novel.

You can find out more about the author at www.codeofdarkness.com.

Made in the USA
Lexington, KY
15 May 2012